His lips touched hers, the contact so light it was barely there. They were both working hard for breath, both tense and troubled just as much as they were burning with craving.

"I just need a moment, Marissa. Just one little moment where who and what we are doesn't matter. Because it has been just as hard for me to accept all the things you are trying to accept right now. But in all this upheaval," he breathed, the softness of his mouth brushing over hers as he spoke, "the only thing that comes crystal clear to me is the way I burn for you."

Then he swept up her mouth with his, holding her so tightly to himself with the wrapping strength of his arms, his hands running fiercely hot across her back.

She should have pushed away from him, but there was no strong, instinctive desire to do so. In fact the ultimate opposite desire was in play, until it felt as though her actual soul was craving to feel him kiss her.

By Jacquelyn Frank

The World of Nightwalkers
Forever
Forbidden

Three Worlds
Seduce Me in Dreams
Seduce Me in Flames

Nightwalkers
Jacob
Gideon
Elijah
Damien
Noah
Adam

Shadowdwellers
Ecstasy
Rapture
Pleasure

The Gatherers
Hunting Julian
Stealing Kathryn

Other Novels
Drink of Me

Anthologies
Nocturnal
Supernatural

FOREVER

The World *of* Nightwalkers

JACQUELYN FRANK

BALLANTINE BOOKS • NEW YORK

Forever is a work of fiction. Names, characters, places, and incidents are the products of the author's imagination or are used fictitiously. Any resemblance to actual events, locales, or persons, living or dead, is entirely coincidental.

A Ballantine Books Mass Market Original

Copyright © 2013 by Jacquelyn Frank

Excerpt from *Forsaken* copyright © 2013 by Jacquelyn Frank

All rights reserved.

Published in the United States by Ballantine Books, an imprint of The Random House Publishing Group, a division of Random House, Inc., New York.

BALLANTINE and colophon are trademarks of Random House, Inc.

This book contains an excerpt from the forthcoming book *Forsaken* by Jacquelyn Frank. This excerpt has been set for this edition only and may not reflect the final content of the forthcoming edition.

ISBN 978-0-345-53490-3
eBook ISBN 978-0-345-53890-1

Cover illustration: Craig White

Printed in the United States of America

www.ballantinebooks.com

9 8 7 6 5 4 3 2 1

Ballantine Books mass market edition: June 2013

For my sister Laraine
My hero

ACKNOWLEDGMENTS

To the Saugerties police:

Yeah, I did it again. I took poetic license with your lovely police department. But I promise, this is the *last* time. (Unless, of course, there's a next time.)

GLOSSARY
AND PRONUNCIATION TABLE

Apep: (Ā-pep)
Asikri: (Ah-SEE-cree)
Chatha: (Chath-UH)
Docia: (DŌ-shuh)
Hatshepsut: (Hat-SHEP-soot)
Ka: (Kah) Egyptian soul
Kamenwati: (Kah-men-WAH-ti)
Menes: (MEN-es)
Odjit: (Ō-jeet)
Ouroboros: (You-row-BORE-us) a snake or dragon devouring its own tail, a sign of infinity or perpetual life.
Pharaoh: (FEY-roh) Egyptian king or queen. This is used in reference to both male and female rulers.
Tameri: (Tah-MARE-e)

FOREVER

PROLOGUE

Agincourt, Friday, 25 October 1415

"Here is war at its most profound," Menes mused as he leaned forward from his seat high on horseback and peered down at the vast field below. "An army of so few making bold against an army of so many."

"Methinks you are seeing parallels, my friend."

Menes turned to look at Ramses, who was a befreckled, redheaded adolescent boy. More of a young man, in truth, but he had yet to fully grow into his body and his looks. Although, with one of the greatest pharaohs of all sharing possession of that gangly frame, it lent an air of surety and power that had no doubt been lacking before. An air that forced others to obey his commands, even if they weren't always sure why they felt compelled to do so. The fact that he was ever at Menes's right hand made it very clear to other Bodywalkers exactly who he was and exactly why he should be obeyed at all times. And in the event of utter stupidity, Ram had his ways of making himself very, very clear on a matter. Ramses may have conceded the throne of the Bodywalkers to Menes, long ago acknowledging him to be the better ruler of the Nightwalker breed, but Menes did not count himself above Ramses in any way other than by

Bodywalker law. They were as equals. They had always been so. Always would be so.

"You only say that because the Politic is outnumbered by the Templars four to one at the moment." Wry amusement touched his lips. Their war, the civil war between the Templars and the Politic, would never end, it seemed. Century after century, death after death, it always turned the same, grinding like millstones. But for the first time the Politic was in danger of losing everything. If that happened the Bodywalkers would fall under the feverish rule of Odjit and her followers, who would rule the Bodywalkers with a zealous fist.

"You know their prophecy as well as I do. The day the Templars wrest power from us, Amun will rise to champion the underdog Templars, gifting them with power and rule for their devoted service to the gods."

Ram snorted derisively. "That's the prophecy as told by *their* oracles . . . not by any oracle we have ever known. If it held any truth, Cleo or one of our other powerful oracles would have concurred."

Menes nodded. He knew that as well as Ram did. However, part of what made him a good pharaoh was that he never dismissed anything out of hand. Over his many lifetimes, while sharing bodies with a great variety of hosts, he had learned that there were rarely any absolutes in the world. Even death was not an absolute. Not to their kind anyway. It was to humans. Which proved another point. One man's absolute was another man's maybe. To the Templars, Amun's prophecy was an absolute. To them, it was a big maybe. Or in Ram's assessment, a huge "not bloody likely."

"The longbow," he said, shifting attention back to the war between the French and the English. The English king, Henry, was proving to be a master tactician. Or perhaps just a dogged one. Menes could not decide. But watching the English decimate the French from a distance with the impressive use of the longbow in spite of having an undermanned army riddled with dysentery and other illnesses, he thought it was perhaps a healthy dose of both. "I once thought it an awkward instrument. But I see in proper hands there is much to be said for it."

"You could say the same about Bodywalker rule," Ram teased him.

Menes reached out to cuff him but froze mid-action. He took in a sharp breath, drawing Ram's quick attention.

"She's here," he said on a rushing exhalation. There was no need for him to explain. Ram knew whom he meant just as assuredly as Menes's quickening heart and soul did. Menes had waited so patiently these past few months, his life feeling void and half present even as he spent the time Blending with his new host and familiarizing himself with the state of Bodywalker affairs after a century of his absence . . .

He had always known her. Lifetime after lifetime they found each other, connected to each other, loved each other in ways no one else could possibly ever understand, though he saw the envy in their eyes as they wished that they could. There was nothing so satisfying, so comforting, as knowing that one's soul mate existed and would follow him from lifetime to Ether to new lifetime and back to Ether again. And though they could not touch in the Ether, just the presence of each other was beyond comforting. Beyond simple pleasure. And patiently they would wait for their next lives, their next bodies, when they could touch each other once more.

He could feel her now, her presence like sunshine burning through full armor, and a bead of sweat rolled down the channel of his spine. He felt like a child anticipating the sweetest of sugar, all gap-toothed and silly grins and grasping, eager fingers. Oh yes, his fingers would be grasping and very, very eager.

But softly now . . .

He whispered the warning into his eager brain, using more forceful methods to quiet his libido. She was newly born, not even begun to Blend with her new, unsuspecting host. And that was perhaps the best of it. Every time he got to coax a new woman with an old soul inside of her to love him. He would woo and romance her, convince her to love him while the soul he loved was being reborn inside of her.

"This is the part I love best," he said softly.

"I am well aware," his friend said with amusement. "One day she will be born into a woman who will not fall for your charms so easily," Ram said.

"Oh, I but live for the day!" With a whoop he kicked his steed into motion. Over his shoulder he shouted, "Where would the fun be in an easy conquest?"

Ram looked down at the forces at war below.

No doubt King Henry would have enjoyed an easy conquest right about then. As it stood, he would very likely be dead by night's fall . . . and all his forces with him. But he would not go down easy, a trait he admired in both the English king . . .

. . . and in this.

THE LOST SCROLL
OF KINDRED

. . . And so it will come to pass in the forward times that the nations of the Nightwalkers will be shattered, driven apart, and become strangers to one another. Hidden by misfortune and by purpose, these twelve nations will come to cross-purposes and fade from one another's existence. In the forward times these nations will face toil and struggle unlike any time before, and only by coming together once more can they hope to face the evil that will set upon them. But they are lost to one another and will remain lost until a great enemy is defeated . . . and a new one resurrects itself . . .

CHAPTER ONE

Dr. Marissa Anderson sat tapping a pencil against the corner of her desk with a very uncharacteristic fidgetiness that reflected the utter turmoil of her thoughts. She was trying to figure out what had so unsettled her. Her life, as a whole, was going along swimmingly. She had settled into her position as the precinct's head psychiatrist very well. She was even learning how to balance that difficult line between professional relationships with her coworkers and the extension of it into personable, casual ones. Making friends in a predominantly male precinct full of alpha-type personalities who hated being reminded they had emotions . . . yeah, that had its difficulties. Especially when she often stood between them and their reinstatement or continuation of their duties. But they were beginning to get the picture that she didn't take some kind of sadistic pleasure in holding that kind of power over their heads. Quite the contrary. As long as they confronted and dealt with whatever issues they had, she was happy to be a strong advocate for the continuation of their careers.

Career. Check.

Her sister, who had been known to get into trouble now and then, had been blessedly well-behaved and had managed to obtain at least a part-time job.

Family. Check.

And while Marissa wasn't in a relationship at the moment, she was fine with that. She had never felt the need to define herself by the regard of a man, as some of her friends and relations were wont to do. She was comfortable with herself, her home, her lifestyle, and did not feel she was somehow failing in life because she didn't have a significant other.

Personal life. Ch . . .

She hesitated in her thoughts, the tapping of her pencil reaching critical mass.

Three weeks . . .

The thought whispered with an insidious sort of mocking in the deeper corners of her mind. Her skin went a little hot and her face tinged with heat immediately after. The response made her growl under her breath in frustration and she chucked the pencil across the room in a rare fit of pique, watching the thing bounce off the window and land in the potted plant beneath it.

With a sigh she made herself get up and cross the room, bending to peer into the wilds of the ficus. She didn't quite make it that far. Through her windows, she caught sight of a streak of brown and black bolting across a not-too-distant field, leaping so high off the ground it was astounding, before barreling into the man in its path and sinking vicious teeth into the nearest appendage.

"Get down! Get down on the ground *now*!" The command made her freeze, the deep, authoritative voice washing over her and giving her that queasy mixture of fear and admiration in the center of her stomach. Chills raced across her breasts even as heat raced into other places.

Her eyes yanked away from the dog and its victim and zeroed in on the owner of that voice. The victim was dressed in a thick padded suit designed specifically to withstand the majority of a dog bite. However the man commanding the dog, the man training him, was in full uniform.

Jackson. Sergeant Jackson Waverly was one of the two K-9 officers in the Saugerties, New York, police department. His former canine partner, Chico, had died about six months earlier in the line of duty. Sergeant Waverly had not taken it well at all. To him it had been no different than if he'd lost a human partner. And considering Chico had laid down his life to protect his partner's, she'd say he'd earned that sort of respect.

For a while there she'd been pretty sure Jackson wouldn't be able to bring himself to continue on as a K-9 officer. He'd been putting off training with his new dog, showing very little interest in the handsome German shepherd named Sargent. But three weeks ago . . .

Three weeks . . .

Three weeks ago something had changed dramatically in Jackson. If anyone had asked her to explain, she probably couldn't have done so with any real clarity . . . not without sounding like a goofy schoolgirl with a demented little crush on some boy.

Oh, she had to admit that on some level she'd always found the man appealing. How could she not? He was damn beautiful for a male and any woman with half a brain and at least a partially working libido would accede to that. He was tall, but not overly so. Tall enough to be several inches taller than her lofty height of 5'7" with the constant addition of three- to four-inch stiletto heels. It was such a rare thing, really, for someone to make her feel smaller and more delicate than she truly was. But he also made her feel . . .

Scorched was the only word she could use to describe it. It was how she had felt that day, three weeks ago, when he had gone from being this sometimes-appealing/ sometimes-pain-in-the-ass man to . . .

"I'm putting you on notice, Marissa . . . I've come to realize that there is no one on this planet, in this time, more intriguing than you are. You are a puzzle, and a pretty one at that. I think perhaps it would be a terrible shame if I were to let you slip away from me."

Who the hell says that to a woman? It ought to have been obnoxious. Or at the very least corny. It ought to have been offensive and uncomfortable, considering he was technically a patient of hers and it would be a serious breach of ethics to entertain what he was teasing her with.

So no. She'd shut herself off from it. Pretended that it had been his idea of a mean little joke, of wielding male authority over a woman he hadn't been able to conquer with his charming smiles and ridiculously beautiful green eyes. Those clear as glass, bright as a turquoise ocean eyes, eyes so brilliant they jumped out of his nobly featured face. Even more so, it seemed, than usual these past three weeks.

Poppycock, she thought fiercely. He rattled her cage and made her take notice and now she was having flights of fancy every ten minutes . . . not to mention quite a few steamy dreams with Jackson as the headlining star.

Part of the problem, she realized, was that he was always there. Every time she turned around she could see him or hear his deep resonant voice. Like now, as he recalled his dog with a sharp, strong command, sending the powerful animal gamboling back across the field to his side where Jackson kneeled and gave him praises, tousling his ruff, and giving him his favorite toy as a reward.

It didn't help that the practice field was right outside her windows. It was damn distracting, watching him be stunningly authoritative and then, by turns, goofy and fun-loving as he played with Sargent between rigorous training sessions.

But in no time at all the intensive training would end and so would her equally intensive immersion in the tempting Jackson Waverly sightseeing tour.

Yay.

Darn it.

"Hell," she muttered, giving the blinds a frustrating yank, dropping them hard into place and blocking out half the sunlight in her office. "All it was was one stupid little moment of flirtation," she muttered.

Well, that wasn't exactly the truth, either.

Shoving herself back toward her desk, she decided not to dignify that with any further mental discussion.

Twenty minutes later, Marissa was doodling absently on a scrap of paper, her pen swirling almost frenetically. Almost as if it was matching the frenzy of the thoughts racing through her mind . . . or the fierce effort she was exerting trying to *not* think. The phone rang at her elbow, the cell vibrating into movement, trying to travel across the desk. She picked it up and glanced at the screen. A bright, beautiful picture of her sister was displayed, the pure sunlight on her hair making the brilliant red light up as if on fire. That brilliance was nothing compared to the explosive beauty of the smile that had been captured with it. And that smile said everything that needed to be said about the type of person her sister was.

Smiling in return, she answered the call.

"Whadayawant?" she drawled into the phone, using the heaviest Brooklyn accent she had in her repertoire.

Angelina laughed right off the bat, the ebullient sound dancing across the tension in the back of Marissa's neck and shoulders, instantly releasing and relaxing it.

"Whatchadoin'?" Angelina bounced back to her in

the same exaggerated accent. The amusement was that neither of them had been born in New York, but Lina kept insisting Marissa was starting to sound like a native, so . . .

"I'm working of course," she replied in her normal voice. A voice that had been cultivated to sound sophisticated and free of all accent.

"No, you aren't. You wouldn't have answered the phone if you were trying to pluck the crazy out of someone."

"I do other things besides 'pluck the crazy' out of these cops. The paperwork alone . . ."

"Sure, sure," Lina drawled. "You're probably just sitting there staring out at Mr. Tall Dark and Dangerous."

The remark took Marissa so by surprise that she hesitated, her words trapped in her throat. "I most certainly am not staring out at him!" she protested.

"Liar," Lina accused knowingly.

"Shut up," Marissa groused, hating that Lina knew her so well . . . and beyond grateful for it at the same time. They both had other friends and companions in the world, but no one was closer to Marissa and she knew the same stood for her sister. "So tell me why you feel compelled to torment me in the middle of my workday."

"You mean besides it being fun?" But Marissa could hear the smile fading from her sister's voice in the next sentence. "Actually, I do have kind of a small teensy little problem," she confessed.

Marissa rolled her eyes. Angelina never had a small problem. And the more adjectives she used to minimize it, the more Marissa knew she wasn't going to like the favor she was going to be asked for.

"What is going on, honey?" she encouraged her, sighing silently.

"Can I come see you? I'm not far away."

Marissa glanced at the clock.

"I have an appointment in an hour . . ."

There was a knock on Marissa's door, interrupting her. She got up and hurried over to it.

"Hold on a sec, Lina, I have—"

She broke off when she opened the door and saw her sister standing there. Angelina lifted a hand, gave her a sheepish version of her winning smile and wiggled her finger in hello.

"Oh for Pete's sake," Marissa huffed, shutting off her phone with a click. "Why didn't you just . . ."

That was when she noticed the large, surly looking officer standing behind her sister. Officer Weiss she thought his name was. Marissa slowed down a moment, taking in the details of what she was seeing.

"Oh *hell* no!" she exclaimed.

"Yeah. I kinda got arrested."

"How do you *kind of* get arrested?" Marissa demanded, using every last remnant of professionalism and patience she owned to keep from losing her cool in front of the entire bullpen. Just a few yards away everyone she worked with was milling about and any of them, most probably *all* of them, were witnessing this developing debacle.

"She *kind of* punched a cop in the eye," Weiss growled churlishly.

Marissa's eyes flicked back to the officer, and sure enough he was turning black and blue around the orbital bone of his left eye.

"Angelina!"

"I didn't punch him!" she exclaimed. "I sort of . . . flailed. It was an accident!"

"She was at the MaxCon rally."

Now things were starting to make sense. MaxCon was a notorious textile company on the Hudson River, just north of the village of Saugerties. They had recently been fined for illegally dumping chemicals into the Hudson River. MaxCon's press release claimed it was an accident, a malfunction of some piece of equipment or other. There were a lot of people who didn't believe that for a second. Clearly, her sister was one of them.

Leave it to her sister to be in the thick of trouble. Angelina was a blunt, outspoken, and confident person. She didn't prevaricate. She didn't keep her opinions to herself and she always, *always* fought for what she believed in.

Needless to say, it wasn't the first time Angelina had had a run-in with the Saugerties Police Department.

Well, she wasn't in cuffs. She was holding her cellphone, so it hadn't been confiscated. And Officer Weiss had brought Lina straight to her. Marissa winced inwardly when she realized he'd probably been privy to Lina's entire conversation, including the part about her staring out the window at Jackson Waverly. She hadn't mentioned him by name, but still it didn't take a genius . . .

Oh *man* she was going to commit sororicide!

"What else did she do?" Marissa asked wearily, deciding not to waste energy worrying about that. Her sister had offered far more fodder for worry at the moment.

"She trespassed."

"I climbed the fence and sat on top of the wall! I didn't even touch the damn ground!" she argued fiercely, hands on her hips as she rounded on Officer Weiss. "At least I didn't until you grabbed me and yanked me down! And that's when I flailed." She waved her arms around wildly. "I was trying to get you off of me and get to my feet at the same time!"

"Lina!" Marissa hushed her through her teeth and stiff lips. Angelina was in the process of embarrassing her in front of the entire precinct. And of course she picked shift change to do it, when everyone was present in the building for clocking out or briefing before shift. There was an audience growing in the distance behind Weiss and Lina.

"Is she under arrest?" Marissa asked coolly.

"Well . . . not yet."

"Why not?" Marissa wanted to know.

"Hey!" Lina protested.

"Hush!" she commanded her sister. Then she looked at the bruised officer. "Why isn't she under arrest?"

"Because *she* didn't do anything wrong," Lina grumbled, absolutely unable to keep her own countenance. It was perhaps her most infuriating trait.

"Well . . . uh . . . the incident in question . . . it's kind of a gray area."

Lina turned back to her sister and looked smug. The girl didn't have the first idea how to be careful for her own good. But it did seem as though her sister was perhaps in the right here. If Weiss had been convinced of malicious intent he wouldn't have brought her to Marissa. The department was very strict about giving preferential treatment to friends and relatives. The town was too small and everyone knew everyone. They had to stay as professional and as impartial as possible.

"You mean you don't believe she hit you on purpose."

Weiss hesitated, clearly debating with his injured ego for a moment, but Marissa believed that he would be fair if it was warranted. She did know him a little and had never heard of him being accused of being a hard-nosed cop.

"I'm willing to believe it was accidental," he grumbled at last.

Angelina exploded into a beaming smile and, instead of gloating over her victory, she leapt up with a bounce and hugged the officer so hard he grunted.

"Thank you!" she exclaimed. She pulled back and

patted his cheek as if he were a child. "You're a good man, Officer Weiss."

And the burly officer colored, his entire posture turning "Aww shucks!" as a smile grew across his lips.

"Just you stay out of trouble, little miss," he scolded her, reaching out to pinch her on her chin. Then he turned and walked off, shaking his head and grinning.

Lina wins again.

Always. It was that ingenuous face and disarming smile, Marissa thought. Not to mention the rest of her ebullient personality. She didn't blame Officer Weiss for his reactions to her sister. He wasn't the first to be taken with her charm and spirit.

Lina turned back to her sister, all white smiling teeth. "So? Show me Mr. Delicious!"

Marissa grabbed her sister by the arm and yanked her into her office, slamming the door behind her.

"I wish I'd never told you about him," Marissa hissed at her. But she was talking to Lina's back. Lina was already hurrying across to the closed blinds that blocked Marissa's view of Jackson Waverly. At least Lina was circumspect enough to peek out between the slats and not press her whole face and body against the glass. Marissa needed to be glad for small favors.

"Oh my freaking god!" Angelina exclaimed.

"Will you lower your voice," Marissa hissed, her face burning with inexplicable embarrassment. Well . . . actually . . . it wasn't exactly embarrassment that made her skin heat up. She knew exactly what Angelina was seeing. She'd peeked out that window endlessly these past weeks. And that moment didn't turn out to be any different. She moved up beside her sister and peeked out at Jackson right along with her sister.

"Jesus, Mari, he's gorgeous! Look at that ass! You could bounce a quarter off that thing."

"Lina!" But the scold was ruined when she laughed

behind it. "He *is* pretty," she said as she made herself move away from the window and pick up her tepid coffee. "I'll give him that."

"Pretty? He's a *god*. He's the kind of guy that makes you wish to be a bar of soap in his shower."

Coffee sprayed across Marissa's desk as the remark hit her mid sip. Marissa dissolved into a coughing fit and half-inhaled coffee swam in her lungs. "Oh my god!"

"You said it, sister," Angelina said with a giggle as she turned away from the window. "So what are you going to do about it?"

Angelina waited patiently as her sister recovered a normal breathing pattern.

"I'm doing nothing about it of course!" she croaked out. "Jackson is a patient. Doctors don't date patients. It's a matter of ethics."

"Please," Lina said rolling her eyes. "I'd quit for that." She nodded toward the window.

"Well, I'm not you. And it's a good thing too because someone has to pay the rent."

"Oh. Ow. Low blow, sis."

Marissa frowned. It was a low blow. Times were tough across America, and Angelina's personality couldn't fill just any kind of job. Oh, her smiling eyes and sunny strawberry-blond looks made it easy for her to *get* a job, but the opinionated champion of underdogs and lost causes everywhere eventually got on nerves and infuriated or exasperated her bosses. The fact that Lina was just too sweet for words and was as compelling as the day was long . . . that made it really hard to fire her as well. But eventually she got on a last nerve or crossed an inappropriate line and the employment opportunity would dissolve around her.

"I'm sorry. I know you try."

That was part of the problem. Lina tried too hard to

champion the world. She came dead last on her own list of things that needed taking care of. Everything else came first, whether it was the Hudson River, the homeless, or the extinction of Siberian tigers . . . just to name a few.

"Angelina, you really need to be more careful," she said with a sigh, fingertips rubbing at the ache throbbing at her temple. Marissa knew she was wasting her breath, and in a way she was proud of her sister for that. She stood for something. She wasn't ever afraid of anything.

Marissa couldn't say the same. In fact, she was the overcautious, strait-laced, serious one of the family. Yes, that's exactly how she would describe herself.

"You need to loosen up," Lina said, for the thousandth time. "Before you know it your youth will be gone and bam!"—she smacked her hands together— "You're old and decrepit with cobwebs in your vagina and you'll be sitting there wondering why you never actually lived your life. I constantly hope you'll throw caution to the wind one day and just *embrace* your life."

"And I constantly wish you'd tread a little more carefully." Marissa sighed. "Let's face it, we're never going to be what the other wants us to be."

"Never say never," Lina said with a mischievous wink. "If you're up against the glass drooling over that, then I have tremendous hope for you!"

"That," she said, pointing to the window, "is never going to happen. Not in a million years. So give it up."

"Humph. Maybe so. Maybe not." Lina moved toward the door. "You never know what the future holds."

"Never, Lina. So stop bringing it up," Marissa said sternly as Lina pulled open her office door.

"I've got to jet. Later, sis," she said waving as she breezed out the door. "Hey Weiss!" she shouted across the bullpen. "Coffee and donuts on me!"

The office door clicked shut.

Marissa dropped down into her chair, as usual completely exhausted by the tempest that was her sister. She sat back with a deep exhalation.

Then, unable to help herself, she glanced toward her closed blinds.

"Never gonna happen," she muttered to herself in reminder.

CHAPTER TWO

Jackson looked to his left, a flash of movement briefly catching his attention. Rising to his full height, he smiled as he watched the blinds drop behind Marissa's windows. A snap of his fingers brought Sargent to his heel. The dog took his position and gazed up at him, tongue lolling out of his mouth as he panted from his exertions and his excitement.

"Wow, Jacks, that dog's a beast," Officer Carl Manheim panted as he came toddling and hopping up to them, the bite suit he was wearing too bulky to allow for any grace and even less dignity. There were better made suits these days, but their tiny little department with only two K-9 units in training didn't rate such costly equipment. They had to make do with ancient leftovers inherited from the Albany police department.

Jackson pulled his cap down to shade his face, his sunglasses protecting his burning eyes from the sunlight. He felt heavy and tired, as though he were slogging through a marshland full of thick, sucking mud. He would be glad when training was finally complete. This weakness to sunlight he'd inherited along with a certain Egyptian monarch was beating the Christ out of him. And from what he had come to understand, he was lucky to be moving at all. According to Ram and to Menes himself, the only reason he was able to move at all was because Menes was slowing down the Blending process to an infinitesimal rate and because Menes himself was incredibly powerful and had the strength necessary to buck the one weakness that dogged a Bodywalker's heels.

This was perhaps why Menes was pharaoh over all the other Bodywalkers. Even above powerful, dominant men in their own right like Menes's best friend Ramses.

Ramses II.

Holy hell. It had been three weeks since Jackson had nearly died, only to be saved by making a strange deal in order to save his own life. He remembered every single detail of everything that had happened. He remembered the agony of being hit with a searing blast of power known as the Curse of Ra. He remembered the force of it propelling him back through yards of air, and he very clearly recalled the feeling of crashing violently into a car windshield.

Then there had been nothing. A world of floating, disembodied nothingness. The Ether, they called it. A dimension of foggy clouds and barely existent beings you could feel rather than see. But then he had seen Menes, a tall, dark-skinned warrior, a tower of strength and well-defined musculature and very little in the way of clothing.

Then he remembered the proposition.

Die now . . . or live as host to me. We will share your body; Blend our spirits. One man made of two souls. I am a king, a powerful central figure in a world beyond anything you have comprehended before this. With this position comes not only heavy responsibility, but also very persistent enemies. Enemies who will want us dead.

It had not been a prettied-up offer, had not been glo-

rified, and Menes had made him no promises save
one . . .

*Join with me and I will show you many things you
never would have expected to understand . . . but most
of all, I will show you a love like no other. I will intro-
duce you to the most perfect woman in all known history. You will know a love that will transcend anything
you can conjure in your mind.*

There had been many factors that had intrigued him
into agreeing, but he secretly admitted to himself that
this particular one had held a curious amount of appeal
to him.

"Thanks, Manheim," he said absently as he bent to
scrub at Sargent's ruff. The dog grunted and groaned
happily.

This would be the last safe day in the sun for Jackson.
It had been three weeks since that bargain had been
struck. Tonight the Blending would become complete,
according to Menes, and daylight would be taken from
him for the rest of his life. It had surprised Landon, his
boss, when he had volunteered for third watch. Usually
night watch was for rookies who hadn't earned enough
seniority to get the day shift. But it was the only option
open to Jackson if he wanted to continue at his job.

Oh, he understood he would have to give up his position in the Saugerties, New York, police department
eventually. Perhaps sooner than later. The Bodywalker
seat of government was somewhere in New Mexico, the
desert apparently feeling very much like home to these
ancient Egyptians.

But he had some unfinished business that needed taking care of, and Menes was inclined to agree. Together,
he and his Bodywalker looked toward the set of windows that would have allowed him a straight view into
Marissa's office, had she not dropped the blinds in an
effort, he imagined, to shut him out.

He didn't know why the psychiatrist was a cause for delay exactly. After all, she'd been within reach for the better part of two years and, other than ogling her backside and other deliciously hot curves of her body as she'd walked back and forth past his desk, he'd never felt compelled to do anything more about his attraction to her.

But then his sister had disappeared—or so he had thought—and his entire outlook on the world, including his perspective toward Marissa "Hotbody" Anderson, had changed. How much of it was her doing, his doing, or because of Menes's hijacking of his body, mind, and soul was truly unknown to him. All he knew was that he wanted her. Bad. Really, really bad.

Menes looked through his new host's eyes, studying the drawn shades of the good doctor's windows. As his and Jackson's Blending neared the finish, Menes grew more and more aware of the strong attraction his host had for the redhead beyond the glass. Jackson may not understand his sudden compulsion to sniff after the resident shrink, but Menes did. Menes did because he was encouraging it. He was fanning the flame of it.

When he had first been reborn in Jackson, he'd been drawn too quickly to the surface, had exploded with an unexpected and dangerous surge of power. He had sublimated his host in order to speak and be heard. It was not something he was in the habit of doing. He was in the habit of unifying with his host, sharing the world they now lived in symbiotically. He gave Jackson enhanced strength, retarded aging, leadership of a great people, and a power the likes of which no one else among the Politic had claim to. Jackson gave him breath and body, sight and smell, and the resurrection of life so that there may follow a resurrection of his heart . . . so yes, it was a perfect symbiosis. They each brought something to the table. It would be wrong for

*him to reward Jackson's invitation with an internal
slavery, dominating him and forcing him to his will.*

*But Menes knew he would be sorely tempted these
first years. It was so difficult in the beginning when
two strong personalities had to learn the perfect
rhythm to coexisting as one. Rather like a marriage or
a great love. The first part—the infatuation and the
fascination—was easy. The second part was where all
the work lay. As many marriage vows have declared, in
one version or another, throughout the ages he had
lived in . . . in prosperity and in famine, in health and
in sickness, in the daily cost of living and the tribula-
tions of every soul, that was where the difficulties and
best rewards were to be found.*

*And he would find it. But first . . . first he had to find
a suitable host for his beloved queen.*

*He had delayed his return to mortal life even after his
hundred years of waiting between resurrections had
passed because his love, Hatshepsut, had been reluctant to return this time. Not through any weakness of
her own, but because of his. In their last lives he had . . .
well, that was neither here nor there. What it boiled
down to was that she had finally claimed to be ready
and he felt he must act with haste to find her a suitable
host before she wavered and changed her mind once
more. He did not have the luxury of waiting for
Hatshepsut to choose in her own time when time was
now his enemy. Besides, who would know better what
kind of host would best suit Hatshepsut than himself?*

*And, he considered, wouldn't it be best if he chose
someone his new host was already heavily attracted to?
There was nothing wrong with stacking the deck in his
favor, and he was not above it in the least. It was what
marked the greatest of leaders, the ability to use whatever one could to bring harmony between two disparate worlds and make them as one in purpose.*

"Time to give this pup some dinner and well-deserved rest," Jackson said to Manheim after clearing his throat so the sudden licks of desire sliding through him at the thought of Marissa wouldn't come out in his voice.

"No kidding. Want to catch a beer at Pauly's?"

Jackson shook his head in the negative, even though part of him was wondering why he was no longer interested in going to have a beer with the guys. He used to like doing that. A lot. And from the look crossing Manheim's face, *he* was wondering what was up with him just as much as Jackson was. That wasn't good. He was supposed to be keeping a low profile, so that no one questioned him about any differences in his character. He understood why, of course. During the Blending process he and Menes were extremely weak and extremely vulnerable, even despite Menes's great powers. So it was best to remain inconspicuous until it was complete. As it was, and as he had been made to understand it, the huge display of power he'd shown moments after waking up with Menes inside of him had done damage to the Blending process, slowing it down considerably. It had taken his sister Docia only a week, maybe two, to fully Blend with her Bodywalker. That was not the case with him. Although Menes was apparently doing some of this on purpose so Jackson could maintain life in the sun for a little while longer. Or so he thought. The former and present pharaoh was not exactly a wordsmith. Which was good, Jackson supposed. It would suck to spend the rest of his life chained up with a chatterbox.

He walked away from the field after a wave of acknowledgment to Manheim and some of the officers who'd been watching at the edge of the arena. He'd practiced in full uniform, as usual. It helped define for the dog the difference between friendly combatants in a situation and unfriendly ones.

It was peculiar, really, Jackson thought for the hundredth time as he looked down at his dog in bewilderment. Until recently Sargent wanted to obey him just about as often as a rabbit wanted to jump into a roasting pan of its own free will. Then it had been like someone had flipped on a switch inside the little bugger and now he was doing everything and anything in his doggy power to do all that Jackson asked of him. Eventually Jackson had to concede that perhaps Sargent hadn't been the problem. Animals were very intuitive. In all probability Sargent had been able to tell right off that Jackson hadn't wanted anything to do with him. Not through any fault of his own, but because Jackson hadn't been over Chico just yet.

Funny how that all felt so distant now. As though it had been another lifetime. He had been so consumed with the strange experience of having to share his consciousness with someone else . . . someone very dominant and very powerful, that he hadn't had time for wallowing. He had moved on with his life. Or rather, his post-near-death. He supposed that was the most sobering thing about all of this. If not for Menes's interference and selection of him for host, he would be dead. He would have left his sister all alone in the world. No parents. No siblings. No . . .

Well, there was Ram, he conceded reluctantly. And because Docia was host to another Bodywalker, named Tameri, he supposed she would never be alone again for the rest of her life. But outsiders were one thing, and family quite another. He for one didn't know what he would do without Docia. She was the only family he had left . . . outside of Leo. But the badass mercenary wasn't blood. He was more like a brother of the soul. The two of them had raised Docia together and Leo had been there for him through some of the toughest times of his life.

He had been avoiding his best friend ever since the

scene of his "death." He didn't know what Leo had made of what he had seen, and he had seen a lot. He had also killed Odjit, the vicious leader of the Templars, a sect of the Bodywalkers that was actively carrying on a civil war against the Politic, the lawful part of the Bodywalkers of whom Menes was the ruler. But Leo, as well as Marissa, had been made to believe everything they had experienced in that moment was nothing but a dream. So neither had any idea that Jackson had died and that Odjit had been killed.

But Menes had assured Jackson that like a hydra, the Templars would grow a new head quickly. This came as no great surprise to him. Knowing what a never-ending battle that was, he did not envy Menes his position.

Their position.

You will have to quit soon, Menes said with little gentility. *Surely you realize that? The Politic awaits our leadership in New Mexico. Even your sister has left to go there with Ram as he holds the government center for me during our Blending. What is the purpose of training this animal when you know you must leave him?* Menes reached out with Jackson's hand and rubbed at the dog's ears. *He is a fine beast, and you are making it difficult for him to do his job well if you don't transition him to a new owner as soon as possible.*

Jackson didn't respond. He knew he was in some sort of denial, and he knew every word was the truth. That didn't make it any easier. To leave everything he knew? To leave a lifetime's work behind and force new, unappreciable goals onto himself? He resisted the thought of it with every fiber of his being. He loved being a cop. The law is what he excelled at. What he thrived for. And the K-9 unit . . . he would have been content to stay in the unit until he retired.

But he'd made a deal with Menes, and now he must

honor that. Menes had held up his end. He had brought him back to life. Now . . .

He knelt down beside Sargent, tousling him roughly, patting his dense, muscular body until the dog was grunting with pleasure. It was then that he realized just how attached the dog had become in spite of Jackson's months of recalcitrance. Jackson wouldn't be the only one affected when he was compelled to quit, leaving the dog behind to connect to a new handler. Perhaps he *was* being selfish, training Sargent now and allowing him to imprint on him as a companion, as if they truly were going to become a warrior team when he knew there was no enduring future for them whatsoever. The understanding made him frown as he stood up, his heart feeling a bit heavier as he entered the building, Sargent trotting perfectly at his side.

Sargent's training was showing impressively as the dog resisted all the smells of the food the dinner shift was partaking of. Jackson's dog was especially fond of hotdogs, and Detective Wells had two sitting in a take-out box on his desk. But Sargent simply walked by, only his nose flaring in recognition of the coveted scent.

Then, unexpectedly, Jackson was pulled back by Sargent's leash. The dog sat dead still, his butt hitting the floor and his heavy body becoming suddenly unmovable. "Come on boy," he instructed, his hand signal to retrieve the dog automatic as he made the command.

Sargent stayed.

The door he was near opened, and out stepped Marissa Anderson. She came up short at the sight of the dog, rocking back a little on her fiercely high heels. Honestly? As tall as she was, why the heck did she have to wear those killer heels? Other than to accentuate her long, gorgeous legs and the way her snug skirt loved up against her delectable backside, that is.

He saw her hands lift up in withdrawal, as if she were afraid Sargent would bite her.

"He won't hurt you," he felt compelled to say, even though she should've already known that given all the time she spent among cops and, most especially, her time talking to him about Chico's death.

"I know. I'm sure he's a very nice dog," she said, a tremulous tone underlying the stern bravado she was mustering up. Still, she couldn't hide the stressed tension in her body as she leaned away from the dog.

"Are you afraid of dogs?" he queried her directly, studying her face carefully for tells. The desperation in her eyes on his told him that he was right.

"Not at all," she lied. "Could you please move him out of my way? I do have things to do."

Damn. Damn damn damn. Why was it the more tightly wound and aloof she acted the more he wanted to rip it all down, leaving her vulnerable to him and opening her up to the idea that a grunt cop had a hell of a lot of *physical* therapy to offer the highly educated, perfectly poised, and consummately professional doctor.

"Chico, come." Jackson commanded his dog.

The entire corridor seemed to go still. Marissa. Jackson. The two cops that had been chatting it up a few feet away. Jackson felt a chill walk up his spine and a sickly rush of regret and pain swam in his gut. It was a command he had given over and over again for years. It was still second nature.

And, God love him, Sargent stood up and came immediately to heel, clearly knowing what Jackson had meant to say and making no notice of the slip. He took no offense. It only solidified Jackson's admiration and connection toward the canine cop.

But the humans around them were another story. They were suddenly watching him with an almost eager sort of wariness, as if they were staring at the high adrenaline danger of a ticking bomb.

"It's only natural to become victim to longtime habits," Marissa said softly, soothingly, as she put a gentle hand atop his biceps, her fingers warm through the fabric of his uniform shirt. He could smell her now and almost instantly the calamitous emotions caused by his faux pas were forgotten and other sensations rushed up to replace them. She smelled of sweetness, like fresh-baked cookies made with warm, gooey chocolate. It made him want to nibble and lick and . . .

He jerked his thoughts away when he felt himself getting hard. He drew away from her, turning his back to her, shutting down her empathy and ignoring her nearness the best he could.

"It happens," he said with a shrug. He paused to give a hard look to the other two cops in the hall who immediately moved along and resumed their conversation.

"Do you want to . . . ?" Marissa began predictably.

"Jesus, Doc," he snapped shortly, "why does every little thing need to be talked about? That's a hell of a world you live in. If I took time to kick around every stray feeling or negative thought I had I'd never get anything done."

She bristled, as she invariably did when he dismissed the effectiveness of her work.

"I was just—"

"Well don't," he bit out, cutting her off. "I don't need your mothering and fussing." Then, without understanding why he did it, he turned back to her and stepped into her personal space. She immediately took a step back, but the wall was directly behind her now and she found herself pressed back into the painted cinder blocks. Oh, he knew it was playing with fire, bordering on insubordination and about to cross into sexual harassment, but he also couldn't seem to make himself care enough to back off. "Unless you have other ways you'd like to fuss over me," he said, his voice dropping so only she could hear him, and so there was no mistaking the intent of the remark.

She drew in a small, startled breath, holding it as she stared up at him and searched for a response that wouldn't immediately come. As he looked down into her eyes he confessed to himself that he'd always found the blue-green color of them to be compelling and beautiful.

Pupils dilated. Pulse beating rapidly at the base of her long, beautiful neck, he heard ghosting through his thoughts. *Whatever she says, she is aroused by our suggestion.*

Our.

The pronoun in his mind caused him to falter and he stepped back awkwardly. Our. He was no longer a "me" or an "I." He was a "we" and an "us." He no longer spoke for only himself, and he no longer had his own mind and solely his own impulses to control.

He was searching for a graceful exit out of a situation of his own making when someone came running up to him, out of breath and clearly overexerted. Then again, Tim McMullen was always out of breath and overexerted. He'd put on quite a bit of weight over the years and probably hadn't seen the inside of a gym since academy training.

"Jacks! Jacks, there's a kid missing. Riley's on vacation in Albany with his family," he puffed, even though Jackson already knew the other K-9 officer was away. "The captain wants to know if you think Sargent is ready to help us out."

"Whether he is or isn't," Jackson said, "it's better than nothing."

"I'll come too," Marissa said. "The family is going to need someone."

"Took my next words out of my mouth, Doc," Tim said with a toothy grin.

Marissa hadn't realized that going to the scene of the missing child meant she would be forced to ride shotgun with the very officer she'd been trying to avoid for weeks. She supposed she could have taken her own car, but then he would have known just how much he was getting to her and she refused to give him the satisfaction. Let him stew and wonder, the little bastard. She was tired of this whole situation. Tired of having her sleep ruined every single night because he had wormed his way into her subconscious. And because of that disturbed sleep, she was just plain tired.

In the backseat Sargent was pacing back and forth, getting on her nerves with his whining. Jackson must have noticed her tension because he said, "He knows something is up."

"I imagine the siren is a dead giveaway," she said dryly.

"It is, actually, even though he hasn't got too much experience with it. We've exposed him to it several times already to get him used to the sound, and he associates it with training, which is exciting and rewarding as far as he's concerned."

Marissa stole a glance at him. Although he was trying to adopt a laissez-faire attitude, he had a white-knuckle grip on the steering wheel. She wished she could read his mind and figure out why. Was it anxiety about working in the field for the first time with a new dog since Chico's death? Was it tension from the interrupted moment of sensuality between them that still had her heart beating wildly?

She should have been offended. She should have slapped his face off in a single blow. But she hadn't. She had been paralyzed as his heated suggestion caused her to get weak and wet in all of a heartbeat. And she had been terrified that he would know it. He seemed to perceive a lot of things lately. Ever since . . .

She shook herself mentally and then forced herself to converse with him, trying to prove to herself that he didn't rattle her in the least.

"I heard your sister is getting married," she blurted out—an obvious stumble for conversation.

He smiled with one side of his mouth, his entire face changing from a guarded expression to one so warm that it peeled years away from him.

"Yes. To Vincent Marzak."

The man who had "kidnapped" his sister three weeks ago. Only it had turned out to be just a very big misunderstanding. She didn't know all the details . . . she just remembered Jackson apologizing to everyone for his behavior and then eating a lot of crow and taking a lot of shit from the brotherhood of the SPD. There was very little room for error in an environment like the one they worked in. If you made mistakes you paid for it. But Jackson had withstood the weeks of ribbing and practical jokes far better than she would have expected from him, considering the short fuse he'd been displaying at the time of the incident.

But it was like . . . it was as if she were dealing with an entirely different man. As though the incident with his sister had flipped some kind of switch inside of him that made him recognize where he had been coming up short . . . or perhaps it finally forced him to reconcile with the recent loss he'd suffered.

Or so she had thought. But that move a few minutes ago of trying to throw her off balance and disturb her line of concern when he had called Sargent by Chico's name, that was a classic avoidance maneuver. He was throwing up a smoke screen of sex and inappropriate-

ness to obscure her focus on the one thing he didn't
want to address.

Ahhh . . . so that was it, she thought. The ultimatum
he'd given her had been his way of trying to cut off her
access into his mind and emotions! Why hadn't she seen
it before?

*Because a little part of you wanted it to be genu-
ine . . .*

Marissa ignored that nagging little whisper in her
subconscious. She couldn't afford to indulge it. And
honestly, Jackson couldn't afford it either. He needed
her to be far better at this game than he was. He didn't
know it . . . but he needed it.

"It must be a very big change in your relationship
with her," she observed.

"Not really." He shrugged. "Vincent treats her like a
queen." For some reason she got the feeling she was
missing an inside joke when he smiled rather mischie-
vously. "Ram would rather take a bullet than let any
harm come to her. She's in very good hands."

"Ram?" she queried.

He blinked, a small line of tension tautening up the
length of his arms and his grip on the steering wheel.

"Nickname. I think it was football related or something."

Okay now that was weird. Why did it feel like he was
lying to her? If so, it was a really silly thing to lie about.
What the hell did she care where the name came from?
He could have said it was his alter ego's name for all she
cared. She'd heard stranger and weirder things in her
career.

She decided to let it go. She told herself she was being
oversensitive. After all, she had been on edge around
him lately, waiting for his other promised shoe to drop.
She'd been envisioning hundreds of scenarios, a thou-

sand ways to face the application of his promised assault on her, and it had made her hypervigilant.

"We're here," he said abruptly, throwing the SUV into park. Sargent went wild, pacing in the back of the car, whining at an earsplitting pitch and consistency.

Marissa fumbled for the door handle on her side, determined not to look at the lean, powerful line of his athletic body in uniform with the autocratic weight of his gun belt and vest lending a quintessential air of powerful masculinity. She would not allow herself to devolve into some kind of girlish flirt who giggled and twirled her hair as she checked out the cop's hot bod. Nope. That was so not her.

Mostly, she amended as she watched the sexy cop clip a leash onto his dog, bring him out of the car and, with a deep-throated sound, command him to heel. She would have to be dead not to notice how truly fine a male specimen he was. Watching him hold all that frenetic canine energy in abeyance was practically primal. Man and beast, moving as one, a team of ultimate power and strength.

She looked over the crowd of people assembled. Cops, civilians, EMTs, and every other sort of official she could imagine had been drummed up for the search. Something like this was a big deal in such a small town, and the local news crew was there right on schedule. But what she was looking for was . . .

There. Loss. Abject horror dulled by the weight of ultimate shock. Tears of disbelief quivering in the lashes of a woman being comforted by nearly a half-dozen people. The mother. The phalanx of loved ones surrounding her was keeping her protected from the media. There was that at least. But those loved ones would eventually become obstacles, in one way or another, that she would end up in contention with unless this situation resolved in a quick and harmless manner.

"How long?" she heard Jackson ask the chief of police—a tall, autocratic man with salt-flecked black hair and a pair of serious dark eyes. Devlin Morris was a good chief. He was just the right mix of hardcore cop and clever, diplomatic politician. He was accessible to the policemen and -women who worked under him, revered by them in many respects because he was a legendary figure on the force. Just the other day she had heard a story about him her patient had dubbed "The Polka-Dot Dress Story." It said something about how far you had made it in the world, when people referred to your adventures in work and in life with a title.

"Best guess is three hours. She sent the kid to his friend's house to play about four p.m. She figured he might have stayed for supper when he didn't come back after a couple of hours and says she tried to call him then. When she finally got seriously worried, she called the friend's house and found out he'd never gotten there."

"Three hours then," Jackson agreed grimly after a glance at his watch. She looked at hers even though she already knew it was close to seven p.m. They would assume the last sighting was at the time of the incident . . . whether that incident was accidental or by nefarious means . . . and work all following courses of action outward from there. For her part, she was looking at a mother who was no doubt kicking herself and asking why she hadn't called the friend's house sooner, why she hadn't walked him there herself, why she had ever let him out of her sight in the first place.

But Marissa was also there for another reason. She looked carefully at each and every face that was there and was not obviously an official. She would consider them later on if it came to it. For now, she was focusing on the lookie-lous and those seemingly close to the family. Especially those close to or part of the family.

Statistics showed that a high percentage of child disappearances were instigated by another family member. Uncle. Cousin. Brother. Mother.

Mother. Marissa hung back from introducing herself to the mother just yet. Instead she leaned back against the warmth of the SUV's hood, the spring night coming in a little chillier than it had been. She had been in such an all-fired rush to jump into the car with Jackson that she had forgotten to grab her coat. Or her purse for that matter. But she wasn't going to waste time examining the reasons why she had done that. She had bigger fish to fry.

The mother looked suitably distraught. There really was no right or wrong way for a parent to act after their child disappeared, but there were certain things you wouldn't expect to see in their behavior.

For instance, the mother pulling out a compact and checking herself before allowing a reporter to speak to her. She dabbed at her eyes, pulled out a lipstick, tugged at her curls in order to make them settle better and more attractively. Now, it was highly possible that these behaviors were rote, that in her shock she was resorting to motions and actions that were comforting and familiar. But there were also triggers for certain behaviors. The trigger here, she imagined, was the desire to look at her most appealing to anyone watching her. Now why would a mother care about that when her child was potentially lying dead in a ditch somewhere?

A cold dread clenched in Marissa's stomach. She flicked her attention to Jackson, who had Sargent out of the car. The dog was twisting and turning around after having been given the scent he was supposed to search for. Jackson's brow was drawn in a wrinkled wave of perplexity and concern. He kept tugging at Sargent, redirecting him, but the dog seemed to be lost. Either that or he simply wasn't as well-trained as he needed to be yet.

She found the latter very hard to believe. She had watched out of her window for three weeks solid as Jackson had run Sargent through drill after drill after drill, ending every one with triumphant praise and the genuine pleasure of a job well done. She moved closer to him.

"Jackson?" she hedged, not wanting to interfere. She didn't even realize she had called him by his given name rather than "Officer Waverly" as she usually did.

"He's not catching on," Jackson said, the frown deepening.

"Jackson," she said more softly. "The mother."

That brought his attention sharply away from Sargent and up to her face. She couldn't help but jerk in a short breath when she found herself the center of his attention and staring dead into his brilliant turquoise eyes. They were that bright tropical ocean blue that made you jealous of their beauty and the power behind them could either scare the bejeezus out of you or make you melt into a puddle of hormones.

She was trying hard to resist doing the latter. Very, *very* hard.

And it was strange, but she had never thought they were so sea-colored before. She had always thought they were more of a classic blue. How strange . . .

Jackson redirected Sargent without looking at him and the pup obediently sat at his heel. He released her from his penetrating regard for all of a second to steal a glance at the missing child's mother. But then he was back to her, the intensity of his gaze boring through her, making her feel naked and shivery.

Crap! Get it together, Marissa! she scolded herself.

"What are you seeing?" he asked quietly.

She licked her lips.

"I could be wrong but she seems a little off. But let me talk to her before I pass summary judgment. However, you might want to move Sargent closer to the house."

He nodded curtly.

Marissa went to speak with the grieving parent.

CHAPTER THREE

Kamenwati was slowly turning the pages of a prayer compendium. It was dead silent in the room, so the rasping sound of one page against another filled the otherwise vacant air. There was one other sound. Breathing. There was an inadequate touch of comfort in the sound of her breathing as she slept. Sleep being a subjective term.

At least she was alive, he kept telling himself. But Kamen could not rejoice overmuch in the understanding that it was a matter of semantics in Odjit's case. Her host, Selena, who had given his mistress new and glorious life, was now Odjit's warden. Her prison.

When he got his hands on that mortal who had dared to injure her those three long weeks ago, his blade nearly severing Selena's head from her body as he had cut her throat, he was going to destroy him slowly, molecule by molecule, so he would know the same pain that Kamen was feeling and had been suffering from ever since Odjit had been wounded.

Her body was healed, finally. The process of drawing her away from the brink of death had been arduous and he had come close to failing in spite of her Bodywalker ability to heal rapidly.

Yet she lingered in a coma. Dead but alive. Alive yet

dead. It was an infuriating limbo and she didn't deserve such an ignominious existence. Odjit was the most powerful and beautiful priestess of her time. She communed with the gods whenever she walked on this earth, providing the Templar Bodywalkers with a conduit to them. All she had ever done, all she had ever tried to do, was bring the Bodywalkers closer to their gods.

But Menes and his foul followers in the body Politic thwarted her efforts time and again, leading the so-called "lawful" Bodywalkers further and further from the only resource open to them that could perhaps, one day, bring a peaceful end to this interminable existence where they resurrected over and over and over.

Life had become so empty for him. He would do any-thing . . . anything at all to finally find a sense of peace and finality. And he believed with all his heart and soul that Odjit was the only way to do that. Only her fervent belief could bring them there.

He turned the page and found what he had been look-ing for. A translation of the Bodywalker prophecy they called the Resolution Prophecy.

> *The children of the sun will fall into misguid-ance, will pervert the natural order of things, and find themselves knowing only night. There will be no final peace, no resolution, until Amun rises and holds his hands out to the most repentant and most deserving of his children. Love, blinding and pure, will guide Amun home at last. But should he find poison and acrimony amongst his children, then his fury and punishment will know no bounds.*

All scholars and historians, on both sides of the civil rift, agreed that the falling into misguidance had al-ready occurred. It was what had created the Bodywalker species to begin with. Their elaborate mummification rituals, meant to bring their wealth and households into the afterlife with them and preserve them for their glorious rest had, in fact, ended up tethering their souls to the mortal world. They had suffered for angering the gods with their hubris, waiting in the Ether, numb and in limbo, for hundreds of years before they had evolved enough to learn that they could exit the mists by luring to them a living mortal on the cusp of death. The lesser mortal souls were honored and graced with the Bodywalkers' powerful presences. They gave them new life and extraordinary power in trade for the dominant control of their mortal flesh. In essence, they paid for their near-immortality by moving to a submissive position and allowing the host full reign over all thoughts and actions.

And even so, they could never look upon the face of their beautiful sun. They who had been born to the deserts of Egypt and Mesopotamia, the absolute children of the sun and the great god Ra. It was a painful and bitter punishment, and Kamenwati, as well as all of the other Templar followers, longed for the day when this curse would end.

But here was where interpretations divided. The Templars like himself and Odjit believed wholeheartedly that if Amun rose and found the Bodywalkers at war he would be further angered and there was no telling what greater punishments it would earn them. Templars like Kamen believed that prayer, rituals, and absolute devotion to the gods and to a unified peace was the only way to earn Amun's blessings and, finally, a place in the afterlife.

The godless Politic with their modern ways and blasphemous practices would be the ruin of them all. Kamen could not see that happen. Refused to see that happen. He was tired. So very damn tired. He longed for the end of all of this. Sure, he had thrilled in the immortality of it all in the beginning. But it had not taken but two long lives for him to feel disenchanted with all that had once given him joy, like material things and prestigious power. He had been wealthy and powerful in his original life and continued to enjoy those same powerful positions with every rebirth. It was just as easy to pick a wealthy host as it was to pick an impoverished one. When hosts rose into the Ether and touched souls with the waiting Bodywalkers, they learned a great deal about them. It allowed them to choose the most compatible soul they could find.

For Kamen that had meant physical strength, a position of wealth and power, and, most important, very few human connections, such as family or siblings. He wanted nothing to do with his host's former life. He had no patience for the petty things mortals worried and squabbled about. His host, an entrepreneur named Thomas James, had been married. It had taken two weeks for him to Blend enough with James to dissolve the marriage. He had made certain to be cruel and do and say the most unforgivable things he could imagine, compelling the wife to walk out and never consider returning.

He had methodically alienated himself from his host's former life in all ways except the financial and business aspects. Those he kept afloat, albeit from a distance, by using others to manage the day-to-day affair of maintaining a steady flow of income.

Because as powerful as the Templars were, they could not simply conjure the means needed to buy them the land that sheltered and secluded them or the food they needed to sustain their hosts.

"Your pardon, my lord."

Kamen looked up sharply, seeing a hesitant acolyte standing just outside of the doorway. He had given strict instructions that no one was to cross the threshold into Odjit's chamber—aside from himself and whomever was chosen to wait upon them. They also should know by now that he was in a perpetually surly mood and would remain as such until Odjit returned to them in her full glory.

Perhaps not even then.

Damn this never-ending existence, he thought heatedly.

"Well? You've come this far to test my patience. I suggest you speak with more alacrity." He shut the compendium in his lap and moved it onto the table. It was heavy and quite old and needed to be treated with a great deal of care.

"I think we have found him, my lord."

The heat of instant fury raced through him. His immediate thought was that by "him" the acolyte meant the nameless, as yet untraceable human who had mutilated their mistress. Then he recalled that he had not set that task to the Bodywalkers, but instead to humans. He had sketched the face of the Latino man to the best of his ability and had presented it to three different private detectives, two of whom lived in the area where the attack had taken place. As natives, they had to be able to find some clue as to who this man was. He was not a ghost after all.

"Menes," Kamen said quietly when he realized the actual "him" that was being referred to. "Where? New Mexico I take it." He had been hoping to get a shot at the Politic bastard while he was weak and still in the Blending process. If he was already in his stronghold with Ramses and his contemptible traitor bride to protect them, there was no point in making an attempt on him while Odjit was so indisposed.

"No," the acolyte corrected him gently. "It turns out

he's been hiding in plain sight all this time. Sybelle the chantress has seen it clearly, although she is not of equal power to our great mistress—"

Chantresses were powerful spiritual women, also known as prophets—or a human might call them psychics. They could see things beyond normal ken. The future. Danger. Sometimes messages from the gods themselves, although it was rare for anyone in Templar ranks other than Odjit to lay claim to such a power. Odjit was easily threatened by anyone who harbored the potential to outgun her.

"Where is he?" Kamen demanded, cutting away the effulgent praise the acolyte was about to heap onto Odjit.

"Saugerties. New York."

"Get Thorn. And my lead Gargoyle."

"Of course, my lord," the acolyte said, bending to enter a deep bow, as if the depth of his ability to bow before Kamen were equal to the amount of loyalty to be expected from him. But Kamen was no fool. If there was one thing he had learned in his many lives, it was that no one could be trusted.

No one.

The acolyte turned, but Kamen halted him with a sharp snap of his fingers.

"Fetch Chatha to me," he said darkly. "I have a special task for him."

The servant paled by three shades and his fingers almost instantly began to tremble. Kamen watched him with genuine curiosity. Would the acolyte brave Kamen's wrath by refusing the request, or would he brave the unpredictability of the psychopathic killer? It was an intriguing contest.

The repeat of a deep bow gave him his answer, and just like that the moment of fascination was gone. Like all the moments before it, fleeting and ephemeral and nothing. Always such vast nothingness.

He glanced at Odjit.

Nothingness. But there was going to be a price to pay for this nothingness. And like anything else, he knew no one source could be trusted to complete the task, so it was best to sic all his best dogs on the problem at hand. Kamen walked over to his mistress, his fingers reaching down to brush over her forehead and over the fading scars at her throat. He knew that if he set a dog like Chatha on the trail of Odjit's would-be killer that he would go after the quarry with rabid delight, but only for as long as it amused him to do so. Kamen's job would have to be to make the process as entertaining for him as possible.

Someone had taken the last vestiges of light from his world . . .

. . . and that someone was going to pay.

Leo Alvarez opened his eyes to utter darkness and the smell of musty perfume.

"Shit," he grumbled under his breath as he fumbled for his watch, trying to do it as gingerly as possible. The owner of the perfume, not to mention the bed, was asleep against him, snoring a little on every breath.

Six p.m. Or eight a.m. Tasmania time, which is where he'd just spent two weeks routing out the remains of a drug cartel that had been in hiding on the otherwise harmless Australian island. Depending how you looked at it, he had either overslept or was waking just in time to start his day. He groaned softly when pain shot through both the back of his skull and his eyes. No doubt a recollection of the tequila he'd been pounding back, trying to drink some fricken lumberjack under the table last . . . yester . . . ah fuck it. He just took pleasure in the idea that the lumberjack was probably still throwing his guts up. Luckily the lady of the stale perfume hadn't cared whether or not Leo was drunk, she'd brought him home anyway. Which was good last night, but not so good this morning . . . evening . . .

"I fucking hate time zones," he grumbled under his breath.

Now the trick was to find a way to extricate himself from woman and bed without waking her up. In his favor were vague memories of her drinking pretty heavily herself the night before. Odds were she was down for the count. He also seemed to recall some heavy-duty drunken sex in there somewhere. Actually, he was pretty damn proud of himself for it. Performance under the influence of alcohol could be a hit-or-miss situation. Especially that much alcohol.

He had danced through more than one bottle of Jose Cuervo Especial during this particular contest. And if he remembered correctly, he'd won a fuckton of money when Mr. Lumberjack went down like a felled tree, the wooden floor of the bar shuddering with the impact. *People could be so predictable,* he thought. They figured the man with the height and girth was going to handle his liquor better than a man half an inch over 5'10" with lean, whipcord strength and no fat to help absorb the tequila.

They had figured wrong.

Unfortunately, there was a price to be paid for being right. Actually, it was more like a steep cover charge. Number one, a hangover. Not a bad one because he'd remembered to drink a lot of water along with his shots and he'd taken aspirin before finally falling asleep. Number two, slipping out of bed without waking his hostess. Luckily this was something he'd had a lot of practice in. Infiltrating and extracting, without his targets being any the wiser. Honestly, they had both known this was going to be a straight-out tumble and nothing more, but he wasn't interested in any pillow talk. She had already run through a lifetime's worth of beauty-shop drama from where she worked, with the occasional segue to toss some serious venom her ex-boyfriend's way. It was a good thing he'd been so hammered or he might have developed momentary discretion, looking for someone who had less juvenile drama in her life. Of course, those kinds of women were either A) taken or B) wouldn't be caught dead in the seedy joint he'd sauntered into. And since he'd had no desire to juggle the difficulties of a better class of woman, this one had more than served her purpose.

And it wasn't as though he'd used her with no regard for *her* needs. He'd made her pretty damn happy. And to be honest he hadn't originally planned to bed her. He'd been really wiped out from the flight back to New York from the land of Oz. But when a woman puts her hand down the front of his pants, what's a guy to do? She'd have been insulted if he'd turned her down.

Leo gingerly moved over her since his side of the bed butted up to the wall. She didn't so much as stir as his catlike movements kicked into autopilot, years of training to move with silence and efficiency doing him some justice.

As he pulled his jeans on he looked around, trying to remember what he'd done with his sidearm. Under the pillow. Of course. He sighed, making a note to lecture himself on the all-around foolhardiness of his actions these past twenty-four hours. He quickly pulled on his boots, resituating the dagger sheath in his right one so it wouldn't chafe him. Then he snagged his shirt and headed for the door, making his way out, and shutting it quietly.

Once he was out in the open air and the last fading light of the day, he scrubbed a hand through his hair and shrugged into his shirt. It wasn't until he was off the porch steps that he realized he didn't have his truck.

"Slick move, jackass," he muttered to himself. Faced with the choice of going back inside or hoofing it, he started to walk.

CHAPTER FOUR

Marissa looked up from her conversation with the missing boy's mother to see Jackson and Sargent running along the edge of the woods set back behind all of the properties on the street. Even as inexperienced as she was, she could see that Sargent was serious about whatever it was he was tracking. If Jackson went into the woods she would lose the chance to give him her impressions on the situation. She looked down at her shoes, wincing inwardly. She wasn't wearing stilettos, but there was a good two inches on the heels of the shoes. Her only consolations were that they were a sturdy pair of wedges and that they weren't exactly a favorite pair.

"Excuse me, Becky," she said gently to the mother.

Becky was watching Jackson now, too. And Marissa hesitated just long enough to see the woman start biting on the inside of her lower lip. The nervous gesture only confirmed what she had suspected all along. In a way she felt bad about suspecting the mother. She could always be wrong and it was a terrible thing to accuse an innocent mother of. But statistics didn't lie. An overwhelming percent of child disappearances and deaths were from the violence or nefariousness of a family member or close friend. It could just be that she had a form of Munchausen's, where she thrived on the attention she received through the plight of her child. It didn't mean necessarily that she had had anything to do with it. But it was enough of a suspicious behavior to mark how she wanted to approach this search. The more efficient they could be, the better. Especially since Jackson was, at present, the only dog handler in the area. Every hour that passed would make the situation bleaker and bleaker for the child, provided he was still alive.

She moved toward Jackson hurriedly, but not so much as to alert the mother of her suspicions.

"Officer Waverly!" she called out just as he was bending down to unhook Sargent from his leash.

"I think he's got something," Jackson said. "And don't call me that," he said with a frown. "We're a little beyond official titles, wouldn't you say?"

The remark paralyzed her throat momentarily, causing her to stare at him openmouthed for a good five seconds.

"I don't see why—"

"I don't see why everything needs to be an argument," he cut her off, regaining his full height, the leash still attached to Sargent's harness.

"Jackson, please," she said, frustration lacing her voice.

"There. Was that so hard?" He grinned, completely pleased with himself, the infuriating ass. For a moment she seriously thought about committing cop-icide . . . or something like it. No. Better yet, something really juvenile like putting motor oil in his coffee. The smug bastard.

Then again, knowing what the station coffee tasted like, he wasn't likely to notice the difference.

"I came to tell you that I don't think the mother is telling us the whole story," she said icily. "Not to get poked and teased and have you pull my pigtails like some bully in the school play yard!"

"I had a feeling you were going to say that," he said grimly. Then he looked at her with amusement. "Pigtails, huh? I bet you wore pigtails, didn't you? Cute little red-haired girl with scabby knees from falling while playing jump rope, freckles on her nose . . ."

"I did not have freckles!" she hissed in a low voice when a pair of cops walked past them. "Do you see any freckles?" She gestured with the blade of her hand at her eye-line, over her nose. "It's not like they magically disappear, you know."

"You never know, what with the miracle of makeup and all." His voice dropped as well. "So you're thinking foul play by the mother?"

The question was grim, reminding her that he had a job to do. That he was potentially the one who'd find this poor kid dead in a ditch somewhere or under a copse of trees. It made her realize that he'd been teasing her perhaps as a way of coping with that knowledge.

Great, Marissa. Some shrink you are.

Jackson leaned over and cut Sargent loose. He made a deep sound in his throat and Sargent took off into the woods.

"Keep working the mother," he said before heading off after his dog.

She did exactly that. Subtly, slowly, waiting for the woman to do something to give herself away.

"I just don't understand," she said, dabbing a tissue under red-rimmed eyes. The tears had been genuine at least. Whether it was actual grief or due to fear, that part was hard to tell. It was past three a.m. and as far as she knew, Jackson had only taken two breaks, and both of those breaks she suspected were for Sargent's benefit as opposed to his. The other dog teams from Albany were tied up and still hadn't arrived. Apparently there was no shortage of missing people that night. Since the Saugerties dog handlers covered a great deal of the townships in the area, the next closest town with a team had been notified. It was spring so the ski teams had come off the mountains and were being called back to join the search. They were just now starting to arrive.

"Damn him, I'm going to nail his ass to the wall," barked Avery Landon, the precinct captain. "He's ignoring me on purpose!"

"Tommy was such a good boy," the mother was saying. "He always, always listened to me. Never did a single thing wrong."

"I'm going to go out there and get him myself."

Uh-oh. Trouble. And she knew there was only one person "out there" who would pretend he didn't hear his captain recalling him if he didn't want to hear it. He would work himself until he dropped, the noble idiot. He'd let that dog rest, but he'd probably work himself into a—

Was.

Cold seized Marissa by the heart, freezing her breath in her lungs.

Was. Tommy *was* a good boy. Not *is*, but *was*.

And that was when she knew Tommy was most likely dead already. It could have been days ago . . . who really knew? The only other person to see him had been his teacher on Friday. Two whole days ago. And here he was, missing quite conveniently before he was due to show up in school the next day.

"Excuse me," she said numbly, standing up and walking over to Landon. "Captain, I know where Jackson is." She didn't actually, but she suspected what she had to say would flush him out far quicker than his railing captain would. But she did have his cell number and as soon as she got into the woods and far enough out of earshot, she was going to tell him to come in.

Because as far as she knew, Sargent hadn't been trained as a cadaver dog. It took a very special type of training for that.

"Where?" Landon demanded on a growl.

"Firstly, Captain, I can appreciate that it's late and we are all very tired, but snorting like a bull isn't going to help. Secondly, if you think I'm going to tell you so you can extract your pound of flesh you clearly don't know me very well. Let me go. There's as much chance of me talking sense into him than anyone else, I guess."

"You get him and you bring him back ASAP, Doc," Landon ordered. "I swear I'm writing him up this time. He's gotten more and more insubordinate this last month . . ."

Marissa tuned out the rest of the tirade, hunching into her sweater, and moving toward the trees quickly before Landon changed his mind and sent someone with her. Actually, it was pretty thoughtless of him not to do so. She probably should have told Landon her suspicions, but a few minutes either way wasn't going to make much difference. It had been hours, actually, since anyone had made anything resembling headway. Anyone but her.

Was.

It was a horrendous word to use when referring to a child, she thought as she picked her way carefully through the trees and brush, keeping her back to the house and the command station as she moved out of sight. Usually a mother would deny the idea of her child's death for as long as was logically possible . . . and even then some. She knew mothers of missing children who never stopped looking, not even decades later. Never stopped hoping that one day their doorbell would ring and there their child would be, all grown up, children in their arms, some miraculous circumstance bringing them home at last. Denial was a painful coping skill. But it was almost always there. Sometimes until the bitter end.

Once she was deep enough into the woods, the terrain suddenly steep and indicative of her having begun to travel up the mountain, she pulled out her cell. Belatedly she realized she might not get a very good signal there. That could be why Jackson wasn't answering his cell or his radio. Well, the radio was less likely . . .

"Marissa?" He picked up on the second ring. So much for that theory.

"Landon is so hot you're going to need to call the fire department to put him out," she said wryly.

"Yeah, I figured he would be."

"You can come in now. You're not likely to find him, Jackson."

There was a long minute of silence.

"Fuck. Are you sure?"

"Pretty sure."

"Double fuck." She winced. She didn't think she'd ever heard him swear before. He had once told her that if he swore in private it made it too easy to revert to it in public and during the job, when he needed to stay cool or risk enflaming a situation. "Where are you now?"

"In the woods. Actually, I think I may have gotten a little turned around," she said. It wasn't the truth, but Jackson needed someone to rescue, no matter how small. It was a silly thing to do, and maybe she was treating him like a child who needed his hand held, but hell . . . someone had to do it. And if that wasn't the definition of her job then she sure as hell didn't know what was.

"Okay, stay where you are. We don't need to be looking for you as well."

"It's not that bad," she laughed. "It's not like I'm lost in the badlands or the Grand Canyon or something."

"Just the same. Let us come to you."

"But how are you going to know—?"

She realized she was talking to herself when her phone clicked off in her ear. Okay sure, so he had a supersniffing dog, but it's not as though Sargent had a sample of her scent to go on. It wasn't as though they were going to make a beeline straight to her in a matter of minutes.

"All right, so much for that idea," she muttered to herself when, minutes later, Sargent came bounding out of the trees at her, barking happily, his master sharp on his heels.

"How do you do that?" she demanded to know. "You couldn't possibly—"

"Two words. 'Find Marissa.' That's all it took. This dog has a jones for you, Doc, or hadn't you noticed he plants his ass in front of your door anytime I'm not paying close enough attention?"

She'd noticed. And it had unnerved her every time she'd come out and found the dog staring and waiting for her to appear, like some kind of canine stalker.

"You probably taught him to do that because you know I'm nervous around dogs."

That earned a lifted brow. He'd been working at getting her to admit it for three weeks now. His sea-green eyes narrowed on her, the sharp relief of color in the darkness more than a little eerie. She shivered, lecturing herself for letting the woods creep her out. For letting him see any weakness in her at all. She normally wasn't afraid to be human in front of her coworkers and patients, but when it came to Jackson she felt the need to always be on guard and to always project a wall of strength. It was sometimes like dealing with a wild animal . . . if you showed any kind of fear it might turn on you.

That was incredibly unfair of her, she thought in the next moment. Jackson had never done anything to her to deserve her cautious behavior.

Unless you counted propositioning her . . .

"There's no need to be afraid of Sargent," he said, his tone gentling. He reached down and patted the dog. Sargent ate up the attention, his tongue hanging out of his mouth and his panting goofier than usual. She realized then that it was because he had been working nonstop for hours and was visibly tired. So was Jackson for that matter.

"Come on," she said coaxingly to them both. "It's time you two got some rest."

The sound of a shot rang out an instant after some kind of red projectile hit the tree next to Marissa's kneecap, bark spitting out at her and Sargent. The canine reacted, jumping back, and immediately barking an alarm. Marissa's heart leaped into her throat and she froze, unable to move, unable to react. Had someone just shot at her? On the heels of that thought was the understanding that had the projectile been an inch more to the right she would be missing a knee and an inch more to the left and Sargent . . .

She quickly looked up from Sargent and into his master's gaze. The understanding she had come to was already written clearly in his eyes, and she could see the rage flooding and darkening his beautiful green-blue irises. The darkness in them took her breath away. The idea of coming within an inch of being shot was nothing compared to the heart-clenching alarm that filled her soul. What she was seeing was something so virulently dark that her human instincts, watered down by centuries of domestication, came racing to the forefront, warning her to hightail it out of there.

She watched his head whip to the side, watched as he narrowed all of that rage in a single direction as if he knew exactly where it had come from. No guessing. No debating. He seemed to just know.

A second projectile snapped out of the trees and right before her eyes she saw it tear open a massive hole in Jackson's chest, the force of the shot jolting his entire body back into a tree.

Yet he did not go down, did not flail. Did not panic. How? How was he standing when it was clear the attacker had just tried to blow a hole in Jackson's heart? The only thing that had saved Jackson from an instant death was his flack vest.

Thank god, she thought fervently. Oh thank god he had that vest. And then, in the very next instant she realized the exact thing Jackson was realizing. *She* did not have a vest.

Jackson did not so much as flinch. Not a single motion in response to the fact that someone had just tried to kill him. He didn't drop down into the brush like she did, her hands covering her head . . . as if that would do anything to stop a bullet.

Marissa opened her mouth to shout at him, to yell at him to get down before he got his fool head blown off. But before a single sound could pass her lips she watched him unfurl his hands from the fists that they were in, watched him throw up both of his rigid palms and, with a deep, roaring shout of pure outrage, jolt forward as if shoving against a wall.

A huge blast of energy exploded outward, coming from nowhere and blossoming out from Jackson's capable body so roughly that every single tree bent under the power of it. Some even snapped in two, making the woods in front of Jackson come alive with the sound of cracking, falling branches. She watched gape-mouthed as he clenched a thick dominant fist, and as though he were yanking on an invisible rope, he jerked the whole of his powerful body back. Then, as if the other end of that invisible tether were wrapped around it, a huge pine tree came tearing toward him, plowing through other trees and bracken, rich loamy soil churning up in a dark black path behind it. It came screeching to a halt mere inches from the tips of his toes, a shower of old and new pine needles raining down on him. The roots of the tree remained buried in the soil, as if it had grown up in that very spot all along.

Sounding slightly hysterical in her own head, Marissa found herself thinking that the act gave a whole new meaning to the phrase "moving heaven and earth." And there, up in the mid branches, sat a man who was clinging to the trunk of the tree.

However, the instant the tree came to a halt the attacker within it burst free of the branches, a power-filled explosion of cracking wood and even more pine needles raining down on Jackson as he leaped up from the ground and into the tree with a mighty flex of uniform-clad thighs. But strong as he was, human strength couldn't account for the distance he covered in that single leap. He made it all the way up to the attacker's former position. Then, using it as a secondary launching point, he burst into the air with a roar of fury that made her blood run cold. The two men connected in midair, a sharp punch of sound echoing back down to her, forcing her to recognize that it was the savage sound of flesh and, more important, bone snapping as force met resistance. Jackson grabbed the man by the length of his hair and slammed a vicious elbow into his face right before both men went plummeting to the ground. Marissa screamed in abject horror as she realized gravity had taken over the situation and she was going to watch two men hit the ground at full force.

They hit the ground all right, but both landed on

their feet, the impact so hard she could feel it under her. Suddenly they seemed larger than life, like two mighty titans at war with each other. She knew she was bearing witness to something that could never be unseen, a secret that could endanger her life. Suddenly Jackson's adversary spat out a pair of words, the language beyond foreign to her, and a charge of red light enveloped his hands and then exploded like a bomb when he used them to shove at Jackson's chest.

Jackson went flying back, tearing through the air until his shoulder and the right side of his back impacted a tree. Once again he landed on his feet, the only hint that he had been injured was a grunt as he regained balance.

The enemy, whoever he was and for whatever reason, attacked once again, more words spitting past his lips and more red, fiery light bolting from his hands in a massive ball of energy. But this time Jackson was ready for him. He leapt aside, propelling himself into a running charge and plowing into the attacker. They cracked their heads together, like two mighty rams challenging each other for the right to a mate.

"How do you dare?" Jackson roared into the other man's face. "How do you dare try and injure what is under my protection!" He gave the man such a vicious shake that he squawked like a dying bird.

"J-Jackson . . ." Holy hell, was that her voice? Was she actually going to try to reason with . . . with . . .

She had no idea what they were. She should just shut the hell up and figure out how to get away and run really, really fast in the other direction. But logic said, after witnessing what she had just seen, distance wasn't going to make all that much of an effective advantage.

"I will tear you down, Menes, and reap the reward and infamy for it! I will destroy you so thoroughly you'll find permanent end! This I do in the name of Amun!

And when you fall under our blades, I will take your human doll and use her until she swells with my get."

Well, apparently that was the wrong thing to say, Marissa thought. The roar of fury that ejected from Jackson was, in a strange surreal way, very flattering, as was the beating that commenced instantly after. There was a sense of being championed that she'd never felt before, and as terrified as she was of them and of what the other man had just vowed to do to her, she felt a wave of reassurance and faith in the power of the man fighting for her safety . . . as well as his own.

Jackson's shirt, she realized, had been burned away across the front. Charred, ragged edges in a large circle exposed the bulletproof vest he wore and it too was scorched to black. He was trading blows with the other man in earnest now, perhaps a little too earnestly, obvious signs of wrath causing him to overreach, to miss his mark. But after just a minute he must have realized this as well and grew intent and serious, taking more time to plot not only his attack, but his defense. The two men grappled, struck, and crashed through the brush and trees.

Our.

It struck her just as suddenly as "was" had when Tommy's mother had spoken it. Jackson's enemy had said "our."

"Jackson there's another!" She screamed the warning to be heard over the din of their fierce battle.

He looked up, distracted momentarily by the warning, looking to her as if the other was possibly coming after her. But he wasn't. Marissa suddenly grasped that this was all about Jackson, as something enormous and heavy dropped out of the sky to land behind him, with wings of terrifyingly large proportions. The wingspan of it must have been at least twelve feet wide.

Its *wingspan.*

It was a creature as ugly and horrific as any demon she'd ever seen illustrated in fantasy. Its gnarled hands, giant wings, and massive body looked as though it had been carved directly out of stone.

"Oh my god," she whispered, fear freezing her to the spot, gripping her so thoroughly she couldn't even scream. But what terrified her, mobilized something else.

Sargent.

The dog, she realized, had been barking viciously since the start of the fight, but Jackson had not commanded him or signaled him to move and Sargent had fought his ingrained nature in order to obey his master's training. But he must have decided enough was enough when the demon creature fell onto Jackson's back. He tore through the undergrowth, all savage teeth and snarls. He leapt for the first assailant, his teeth finding a mark on the man's left thigh and latching on ferociously. The titan, for all he was built like a linebacker, bellowed out a roar of agony even as a massive burst of red energy was exploding out of him. The demon had wrapped an arm around Jackson's throat, yanking him up from the ground and back against his massive stone chest. He'd been holding him still for the blast his partner was about to release, but Sargent's interference pulled the energy off center. It still hit Jackson at full burn, but the off-centeredness of the shot may very well have saved Jackson's life as his clothing burst into flame. His pants, vest, gun belt . . . it was all incinerated on contact from the front, the fabric trapped between his body and the beast's was all that remained.

Of all the times she had imagined scenarios where she might see Jackson naked, this one had certainly never crossed her mind. His skin was burned, but nowhere near what it should have been for having his clothes catch fire. It was red, more like a decent sunburn than anything. Pulled back and up, his back bowing, every single muscle, of which there were considerably many, stood out in stark relief, portraying quite clearly just how much he was putting into the struggle with the new adversary. Far leaner than those he fought, she didn't see how he could possibly survive against so much weight, strength, and inexplicable power.

A percussive blast exploded out from him, sending his enemies flying, Sargent dropping to the ground with a pained whine. But before either of his adversaries could impact anything, Jackson landed on his feet, reached out with both hands, each targeting an enemy and his fingers fisting hard. Each male body jerked to a halt in midair, both trapped by an unseen force, both struggling as if to breathe. Neither could move. Jackson stood with his thickly muscular legs braced apart, his body straining outward in both directions as if the effort to hold them took monumental strength. Then he whipped his left arm toward his right until his fists slammed together. And as he did that both suspended bodies careened into each other, a loud, sickening smack filling the air. He let them fall, leaping forward to get between Sargent and them when the dog tried to jump back into the fray.

"Out!" Jackson commanded roughly, a hand pushing toward Sargent and the telekinetic power he wielded snatched Sargent by his collar hard enough to halt him, forcing him to listen to the command. Then he turned back to the male who had wielded the deadly red energy, grabbing his enemy's head between his hands. "Suck Ether," he hissed as he wrenched the man's head around 180 degrees and shoved his face into the dirt. Then he sent another of those percussive blasts into his enemy's body, this time blowing him apart on a molecular level.

Marissa watched the man disintegrate into thin air.

* * *

Jackson couldn't keep himself from looking for Marissa, checking on her in a costly distraction as he looked over his shoulder at her. It allowed the Gargoyle the opportunity it needed to launch away from him and into the night sky. Gargoyles could fly at blinding speeds, despite the weighty stone of their bodies, and the creature was out of his reach within instants.

Later, Menes ground out in his mind. *In the future we will grow strong enough where they cannot escape us so easily.*

He was drawing hard for breath, in desperate need of a moment to pull himself together, but knowing he couldn't risk the luxury. Sargent was whining, a little put out that Jackson had pulled his leash, in a manner of speaking. But the dog couldn't possibly have stood up in a battle with these supernatural and powerful enemies. Jackson had tried to protect him just as he had tried to protect Marissa.

How had they found him? How had they known?

It was a trivial point of interest. They had their way of discovering things just as his people did. He had thought himself well hidden, safe in his anonymity, and it had been a foolish way to behave. Menes had allowed it in order to help Jackson's spiritual transition as well as the Blending process. There was comfort in the familiar, and he hadn't wanted to throw 180 degrees of change at him all at once. The Blending process was overwhelming enough as it was . . .

And he had lingered for other reasons. One of which, he confessed to himself, was sitting right behind him. But one step at a time. He couldn't guarantee that the Gargoyle wouldn't try another run at him or that they didn't have reserves out there somewhere.

Slowly, he turned to face the wide, wild blue eyes of Marissa Anderson.

Marissa was panting for air, the world swimming around her as she stared with wholehearted disbelief at Jackson. He took a slow breath, steam lifting from his bare skin and into the cold morning air. She didn't know that not all of it was from his exertions of the moment. What she didn't realize was the coming sun was lightening the sky, and when it finally began to touch his skin she would watch him slowly go numb, one second at a time, the obvious signs of life bleeding away from him until he was little more than a paralyzed husk, his consciousness trapped within and unable to do anything but scream and scream and scream for freedom. Because, even though he knew logically it was temporary, even though he knew that night must always follow day and that, with the darkness would come release and succor; that poisonous, deep paralysis and that long stretch of helplessness ripped at everything that Menes and Jackson were. Men of strength. Beings of power both physical and mental. Men of action. They were the men who others hid behind, taking comfort in the protection they could deliver. To be so exposed and vulnerable was the very worst of all things to men like them.

Marissa watched Sargent sit, his tail wagging in a *swish-swish* that kicked up old pine needles underneath a nearby tree, little cries eking out of him as he inched closer and closer to Jackson in an effort to win his attention. Sweat rolled down Jackson's skin, wending rivulets that tracked around thick, beautiful muscles and the veins and vessels that roped all along them. He was not overbuilt by any stretch of the imagination, but he was formidable just the same. And beneath a solid six pack of abs, was a tattoo. A dagger, pointing down toward a whole different sort of dagger, and two entwined snakes wrapped tightly around it—each snake devouring the tail of the snake before it in a never-ending circuit. There was something so primal about that emblem, and something so intimate about being able to see it like she was. See him. All of him.

And standing utterly naked as he was, there was nothing . . . absolutely *nothing* she needed her imagination for any longer. Except, perhaps, in the way furtive parts of her mind began wondering things like . . . how would his lean, sexy body feel pressed to hers, his hot wet skin slick against her and all that delicious muscle clasped around her . . . holding her . . . moving and shifting within her and making exquisite love to her?

She wanted to laugh at herself for the utter absurdity of it all. How could she possibly be thinking about any of that after what she had just seen him do? After she knew what deadly things he was capable of? She didn't even know who he was anymore . . . if she ever had at all. She didn't even know *what* he was anymore. In the flesh as he was he looked all human . . . or actually, fairly godlike as he seethed with power and energy.

He advanced on her and she skittered back, barely keeping herself on her feet as she snagged herself on the bracken and underbrush. Oh Christ. She was out there all alone with him. This was one of those moments when she wanted to curse herself for her foolhardy devotion to doing a thankless job. She had no business being out there, just as he had said. Maybe now she knew why.

"I-I didn't see anything," she stammered out. "I swear . . . I'll-I'll . . . I won't say a word. You know, therapeutic confidentiality and all that." She laughed, the sound weak and tinny.

"Aw c'mon, Doc. You and I both know that flies out the window if you think I am a danger to myself or others."

Damn. Damn, damn, *damn*! He was too smart for her own good, and she had always known that. It was, perhaps, why she had worked so hard to give him a wide berth. Or maybe it had been an instinctive reaction, some sort of flight mechanism that had kicked into effect for her, recognizing an apex predator subconsciously and working hard to keep herself far away from the danger he represented.

Only that was a bald-faced lie in part. Never, in all the times she had seen him, had she thought of him as being an unmitigated danger. She had come to know this man. He was thoughtful, conscientious, and, she had thought until this moment, he was perhaps the most law-abiding creature on the planet. His seeming devotion to doing the lawful thing, even when that lawful thing was contrary to what was very obviously not the *right* thing, had always struck her. Like setting a man loose he had known in his soul was a pedophile, a predator of small children, because he had no sure proof . . . or rather not enough to convince the DA to prosecute the case. But what he *had* done was spend his time off doggedly watching the man's every step until he did have that proof and could see him prosecuted. It was why he ought to have been detective grade by then . . . only he had held himself back, and she had always thought it was because he felt far more valuable as a K-9 officer.

She didn't very much trust all the things she had thought at the moment.

"Well," she edged out, "subjectively, he was a very *very* bad man. I mean, okay, so it would have been better if he'd had a trial of his peers, b-but clearly . . ." She trailed off, unable to finish because they both knew she was making it up as she went along and there was no passion of conviction behind her words.

"There are things in this world, Marissa, that you have no comprehension of," he said softly . . . dangerously . . . as he stepped toward her persistently, putting her into a steady back-stepping retreat.

"Clearly," she said dryly. "It's not every day a gal watches someone evaporate into thin air."

"You know something, that pluck of yours is probably the reason why we've had a jones for you for just about as long as we can remember."

"W-we?" she hitched out. Like the royal We? Or we as in . . . dissociative identity disorder we? Great. Not only could he wield deadly power at a whim, he was also mentally unbalanced.

He hesitated for an instant but then he was stepping forward again, twigs snapping under the weight of his movements. It made her look down at his bare feet and wonder how it was that he wasn't torn up by the underbrush. Of course that was perhaps a silly consideration under the circumstances. Obviously he was a god. Or maybe a demigod. From that powerful ability right down to that awe-striking physique . . . not to mention the total arrogance he was seething with. He simply couldn't be anything less. He'd always been notably confident in the past, but the sensation she was feeling from him now could have bordered on hubris. He was a living, breathing Hercules. Prometheus born to give the gift of fire to mankind. To her. God, what fire would he stir in her? It couldn't be much more than she had already entertained in her most secret fantasy life. Or could it?

Oh Christ. She was out of her mind. She was worried about *his* mental stability? She was the one who had clearly jumped right into the deep end. Her life was in the utmost danger and yet she was still obsessing about . . . about things she had never had any right to obsess about. No matter what their relationship, even if he had never walked through her office door, she was the department shrink. Any officer who might end up crossing her professional path must be treated as a patient at all times. Treating the precinct like a possible dating pool was absolutely out of the question. Now it was even more so. He was a killer. A stone-cold killer. A powerful killer. He had wielded a power that no man should ever have at his fingertips. Humanity was far too flawed and far too infantile to have such power in this world.

"Now there you would be right," he said quietly. "No ordinary man could do what I do and be considered anything but dangerous. But we . . . I . . . am no ordinary man."

"Well excuse me if I spit out a big fat *duh* on that one," she bit off, her ongoing panic beginning to make her a little surly. There was only so long a woman could tolerate being utterly scared to death. Given enough time, she was going to push past fear and move straight into bold foolhardiness . . . if she hadn't already. "And who is this 'we' we're talking about anyway? Because I must say it sounds a little crazy from the shrink perspective."

"I thought shrinks weren't supposed to say their patients were crazy," he said, amusement shaping his fine mouth into a broaching smile. It kind of pissed her off even more.

"Well I think I'm staring at a big fat exception to the rule," she spat.

"No doubt. Are you going to let me explain?"

"Do I have a choice?"

"My my, Marissa, you do get plucky when you're nervous. Your defense mechanism is showing."

"You're an ass," she bit off. Then she realized she was insulting a very powerful ass and she swallowed audibly.

"And you are either very, very brave, or very, very foolhardy."

"I'm teetering on a little bit of both," she said with a weak, breathy sort of laugh.

"I'm not going to hurt you," he said. And in that tone of voice, with all that rich bass reaching out to cuddle her up in its unexpected tranquility, she felt herself craving the ability to believe him. The desire frustrated her to no end. She was a strong, independent, professional woman! She shouldn't get all googly-eyed and mushy-hearted over the charming, handsome demigod who could smite her with a dirty look.

She swallowed noisily.

"You'll forgive me if I don't believe you," she said, thinking it would have sounded much stronger if she weren't breathing so damn hard. Her blood was racing through her veins, just as her breath raced in and out of her lungs.

"Oh, but you do believe me," he said, his tone even more coaxing, his hand lifting in a supplicating gesture. "If you didn't, you would have run away from me long before now."

"Well, as you're always pointing out, I'm not exactly wearing the right shoes for a foot race."

Jackson watched her tip a foot forward onto the ball of the black suede wedges she wore. They, like most of her shoe wardrobe, were no shorter than two inches in the heel, albeit not the four inches he was used to seeing her in. When she wore those shoes, she could look him dead in the eye. It was strangely erotic. She was not petite . . . not delicate. She was athletic and wickedly curvy, like a seductive Amazon woman, and he'd always had a weakness for women who could hold their own in a wrestling match with him.

And wrestling with Marissa was getting delightfully trickier with every passing moment. Jackson supposed he should be more concerned. After all, his secret was out . . . and to the worst possible witness he could have imagined. Instead, he felt as though his entire body was revitalized, even beyond the typical rush of adrenaline.

"Good point," he said almost absently as he scanned the woods around them. Something was a little . . . off. He didn't really know what it was, but it just was. Whether it was a cop's gut instincts or the paranormal sense of the Bodywalker inside of him, his skin began to hum with the need to get them out of there.

Problem was, he was as naked as the day he was born and the entire police department and a good portion of the town lay less than a mile away from them. Even now he could hear the distant disturbances in the trees and underbrush as clumsy men and women stomped all over the woods looking for a lost child.

The last thing he should be doing was wasting time toying with Marissa. But apparently he had zero self-control in the matter. Maybe it was because, in spite of all the damp pungent odors of the thick woods, he could smell her. Sweet and strong with an underlying streak of something undeniably sexual. It was how he had always imagined Marilyn Monroe must have smelled like. Living, breathing, oozing feminine lures. She was dazzlingly perfect, somehow having managed to keep herself from looking like she'd spent the past few hours tromping through the woods. It was one of the things that fascinated him. How did she manage to look and smell so temptingly perfect all throughout the entire day? And night.

And day.

He looked up at the lightening sky around them.

"Listen to me Marissa. I have to get indoors, away from the touch of the sun before it breaks fully above the horizon line. If I'm caught in the sun it will paralyze me."

Her guffaw burst out in two paths, half by mouth and

the other through her nose as she started to turn visibly pink along her skin.

"If you tell me you're a fucking vampire I'm going to find a very big stick, aim for your heart, and make you prove it."

"There's no such thing as vampires," he said with a wry little laugh of his own. "But you've already borne witness that there are more things in this world than the average human being is capable of understanding."

"I've seen you in sunlight," she scoffed at him.

"And yesterday was the very last day I could let myself go out in it. From this moment onward the touch of the sun is like poison to me." He hesitated, and she leaned in toward him with unabashed curiosity. She knew there was something unexplainable about him, knew he was, indeed, different. Dangerously different. And *still* she leaned closer.

"Poison?" she echoed. "Like . . ." She narrowed her eyes on him suspiciously. "Like turning to a poof of ash?" She made a small explosive sound with her lips, her hands blossoming outward to illustrate a mushrooming blast.

"Nothing so dramatic," he lied. As far as he was concerned, falling into a deathlike coma unable to move a single inch probably had its own moments of drama. Especially to an inexperienced onlooker. "I'd be happy to explain it after we find some kind of shelter. And"— he indicated his naked state—"I can't exactly march out of here past the base of operations and not draw attention."

She giggled at that, probably in an attempt to hide the scorching blush blooming over her cheekbones as she let his encompassing hand gesture invite her to yet another eyeful of all things Jackson, including that wickedly naughty tattoo just begging to be touched, stroked, inspected . . .

When he realized she was staring at him, openly con-templating him, it was all Jackson could do to keep himself from grinning. Or teasing. Either was bound to earn him a projectile shoe upside his head. He fiercely pushed away the awareness that threatened to crawl up inside him, along with a host of illicit thoughts.

Marissa nibbled nervously at the inside of her lower lip. She *could* just march off to safety, leaving him there vulnerable and butt-ass naked and make him entirely someone else's problem. If she had an ounce of brains in her head that was exactly what she ought to do. But . . .

"You can leave me if you like," he offered her quietly. "This really shouldn't even be your problem."

Okay, now that was creepy. How'd he know she was just contemplating that as a possible option for action?

"I can't just leave you here," she said, brushing flecks of bark off her skirt in a nervous gesture she didn't usu-ally allow herself to indulge in. Then she realized there was probably a whole hell of a lot of the stuff stuck in her hair. The man had wrecked half a forest, after all.

Among other things.

She had to be in shock. It was the only explanation for her inappropriate, leapfrogging thoughts. And to be honest, this whole holding on to her sanity thing was beginning to wear a little thin.

Looking back she wasn't sure what finally compelled her to run, but some stupid part of her PTSD brain thought it was a good idea and somehow thought she might be able to make it to some of the humans she could hear in the distance. As if they could actually help her.

She made it all of five feet before he was on her.

She lashed out wildly, connecting with something.

"Ow! Marissa!"

"Let go of me! Leave me alone!" she screamed at him.

"Marissa, knock it off!"

She didn't. She stomped down hard on his foot, for all the good that would do. And she couldn't believe he'd just said "ow." Those other two had beaten him, burned him, and practically blown him up and he'd barely flinched. But one little elbow from little old her and he was supposed to believe she'd hurt him?

Not freaking likely.

Then in a sudden flight of movement her feet came up off the ground and she went hurtling forward. All of a sudden, there was a rock face in front of her and she screeched as they blasted right into it.

And through it.

A cave or cavern, hidden by all the overgrowth, barely big enough to walk around in.

But she didn't have the opportunity to take even a single step. He launched her straight into the back of the little cave, smacking both their bodies up against the wall, with her front pressing into the cold stone and his front pressed hard and hot all along the back of her body.

Marissa gasped for every breath, the wall cold against her cheek and breasts. She watched his hand touch the stone near her face, just the tips of his fingers, drawing close to her while his other hand was on the other side of her, caging her in. And if the stone was cold, the looming strength of his body at her back was hot. He wasn't touching her right then, but all she had to do was push away from the wall by just a pair of inches and she would find herself curved into his whipcord-strong body. It took everything she had to keep from doing exactly that. She forced herself, instead, to remember just how terrified she was of him. She was. Wasn't she?

"Marissa," he breathed just behind her ear. "Marissa, Marissa, Marissa." He said it so slowly. Just her name. The first one reproving. The second exasperated. The third calm. And the fourth . . . suggestive. It was just her name, but it was so much more than that.

"You think you know me," he said in a whisper. "You think I'm still the man who sat in your office struggling to deal with grief and loss. You still think I'm a patient. I'm wounded. I'm . . . human."

"A-aren't you?" she stammered. She definitely wasn't at all sure of that. Not anymore. Never again.

"Fair question," he said, his breath washing hotly down over her shoulder. "I'm willing to explain if you are willing to listen."

"I-I don't see how I have any choice," she said, struggling to speak as chills of fear and excitement chased each other down her skin over her spine. *Just a little closer*, part of her whispered. *Run away, run far far away*, another part whispered.

"Now, there you're wrong. With me you will always have a choice. I can't promise a lot of things, but I can promise you that. Go on. Ask me to let you go. See what happens."

Marissa's heart thundered against the press of the wall, her palms sweaty where they were braced against the cool stone. There it was, the perfect opportunity to get away, to be free. If he meant what he was saying she could leave. She could run away. She had that choice.

She opened her mouth. She had every intention of asking him to let her go. But instead a shaky whisper left her.

"If you're not human, what are you?"

Goddammit, her curiosity was going to be the death of her, she thought fiercely.

"Oh, I'm human," he assured her. "But I'm more than just the human male you know as Jackson Waverly. So much more."

"So I gathered," she said roughly.

His lips were against her temple and she felt him

smile. For some reason it calmed her to know he was smiling. It was a ridiculous reaction, but it was there just the same.

"I want to tell you a story, Marissa. Short and sweet. Something to help answer a few of the questions swimming around in your head." He lifted a hand away from the wall and brushed cool fingers across her lips. The coolness turned to fire, as though he'd turned to flame against her, only this reaction was all her, coming from within her. Could he manipulate her body? With all she had seen him do . . . what couldn't he do?

"Once upon a time, a very long time ago, when pharaohs walked this earth and built tremendous monuments in the scorching desert sands, there lived a powerful and intense man . . . a king . . . named Menes. Menes was a great warrior as well as king. His great campaigns unified upper and lower Egypt. Brought disparate nations together under a single monarchy. It began a long age of Egyptian prosperity . . . and he was revered for it. They called him Scorpion . . . deadly . . . respected . . . acknowledged.

"And though he had two wives, he never knew love in his original lifetime. No . . ." She felt him breathe a sigh across her cheek. "He didn't even know the love of his son. He was foolish. He was focused on conquering the lands within his reach, thinking that was a value that was needed to make a life truly satisfying."

"But what . . ."

"Shh," he said against her ear. "Wait for it, angel. You'll ruin the story."

The truth was, his story was having a calming effect. Although how calm she could be with all that intense male power against her back was relative. But he was distracting her from her fear of him. And it occurred to her that this was probably precisely why he was doing this.

"Do you know what happens to great men of such hubris?" he asked her, his lips moving against the shell of her ear as he spoke.

"They fall," she answered breathlessly.

"They fall," he agreed. "They die in ignominious ways. They fail to be remembered for what they wanted to be remembered for. They become a punch line. Did you hear about the great pharaoh? Oh, yeah . . . didn't he get mauled by a hippo?"

She didn't want to laugh. At least she didn't understand how she could possibly find humor at that moment. But the breathy laugh escaped her just the same.

"Life can be so bitterly amusing," he said, and she could imagine the grim expression to match the tone of his voice. "But death can be ironic. As can rebirth." His lips turned against her ear once more. "I was given a second chance I did not deserve. I was given a love for the ages that I did not deserve. I was given all of this, angel, and all I had to do was trade away ever knowing the finality of peaceful death. Instead I live forever, and die again and again and again. Each time more painful than the last . . . or so it seems. This time I was reborn in this body, my soul sharing this space with the man you know as Jackson Waverly. We have since become one in most ways. And we are called the king of all of our kind. We are pharaoh of all the Bodywalkers."

It took a long minute after he stopped for her to grasp that he was dead serious about this claim.

"Okay, wait a minute. A pharaoh? A king? Jesus Christ, I would never have taken you for having a god complex," she spat out. "This is preposterous!"

"This is real. As real as the strength and body pressed against your back." He leaned forward into her to illustrate his point. "As real as the heat of life that burns inside of me. A heat that rises every single time we lay eyes on you."

"Will you stop calling yourself a we?" she barked at him, trying to throw her temper at him in order to cover the liquid burn of arousal that splashed up against her every nerve ending just from the feel of him. "I swear to god I'm going to have them put a psych hold on you!"

"And what about you, Marissa? Are you crazy? Or did you really see what you saw only a little while ago? Did what you see have any human explanation? When you tell someone else about it, will they believe you or threaten you with a psych hold?"

Tears, inexplicable and wild, leapt into her eyes, her heart racing once again as she realized just how right he was. She wished, oh how she wished, she could unsee what had been seen. She wanted to go back. She wanted to once again be ignorant that these deadly things truly existed in their world. She knew without a doubt that ignorance was bliss in this instance.

"Menes," she whispered.

"Yes," he whispered back, again ending with a warm wash of breath over her that caused her nipples to tighten painfully against the wall she was still leaning on. "And Jackson," he added. "Two souls, one body. We call ourselves Bodywalkers. And you do not remember this, but you were there the moment I was reborn."

She scoffed . . . well, half a scoff because he chose that moment to run the knuckles of his hand over her cheek and the sensation was ridiculously electrifying.

Why? *Why*, she demanded of herself, *does his touch always seem so electrifying!* It was just a touch!

"I don't know what you're . . ."

"Dream. Remember the dream you had when a blast of energy sent me crashing into a windshield. You cried over my body—"

"Oh my god! Oh my god, please shut up! Let me go!" She had already been trembling from head to toe, but now she was shaking because she was so incredulous and upset by his words . . . by the implication of his words. "It was just a dream! Just a—"

"If it were just a dream, then how would I know about it?" he asked, completely ignoring her request to be freed. "How would I know that you cried over me, dropping beautifully tender tears onto my face?"

Marissa's chest ached, partly from the way her heart was racing and now also because the emotion she had felt from that dream came rushing back over her. She wanted to push it away. To run away. To be anywhere but there and feeling what she was being forced to feel.

"Please. Please," she whispered. "Please stop."

Then Jackson's hands were on her shoulders, and she felt him stepping back half a step. The relief she should have felt didn't come because her traitorous body whimpered like a child who'd just had its favorite teddy bear taken away. Jackson pulled her away from the wall, but only enough to turn her around, his hands sliding up, his thumbs touching the underside of her chin and tipping her head back so that she was coaxed to look up into his eyes.

"My people have lived among and within your people for centuries," he said, the gentility of his voice reassuring and comforting in spite of her need to hold on to her panic and fear, because she knew that letting them go would mean acceptance and she did not, under any circumstances, want to accept what he was saying. "I will not claim we never harm anyone."

"Ya think?" she bit out.

It made the right corner of his mouth curl into a smile that reached into the stunning blue of his eyes.

"Like any society we have our villainous element. If anyone can appreciate that it would be a psychiatrist who tries to ease the souls of officers who have become jaded and bitter when they see just how horrible humanity can get. But lawful Bodywalkers always ask for permission to reside in the bodies of their prospective hosts. The day Jackson's life was being stripped from him, as you shed tears for him, he was in the Ether, meeting me, accepting my proposal of a newer, longer lifetime and a position in it that will influence the well-being of thousands of people, be they original humans with a single soul or those of us who have been given another chance at life. You were witness to all that led to that. The battle. My death. Your grief. And we could not let any of you go out in the world with knowledge of us, putting us at risk, so your minds were nudged into believing it was nothing more than a dream."

And she knew the very dream he was talking about because it had been the realest thing she'd ever experienced in her sleeping life. She had seen him go flying through the air, crashing back first into a windshield and then . . . dying.

She was shaking her head in negation even as his thumb came up to stroke the width of her bottom lip, sending more of that electrical awareness through some very private nerves inside her. If she accepted what he said, accepted what her very own eyes had just seen, then maybe his touch truly was full of magic. The idea made her shiver, warring with her still-healthy fear of the man touching her.

"I will not hurt you," he promised her in deep, gentling tones. "You mean too much to us, Marissa."

The sentence took her breath away. And it wasn't because his use of alternating personal pronouns was disturbing to her. Well, it was, but that wasn't what she was reacting to. Was he implying that he had feelings for her? Was she excited by that insane thought? There were thousands of reasons why she shouldn't entertain or encourage something like that, but what she had witnessed him do to that other person was really all she should need.

So why was her heart leaping with excitement?

"I want to tell you you're insane. I want to say you are delusional and hallucinatory. Hell, I want to say that about myself. But I know this isn't a dream. I know what you are capable of is not normal or human."

"On the contrary," he argued quietly. "It was the most basic act of humanity you will ever see. A being with good morals and conscience eradicating one without. He was from a sect of Bodywalkers called the Templars. Somehow he must have discovered that we are Menes, the leader of the Politic Bodywalkers. The lawful ones. He was an assassin bent on destroying me, hoping that my death will give them an advantage in the war we fight against his kind. If he had succeeded in killing me Jackson would be dead, and I would have returned to the Ether, trapped there for another hundred years."

"Why a hundred years?" she asked. Of all the things she should be asking . . . questioning . . . it seemed to be the safest choice.

"It is as the gods decide, Marissa. We are powerful as a species, but we are not omnipotent. Far from it. I am not a god," he said as he gently brushed her hair back with his fingertips. How, she wondered, could a touch be so comforting and disturbing at the same time?

"I don't want to believe anything you are saying," she confessed to him fiercely. "I want to be a thousand miles from here and I want to wish I had never laid eyes on you, Jackson Waverly . . . or . . . Menes. Whoever you are! I just want you to let me go. Are you going to let me go? Now that I know this incredible secret, are you going to let me go or . . . or do you have to d-do something to make me not remember any of this?"

"It cannot be done twice, Marissa. The human brain is too fragile to be manipulated in such ways too often.

And yes, I would set you free and I would trust you to keep your countenance."

"I sense there's a 'but' coming," she said wryly.

"But," he obliged her, "I believe you would not be safe unless you were under my protection from now on, Marissa. The creature that escaped has seen you. He will report to his masters about this battle, and part of that report will include you. They will assume you"— he paused with difficulty—"are of importance to me. If I let you go, they would seek you out and try to find a way to use you against me. Whether as a bargaining chip or as a corpse meant to shatter my calm, they will see to it your value is used for their benefit."

"So you mean just because I was standing next to you I'm going to be a target for the rest of my life?" She sounded angry now, and maybe that was a good thing. She desperately wanted to feel something else other than fear or . . . or . . .

"No. Because I protected you. Because I reacted emotionally to you possibly being harmed. That is how they know you mean something to me." He was touching her lips again, looking at them as though *he* wanted to use her for his benefit. And the thought made frissons of heat slip through every last vessel in her body. "But I will not let anyone hurt you, Marissa. I promise you that."

"You can't. You can't promise me anything of the kind! You can't be there every second of every day! And I don't want you there every second of every day!" She tried to pull away, to back off from him, but he followed her until she once again found herself trapped between him and the wall. "Please," she breathed, not knowing what else she could say or do. She was completely at a loss as to how to handle this situation. All of her training and professional experience meant absolutely nothing because *things like this did not happen.*

All her training and education told her was that she must have gone right off the deep end. She must have suffered a psychotic break along with the full boat of hallucinations and denial because it felt pretty damn real and she felt pretty damn sane.

"Please? Are you begging me to protect you or are you begging me to watch you die?"

"Stop. Stop saying things like that! Do you have any idea how crazy this all sounds? Jackson, you aren't an Egyptian pharaoh! You aren't a body snatcher o-or anything else. You're a cop. A really good cop with a really good heart and you have what it takes to go really far in the department i-if you would just . . ."

"Is that how you think of me?" he asked, sounding genuinely pleased to hear her assessment of him. "Isn't that funny? I always thought you didn't think I could cut a lifetime career in the SPD." A short, rough laugh popped out of him. "How strange. All I've ever wanted was your good opinion, Marissa. And now here you are giving it to me . . . but only so long as I deny the truth of who and what I am. Only so long as I allow you to deny it because you aren't equipped to deal with the understanding that there are more things in heaven and earth than you have ever conceived of before this. You approve of me only if I am the sum of your ideas of who I am or should be."

Marissa's breath caught in the back of her throat at the backhanded accusation that she was being close-minded. He couldn't have known that it was the one thing she couldn't bear feeling. The idea that she was being intolerant of another human being . . .

Human being.

She didn't know why she reached out to touch him. All she had tried to do since that horrible fight had ended was try to get away, push away, repel and resist. But now she reached to touch him, her fingertip resting shakily against his chest and then, a moment later her palm followed to press against his bare skin.

There. There it was. A powerful, steady heartbeat.

"A single heart . . . two souls. Human in almost every way, Marissa. Human and *more*," he said as though he could read her mind. Hell, for all she knew he *was* reading her mind. Unable to check the impulse, she let her eyes drop down the length of his torso. Naked as he was he was completely exposed to any inspection she wanted to subject him to. But the minute she laid eyes on his sex she whipped her gaze back up. Oh yeah, he sure seemed human to her. And he was definitely *more*!

"I want to believe you. I-I have to believe you because if I don't it means I've lost hold of reality. And at the same time everything inside me is screaming at me to push it all away. To shut it all away, because if I accept this craziness . . ."

"Then you must be crazy yourself. And who wants to admit that to themselves? Who wants to face the prospect that they might not be as in control of their own lives as they thought they were."

"Yes," she said softly. She looked back into his eyes, the sea-foam color of them so clear and sharp. And that was when she realized that he was so obviously *more* than Jackson Waverly had been. Jackson had been handsome and vital, dedicated and loyal, devoted to his work and those whose lives he held in his hands every day. She had always considered him to be intelligent, but not in an existential way. The man standing before her was everything Jackson was . . . and so much more. After Chico's death he had been growing increasingly less patient, his bitterness taking its toll on him. But she realized that for the past three weeks he had not had a single incident of short-temperedness. And psychologically speaking there was nothing that could have triggered a spiral in his behavior more than the act of training Chico's replacement.

"Why hasn't anyone noticed?" she heard herself asking, her tone softly astonished. "How could all of your friends and family spend day after day with you and not notice something was different?"

"Because I'm still everything that Jackson is. And they probably have noticed things, but certainly not enough to make them question me about it. But that will come soon enough. And as for my family . . ." He trailed off and she could tell he was debating something within himself for a moment. "Three weeks ago my sister died, Marissa. When she came back . . ."

"Oh my god! Docia is a-a—"

"Bodywalker."

"Body . . . Bodywalker." And as though saying it aloud was like speaking a spell, her mind and heart finally settled into acceptance. Whatever else happened, she knew she was going to accept this.

She was going to believe.

CHAPTER FIVE

Jackson was looking down into her face when he saw understanding blossom into her features and eyes like a drop of ink released into crystal clear water. It was understanding and, more important, it was acceptance. He knew that because her other hand lifted to touch his arm at the biceps, and for the first time she wasn't trying to press her body and everything else away from him. He knew she wasn't going to completely grasp all of what he had told her for some time, but at least she was now receptive to the information.

As for himself, he was more than a little confused by his own actions. True, he was only just learning about the power that Menes commanded, and of course there had been no way of preventing her from witnessing him in action. They both would have been dead if he had not shown his hand. But what baffled Jackson was why Menes had gone out of his way to make a show of protecting Marissa. He had said himself that those actions were like putting a bull's-eye on her.

So why had he made it so obvious? And it *had* been Menes in control at that moment. Jackson's first lesson in being host to a being as powerful as Menes was to learn when to step back and let the expert take charge of the moment, just as Menes did when in an element only Jackson could manage because of familiarity and experience. It was the more mundane things in life that found them more perfectly blended, and Menes assured him that would only grow and spread over time as they both continued to experience life and each other. But in spite of this Blending being supposedly finished, Jackson felt there was still much of Menes's mind that he simply could not access, whereas he felt the reverse was much less true. It was a strange thing, this feeling like he couldn't trust himself entirely.

Stranger still was the way he felt being near Marissa like this. It was as though all of his senses had gone into hyperdrive. The smell of her, something musky yet sweet at the same time, had him wanting to inhale deeper and deeper with each successive breath. He even lowered his head, trying to surreptitiously smell the floral shampoo she used in her hair. What was more, he couldn't keep himself from touching her, his hands still cradling her face, his thumb running obsessively over her lips. She had the fullest mouth he'd seen on a woman, other than Angelina Jolie. It begged for exploration, for experimentation. His mouth began to ache with the need to kiss her, his heart hurting in his chest as he resisted the urge. She was disturbed enough without having to fight off his advances.

Let go, he told himself fiercely. *Just let her go!*

"Marissa," he said breathily. *I'm going to kiss you.* "I think it would be wise to find me some clothes."

"Oh," she said softly, seemingly caught up in the same craving that he was.

She wants it, Jackson. Just kiss her. Kiss that delectable mouth and taste her.

Jackson stepped back, forcing himself to let go of her. He turned his back to her, closing his eyes as he clenched a fist against the desire riding him hard. It wouldn't be the first time he got hard from craving Dr. Marissa Anderson. But it would damn well be the first time she would know about it because, being completely nude, he couldn't conceal the result of his lust for her.

"Go. Out of these woods and to my car. I have a gym bag in the trunk," he said, keeping his back to her as he pressed hard palms against the wall, trying to erase the feel of her from his hands. "No one should stop you, but if they do just tell them the bag has supplies for taking care of Sargent."

"O-oh okay," she said. "I . . . I thought you said I wouldn't be safe without you," she hedged nervously. He glanced over his shoulder at her, turning only just as far as he dared.

"It will take time for the Gargoyle to make it back to his masters. Just do this quickly. I'll follow behind you and meet you in the woods once you're clear of witnesses."

He was so grateful when she nodded in agreement and moved toward the cave entrance that he thought he could cry with relief. He watched her push through the brush guarding the place, and then she was gone. He exhaled hard, finally turning around and leaning his back against the cold surface of the wall.

"What the hell are you doing?" he demanded of himself.

Being human, Menes, his new conscience answered. *There is nothing shameful about craving a thing of beauty.*

"I thought you were a one-woman man," he muttered petulantly.

My woman . . . There was a distinct hesitation and Jackson felt as though there was an omission taking place . . . *My woman is not here as yet. When she arrives you will know it without a doubt. You will feel the power of what I feel. In the meantime . . . there is no betrayal if you have desires counter to my own.*

But Jackson found the idea settling ill within him. He wasn't about to make advances toward Marissa when he knew there would be no future in it. Marissa Anderson was a forever kind of woman. She didn't strike him as the type to have casual sex just for the sake of scratching an itch. She would be looking for more. More than what he could give her.

No. Marissa was off-limits. And the sooner he reconciled himself to that the better off he would be.

And on that thought he left the cave, following behind her.

Marissa broke free of the tree line and hurried directly for Jackson's vehicle. Luckily she had seen him use the concealed trunk release earlier when he had gotten water for Sargent. She reached into the car and engaged the release. When she straightened and turned, it was all she could do not to scream when she nearly ran into Captain Avery Landon, Jackson's boss.

"What are you doing? You're not allowed in the front of an official vehicle, Dr. Anderson, without an officer. And there are weapons in the trunk." Langdon reached back and put a hand on the trunk lid, slamming it down into place again.

After all she had been through in the past half hour, it was the straw that broke every single ounce of self-control she had. She rounded on the captain with a fury.

"Of course I know there are weapons in the trunk!" she spat out. "And I also know that I don't belong in the front of this car without permission. But did it ever occur to you, you pompous jackass, that I was sent here to retrieve something for Officer Waverly? He's in the field with his K-9. And I know you know how dedicated he and that damn dog are. Too dedicated to take a break and fetch the supplies they need to keep hydrated and their energy up!" She reached back into the car and snapped the lock release again. "Jackson sent me for his supplies, and I damn well am going to bring them to him. Now back off and stop getting in the way of his work. Christ, you're your own worse enemy, Captain," she ground out at him as she pushed past him and looked into the trunk. "You're so busy trying to tighten your control freak noose around everyone's throat that you don't even realize what a hindrance you are to these men and women beneath you." She found the bag and snatched it up. She reached to slam the trunk closed, putting so much force into it that the patrol car rocked. "These are good cops, Captain Landon. If anyone would know that, it would be me. And I'm telling you what they can't, that you need to back the fuck off!"

With that she pushed her way past the flabbergasted captain and stepped toward the woods. Only there was a phalanx of officers standing in her way, the group having gathered, obviously, when they had begun to overhear her tirade. She faced them, her entire body flushing hot with embarrassment because she knew damn well how unprofessional she had been. But she would worry about the consequences of that later. She had more important worries on her mind at the moment. But just as she was about to bulldoze her way past everyone, one of the officers began to clap his hands together. Like wildfire it spread, until she was facing a platoon of applause. She winced, picturing in her mind exactly how furious the captain behind her would be because he was head to toe a classic narcissist who defined himself by the value of his position and his job. He would not appreciate anything that undermined that. He just wasn't the sort to see the errors of his ways.

Odds were, she would be fired by the end of the week.

She pushed free of her admirers and ran for the woods. Avery Landon was a worry for another day. Right now she had to bring clothes to a naked man. As she struggled through the bracken to get deeper into the woods and farther away from potential witnesses, she suddenly heard the snapping of branches and Sargent bounded out of the brush, barking happily at her arrival. She moved quicker at the sight of him, headed in the direction he'd come from. Suddenly a hand grabbed her by the arm, pulling her to a stop. She was such a jumble of high-strung nerves that she shouted out in surprise.

"Easy," he soothed, reaching to take the gym bag from her tightly clutched fingers. "Is everything all right?"

No. Nothing is all right, she thought. "It was fine. Nothing of note happened."

"Damn, that's unnerving. There are weapons in that trunk."

"Yes. I kind of figured that out," she muttered.

He unzipped the bag, and after withdrawing a uniform let it drop to the ground.

"You carry a second uniform to work?" she asked, surprised that it wasn't street clothing. On her way back she'd been wondering how he was going to explain his missing uniform.

"We all do, if we're smart. I can't even tell you how often I've had a drunk puke on me."

"Oh I see."

Yeah she did see. She watched, unable to even give him the courtesy of turning her back to him, as he stepped into his pants and drew them up over extraordinarily defined calf and thigh muscles. Apparently undershorts weren't a part of his backup bag because he zipped himself in with caution, going utterly commando. Marissa ignored the part of her brain that pouted heavily as he hid all that tanned, glorious strength. He quickly drew on an undershirt and then his uniform shirt, taking the unimpeded beauty of powerful biceps and shoulders away from her.

More internal pouting. *Damn him*, she thought a bit grouchily. How was it that she constantly felt like she was being pushed and pulled at the same time whenever she was around him? It wasn't as though she'd never seen a beautiful, lean, muscled, deliciously male person before.

Marissa went hot and wet in one second flat and she forced herself to turn away, lecturing herself for being so weak and so damn pathetic. Okay, sure it had been a long, long, looong time since she'd gone to bed with a man, but she'd somehow managed to keep from panting over just any man in sight for all that time. Or any man at all for that matter, she amended.

He's a patient, she reminded herself fiercely. An alien patient from some sort of cosmic lab experiment. It was all she could do to keep from biting at her lip, shifting her weight, or chewing her damn nails off, she realized with no little irritability. She had worked so hard to eradicate all of those kinds of fidgets and tells. It was so important to her to demonstrate the level of competency and professionalism she needed in order to work with these alpha men and women. All it took was a single impression of weakness and any chance of them respecting and trusting her strength and guidance would crash and burn. Some of them even went for her throat, casting her as the villain who was trying to rob them of the job they depended on for self-definition and self-worth. She had to hold on to her competence even more now that she was faced with this potentially paralyzing situation. She was, she knew instinctively, going to need every moment of calm and strength she could muster up in order to cope with this unbelievable turn of events.

"S-so . . . you have a, um, dead pharaoh living inside

of you?" she asked, looking for a more focused explanation of what he'd been telling her. Bodywalker 101 for dummies . . . or at the very least a completely dumbfounded doctor who'd always thought the planet housed only one kind of humanoid species. Now she'd been exposed to at least two others and was struggling to make herself accept it. "And that other creature . . . the thing made of stone . . ."

"A Gargoyle. Gargoyles are . . . well, the gist of the story is that the Templars used their spell-casting abilities to create the Gargoyle race in order to have powerful protectors and servants."

"You mean slaves?" she asked, turning back to him.

"Exactly," he said, a grim expression on his face as he finished strapping another flack jacket across his chest. She had witnessed how little of a help his other one had been against that fierce red energy his attacker had wielded against him. But a little bit of help was better than no help at all and it made her feel better to see him somewhat protected.

"That's horrible," she said, her stomach feeling sick in sympathy for the creature she'd seen.

"Long ago, however, a large amount of Gargoyles escaped from the Templars' control." He looked directly into her eyes. "It was a very brave and risky thing to do. Their masters created them in such a way that each Gargoyle is prevented from attacking their individual creator, and their creators had linked them critically to an object called a touchstone. If a Gargoyle does not return to their touchstone with a certain amount of frequency, they will very quickly lose control of their bodies and their minds. It only takes a matter of days before that happens. So not only did they have to find a way to rise up against their masters, they had to retrieve their heavily guarded touchstones. The Templars knew that to control the touchstone was to control the Gargoyle."

"If they couldn't fight their creators, then how were they ever able to escape these horribly powerful Templars?"

"There was only one way. They had to enlist the help of the Politic Bodywalkers. They had to pledge their loyalty to another Bodywalker and ask them to help free them."

"And . . . did you? Did your type of Bodywalker fight the Templars to free the Gargoyles?"

"Oh yes. We did. In fact," he said, so quietly she could feel the deep gravity emanating from him, "the exodus of the Gargoyles and the fight for their freedom was the catalyst that began the war between the Templars and the Politic." He moved a step closer to her and, like all the other times he put himself into her personal space, her breath caught in her throat. Marissa forced herself to breathe, but all that managed to do was bring the rich scent of potent male onto her suddenly keen senses. "The Templars are ravenous for supremacy. They are also inhumanly callous. They do not respect the exquisite intelligence of the Gargoyles, or the culture of tribes they have created for themselves. Templars don't even respect the host souls they share a body with."

"But . . . that Gargoyle was . . . is he still a slave?"

"There are several generations of Gargoyles, each different in some way from the last as the Templars tried to improve on their design, along with improving their methods of enslaving a Gargoyle's loyalty."

"Oh my god," she breathed, sickened and disturbed to her very core.

"That is the nature of each Gargoyle tribe, Marissa. Each tribe is a different generation of Gargoyle. So far there are six different tribes. Apparently the Templars have grown another generation, which leaves me to believe that the free Gargoyles will soon find themselves ferrying the seventh tribe-to-be along their underground railroad. Those who are free endanger themselves nightly in order to help liberate the enslaved."

"You said they pledge loyalty to Politic members. Do you mean they let you hold their touchstones? And if so, how is that different from being enslaved by the Templars?"

Jackson was always impressed by Marissa's quick and thoughtful intellect. The workings of the Bodywalker world could be very complex. Just as complex as the relationship the Politic had with the Gargoyles.

"The Templars created the Gargoyle touchstones in such a way as to force a Gargoyle to be closely connected to either their creator or another Bodywalker. The energy of our entwined souls revitalizes the power of a touchstone, which then transfers it to the Gargoyle. They are closely attached to us, it's true, but they are not slaves to those of us who are Politic. We deny them nothing, give them total freedom to the best of our ability, and enjoy and respect them just as they enjoy and respect us. They are our bodyguards, our companions, and our closest friends in some cases."

"I see. That's very good of you," she said softly. Jackson could see the empathy for the Gargoyles' plight in her eyes, even though she was trying to come off as nothing more than analytical and thoughtful about the situation. It made him wonder why she always felt the need to project a sense of flawless self-control to everyone. The fear she had shown in the cave was only the second time he had seen her become emotional. The first time had been during Docia's disappearance when she had set him back on his pompous ass, as was rightly deserved.

There was a creature of fire and feeling beneath all of her cool beauty and powerful professionalism. What she didn't realize was that this veneer she clung to so desperately made her come off as arrogant and cold. Oh, she sympathized with her patients—he could attest to that—but always in a controlled manner. He wondered what had happened to her that made her feel so compelled to project perfection at all times.

It also made him crave the opportunity to tousle her up and ruffle her feathers. It made him want to strip away the layers of her psyche, her always-neat appearance, and tumble her across his bed until she absolutely shattered for him. The simple thought of it had him craving her all over again, had him leaning in closer to her so at the very least he could feel the radiance of her warmth and smell that sweet, feminine scent of her hair.

Marissa felt the change that came over him like any prey would feel when faced with a predator. He was so close again that she had to tilt her head back in order to look up into his eyes and she watched as his teal-framed pupils widened a little. He was one of those men who had been gifted with thick, beautiful lashes. Their blackness the perfect foil for the color of his eyes. There was no innocence to his features, no boyishness. He was every inch the mature and vital male.

A *dangerous* male.

"What do we do now?" she asked in a voice so close to a whisper.

He smiled then, a wolfish quality to it that made her heart skip a few beats. His hand came up and once again his thumb traced over the rise of her cheek and then the shape of her lips.

"I have such amazing answers to that question," he said to her.

There was absolutely no mistaking the entendre of his remark. She should have laughed and set him down, putting him back at a safe distance. She was actually quite good at that. There had been a great deal of practice over the years as she had been the object of a lot of unwelcome attention. What she had intended to be a projection of a neat polished appearance was, for some reason, seen as some kind of invitation to the opposite sex. Or perhaps challenge was the better word for it.

But until that moment when he had bluntly told her that she was in his crosshairs, she hadn't lumped Jackson in as a source of unwelcome advances. She had handled the whole thing badly, become stupidly flustered and at odds with herself over it.

Now she had the most powerful argument against him she could possibly have conjured. He was a Bodywalker. He wasn't entirely human anymore. She simply was not adventurous enough to get tangled up in something like that. Not to mention all the other reasons that were still in play. He was a patient. They worked together. It was just a bad idea all around.

She opened her mouth to speak, but the act of parting her lips brought the touch of his thumb a little farther inside her mouth, as though she were inviting him in. The smoldering hot look that entered his eyes made the touch erotic, for all it was a simple and unintentional thing. His thumb hooked on to the tips of her lower teeth and his remaining fingers curled to grasp her by the chin. The capture, as simple as it was, made her heart and breath seize in her chest.

But the instant his head dropped toward hers, his attention fixated on her mouth, she shoved away from him, nearly tripping herself and falling on her backside.

"Stop it! Stop this," she panted, righteous anger warring with the jumble of feelings his small movement of intent had given birth to inside of her. Her face felt hot from the sudden heat erupting all along her skin. Goddamn him, why did he have to be so inaccessible! So ethically out of her reach. "You *know*. You know how many reasons there are why you and I cannot even entertain . . ." Marissa had never been so at a loss for words in her life as she was whenever she was clashing wills with him. It was completely flustering and infuriating.

"Knowing doesn't always dictate desires," he retorted quietly, his hand coming out with blinding speed, snagging her by her upper arm and yanking her forward until she crashed up against him, her feet jumbling up together beneath her. But before she could fall his other hand was at her back and jerking her up completely off the ground. "You think I don't know what I'm doing? You think I haven't weighed all the possible rights and wrongs of it? Do you think I'm really that thoughtless? I've thought of nothing else for weeks. Fought myself into wild circles of confusion as the part of me that craved you warred with the part of me that knew you should be off-limits. Even now I hear the voice of my conscience telling me to stop this, but it can hardly be heard over the voice screaming at me to take you in every way I can possibly imagine."

His words were like hot honey being drizzled all over her skin, burning and sweet at the same time. Marissa couldn't breathe. She couldn't speak to stop him again.

It was probably because she had the very same voices holding the very same argument inside of her. And somehow, knowing he couldn't heed them despite his better judgment made her whole existence go up in flames. By the time he had dragged her up to meet his mouth, she had confessed to herself just how badly she had wanted it.

His lips touched hers, the contact so light it was barely there. They were both working hard for breath, both tense and troubled just as much as they were burning with craving.

"I just need a moment, Marissa. Just one little moment where who and what we are doesn't matter. Because it has been just as hard for me to accept all the things you are trying to accept right now. But in all this upheaval," he breathed, the softness of his mouth brushing over hers as he spoke, "the only thing that comes crystal clear to me is the way I burn for you."

Then he swept up her mouth with his, holding her so tightly to himself with the wrapping strength of his arms, his hands running fiercely hot across her back.

She should have pushed away from him, but there was no strong, instinctive desire to do so. In fact the ultimate opposite desire was in play, until it felt as though her actual soul was craving to feel him kiss her.

She wanted the kiss to pale . . . to be less than her illicit fantasies had made of it. She wanted the reality to help her find a reason to never let this happen again. It was a wish that would never be fulfilled. The painfully soft and powerful strength of his kiss, the poignancy of the struggle within them both, made it everything it could be and more. He smelled of the woods around them, so unbelievably earthy, as if this were his natural habitat and she had been caught trespassing. She had been cold before, as the waning spring night bit at her poorly clothed body. Now her chilled skin gave way to the heat that had been flirting beneath it for every last moment she had been in his presence. It was like pressing herself up against a radiator, his heat enveloping and permeating her. He took no half measures, his mouth testing hers for all of a few moments before his tongue came into play and commanded ownership of hers. She'd never liked men who assaulted her with all tongue from the start of a kiss, but what others had made offensive, he made a seduction. His hand came up to cradle the back of her head, his fingers burrowing into her hair and he used the possession of his hand to turn her into his kiss more fully. He did not invade, but conquered just the same as the taste of him was swept into her mouth and against the buds of her tongue.

Marissa drew breath in little shots, only to let it slip away again just as quickly in stunned hitches. She couldn't think as the heat he delivered burned away all thought, burned away all reason, leaving nothing for her but the feel of his mouth and the touch of his hands bringing her more and more tightly against him. Her hands lifted to the backs of his taut, muscled upper arms, her fingertips clinging weakly to the crisp fabric of his uniform shirt. That his kiss was a pure seduction was never in question. The way his tongue stroked hers was nothing less that an exotic spell compelling everything she had into the connection. And there was darkness there. An indefinable element to him that was so incredibly deadly if he was not respected or did not get what he demanded. The fear that came with that thought only made her body react more strongly, her nipples tightening fiercely, her breasts screaming with sensitivity inside the lace of her bra.

His hands were in neutral territory still, but they may as well not have been because the demand of his kiss set sensitive sexual places alight with passionate fire. She became tantalizingly wet, a startling reaction for her because things like that did not happen so easily for her. What was more, she could feel him, a wall of powerfully taut muscle and hips framing an undeniable erection pressed to her. The soft fabric of his uniform pants made it impossible to hide . . . but his boldness told her that hiding was the very last thing on his mind. On the contrary. She knew he wanted her to feel it. Wanted her to react to it. Wanted her to know there was no denying what she did to him.

He broke from her mouth just far enough to allow

breath between them. She was panting for it. For everything.

"I never knew," he said roughly. "If I had, I would never have let you hold yourself from me."

The sentence frightened her just as much as it melted her with excitement and arousal. He made no show of asking for further permission, taking what he felt was his as he swept her up into a new kiss, this one twice as aggressive as the one before it. She felt him move, felt him turn, but she was blind as to the reason until she felt her back come up against the rough bark of a thick trunk. The woman she had been before that kiss would have complained that the roughness could catch and ruin the cashmere of her sweater, but she was no longer that woman and, she feared, she never would be again. The woman she was now no longer cared about that triviality, and instead she craved his hands on her sweater, dragging it from her, making way for his hands to touch her craving skin at last.

Instead his hands slid down her sides and around her hips, his fingers gripping her ass through her skirt and dragging her hips tighter to his. *Are you feeling what you do to me*, the action demanded of her. *You thought you could deny me this?*

And still it was just a kiss. A fierce, unbelievable, soul-stripping kiss. It shoved aside all the bullshit they had been trying to protect themselves with and went for the throat of their craving for each other. His mouth wrestled with hers, devouring her six ways from Sunday. She felt her hair dropping down against her neck and shoulders and realized his hand was combing through it, unraveling the strict twist it had been in. His other hand, however, was on her thigh, grabbing possession of it, dragging the inside of it along his outer hip until somehow they were both wrapping around his waist, opening her up to the aggressive press of his sex against hers. It was through layers of clothing, but it may as well have not been, that was how ferocious the flame inside of her became at the connection. She gasped into his mouth, her fingernails curling into the flesh of his arms.

"Easy," he breathed against her lips. "God, Marissa, go easy."

Go easy, Jackson thought. Otherwise he was going to try to fuck her right where they stood, only a few kisses into learning each other. That was how blinding his desire was for her. Hadn't he told himself he wasn't going to do this? Hadn't he told himself there was nowhere for this to go? Hadn't he realized that she wasn't the type of woman he could throw up against the nearest hard surface and tear a path into her with no thought for the consequences?

She will be ours one way or another . . .

Jackson didn't understand what that meant. He wasn't exactly in the right mind-set for clarity of thought. Of all the times he'd thought of getting his hands on her, even the instances he wouldn't admit to himself, he'd never conceived the power of what his reaction would be. She smelled of summertime, hot and sultry, as though the air were so heavy with heat it clung to all of the senses. How her legs had ended up around his hips, he simply couldn't comprehend. Had he done that? Had she? Did it matter?

Her fingertips released from that clutch on his arms and slid up into his hair, the sensation of them running through the crisply short strands sending clenching heat stripping over him like the lash of a whip. He couldn't make himself draw his mouth away from hers, couldn't make himself move slower and softer. He was famished for her and she was utterly divine. In feel. In taste. And, oh god, that smell. That sweet, lusty smell of her.

It was Sargent's sudden bark of alarm that forced reality into the situation. He had spent weeks in training learning and teaching the requirements of that bark. He jolted away from her mouth, his body jerking into a turn even before he was sure she had her feet back under her. He drew hard for every single breath, trying to shake the fog of need from himself, like trying to break the surface of heavy water in order to pull in much needed oxygen. He raked his eyes around the perimeter, including the sky. He would not be taken by surprise again by thinking in human, linear ways. He kept himself against her otherwise, turning front to back, keeping her pressed between his back and the armor of the thick tree behind her.

"What—?"

"Shh!" he hissed softly, his hand reaching to touch her on her hip, the act possessive and ebbing a powerful warning in case she didn't take the verbal one in the spirit it was meant.

"Waverly!"

There it was. Distant, still out of normal human earshot, but clear as hell to him. The rest of the searchers were looking for him. And that was when he realized just how light the night sky had gotten.

"Shit," he hissed. "I have to get out of here. They're looking for me and Sargent, but . . ." He turned back to her and winced when he saw the embarrassment coloring her face, the hands that had been in his hair with such abandon now pressed to her cheeks in mortification. He didn't have time to unravel the knots she was tying herself into as she realized just how far out of control she had allowed herself to go. If there was one thing he had learned about Marissa Anderson, it was that she despised losing control. Not only of any given situation, but most definitely of herself.

"Marissa, sunlight can kill me." He cut straight to the chase, time too short to do otherwise.

"*What?*" she demanded. "What do you mean . . . ?"

"Think of it like kryptonite, Marissa. The touch of the sun paralyzes my kind. We don't turn into solid stone statues like the Gargoyles do, and therefore the only protection we can provide ourselves is whatever pitch-black room we lock ourselves into. I don't have time to explain and I don't have time to be debriefed by the captain before sunlight crests over the horizon."

She must have realized that his precarious position had been brought about, largely, because of his need to deal with her. He had wasted precious time comforting or explaining or . . . *touching*. He could see all of it playing over her features and wanted so badly to reassure and comfort her.

"Sargent," she rasped out roughly, her voice still sounding full of the arousal that had so overwhelmed them both. "Tell them he's injured."

He couldn't help but explode into a grin. So simple. So perfect. The caretaking and well-being of his dog was Jackson's largest priority when in the field and everyone knew that. It would not be questioned if he dismissed everyone and hurried to take care of the canine that had been entrusted to him by the department. He commanded Sargent to his side and stooped to hoist the solid shepherd into his arms.

"You need to drive me," he told her. "I can get us out of sight of the searchers, but then I have to . . . I can try to stay mobile, but the longer I fight it the more strength I lose and the longer I will need to recover. I have to . . . I have to . . ."

Trust you. He didn't speak the words aloud; thereby making it known how difficult a concept it was for him. And all he could do was hope that she understood it had nothing to do with her and everything to do with being that vulnerable.

"But I saw you in sunlight just yesterday . . ."

"It was the last day before Menes and I finished the Blending process. And believe me, forcing myself to keep mobile in the sunlight was getting harder and harder every damn day. Fighting it now . . . it's deadly. If I don't sleep it can be deadly, Marissa. And I haven't slept in . . ."

"Oh my god!" she cried. "Why would you risk yourself like this?" she demanded.

He looked at her as if she had lost her mind.

"Marissa, there's a child missing."

He said it as though it was entirely self-explanatory and Marissa supposed that it was. And how could she have forgotten what had brought them out there in the first place?

Well, getting attacked by supernatural beings could easily make that happen. And she saw by the expression on his face that Jackson was torn up about that fact. He didn't want to quit. He didn't want to leave. He wanted to keep going until that child was found. She watched him hoist Sargent higher onto his chest, the dog's tongue lolling happily, the shepherd perfectly comfortable being held by his master and probably much in need of a good rest himself. Jackson started making his way toward the base of operations where he had left his car, his long legs devouring ground as if he were walking over a manicured lawn, rather than through the tough, uneven bracken of the forest floor. They met Officers Hampton and Reese very shortly after they began.

"What's going on? Where's your radio and cell?" Hampton demanded. "We've been trying to reach you."

"The radio is at the bottom of Ranger's Cliff," Jackson lied easily. "Sue me for butterfingers. Cell must be dead."

Oh it was dead all right, Marissa thought. It was burned to dust along with the radio and his original uniform.

"Sargent's hurt. He tumbled ten feet down Ranger's Cliff. It's a damn lucky thing I had a good hold on his leash at the time." It was also lucky that most cops wouldn't think it was odd that his dog was in search mode with his leash on. In woods like this the likelihood of the leash getting tangled up on trees or brush made it more efficient to remove the leash and give the animal his head.

"Is he okay?" Hampton asked, reaching to tentatively ruffle the dog's fur. Jackson didn't blame him. The entire precinct knew exactly how hard Sargent could bite. They'd all watched him in action these past weeks. But they should also know he was extremely obedient and well trained.

"Just a sprain I'm sure. I'm going to take the little bugger home and get us both some rest. Sawyer's here now, right?"

"As well as two dog teams from Albany," Hampton agreed with a nod. "You guys get out of here. Get some sleep. You've both been at it way too long. I'll tell the captain."

"I'm sure we'll see him on the way out," Jackson said, unable to help looking over his shoulder toward the breaking dawn.

"Oh and hey," Hampton said, nodding his head toward Marissa. "Doc, I couldn't have said it better myself."

That distracted Jackson just enough to look at her questioningly. She muttered a thank-you before reaching to touch his arm and urge him forward. Oh, now he *knew* he'd missed something. He was going to have to pursue the question at a later time. A much later time. He could feel it . . . the sun . . . all along the skin of his back and legs, a tightening in anticipation of his unprotected position in the open.

They weren't going to make it. If he fell in front of everyone . . . it would be really goddamn bad.

That was the moment he realized it was time for him to quit this job and go on about the business of becoming the Bodywalker he was meant to be. Becoming Menes, the pharaoh and ruler of the Bodywalkers. Living and behaving like a Bodywalker, aware of his strength and weaknesses, and leaving the world of his humanity behind him.

The understanding damn well stung him. It sucked in every major way. That wasn't to say that the prospect of the new life awaiting him wasn't something he could get excited about, it was just . . . it was just mourning the loss of that which had once made him content and comfortable.

"Come on, Jackson. Let's get this guy some kibble and a soft bed," Marissa said, reaching to lay her hand on his back, pushing him forward. She didn't have to ask or urge twice. They both knew what was about to happen and how crucial it was that it didn't happen in front of witnesses.

But what burned, what really chafed him . . .

She would be protecting *him* when, in truth, she was going to need him to protect her. As they broke from the tree line and made their way quickly to Jackson's car he made the barest of excuses before getting dog and doctor into the car and getting the car on the road. The sun broke about five minutes later and Jackson slammed on the brakes, his entire body clenching with spasms of rigidity.

"You can't bring me to my house," he rasped as he grabbed her by the arm and yanked her bodily into the driver's seat. He left the seat as he put her into it, getting out and stumbling around to the other side of the car.

"Or yours. Somewhere else," he ground out. God almighty this was painful, he realized with no little shock. He hadn't realized it would actually hurt. "Darkness. I need the dark in order to move. You aren't going to be able to manage my weight so you need to get me into the dark in order to get me out of the car."

"Jackson," she said, reaching to grip him by the wrist, making him look into her eyes. "Trust me. I understand and I will keep us both safe."

He laughed a little painfully. "Marissa, I don't doubt that in the least. I just . . . I'm just trying to remind you things have changed. I've changed things for you."

"I know."

"And I'm damn sorry for that," he said tightly as she threw the car into gear and began to race them off of the mountain.

"I know that, too," she assured him. "Stop fighting it. I see how much it's hurting you. Please, Jackson, just trust me."

She was right. The more he fought it the more it hurt. He exhaled and tried to relax, tried to let the stiffness wash over him unimpeded. The helplessness of his numbing body was terrifying. It crept over him as if he had stared Medusa in the eyes and was now turning to stone. He had once wondered how that must have felt for those heroes of myths, to have moving life bled out of them, snatched away, making them forever helpless. It terrified him that now he knew.

It was the most horrifying feeling in the world.

Ram sat up suddenly and sharply in bed, gasping for air as a sensation of absolute terror and agony whipped through his senses. Docia was asleep curled up against his warmth and strength, the darkness of their protected home keeping them safe from the bane of the sun. They had only just fallen asleep, after much flirtation and then, finally, a great deal of fervent lovemaking. Docia had proven lately to be . . . how had she put it? "A total horndog." It was yet another amusing turn of phrase in his mate's vast repertoire of colorful phrases.

Docia came awake more slowly than he had, her hand reaching for his back as she pushed up and laid her sleepy weight against him.

"What is it?" she mumbled into his skin.

He wished that he knew.

"Nothing. Lay down, sweet, and go back to sleep."

"Mmmno," she said. "Not till you tell me what's wrong."

"A nightmare, I think," he answered with a sigh.

"About?"

Menes. It had been about Menes. Or rather, Jackson, who was her brother. The absolute feeling that he was in grave danger was still clawing through his body. The problem was, Ram wasn't exactly known for being clairvoyant. His power was command of the weather, the crash of thunder and the sear of lightning. The only prophetess in their house, or chantress as she was often called, was Cleo. Perhaps it had been a subconscious thing. As every day passed he'd grown more and more anxious about Jackson's reluctance to take up Menes's mantle of leadership, and even more so since Jackson had sent him and Docia away to ready a new household for him in New Mexico where so many of the body Politic resided. Jackson had insisted he was safe, that his anonymity protected him from Templar assassins. But the entire idea sat ill with him. He had been separated from his good friend more than long enough. And he knew Docia had been chafing for his appearance as well. She loved her brother a great deal and, although she was now a Bodywalker herself, she had been very upset about Menes taking up a position in her brother's body. Even she had known the risk involved, that just his existence painted a target on him as the two warring factions tried to gain the upper hand.

But Ram felt the tide of this interminable war might be turning at long last. The Bodywalker inside of his mate was a priestess. A Templar. She was also niece to Odjit and a being of such great power that when the priestess had tried to defect to the Politic, Odjit had hunted her down for it. It was in the process of that battle that her brother had nearly lost his life, sending him into the Ether where he had found Menes and the promise of a continuing existence.

"Menes," he finally said to her.

That made her sit up a little straighter at his back. He felt the change go through her as tension took away the bonelessness of sleepiness.

"Jackson? What was it?"

"Ram!" The door to their outer suite crashed open as Cleo's panicked voice filled the room. He was out of their bed in a flash of movement, Docia following a little more clumsily behind him as she pulled herself the rest of the way into the woken world.

"Cleo, what is it?"

"It's Menes! I've had . . . there's danger! Oh, so much danger! I can see the blood. The fire! Oh god, it feels so painful!" Cleo's cerulean eyes had gone wide with fear, the wild tousling of her hair showing she too had been asleep when this had occurred. Cleo was not known for allowing herself to be seen unkempt. Nor was she prone to fits of panicked emotion. She had once been one of the greatest of Egyptian queens and she did not rattle easily. But when she spoke of fire burning she was holding out both of her arms and staring at them in abject horror as if she were actually on fire.

"I have felt this sense of danger myself," he told her, while at the same time taking hold of both her hands and pulling her arms up against his bare chest. He made her look into his eyes, drawing deep steady breaths until she was subconsciously mimicking him. "I will go to him this very minute and fetch him back to us. It is beyond time for him to be safely within these walls and within our reach to help him. Now, other than the things you described to me, was there some kind of clarity? You know a great many of your visions are symbolic and not necessarily accurate. So be calmed, Cleopatra. Be easy."

"You must take this seriously," she said, a tone of petulance entering her voice and turning her expression to one of consternation.

"I am taking this very seriously," he assured her. "Did I not say I was going to fetch him? I would never take you less than at your word."

"I did not speak of it earlier," she said, "because there was only the sense of imminence, not alarm. I thought it was because you had told me that the Blending was almost complete and that he would continue to go about the business of withdrawing from Jackson's old life in Saugerties. But it's been stronger every day, this sense that something is on the horizon. Something . . . something is coming toward us."

"Do you mean this danger?"

"I don't know. The danger is new. Before this it was as though . . . as though we would be entering a time of discovery. Everything felt benign until just moments ago, or I swear I would have told you."

"I know you would have. I don't hold you accountable for anything, Cleo. You are of tremendous value to all of us. Your power has been an asset to us throughout the ages and it is very much appreciated."

"Hm. For you maybe," she said with no small amount of irritability. "You aren't the one who has been cursed with this interfering ability." She frowned very seriously. "I feel as though it has weakened me. Where once I was a woman of great strength and conviction, I am now plagued with caution. Worry. Always desperately trying to interpret what comes to me."

"I can understand that frustration," Docia spoke up. "In a way, for me, it's been the opposite. Tameri has given me strength I never knew as a mortal human. It can so easily make me overconfident. She is always so confident, even if I am not. Together it Blends in an extreme push me/pull me manner. I question everything so very carefully now for fear of jumping all in and putting myself in danger."

"Yes. Yes exactly," Cleo said, the comfort of knowing someone else understood how she was feeling helping to calm her further. "Ram, you will go now? This moment? You should make time your enemy in this matter, I beg you. Take Asikri with you. Do not go alone. You must protect him at all costs. The Templars will do anything to take him from us for another hundred years. And to lose Hatshepsut as well . . . it would be a blow that could destroy our position forever." Because they both knew Hatshepsut would not allow herself to be reborn if it meant leaving Menes in the Ether for another hundred years. Perhaps at one time she would have braved the abject loneliness that would have come with ruling alone, putting the well-being of her people above the needs of her heart, but every regeneration had cleaved them closer and closer together until they could no longer bear living, be it in mortal form or in the Ether, without the other.

Jackson had told him that Menes had delayed his return from the Ether because of Hatshepsut's reluctance to go through the pain of being reborn only to face the inevitable rending away of life and, in the same sweep, their love. Being the central figures in their government made them the key focus of their enemies, and their enemies knew as well as all other Bodywalkers that to destroy one was to rid themselves of the other. In the past they had survived because Menes had never allowed himself to go into the Ether without dragging Odjit or her lapdog Kamenwati with him. They were the Templars' magnetic north, and without them the Templars stumbled around just as lost as being deprived of Menes and Hatshepsut would do to the Politic. But what kept the Politic above water was that the strength of Ramses, Cleopatra, and Asikri made it possible for them to keep the upper hand in the war. The Templars were so busy infighting that they could not claim such cohesion. Yet they remained enjoined enough to hold steadily against all efforts to bring the Templars completely to heel. Perhaps that was because the Politic had a nonaggression policy. As long as they were not aggressed upon, they did not aggress in return. This was, Menes had often preached, what kept them from becoming the enemy they fought. Kept them from being just another power-hungry faction trying to force others to their will.

It wasn't a policy Ram had always agreed with. Especially in light of how long the war had continued on. It was, he was beginning to believe, time for them to be more proactive. Especially in light of the information that had come with Tameri's rebirth; that there were many Templars who wanted to come home, so to speak, to follow Menes's teachings and philosophies and move free of Odjit's mongering ways. There were Templars who, as Docia had put it, were no longer willing to drink the Kool-Aid.

"Yes, Cleo, I will leave with all due haste. But if it's all the same to you, I'd like to put some clothes on."

She drew in a little breath of surprise, then looked down at his clothing-bereft body. She laughed then, her

familiar mischievousness climbing into her eyes and
voice.

"Are you growing modest in your old age, Ram?"

"Hardly. But I'd rather not be arrested for public in-
decency."

Cleo clicked her tongue and waved her hand at the
laws of humans as if it were a pesky little fly.

"Honestly. All due respect to progress, and to colder
climes, but I miss the days when we could walk in the
warmth with little more than colorful beads to adorn
our bodies."

At Ram's back, Docia snorted a laugh out of her nose.

Marissa had shouldered a great deal of responsibility
in her life, but she had never felt the intensity of it the
way she did while driving Jackson to safety. She didn't
like not having a game plan prepared for herself way in
advance. Not that she couldn't think on her feet. Being
a psychiatrist required that constantly. But that had
taken a considerable amount of training.

So the first thing she started to do was to make up a
plan of action. It's easy, she told herself. Just get him
somewhere dark. Away from the sun. Like a vampire.
Only, this vampire didn't burst into ash at the touch of
the sun. He merely went stiff and, when she reached out
to touch his wrist to seek his pulse, he was ice cold. He
had curled slightly toward the door, turned away from
her as if to hide his condition from her. Probably because of some instinctive need to conceal his weakness.

"Okay, mister, we have to start with a place," she said
aloud to Sargent. "What about Uncle Bob's? No, wait,
he's got workmen there while he's away. Maybe
Manon's?" Manon was her cousin and he had a very
remote cabin just a few miles northwest, in Sullivan
County. She took a moment to debate whether the patrol car would be able to make it down the rough drive

to the house. It was a good idea to have four-wheel drive when attempting it, especially after snow or rain. It hadn't snowed since the end of February, so it wasn't as though she would be trying to drive through snow. It hadn't rained in the past couple of days either, so the drive wouldn't be pitted with thick mud.

"Sold! To the shepherd and his master," she said, satisfied with the plan. She was talking to Sargent because if she didn't she'd keep looking over at Jackson. There was absolutely nothing peaceful or sleeplike about the way he was just then. He was leaning awkwardly against the door, his skin as pale white as marble even though she knew he was tanned from his time training outdoors with his dog. He lay rigid, no relaxation, as though every muscle in his body was tensed to the breaking point. If he had not had color in his hair and brows, he would have looked like a marble statue. A light, misting steam lifted from him, though it didn't fog the windows or feel like there was a great amount of heat emanating from him. In fact, when she reached out to touch him he felt so very cold that it was unnerving and alarming to her. She wondered if he could hear or even see. My god how horrifying, to be completely paralyzed and yet able to see anything and everything that was happening to you, with nothing you could do about it. No arguments, no ability to express wishes . . . no chance to scream or fight to protect yourself.

"It's okay," she kept saying on small rapid breaths. "It's okay. We'll be in the dark in no time at all and you'll be just fine. You'll be normal again." She couldn't sound afraid. She couldn't sound upset or even empathetic for him. Just like she did when dealing with a patient, she tried to project calm, support, and confidence.

When she made the turnoff onto the rugged drive to Manon's house she felt a small wave of relief wash over her. After successfully traversing the half-mile drive she pulled up to the small cabin. It was deceptively rough-looking on the outside with its frayed log walls, but she knew it was quite beautiful on the inside.

There was an attached garage at the rear of the cabin and she pulled up in front of it. She reassured Sargent she would be right back and ran back around to the front of the house and up the steps. She glanced around before accessing the clever little hidey-hole Manon had built into the wall, a silly thing to do really with the only possible witnesses being the deer . . . or maybe a bear. She let herself in and raced to the back of the house. She went into the garage and hit the automatic door lift. Sunlight broke into the blackness of the garage, the lifting door creating its own sort of sunrise. She was ducking under the door as soon as it was half-way up and back in the driver's seat an instant later. In her anxiousness she gave it a little too much gas and ended up jolting them to a stop to keep from hitting the supply cabinets in front of her. She dashed for the door lift once more and hurried to return to Jackson, pulling open the car door just enough to wedge her body in and push him upright, keeping him from tumbling helplessly to the floor.

"Jackson," she said as soon as pitch-blackness had returned to the garage. "Jackson, we're here. We're safe. Can you hear me?"

How long did it take to reverse this crippling condition? She had foolishly thought it would be instantaneous, but five minutes later he still hadn't moved. What was more, he was only taking a breath once every thirty seconds.

But at least he's breathing, she told herself.

Leaving a hand on Jackson's shoulder to make sure he remained upright in his seat, she reached to open the rear door, letting Sargent out. He jumped out with a very subdued amount of energy and she realized that he must be just as tired as she was. And now that the adrenaline of the past half hour was bleeding out of her, she began to feel that exhaustion. She found herself pushing Jackson's hair back, suddenly realizing he'd let it grow without his usual fastidiousness to a short nearly military cut.

"Jackson?" she said for about the thirtieth time. She could have closed the door and left him in the dark to come around in his own time, but she didn't have the heart to leave him alone like that for however long that would be. She was running her fingers through his hair at that point, a slow touch plowing furrows through the soft, silkiness of it.

"Mar-iss-a." Her name rasped from him in three struggling whispers, and she felt incredible relief blow through her, leaving a sting in her eyes and a lump in her throat. She shored herself up against tears and undue emotionalism.

"Jackson? Are you all right? Tell me what to do for you."

"Dark," he said. "Need darkness."

"It is dark," she reassured him. "It's safe."

"Inside?"

Inside the house, she realized, was what he meant. Crap. She'd forgotten about inside the house. "Are you okay to stay here while I darken the house?"

He nodded a brief, jerky nod, but she didn't know whether to believe him or not. If there was one thing she'd learned about these alpha-male types, it was that they never admitted to their limitations very easily.

But she had to leave him otherwise they'd be spending the day in the garage. And as nicely kept as it was, she wasn't willing to do that. She closed the car door again so he wouldn't fall out, since he didn't have all his strength back as yet. She then began to hurry through the house, dropping blinds and pulling curtains. She had never realized just how many windows there were in the small house. Or how sheer some of the curtains were, all for the effect of bringing as much sunlight into the room as possible. Luckily for her the large bank of sliding doors that led to the deck and ran the entire right side of the house were fitted with thick vertical blinds that covered them completely when shut. Even so, there was still a lot of light peeking in this edge or that, so she ran for towels and began to stuff them into the spaces until the entire house was as dark as she could possibly manage. Then she hurried back to the garage. She flipped on the light switch and found Jackson on his feet, gripping the door of the car with one hand and the roof of it with the other. He looked incredibly unsteady and still very pale. He'd broken out in a sweat, his forehead beaded with it.

"Jesus, you couldn't just wait a few minutes?" she demanded of him, hurrying to lever her body against his under his right shoulder. Once he had her strength supporting him he was able to turn with her toward the door leading into the house.

And all the while Sargent had never left Jackson's side. Even now he sat there with his head tilted, as if in concern, watching every move she and Jackson made. It was as though he knew Jackson was in trouble and Sargent was determined to oversee her actions to help him. When he saw they were moving he stood up and hurried to take up a new position beside the door. Supervising from an entirely new angle.

"You know, I think that dog adores you," she said to Jackson, trying to inject some lightness into the moment.

"No, he obeys me. It's you he adores. He has a crush on you."

"Me?" She laughed the word out with incredulousness. "He doesn't even know me!"

"Oh, he knows you." Jackson's words were more lucid, but it was still a struggle for him to speak. "If I had a dime for every time he's tried to sniff or paw at your office door I'd be rich."

"But . . ." She was perplexed. "Well I certainly didn't do anything to deserve it."

"Maybe he's just returning your admiration for him," Jackson theorized as they neared the door. Good thing too, because Jackson was no small amount of weight even though he was mostly on his own two feet, and she was just about at the end of her second wind. Or was it the third by now?

"Admiration?" He had to be taunting her. Surely he realized she was very uncomfortable around dogs. Especially dogs she had seen in action hurtling into men and dragging them down in a fury of huge white teeth.

"Well, I assumed that's who you were staring at from your office window the past few weeks, since you've made it clear to me you think I'm something of an ass."

Marissa's face felt like it had gone up in flames as mortification tripped through her. All those times she'd been watching him, struggling with herself and her inappropriate urges, he'd seen her?

She was really glad it was dark so he couldn't see the embarrassment on her face.

"I was just . . . it's . . . very compelling, watching him do what he does," she tried to explain with haste, trying to judge how believable her tone of voice was. "The strength . . . not to mention the intelligence he has. He's quite . . . um . . ."

"Compelling," he said.

"Well, yes." She reached to open the door. He tried to take back all of his weight, but he nearly buckled down to the ground. "Will you please just let me help you?"

she demanded with no small amount of exasperation. "God, Jackson, you don't have to be this all-powerful man all the damn time. Maybe if you'd learn to depend on other human beings you wouldn't invest so much of your own identity into your job and your dogs!"

Oops. She hadn't meant to say that. She just hadn't been able to help herself. The man just had a way of frustrating the hell out of her.

"Is that what you think I do?" he asked quietly, leaning into her once again. "I have friends, you know. I have a life beyond what you see at the station."

"Well that's damn miraculous," she said with irony, "because outside of your sister you never mentioned one. And the only reason I know about Leo Alvarez being even remotely close to you is because of the way he had your back when you were looking for Docia. But other than that, with the way you like to pick up double shifts, I could only assume you had nowhere special to be."

They entered the kitchen and she headed straight for the nearest chair. Truth was, she was wiped out and was afraid of falling on her face herself. She dumped him not too gently into the chair and straightened up, smoothing her hair and her clothes as best she could in light of the fact that it had been twenty-four hours since she'd put the skirt and sweater set on.

"Now, neither of us has had anything to eat in ages and I think it would be best . . ."

"Are you hungry, hummingbird? Because knowing you and the way you work at top speed all the time you have to be exhausted. Frankly I can't eat just yet and I think going to bed would be the best thing for us both."

"Well I . . ." she began to argue.

"And you say I don't admit when I'm licked?"

Shoot. He had a point. And she was far more tired than she was hungry. "Okay. There's only one bedroom here. It's the darkest room in the house. I'll sleep out here on the pullout." She gestured to the living room on the other side of the openly designed kitchen. "As you see it's impossible to get all the light blocked out here but the bedroom is dark as night."

"The pullout is fine for me. It's dark enough."

Marissa made an exasperated sound and dropped into the chair nearest him. "God, what a pair we make." She huffed in frustration. "Neither one of us wants to admit to our shortcomings and neither of us wants the other to think they're weak or fragile in even the slightest way. I swear the only one with any sense around here is the dog."

She gestured to Sargent who, upon seeing them safely into the house, had found the nearest rug and flopped down onto it. He was already half asleep.

"Then how about we both take the bedroom. I assume it's at least a full-size bed? I take one side, you take the other, and everyone's happy." And before she could even gear up to argue he vowed, "I promise not to jump your bones while you're sleeping."

Honestly, she was too tired to argue anymore. Too tired to be the strong one. She nodded and moved to help him up. She was grateful to realize he was able to take even more of his own weight than before. It comforted her that he was getting better and it kept her from collapsing under him. She guided him onto the bed, helping him take off his shoes and socks. He pulled his belt free and took off his shirt while she kicked off her wedges.

"Do you need another pillow? I can get one from the—" She broke off with a surprised cry when his arm, suddenly full of all his usual strength, enfolded her about the waist as he dragged her down onto the bed. He drew her completely over his body, dumping her onto the other side of the bed next to him.

"Go to sleep Marissa," he ordered her. "Now."

He didn't have to command her twice. She closed her eyes with a sigh, trying to clear her mind of all that she had been through that day.

She didn't even make it to her fifth deeply indrawn breath before she was asleep.

CHAPTER SIX

Leo Alvarez was sitting at Jackson's desk, his feet propped up on the file cabinet right next to it, his eyes half closed as he relaxed and waited for Jackson to show up for his shift. His friend was a little late, which was highly unusual. Also unusual was the distinct lack of activity in the precinct in spite of the fact that it was shift change. He checked his watch to be sure, but of course he was right. He had an impeccable internal clock.

Yep. Something wasn't right in cop land. Avery Landon, known for coming in early just so he could catch anyone so much as a millisecond late, because the man lived to bitch about something, wasn't in his office. He waited until he spied the nearest mid-level officer . . . not a rookie who didn't know what was going on and not an old salt who knew better than to discuss police business out of school . . . and he stood up with a stretch.

"Hey," he said to the cop, "what's going on here? It's like a ghost town."

"Missing kid," the cop said. "They've got all available manpower on it. Don't you watch the news?"

Not from the bottom of a bottle of tequila he didn't.

"Oh yeah. Must have slipped my mind. So I take it Jackson took his dog out?"

"They were out all night last night. I heard that Sargent came up lame round about dawn so he had to take him out of the field."

"Well, that blows," Leo said with a scowling frown. "Guess I'll catch up with him later. Thanks."

"Anytime."

Leo strolled out to the parking lot, scratching his head. He'd already been to Jackson's house and there was no sign of him or Sargent. Jackson wouldn't be running around doing errands if Sargent was injured and he sure as hell wouldn't put him back in the field with only a few hours' rest, either. So where the hell was he?

He was a big boy and could take care of himself, it was just that . . .

Leo couldn't explain it but, ever since they'd found Docia after she had gone missing, something had been a little bit off about Jackson. Actually, not even a little bit. A lot of bit, as Docia would say. The most notable part being that Jackson had been avoiding him as if he were a plague carrier. Granted, he'd been in Honduras and a couple of other places these past few weeks, but usually Jackson would be the one picking him up at the airport or be game for a few beers the minute he rolled into town.

"See Bud? Leave me alone long enough and I'm nearly two bottles of Cuervo into bleached-blonde trouble. I blame you, my friend," he said as he dialed Jackson's number. "Hey jackass, this is the fourth message since I got back. You're starting to hurt my feelings. If you don't—"

He broke off when a man loped across his path. Or rather, skipped across it. Like a child. And while he was big enough to be a short adult, he—

"Hi! I'm Andy. I know you."

The minute Andy turned to face him Leo put the pieces together. The distinctive shape of his face and eyes and that always definable innocence proved him to have Down syndrome. And Andy was right. He did know him. He'd been involved in some parallel crime, as an innocent witness, the day Docia had "disappeared." He had seen him briefly before someone had come to pick him up.

"That's right, Andy. How are you, kiddo?" Leo looked around, trying to see if there was someone with Andy this time. "What are you doing here, Andy?"

"Looking for Officer Jackson. I'm his deputy."

That made Leo grin. Andy mispronounced deputy, but far be it for him to correct him. Jackson had clearly taken a special interest in Andy if he was coming here to see him with any regularity.

"I'm sorry to tell you, Andy, but Jackson isn't working today. He had to work late last night so he took the day off."

"Oh." He looked absolutely crestfallen. "He said I could turn on his siren. It's very loud, but I'm not afraid."

"That's a very good thing. Nothing you need to be afraid of as long as you're a deputy and on the right side of the law."

Of course Leo wasn't exactly choirboy material, but Jackson liked to carry on their friendship in an "ignorance is bliss" fashion. Back when Leo had been an army ranger and on the side of the white hats, he and Jackson had never had a difference of opinion on anything. They had raised Docia by themselves, Leo paying the majority of the bills while Jackson went to college and the Academy. But by the time Jackson had graduated from the Academy Leo had seen two tours in Afghanistan and was looking at a third if he didn't ring out while he had a chance. It wasn't that he couldn't hack humping around seventy pounds of gear in the scorching desert heat, watching a man being blow up right next to him after he was unlucky enough to step on a land mine. No. What had chapped his ass had been something else entirely.

The things they *weren't* allowed to do. Protect villagers from gunrunners or other such bullies. Keep the local children from being forced to walk a field in order to test for land mines before the enemy moved forward. Or bomb-detecting dogs who were treated as "equipment" in the army, ferried onto planes not properly pressurized, heated, or cooled, and not given the rights of the true soldiers that they were. Including contented retirement with a loving family who would be given the funds for the animal's room and board. Perhaps it was Jackson who had made him more sensitive to that. But more likely it was from his own eyewitness accounts of those dogs' infinite bravery and devotion that saved lives. Outside of their handler's praise and some food, they didn't ask for much of anything else.

But the clincher had been the women. Whether it was coming into a village and seeing the remnants of a raid of killers and rapists and hearing those unforgettable wailing cries, or the frustration of female soldiers being mishandled and maltreated by a bunch of arrogant sadistic motherfuckers, he simply couldn't abide being part of an army that let those things happen . . . and then let it slide by, neatly swept under a red-tape rug and a code of silence that, basically, victimized the woman all over again because she couldn't bring her rapist to justice. Now granted, it didn't happen on a constant basis, it all depended on who was investigating and just how important the soldier accused was to the unit. It had been the final straw for him. He'd gotten out of the army. From then on he'd set his own moral compass, a code of honor really, and gone from there. For a guy like him, mercenary just seemed the way to go. He'd just pick an underdog that appealed to that code and hire himself out. He wasn't Superman of course; he looked for compensation in order to pay the mortgage, buy some beer with a good dose of pay-per-view, and the occasional .44-caliber hollow-point bullet. But sometimes some jobs compensated for the lack of funds of others.

Now, because of the sometimes polar sides of the law each of them operated on, he and Jackson had agreed that, for the sake of their friendship, Leo wouldn't talk about doing anything overtly illegal, and he wouldn't do anything construed as misbehaving in Jackson's jurisdiction.

He could live with that. He knew Jackson would be there when he needed him most, no matter what the circumstances. It was just his job to see that those circumstances never arose.

Since Jackson was the closest thing he had to a brother, Leo's actual blood brothers being contemptible douches, he was inclined to do anything that might make life easier for him.

"Hey, since Jackson is AWOL at the moment, what do you say I take you to my place for breakfast? I'm pretty hungry and I'm just around the corner." He hadn't even been home yet since landing, so he'd have to hit the Price Chopper on the way.

"That sounds great!" Andy said eagerly. He followed Leo to his truck and they both got in. Leo stopped at the store and then went to his house. Actually, it was Docia's house. Or used to be. She'd left it vacant in order to abandon all her loved ones and run off with some golden boy. The man could do no wrong in Docia's estimation and Leo could swear he saw stars twinkling in her eyes when she looked at him. But after she'd moved out she'd let him move in and take over the mortgage. It was a nice little historical bungalow on a nice little historic street. She'd been slowly improving it with

Leo's and Jackson's help and he figured he'd probably pick up where they had left off. It wasn't very big, but it was a damn sight better than his old apartment and it felt a little homier to boot. And it was nice to feel Docia's whimsical touch to the place. It reminded him of her constant attempts to bring a feminine touch into their house as she was growing up. It was like having her there, even though she wasn't.

Well, he was still miffed at her for that. *I mean, who does that?* he asked himself. *Where's the logic in running off to live with some guy she'd just met? Leaving all her family and friends?*

Leo was frowning as he let himself into the house. The keychain had a bright pink rabbit's foot on it, the exact way that they had been handed off to him. She'd said, "Here, you can take it for luck. I've already had the best luck I could ever hope for."

So after letting them in he found himself touching the soft fur, the silly thing chasing his frown away and making him smile. Damn her anyway, she'd always known just how to get her way with him. Growing up, she'd had him and Jackson wrapped around her little fingers. It was a wonder she wasn't spoiled rotten to the core.

No. They'd done a good job with her. She'd always been a little bit shy, a little less ambitious than he'd liked, but almost overnight she had seemed to grow out of it and come into her own.

And perhaps if he hadn't been so deep in all of his thoughts, he would have seen Andy's innocence drop away, the sudden malevolent avarice that filled his eyes.

Leo felt something hit his back hard, the strike astoundingly painful. He jerked around with sharp reflex, reaching to strike out at whatever had hit him. But for some reason his arm and hand on the left side would not obey his command, would not lift and move with

the practiced strength that had become second nature
to him. He saw Andy, saw the wide-eyed glee in his eyes
and for an instant thought the kid had been horsing
around. But then why wouldn't his arm move? And why
did he still . . .

Then he tried to take a breath to scold Andy for his
actions and nothing came. Nothing more significant
than a gurgling wheeze that, at first, didn't even sound
like it came from his own throat. He didn t understand.
Couldn't comprehend. Then he looked over his own
shoulder at the burning spot on his back that still hurt
from Andy's strike and that was when he saw the knife.
A huge hunting-style knife, just like the one in his boot
that very second, wicked sharp on one side and serrated
on the other, its black grip touching his jacket and telling him the blade was buried straight to the hilt.

Straight through his back ribs.

Straight through his lung.

Maybe even his heart, he thought as he fell to a single
knee, fumbling for his own blade in an effort to arm
himself. But he was left-handed and working without
fresh oxygen. It felt like drowning, like a black weight
pressing on his chest.

"No! No-nah-no-nah-no!" Andy sing-songed as he
pounced forward, disarming Leo of his knife as though
he were a child. With a sense of furious outrage Leo
realized he'd just given the little fuck another knife.
Andy pushed at him, his strength surprising and powerful, the impact of it sending Leo skidding across the
wood floor until he slammed into the wall. It knocked
what little breath was left in him right out of his un-
damaged lung and a moment of pure, unadulterated
panic swept over him. It was such an alien sensation
after facing so many forms of death, including the possibility of his own. But none of it had been like this.
None of it had *felt* like this. And then the demented

man-child was scrabbling over to him on all fours, panting at him like a puppy getting ready to play.

"Oh, so many things to do!" he declared. "Where should Chatha start, hmm? Any suggestions? Preferences?" He held a hand to his ear, as though he were listening intently. "No? No-nah-no-nah-no! Well never you mind, dearie. I have many many suggestions." Leo watched his vision beginning to go a little dark around the edges as he felt and tasted blood in his mouth, very likely via his lung.

But he was quite conscious when his knife was pulled free of its sheath, and quite conscious when the tip of it was pressed against his gut right above his navel. Then Andy leaned his weight in the slowest of increments onto the blade, watching with genuine curiosity for Leo's expressions. Leo wanted to shout in agony and fury as the wicked blade eased slowly into his body.

"A little to the left? A little to the right? Come, come, we want to know. Tell us. We only want to make you happy!"

Leo gagged up more blood, the barest of sound choking out of him.

"Left! To the left! Excellent suggestion! We like it very much." The blade pulled free, moved two inches to the left and then slowly, very slowly, reentered his body. All the while Andy watched Leo's eyes, watched his grasp for life as death tried to claw at him and bring him under the surface.

The fight within Leo was his curse. It took two more penetrations by that life-raping blade before he finally lost consciousness.

Jackson woke slowly, something inside of him feeling the fall of darkness, flipping an instinctive switch inside of him that told him it was safe to come awake and face the world. He took in a deep breath, bringing forth the scent of sweetness that instinctively tightened his body with awareness. Then he felt the warmth of her, all along the left side of his body, her back pressed up against him in such a way that he suspected she'd alternated from lying half over him to this attempt at spooning against him. Her head was cradled by his arm, somewhere about the vicinity of his elbow, and he felt her breathing against his skin. She was on her left side, the dips and curves of her body on relaxed display. She had come to bed in her skirt and sweater but the skirt, which had been judiciously knee-length, had crept up her thighs quite a bit. Enough to tease, but not enough to satisfy. He wanted to know what kind of panties she had on. It was the craziest impulse, but he realized he couldn't figure it out. The conservative length of the skirt could mean very plain white cotton briefs, but the CFM heels she constantly wore in the workplace screamed the possibility of a naughty, lacy thong.

Truth was, it wasn't the first time he had wondered about it. And like that other time, he grew unbelievably hard at the thought.

"Christ, Waverly, you're a goddamn pig," he muttered aloud with a recriminating groan. Then he found himself seriously debating the benefits of reaching to inch the hem of that skirt up just a little farther. Just enough to tell but not enough to make him hate himself overmuch. He discarded the idea almost as soon as he entertained it. Being a pig in his thoughts was one thing, being one in his actions was something else entirely.

She wouldn't know, his new, smug bastard of a conscience taunted him.

"Shut the fuck up," he groused at Menes. "You're more of a pig than I am."

More a man of action, Menes argued breezily. *You spend far too much time debating the right and wrong of things and far too little time seeing where your im-*

pulses might lead you. You will not know if she would welcome your touch if you never seek an answer.

Jackson wished it didn't sound incredibly logical. He wished Menes would just shut up and leave him be. At what point had he thought welcoming another being into his body had been a good idea?

When you were facing no other option but death.

Oh. Yeah. That.

Jackson decided to look around the room and assess where he was. He was still trying to get used to his ability to see in the dark. It seemed so unnatural and strange even after three weeks of slowly realizing his acuity in the dark was improving every night. Now seeing in the dark was like daylight, or close to it, all the details of the large bedroom jumping out at him.

This was a man's home. He could tell by the way it was decorated, or rather the lack thereof, and the fact that a man's watch was resting on the bureau across from the bed. The sudden idea that this could be her lover's home entered his mind in a white hot flash of anger and jealousy.

No! She is ours!

There was such passion in the thought that he didn't know for sure where it originated from. Himself? Menes? It was all Blending together more and more and he was beginning to have trouble distinguishing between the two at certain times. The only thing he could do was ask himself whether or not he would have thought something like that before Menes had taken possession. He wanted to say no. Never. And with any other woman he would have known loud and clear what to think. But he had to confess to himself that he had imagined things where she was concerned that he never would have thought himself capable of before meeting her two years earlier. He may have kidded himself before, but ever since Menes had taken up residence inside of him he'd faced the fact that she was the rising star of his fantasies. More and more so every damn day. Especially since she'd given him hell for being an arrogant jerk.

Christ, it was as though getting set down and put in his place had been a complete turn-on.

Maybe it had been. Maybe he liked his women a little bit tough. A little bit dominant. Able to stand up for herself. Perfectly capable of telling him where to go when he deserved it. It sure seemed that way to him at that moment. Maybe that was how he'd been getting it wrong all this time. He'd always chased after the curvy vacuous kind, thinking they would be simple to manage and fun to play around with.

But truth be told there had been no curvy and no vacuous women in his life for a very long time. Truth be told he hadn't been much interested in anyone else since a certain redheaded doctor had walked into the station like a breath of soft, perfume-scented air. He could smell her even now, even after they'd both spent hours in the cold night doing their jobs, he could smell the sweet warmth of her. And maybe that was because he rolled up on his side a little and touched his face to her hair, but just the same . . . only she could manage to smell good when everyone else smelled like sweat and too many long hours drinking stale, crappy coffee.

But she wasn't exactly perfectly kempt at the moment, her glorious red hair spilling left and right and all haphazard directions over her face and his arm. She was wrinkled at the skirt and even a little at her sweater, and peeking over to see her face, he saw the dark smudges of makeup that she had neglected to clean off. He would lay bets she'd rather be caught dead before letting someone see her like this, which made him suddenly realize why she wasn't in a relationship.

No, the man who owned this place might be a lover, but he was nothing important to her. She simply was too tightly wound and it was too important to her to be seen in a flawless manner. Relationships were messy and unkempt, they were about letting others see you at your dirtiest, your silliest . . . the real you that you were.

Wow, Jackson thought, he was getting pretty damn insightful in his old age. And there was the fact that he had a very old soul inside of him now. Menes had walked quite a few lifetimes, seen more things and more women than Jackson might have ever conceived of. But what it always seemed to boil down to for Menes was the one, the only one whom he would ever love.

Jackson was given relatively hefty doses of the feelings that Menes had for Hatshepsut. He could feel Menes chafing for her, could feel a level of patience warring with a level of frustration inside him. Menes missed her. This remarkable creature that had his implicit loyalty . . . he missed her with so much power it left a vacant hole in his heart. And Jackson was forced to remember that it meant one day very soon all of his focus would be directed toward another woman. The thought sat very ill with him, despite Menes's reassurances that all would turn out well in the end. All he knew was that it would mean more of the process of saying goodbye to his former life and all the things in it. And that filled him with what was becoming a very familiar sadness.

The thought made him think of Sargent. The poor dog. To work so damn hard and his only recompense was two humans who let him starve and thirst for an entire day! The thought galvanized him, making him ease his arm from beneath her and move as carefully as he could off the bed so as not to wake her. She didn't have an internal clock attuned to the coming of dusk, so she would sleep for as long as her body would let her and as far as he was concerned she could use it. She might not have been tromping through the woods, but she had worked just as hard comforting the mother while at the same time battling the woman with her wits.

And that thought reminded him of something else he had to do. As he moved into the main body of the house looking for Sargent, he was also looking for a phone. He found both in the kitchen, Sargent in the exact same position they had last seen him take up on the rug. But when Jackson entered the room Sargent's ears pricked forward an instant before he lifted his head.

Jackson instinctively made the sound he used to recall Sargent, which brought the dog quickly to his side. The recall wasn't just about commanding the dog to come, it was about releasing him from his well-trained position. It was a strange house with strange smells and rules, but Sargent, who was always brimming with curiosity, had stayed exactly where Jackson had left him, not even trying to climb up into bed with him like he usually did.

"Hungry? And I bet you gotta pee, too. I'm with you on that one, my friend."

Jackson opened the door, hesitating a moment because he didn't have Sargent's leash any longer. It had gone up in flames along with everything else from his original uniform. There was a snapping piece of leather on his gun belt made specifically for carrying the coiled up leash, much in the way Wonder Woman wore that golden lasso of hers, freeing up his hands for other things. But the belt and all else were gone.

After he had taken care of their most immediate need, Jackson started to look for a pantry or cabinet that might have food stores. He opened the refrigerator to find it completely empty and even unplugged. The first thing he had noticed while walking Sargent was that they were really secluded, since he couldn't see another sign of humanity in any direction, and quite possibly completely off the grid. He didn't see any elevated wiring and there had been a series of powerful-looking solar panels at the edge of the northwest corner of the clearing the cabin was nestled in.

"Ah! Here we go," he said with triumph a moment later when he opened the door to a small walk-in pantry. It had to be the neatest pantry on the face of the earth, with multiples of each can, and, oddly enough, each label was perfectly aligned in a forward-facing direction like a neatly ordered phalanx of aluminum and glass soldiers. The sight made him a little sick in his gut. Maybe he was wrong. Maybe she did have a lover. It would be just like her to pick a man exactly like she was. Perfect. Neat. Every last damn duck in its precisely designated row.

The thought made him so surly he had an extremely powerful urge to shove everything off the shelves. *My god,* he thought with shock at the wave of wrath that had washed quickly through him. *Why am I so hot-tempered all of a sudden?*

Not universally, Menes said to him quietly, *but whenever you feel your Marissa in threat . . . in one form or another. Jealousy is to be expected, Jackson, when the winning prize is so exceptional.*

Jackson had to grudgingly admit that there was some truth in that. Perhaps even more so now that he'd kissed her . . . since he'd learned what she'd tasted like on his tongue and felt like in his hands. Since he'd gotten a glimpse of what she was capable of when she let her hair down.

He found a can of stew and pulled the tab up for it. Sargent started to whine eagerly in the back of his throat as Jackson searched for a bowl. He found two, dropping the first in front of Sargent immediately after dumping the stew into it and filling the second with water. He dropped down onto his haunches and scratched the animal that was the pride and joy of its breed. Chico had been a good dog, a dependable dog. A loyal one. He'd never given Jackson a lick of trouble. But neither had he learned so quickly. And Sargent, pound for pound, packed a serious bite. Those padded suits weren't foolproof when it came to protecting the wearer, and a few of his volunteers had come out of training with a good show of bruising.

"Sorry about that, boy," he apologized, still feeling pretty crappy about the dog going hungry all day long. He would have to start paying much closer attention to this weakness he was vulnerable to, start planning ahead and making provisions for all circumstances. He had to heed the lightening sky and not push it to the limit. After feeling that horrific and hot petrification clawing over him he had known it was not something he would ever willingly let happen to him again. And the vulnerability hadn't been the worst of it. The whole time it had hurt, like someone was scraping up the length of every long bone in his body, the nails on the chalkboard kind of pain taken to the nth degree.

"You could have warned me about that," he said dryly to himself . . . or rather Menes.

It seems to me that I did. On many occasions.

"I guess words can't quite convey the honest intensity of the matter. I know I share your memories, but I can't access them yet. I guess . . . I guess I thought I knew."

You never know, Menes murmured quietly in his brain, *until you experience it for yourself. As is true of most things.*

Jackson nodded even though Menes didn't need the gesture to know he agreed and understood. But whether the Blending was complete or not on a physical level, there was still a lot of space between them on a spiritual level. As he had many times over the past three weeks, he wondered just how much of himself he would end up losing in order to make them a single individual.

Nothing, Menes assured him. *Nothing of your soul, your memories, or the essence of who you are. But in the physical world . . . I am asking you to sacrifice a great deal, I know. I sometimes think we ask too much of our hosts. That asking permission in the Ether is such an inadequate way of preparing a human for what is about to come.*

"Yeah, I have to agree with you there. And I understand what it is I have to do. I understand who it is we have to become," Jackson said, a wistful sigh leaving his body. "There's just things I'm going to miss," he said as they scrubbed at Sargent's ruffling fur.

"You know, normally if I entered a room and heard someone holding what seems like a detailed conversation without anyone else there they either have to A) be on the phone, or B) be a schizophrenic."

He looked up, a smile touching his lips at her words. It grew as he took in her tousled and rumpled appearance. She looked like she'd just been engaging in bedsport, her hair victim to the ravaging stroke of his fingers as he held her in place for—

No, no . . . bad thought, he told himself hastily. He absolutely could not let himself run wild with that thought or he'd get hard, he'd start craving things, and start wanting to kiss her lush mouth all over again. Bad enough that he still hadn't erased the taste and feel of her from the front or the back of his mind.

"Good morning. Or . . . well, I guess it's goodnight at this point."

"Yes we've been here all day." She frowned as she watched Sargent lick the bowl so enthusiastically that, now empty of food, it was moving across the floor with Sargent hot on its heels. "I called Landon on the way here last night. I told him my thoughts on the likelihood of finding the boy. Since Sargent isn't a cadaver dog, do you think you'll still be needed?"

There was a hell of a lot Sargent could do to help find that boy despite his training limitations. But . . .

"I won't be going back out. Not after what happened. It's time for me to leave town. Pack up my shit, quit the force, and just go."

"Quit! Why would you quit? Where are you going? I mean . . . can't you just work third shift? It's at night—"

"In the summer it's light until nine p.m. Third shift starts at midnight, sure, but it runs well into sunrise. It's just not possible. And Marissa, even if it were, I couldn't bring my enemies into a place where innocents could be harmed as they try to take my life."

"But . . ." It was a weak word, with her so obviously wanting to argue and yet her logical and reasoning self already knew it was an argument that could not be won. "Do you mean . . . forever? You can't just . . . I mean you have to be able to come back at some point. You can't possibly run away from creatures like that. No matter where you go they will find you and—"

Apparently she realized what she was saying because her eyes went wide with no little horror over the situation.

"Oh my god, it's true isn't it? No matter where you go those . . . those *monsters* will find you. And with all that power gunning for you, how can you possibly survive such relentless targeting? And don't you think the best place for you to be would be familiar territory?"

Jackson straightened to his full height, leaning back against the counter and folding his arms over his chest.

"Why, Doc, I'm touched. You're practically heart-broken about this."

She gasped in a startled breath, her cheeks pinking up and her eyes brightening fiercely in all of an instant. "You're an ass," she spat.

"Yeah, but I'm good-looking so, it kind of evens things out."

God, he loved poking at her to see what kind of quills she'd shoot at him next. There was something about seeing her in full glorious temper that really turned him on.

All right, you bastard, are you some kind of sadist or something? he demanded of Menes.

I'm not the one who traded desks after Sargeant Kanus retired so I could see right down the hall to her office door, Menes was quick to single out.

Well, shit. The man had a point. At the time he'd told himself the desk had more room and a better filing cabinet. But the move had definitely put her and a really good perspective of her ass right in his line of sight dozens of times a day.

"Stay or go, it makes no difference to me," she snapped at him. "I just . . . I mean to say," she said, her hands suddenly becoming busy smoothing out the wrinkles in her sweater and skirt, "that wherever you go you should make certain you don't isolate yourself. A-and perhaps you should find another counselor as well. I'd be more than happy to forward any records you might need."

Officer Waverly. She didn't say it, but it was right there. Sergeant Waverly and Doctor Anderson. He'd brought them to a personal level by taking her out of her comfort zone and forcing her to break all of her own rules. Now she was backpedaling, trying to find strength in the familiar and in the methods she used to distance herself from others.

"I think you're missing part of the point here, hummingbird. Before you go flitting away, if you recall someone got a good look at you and saw me protecting you. If they think they can use you to get to me they will. So, you're coming with me. For a little while anyway."

"I am *not* going with you! I have a job! I have family!"

"Yeah. And if you want to keep them safe you need to leave them for a little while until I'm sure that no one is focusing on you. Think of it like the witness protection program. How many people have you had to coax and counsel to relocate? To change their identities in order to keep themselves safe? Why would you do anything less than that for yourself?"

"It's not the same! Those people were witnesses to terrible crimes and had to testify—"

"Oh it's very much the same, Marissa. It boils down to this . . . if you want to keep our coworkers and your family alive, then you will leave with me *right now.*"

She drew breath to argue almost automatically, but then the words stopped in her throat. He watched her eyes widen and suddenly she was clasping one hand in the other, making a serious effort not to twist them together with worry.

"What if it's too late? What if they are already in danger? Who says they won't hurt her anyway?"

"Her?" He straightened away from the counter. "Who are you talking about?"

"My sister."

"Honestly, I don't even think they know who you are. But if you go back to the office they will see you there and figure it out really damn quick. That's when she'll be in trouble. And unlike me, you won't have to leave forever. Just to give me enough time to make it known I'm in New Mexico so they'll concentrate their efforts in that direction and no longer need to concern themselves about anyone in Saugerties."

"You mean you're going to *tell them* where you are?" She gaped at him. "That's utter lunacy!"

"No, Doc. I assure you I'm quite sane. The people who will protect me in New Mexico are just as powerful as I am. Some perhaps more so. It's not something you can quantify. You'll see what I mean once we get there. Now if you're going to freshen up, you'd better get a move on. I'm leaving in twenty minutes. I have . . . I have to return some police equipment."

His voice turned quiet and he reached out without looking, knowing the wet nose and thick fur he was seeking would be right there.

It was a damn shame he couldn't promise the same in return.

CHAPTER SEVEN

"What are we doing here? I thought we were going to the precinct."

"And I thought I told you that you going there was a bad idea. I'm leaving you with a friend I trust while I go about handing in my service weapon, my badge . . . other things." She saw him glance in the rearview mirror with no little amount of regret in his eyes. She had seen him tilt it down just enough so he could see his dog. Whether Jackson wanted to admit it or not, he'd grown attached to Sargent. She couldn't help but realize he was going to have to grieve all over again, essentially losing two relationships in under a year. "I'll . . . I don't know . . . I'll just say the dead kid was the straw that broke my back," he said with a shrug. "You can back it up with some shrink talk about my 'inability to accept the grieving process' or whatever it is you want to say."

Tommy Slattery had been found dead an hour ago. His mother was being interrogated probably at that very moment, using Marissa's insights to guide them. Oh, how she wished she could be there to be instrumental in the punishment for the horrendous crime against her own child. The boy had been . . . almost unrecognizable. Whether it was from the initial incident or done afterward to hide one crime by making it look like another . . . it didn't matter. She knew the mother was at the heart of it and any woman who could do something like that to her own child . . .

She reached for the door handle. "I won't lie for you, Jackson. But I won't tell the truth either, so you have no worries there. I'll treat this like I would any other doctor-patient confidence."

He reached out to snag her wrist suddenly, pulling her back when she would have alighted from the car.

"I am not your patient anymore," he said roughly, his hand wrapping around the thick braid she'd worked her wet hair into after a hasty shower. He used the grip to make her look him dead in the eyes. "Do you hear me? Doctor-patient went out the window when I kissed you. You can't shut the barn door now, counselor, so get it out of your head because you kissed me right back. You're a liar if you say otherwise."

He was so full of raw male temperament in that moment that her breath snagged somewhere in the lower reaches of her throat. Not so much anger, but dominance. Full lines that he would not allow to be crossed. Not a challenge, but a firm statement that he wouldn't stand for anyone to gainsay him. Apparently the always polite, always conscientiously lawful Jackson Waverly no longer existed. Now he was half owned by this other entity, this unknown element she was beginning to see in bolder and bolder stretches. Or perhaps it was still parts of Jackson, but much less of a desire to control what was seen by others or what he would do in any given situation. Perhaps, she thought, it was best that he resign after all. Jackson had made the perfect cop. A cross between tough and respectful, mindful of the law and of the job he represented. Whoever she was seeing now, she had no doubt he wouldn't hesitate to rip the head off the next bad guy to come down the line if he felt it was warranted. Not indiscriminately, no. She didn't think he was that far over. But he wasn't pulling punches he felt were needed to be thrown in order to save his life or the life of another. Mainly, her. And that was what had gotten her into this mess. His overinflated white-knight syndrome.

And damn him, she liked him all the more for it.

"Okay, Jackson," she agreed gently. "I'll nix the doctor hat from now on, okay? I can't shut it off, it's who I am, but I'll stop trying to pigeonhole you into the role of a patient."

"Good. Because if you do I'm going to kiss you again. And given the reactions all around from last time, I'm thinking I'm not going to try and stop at just a kiss."

And that's just what he gave her then. A short, powerful kiss right on the lips. No teeth, no tongue . . . hell, it was practically chaste . . . except for the fact that it lit her skin on fire underneath her clothes.

Then he was gone from the car with a jingle of keys. She scrambled to follow, determined to warn him that she wouldn't put up with all his Neanderthal macho man tactics to keep her quiet. No way. She wasn't going to sit around waiting for him to give her permission to move or speak or whatever the hell archaic role he thought she ought to play up there in his alpha-male atmosphere.

She marched up behind him.

"Jackson Waver—mmph!"

His hand slapped over her mouth and she felt him pushing her bodily into the wall beside the door. She was just shy of biting him when he held a finger to his lips and she followed the indicating nod of his head to the door standing ajar. There was a brick-colored streak across the bottom of the door, about twelve inches up from the ground, and she realized with shock and horror that it had been made by a hand being dragged over the door. Then she looked down and saw the swath of brilliant red leading over the doorjamb and across the light wood floor just inside the door. She heard Jackson's weapon leave his holster very quietly, and—turning his back to her so he was between her and anything that might come out of the door—he gingerly pulled open the screen door, then held it open with the toe of his boot as he checked his corners and eased into the room.

He didn't have to tell her to stay. She couldn't have moved even if she wanted to. She had seen a lot of dead, dying, or dissected things in her lifetime, but there was something intrinsically chilling about that streaking handprint, as though someone had reached out to try to hold on, to try to stop from being dragged into hell.

In what felt like the longest five minutes of her life, she waited, trying not to breathe too loudly and trying not to think that whatever had happened here was, by trail of that handprint, very likely on *this* side of the door. Her palms were coated in an icy sweat by the time he came back, reaching for her face, his fingers brushing along her jaw and his thumb on her lips.

"Okay?" he asked, making sure he was looking directly into her eyes.

"Yes but—"

But she could see the grimness tightening his mouth, she could see the rage steaming in his eyes.

"Is there a—?"

"No," he said, as always seeming to know what she was going to ask. "But somewhere there's a body missing a hell of a lot of blood. It's everywhere in there." He looked down at his boots, showing her the boot prints that followed him out the door. "If I leave here without calling it in . . . then resign and leave in the same day . . . they are going to think . . ." He trailed off.

She gasped in outrage. "They would not! How can anyone who knows anything about you think anything of the kind?"

"It happens all the time. People snap. People—"

"You're not people," she hissed at him. "You're better than people! I can say without any doubt in my mind that you would never, ever *snap*!"

That made him smile a little. "Oh sure. *Now* you tell me. After I spent months tied into knots because I thought I had to convince you I was doing 'just swell' after Chico died."

She rolled her eyes, choosing not to dignify that with an argument, especially under the circumstances.

"Isn't this your sister's house?" she asked, suddenly realizing she had been there once before.

"Used to be. A family friend took over the mortgage. I think you met him . . ."

"Leo Alvarez," she said automatically.

"Jesus. I really do have only one friend in the world, don't I?" Again that simmering rage made an appearance. "Or I used to. If this is Leo's blood . . . he didn't make it."

"The blood makes it all the way out over the stoop, but stops just a little way onto the porch. Why drag him all that way, only to pick him up?"

Jackson snorted. "You've seen Leo, right? Nobody's picking him up unless they have—" He broke off for a second and they met each other's eyes.

"A partner!" they said in unison.

"We can't stay here," Jackson said tightly. "If they came after Leo because of me then we aren't safe here. Let the consequences lie wherever they will, we're leaving town right now." He held up a keychain with a bloodstained pink rabbit's foot on it. "Leo's car will be a little less conspicuous to start. We'll trade out later on before they can put a BOLO out."

"Jackson?"

The tiny-sounding feminine voice made Jackson's head whip around just in time for him to see his sister suddenly sprinting up the stairs. "Leo! LEO!" she screamed, trying to push and pull her way out of her brother's arms any way she possibly could. On Docia's heels was Ram, Docia's lover, and a very big, very angry-looking man with the shoulder width of two . . . maybe three linebackers.

"Easy! He's not in there, Docia. Easy," Jackson said, although Marissa knew his reassurances were false. It was clear Ram thought so too as they traded looks over his sister's head.

"But—" She was just tipping past the cusp of crying, large tears welling out of her eyes. "But he's all right, right? If he's not here, he's all right."

"There's a chance he's just fine, Docia," Jackson flat-out lied to her. "We have no idea what happened here. And knowing Leo like we do, I'll lay bets that this isn't his blood." As Ram came up to take possession of Jackson's sister, Marissa watched him surreptitiously drop the bloody rabbit's foot into his pocket. He could fast-talk all he wanted, but clearly Docia would put two and two together very quickly if she saw the keychain. "We'll track Leo down from the road, Docia. I'll have Asikri stay behind and watch out for information." He indicated the large wall of a man standing at the perimeter of the group. "Right now we have to get out of here. This is a crime scene, one way or another, and it's just the kind of attention we don't need."

"Do you think he's all right?" Docia demanded of Ram.

"We're talking about the same guy who slit Odjit's throat and rid us of her, yes?" Ram said as an explanation of his feelings on the matter.

"Even though she was Bodywalker and he was merely

human," Jackson chimed in, making everyone come to a screeching halt except, apparently, her. She ended up stepping on the back of Jackson's shoes and quickly apologizing. But her apologies fell on deaf ears, since everyone was staring at Jackson as though he'd lost his mind.

"What?" he demanded. "She knows."

A uniform "Ohhh . . ." drifted out of Ram and Docia. Asikri, the big hulking wall of surly muscle, just grunted. Or maybe he was breaking wind. It was honestly hard to tell by his expression.

"How did that come to pass?" Ram wanted to know. "You managed to keep this from her last time and for the three weeks following your rebirth."

"I was attacked and it forced me to show my hand. And we compounded the situation by protecting her openly and then letting one of them get away. A Gargoyle. He didn't look like any of the usual Templar lackeys, but no doubt he's reported all findings by now."

"Perhaps. Perhaps not. It depends on the Gargoyle's desires and loyalties. A failure like this could sit ill with his masters, and they are not known for their forgiveness. Possession of their touchstones gives the holder the ability to hunt the Gargoyle attached to it down so it's fruitless to resist, but one might try given the circumstances."

"So you're thinking because they figured out who you are . . ." Ram trailed off, giving Docia's shoulders a squeeze.

"They'll go after my family. My friends," Jackson confirmed in a soft voice that held emotion but dared anyone to see it as a weakness. Marissa could just imagine how he must be feeling right then. Jackson's record and profile showed how often he took a lot of weight onto his shoulders that didn't necessarily belong there.

"Why are you here?" he asked suddenly. "I don't recall summoning you."

Oh, there was a dangerous sound of authority in his tone. Enough to make Ram, a man she had found to be of great strength and conviction, visibly hesitate as they progressed off the porch.

"I . . . Cleo suspected . . . well . . ."

"You're telling me," Jackson said with overtaut tension in his voice, "that you suspected I might be in danger and you brought my *sister* with you?"

Ram looked pained, his expression almost comical. "I could not do otherwise, Jackson. If I hadn't taken her with me she would have gotten on a plane and come anyway on her own steam. At least this way Asikri and I can afford her the protection she needs."

"And this is all you brought for protection?" Jackson asked. "You and Asikri?"

"Hey!" Docia protested.

"Sorry, Sissy, but as powerful as you and your Bodywalker Tameri are, you are still too newly Blended with her to convince me that she can wield her abilities with absolute competency."

"So sayeth the man who has only had his Bodywalker for three weeks."

Everyone turned to look at Marissa and she resisted the gasp forming on her lips. Had she said that out loud? Well, yes, apparently so because Jackson was looking like he wanted to kill her and Docia was looking pretty darn pleased.

"Thank god! Finally another woman on my side! Sometimes it's just me and Cleo trying to make these overgrown behemoths see reason. We're not very successful."

But despite her attempt at levity, Marissa could see her looking over her shoulder at her former house with continued worry for Leo's fate.

"I only meant to inject a little fairness to the situation," Marissa said awkwardly. "I have no ulterior motives either way. Other than to point that one part out, I have to agree with your brother that this isn't a safe place to be on many levels. We should be going."

"On that we can all agree," Asikri finally spoke up to say. Then, as though something about the entire lot of them pissed him off, he turned and stalked away.

"Give it time," Jackson said with amusement. "He kind of grows on you."

"Like a wart or a huge pimple. Big, ugly, hairy, and the last thing a girl wants to wake up to in the morning," Docia said.

This time not even she was fooled by her attempt at levity, so she fell silent and seemed to make every effort not to look back at her house again.

CHAPTER EIGHT

Leo clawed his way to consciousness, the cacophony of agony screaming through his body almost too overwhelming and the gritty taste of bile sharp at the back of his tongue. He struggled, tried to push or pull or move in any way possible, even though he knew it was going to hurt like hell the instant he achieved any of those goals. But there was no movement to be had. Something was different. Anything different had to be an improvement over the last time he'd been conscious in the world. Didn't it?

"Well, it is good of you to join us at last."

The greeting was cordial. Almost refined. Or maybe it sounded that way because anyone with that particular kind of accent couldn't help but sound as though he breathed slightly better air than the rest of the world. It wasn't exactly a British accent, but it was foreign. Perhaps South African. However, placing it wasn't the first thing on Leo's mind.

No. The first thing on Leo's mind was the shriek of new pain that tore through his shoulder as he tried to move again.

Breathing. I'm breathing.

That was different. This was a difference he had to count as an improvement. At first. But each breath hurt like hell and any move he made was like nails from a finishing gun punching down in rapid succession, rather like a dotted line that demarcated one territory from another on a global map. The light hurt his eyes, but it didn't escape him that it was probably shining directly into his eyes precisely for that reason. It wasn't the first time he'd been on the opposite end of that kind of tactic . . . and he supposed he knew where this was headed.

"Sorry I kept you waiting," he said. Wow. He sounded like hell. And talking made him cough and . . . oh yeah, that was a whole new world of hell right there as well.

"Somehow I doubt that. You aren't at all apologetic. Not yet anyway. We might get to that eventually."

Leo fought with the grit scraping between his eyelids and the resolution of his focus. The image that finally crystallized for him was of a tall, athletic man with russet hair that was emboldened by the nut-brown color of his skin. He was seated in a metal chair, some ancient relic from an old office-supply dungeon.

Leo then took note of the fact that he himself was bound at all four points, each wrist wrapped up tight in a leather bracer that not only immobilized his wrist, it immobilized his entire arm. He couldn't bend or so much as flex any of his arm muscles and the same was true of his legs. Leo fought down a wave of panic, knowing that the feeling would weaken him. And he knew by looking into the cold clear irises of his jailer that he was going to need all the strength he could possibly muster.

"Let me explain something to you. Because," he injected in a conversational tone, "it occurs to me that you may not even be aware of the curse you have brought down on your own head."

"Play?" The plaintive word was almost like a pleading whimper off to his right. Leo jerked his head to look in that direction, the sound and tone of that voice sickeningly familiar. It was the voice he had heard giggling over him as he'd been slowly and methodically stabbed to death.

Only somehow he wasn't dead. His body burned with the memory and pain of each of those injuries, as if he'd had surgery and was in a state of healing, but not far enough in to have found relief from the damage. How long had he been unconscious? Had they repaired him only to—

"I want to play," Andy hissed, his feelings of impatience coming through loud and clear, his eyes alight with the fire of his desires.

The desire to cause pain. The fire all too easily defined as psychopathic elation. The very same expression that had been on his face with every slow stab wound he'd created. All of it simmering behind the face of innocence, the sweet roundness of a Down syndrome man. A young man, nearly a boy. Leo had never known that a Down-affected adult could exhibit such violent, lunatic tendencies. It just didn't make sense.

But Andy still had Leo's knife in his hand and he leaned forward now to poke Leo with two fast, sharp stabs aimed for his left biceps. Leo gritted his teeth against the pain of it, the tensing of his body ripping at all the original wounds he sported. Healing but not yet healed.

"In a moment, Chatha," the other man said dismissively. And as if Chatha were a dog on a leash, he subsided and sat, waiting with avaricious impatience for his master to let him loose. "Now, I will sum the situation up as efficiently as possible. You see, you have taken something very precious away from me, and while I wait to get her back, I am going to content myself with watching you suffer the death you consigned her to over and over and over. Do you understand?"

He didn't need details. Leo understood. He was going

to be tortured. It was clear he was going to meet death in the process. But he was going to damn well make it as unsatisfying for them as was in his power to do.

Then the man nodded to Chatha and Chatha pounced, grabbing Leo by the hair and pulling hard until his neck was stretched to the limit. Leo struggled to not make a sound as pain and anxiety scraped through him.

And then Chatha used his hunting knife to cut his throat, the knife so sharp it severed everything with ease and purity, like spreading soft butter on bread.

Now Leo couldn't scream even if he wanted to.

Hours later, Leo woke up. His throat, cut nearly to the bone the last time he was conscious was back in working order. He could breathe and swallow, although both acts felt like he was swallowing razor blades. How was this possible? How was he even alive? Twice now he had experienced what should have been his own death, only to wake up once more . . .

To the same nightmare. The calm, regarding eyes that were so eerily light blue they bordered on colorless, like the facets of diamonds. His expression was equally as hard and as cold as that particular stone.

"Where were we?" he asked aloud, clearly rhetorically speaking. He didn't want Leo's input. "Oh yes. The reason for all of this. You slit the throat of a woman, a very powerful woman whose gloriousness and magnificence so outshines the dingy, pissing existence you call a life. You nearly killed her. Not an easy trick, to kill one of us, and I suppose on some level you are to be commended for your strength and prowess.

"But on the other hand . . . you have sinned grievously against me and mine and I cannot let that stand."

"Somehow I knew you were going to say that," Leo croaked out. Hearing himself was a shock. Maybe it was because he'd worked so hard at his speech and its patterns, worked to rid himself of the barrio influences that could make him a caricature of his heritage. He was an intelligent Latino and he damn well wanted others to show him the respect he deserved. Hearing himself sound so rough hit him on a level that he would never allow this *pendejo* to ever see. "Anyway, you're going to have to be more specific. I've slit a lot of bitches' throats in my day. Just which bitch is yours?"

That was a ballsy bit of lying, but he could play this game, too. He'd shot a woman once. Punched one once, too. But in all fairness to him, one had been holding a gun to his head and the other had tried to stab him. Not that he'd blamed them. After all, in both cases he'd just killed their husbands. But hey, that was the risk you took when you hooked up with a drug kingpin and a sadistic mercenary, respectively. The only time he'd cut a woman's throat had been in his dreams. A very vivid dream at that, he thought with a frown. It'd been a hell of a piece of fantasy fiction with spell-casting bad guys and himself, Ram, and Docia cast as the good guys. That dream had creeped him out in huge ways, mainly because in it Jackson had died.

"The fact is you will only remember the act as a dream. I can tell by the energy surrounding you that your memories have been altered. Let me expedite matters by telling you it was not a dream. Everything you did and everything you saw was absolutely real." The other man stood up and loomed over Leo. What made it so unnerving was that he wasn't trying to bully him, nor was he interested in convincing him. He was just dropping information for factual purposes. "The way you remember it is of little significance to me. It was what it was. It was a lowborn beast, a *savage,* thinking he had the right to rid the world of a queen. There is recompense to be paid for such things." Those icy eyes flicked upward to above Leo's head.

"Again" was all he said.

Chatha pounced, this time the knife slicing so deeply that Leo could almost feel it at the back of his throat. As blood filled his mouth and lungs, as it pumped out of his body once again, he couldn't keep himself from wondering what kind of fresh hell he had managed to find.

"And now I will wait until you are once more on the brink of death, then I will have Chatha heal you, so that we may begin anew."

And for the first time in his life, Leo Alvarez came to wish he was dead.

Unlike Chatha, Kamenwati took very little pleasure in what he was doing. After all, that would make him the soulless bastard the Politic liked to accuse him of being. He would not give them the satisfaction of making a stereotype of himself. And yet, punishment was necessary. He could think of no other way to make the human comprehend the heinousness of the act he had perpetrated. Unlike humans, Bodywalkers did not believe in half measures when it came to their criminals. It was far more efficient to make the criminal truly appreciate what he had done. Only then would he think twice before doing the same thing again. They believed there was nothing better than to make the perpetrator really feel the impact of their actions from a firsthand perspective. It was a punishment, ironically enough, that Kamenwati had not always been a strong proponent of. But he believed that in this instance it was more than justified. The human male had chosen sides with nothing but misguided faith and had decided to act as judge and jury against a woman he knew not at all. It seemed only fitting that he learn what the repercussions of something like that were . . . and what it felt like from the victim's standpoint. In this instance of course he was being forced to act in Odjit's stead, but at least when she roused from this interminable slumber it would be to the news that her assaulter had been justly dealt with.

It was ironic, he thought, that Chatha's Bodywalker power was healing. It was because of this that they could send the message home to this mortal, again and again, and feel content that justice was being dealt without becoming true criminals themselves in return. Of course, Chatha was a wild card. He was no more easily controlled than a spoiled child, and, again, he did not agree with letting him run amok. But he was one of Odjit's pets, a true example of how she was willing to see the worth in even the most irredeemable of characters.

Kamen walked into his chambers, intent on reporting to his mistress. Perhaps if she heard of this justice she would find the will to waken. It was his deepest wish that she do so. The grief he felt in dealing with day-to-day life was becoming heavier and heavier. Without her guidance to keep him afloat, he didn't know how much longer he could bear being in this world. He feared his apathy. Feared it would make him like the thoughtless humans who wasted their lives and their planet in such painfully devastating ways, and feared it would make him like the Politic Bodywalkers, enemy to his own race and displaying a complete lack of faith that would one day be his undoing. And so he returned to her to report his news, and to continue looking through her vast array of prayer scrolls and compendiums made of pressed papyrus as ancient as they were themselves. He had remembered seeing something . . . a long time past now . . . a spell that could possibly help.

And he would not rest until he found it.

CHAPTER NINE

"Hey honey, can you please, please, please call me when you get this message? It's extremely important. Do not blow me off, okay? I'm not going to lecture you or anything. It's just . . . you need to call me."

Marissa hung up the phone and—like she had been doing for the last twenty minutes—continued pacing. Seeing that kind of discord and discontent radiating from her was almost as ominous as dark clouds swallowing up the sun. It was the third message she had left for her sister, in his presence that is, and he could tell each failed attempt to reach her sister was only ramping up her distress.

"Marissa."

She jumped in her own skin, apparently so absorbed in her own whirlwind of thoughts and stress that she hadn't even heard him approaching. Then, as if his presence had pulled the plug, she began to vent.

"I should never have left town. I shouldn't have left without at least speaking to her. What if they know who I am and decide to question her? She doesn't even know she could be in danger. I should never have left!"

"Though I think it highly unlikely that they know who you are or where you live, it is still possible, however remote, that they do know. And considering what has happened to Leo, we can assume they are hunting me in earnest and that anyone associated with me is in danger."

She began to pace faster. "If this is your idea of comforting me, it's really not working!" she hissed vehemently. "What a mess! All of this, everything about you is just a nightmare! Now everything I hold dear, my sister, my home, my job, is all under threat because of you! You knew singling me out could have this effect! You had to know because according to you you've done this quite a few times before, this resurrection process and taking on the mantle of this never-ending war you have going on. So how could you do something so stupid like singling me out? How could you just destroy everything in one thoughtless swoop of action?"

"I suppose I could have pretended to be indifferent to you," he acceded, "but then you'd probably be dead in the woods right now."

"You knew this could happen," she railed on. "Why would you carry out this . . . this farce of being human in a human job? Why would you put so many innocent people at risk?"

"Firstly," he said with more than a little sharpness to his tone as he snagged her by her wrist and with a solid jerk tugged her out of her circuit across the floor, "I was not pretending and it was not a farce. Whatever I have become, I was and *am* Jackson Waverly first. Have I struggled with the right and wrong of it? Have I questioned my own wisdom? Of course I have. So don't stand there and berate me like I did this on purpose with callous thought toward others."

"But you—"

"Secondly," he spoke over her sharply, "you are not the only one here missing a loved one. At least your sister is most likely to be alive, whereas Leo Alvarez is most likely dead in a ditch somewhere, so if you please, spare me your recriminations because I am full to choking on my own!"

That, finally, seemed to quiet her. She stood, her posture tense and surly.

"And do you really think," he added on a softer voice as he pulled her closer to the warmth of his body, pulling her in until her feet were between his and her bowstring-taut body was a hairsbreadth away from his own. So close he could feel the heat of her. Close enough to feel the resentment she was feeling toward him all along the surfaces of his flesh. "That I would leave it up to chance whether or not the Templars will try to use others from my former life against me? Asikri was not on the plane with us because, along with obtaining information regarding Leo, I sent him to your house to fetch some of your things and to ensure the safety of your sister. She hasn't gotten your messages because he has thrown her phone away and given her a new one."

He withdrew the smartphone from his pocket and, turning it on with a stroke of his thumb, typed in a quick code and turned the screen toward her. On it was a short text message from Asikri.

"I've got the girl. Tossed the phone. ETA about four hours."

She grabbed for the phone, wrapping her hands around his and jerking it closer, reading the words again as if there was a great revelation to be found in them.

"Why? Why would you throw away her phone? And why didn't you tell me? I've been sick to death with worry!"

"I did tell you. That text came less than five minutes ago. Until it came there was nothing of comfort I could offer you, other than my complete confidence in Asikri. I didn't think that would be accepted at face value, so I waited for contact from him." He took a breath, timing it and the ones immediately after it in a steady, calming cadence. "He had to discard the phone because it has GPS inside of it. Any smartphone in the world can be traced with the right software, and I assure you, the Templars have an excellent phalanx of geeks at their beck and call."

"GPS?" she repeated a little numbly, all of the wind knocked out of her self-righteous sails. She rubbed her thumb over the phone in their hands. "I didn't realize . . . I mean, I knew, of course, but . . ."

"If there is one thing we have become masters of in our long lifetimes it is how to live off the grid. Sort of like your friend's cabin. Self-sustaining and with as little record of ourselves as we can possibly manage. Our wealth is managed through front companies, our investments grow on their own accord and we track and adjust and give ourselves great means leaving little more than a ghost of ourselves behind. It is not foolproof of course, but we know how to avoid the most common pitfalls. Now, this phone has GPS as well, but the number is unknown and untraceable by anyone outside of the highest echelons of the Bodywalker governing seat. I want you to trade it for the one in your hand."

"But . . ." She lifted the hand holding her phone. "I can't just—"

"You can, and you must. Surely you see that? You don't have to like it, but surely you see the logic of it?"

He waited patiently while she thought about it, her lips quivering with tension as she pressed them tightly together, no doubt forcing herself to think before she tried to argue with him. In the end she opened her hand palm up and handed him her phone. He turned it off, pulled the power supply out of the back of it, and pocketed it for their techs to tinker with. They would either remove the GPS and reuse the phone, or they would simply destroy it.

"I have to ask you to limit your use of this phone while you are in our company. It's just like witness protection," he said, his eyes catching her so he could be certain she understood and complied. "You can call any of us and, now, your sister, but you cannot under any circumstances contact anyone outside of our purview. All it takes is one call to lead them here. By giving you this, I am entrusting you with our safety, hummingbird."

"I understand." She breathed after a long moment. Emotional pain entered her eyes and he felt guilty for it. She shouldn't have to go through this. They had done her a powerful injustice. He and Menes. It was their calling to make these sacrifices in the name of his people, and she should never have been involved.

"Jackson, they're going to think you're a murderer," she said on a rush of injured words. "How can you let that happen? Can't you just call or . . . or . . ."

"We've been over this," he said gently, something inside of him filled with warmth, knowing that in a moment like this it was everyone else she was worried about. He had done her yet another injustice by ever thinking her to be a cold and emotionless cog in the wheels of bureaucracy. In truth she spent all of her time worrying about everyone else. He wondered where she fit her own needs in her grand scheme of things. "As of today Jackson Waverly will have disappeared. He will cease to exist. It doesn't matter what anyone thinks of him because he will, for all intents and purposes, die the death he was supposed to have died that night three weeks ago.

"You ask me why I didn't leave right away? Because I needed the time to grieve one of the biggest losses anyone can ever experience. The loss of their entire identity as they once knew it to be. I know that the important parts of who I am come with me, but that doesn't stop me from grieving what once was mine and now must be let go of. I'm only sorry I didn't leave sooner. I thought I was completely anonymous and that it was safe for me to stay . . . but I was wrong and I'm going to have to live with that knowledge and the knowledge of what it might have cost Leo in the process." He had been speaking in a calm, steady voice, but it broke on Leo's name as guilt threatened to swamp him. They must have known Leo was the closest thing he had to family . . . outside of Docia, who was a Bodywalker and very well protected. It had very likely cost his friend his life, because Leo would rather die than ever give up any information about him. The funny thing was, Leo had been out of the country for the past couple of weeks. He hadn't even had any idea where Jackson was. He certainly hadn't known about him Blending with Menes.

Marissa was looking at him with soft, considering eyes, the blue of them so warm, in spite of it being such a cool color. But her eye color was closer to the blue at the center of a flame, like when a Bunsen burner is lit and it roars with its little storm of fire on the tip. And then, as intransigent as the wind, they would turn toward green, hovering on the brink of it, but not quite achieving it.

"You've come so far since I first began counseling with you," she said, her tone so genuine that he didn't feel she was patronizing or even doctoring him. It was as if she were a friend, and not a doctor. "When we first met you were so determined to not acknowledge your grief. And now look at you. You've come to understand you're allowed to mourn, and more important, to let go enough to move on. You were so determined to punish yourself, to blame yourself not only for Chico's death but for replacing him with Sargent. So much so that you wouldn't allow yourself to connect with him the way you needed to." She smiled softly at him. "Now you love him so much you can't even let him go."

She nodded toward the dog sleeping soundly on the floor near the fireplace.

"I'm stealing him, you know. If I'm going to be a murderer, I may as well be a thief besides." He frowned a little. "You know, three weeks ago, I would have never done something like this. I would rather have died than let someone think ill of me or accuse me of a crime, never mind flat-out commit one. But . . . maybe it's because of Menes's influence, that I am willing to do something because it is right and not just because it's the rules. Sargent belongs with me. He depends on me just as I depend on him. And I have no intention of leaving the department ill equipped. They will receive a donation of two new pups from an anonymous donor to replace him."

"Somehow I knew you were going to say that," she said with a smile, impulsively reaching to hug him. It was an affection he hadn't expected, and he certainly hadn't expected her to initiate it. But, of course, she realized what she was doing and pulled away moments later, her head dipping so her loose hair hid her blush-pink cheeks. She stepped back and smoothed her skirt and blouse, though neither were out of place. It was, he realized, more like her version of donning armor. She did it almost like a reminder to herself that there were protocols to be acknowledged.

He wondered, once more, why she felt the need to hide her true depth of compassion and emotion, not to mention her carnal side. She was so incredibly passionate. He should know, he'd held that passion in his hands and had felt the sensual power of it. He had felt what it was like when she released all her inhibitions and just lived for the sensations of the moment.

Not that her conscience and ethics were inconsequential, but there were other things equally, if not more, important. And while she bestowed nothing but respect and understanding to others, he wasn't quite sure she gave the consideration to herself.

He wanted so badly to kiss her right then. It wasn't about the desire that constantly crawled through him whenever he looked at her. Or the fact that she was unbelievably beautiful. Nor was it the way her gorgeous red hair framed her delicate features hinting at the passionate woman within her. All were present and accounted for, but what compelled him most was her kindness and the understanding he knew she felt toward him in spite of him having screwed up her entire life and thrown her into the deep end of the Bodywalker world with absolutely no forewarning whatsoever.

"I'm so sorry about your friend," she said, her bottom lip pulling between her teeth as though she wanted to nibble on it but caught herself in time to quell the undisciplined action.

Good god, she's wound up tighter than a watch, Menes thought with no small amount of frustration. A feeling Jackson shared. In fact, he was noticing a lot more similarities between him and Menes than in the very beginning. They both had strong personalities and both had this powerful need to do something when they saw what needed to be done. It was just that sometimes it seemed like Jackson wasn't as willing as Menes was to do whatever necessary to see the right thing done. Or what he *felt* was the right thing.

For instance they felt that the right thing to do would be to grab hold of her and pull her close. To kiss her and force her to see the passionate woman she was inside. But they knew it wasn't going to be as easy as that, and they knew that heaping that kind of revelation on top of all she was dealing with bordered on selfishness.

"And," she said, "thank you for keeping my sister safe. She means more to me than anyone else on earth and the idea of her getting hurt just because of me . . ." She shook her head, mute with all the negative things that came after such a thought, too disturbed to voice the possibilities.

"It was the very least I could do, considering I'm the reason you are in this mess to begin with. Come," he said, pulling her with him as he left the room, "let me get you something to eat."

"I'm not very hungry."

"You haven't eaten since . . . good god, when *did* we last eat?"

"I suppose it has been a while," she said as he drew her into the enormous custom kitchen in the center of what had to be the largest home Marissa had ever been in. It was large enough, he had told her, to house several Bodywalkers in comfort. They tended to travel and live in groups, a way of protecting one another from Templars or any number of hazards. This was to be Jackson's new home and, for the time being, hers. She took the seat he offered her on a barstool near the counter and he went to the fridge. He started pulling out enough food to feed an army.

"You can't be that hungry," she said with a laugh as he began preparing what looked like at least three sandwiches. "No mustard, please. I'm allergic."

"Really? I never knew that about you. And I don't think I've heard of a mustard allergy before."

"It's something of a pain in the neck when I go out to eat. I constantly have to ask if they use mustard or mustard seed in something. It's used much more often than you might think. And it's kind of a downer because every time I hear about honey mustard dip or honey mustard dressing it always sounds so delicious."

"What happens if you eat it? Rashes and such or full-on anaphylaxis?"

"Oh, I'm the grand prize winner. I get the whole deal. Blisters, anaphylaxis . . . I almost died the first time I ate it when I was five. Fortunately, since we'd been outside at a picnic, my parents and the doctor thought I might have been stung and that I was reacting to that. The adrenaline treatment stopped the worst part of the reaction long enough for everyone to figure out what had happened."

"Fortunate indeed," he said, his tone seeming to go a little distant, a small frown toying at the spot between his brows. "No one really knows when the fates will decide to end our lives. It is inevitable for us all. Except perhaps Gargoyles. They are virtually indestructible and it takes some pretty specific series of events before it . . . well, that's neither here nor there."

"But in a way, aren't you really the immortal ones? If I understand this correctly, you are the exact same soul, if not the exact same physical rendition, of the pharaoh Menes. Isn't that immortality at its plainest?"

"In simplified terms, I suppose it is. But with every generation, our souls are touched by the soul of another, Marissa. There is nothing to compare it to, I know, but learning someone . . . *knowing* them that completely changes us until, by the time we part from each other, it is as though all of what Jackson is will have been included into my soul and he too will have immortality through that means." He put a sandwich in front of her and came around the bar so he was standing close to her. He reached to touch her chin, tipping her head back so she was looking into the sea green of his eyes. "Think of it like finding a soul mate. Like loving someone on such a visceral level that it becomes almost impossible to think of living without them. To know that they are etched in your heart and your soul for all time, that is how deep an impression they have left. That is how it should be. And everyone should know what that feels like, though I'm sad to say that I know they won't. I think in that way we are truly blessed, we Bodywalkers. Sometimes I look at a human being such as you and I think, how do you do it? How do you move through this world knowing you are so alone in everything that you do? And then Jackson remembers what it was like and that it wasn't so bad. It eases my worry."

That was when Marissa realized she was talking to Menes more than she was Jackson in that moment. Someone else might have found that reference to himself in the third person obnoxious, like some kind of star or something, thinking he was so glorious that he must be referred to as something outside of an individual. But she realized she was coming to understand the fluctuation between the disparate personalities living inside of Jackson. And it was funny, but she could see physical differences as well. Not in form or features, of course, but in mannerisms. The way he held his posture, the deep confidence in his body language. Jackson was a confident man of course, but there was something *more* to the way Menes projected himself. She realized then it was because he was a being who had lived and died in some of the most turbulent times in history. The relative cushy lifestyles that humans had now must be amusingly simple to him.

It was a little unnerving to her, to know she was sitting in front of a great Egyptian pharaoh . . . and that he had been there when Jackson had touched her and kissed her.

She blushed without knowing why. She wasn't exactly known for her lack of confidence. She might feel moments of insecurity from time to time, mostly when trying to find a way to fit in with the rest of her coworkers on a social level; but the nature of her job and the role she played made it very difficult. Sometimes she was convinced they thought the only thing worse than her was Internal Affairs. That made it very hard to cultivate relationships. They couldn't separate who she was as a human being from the threat they perceived her to be professionally.

"Now what's that expression for?" he asked her gently. "That looked like a very troubling thought."

"I was just wondering . . . I thought you told me that you're Blending with Jackson and becoming one in essence. But I can very easily tell who I am talking to from one topic to the next."

He made a small contemplative sound. "I find it intriguing that you do. But we are newly Blended, and over time you will not see any distinctions. Nor will we feel the need to use plural pronouns when referring to ourselves."

He smiled then, all gentle magnetic charm as he touched his thumb to the corner of her lips. It seemed to be a favorite caress of his, she thought as warm frissons of indefinable emotion swam through her. It wasn't arousal or desire, though she did acknowledge that both were also present at that moment. It was . . .

It was enough to make her shy away from him, turning abruptly out of his tender touch. She reached for her sandwich, stuffing it into her mouth before she got some crazy notion in her head like wanting him to kiss her.

Menes watched her shift away from him, drank in the pretty flustered color on her cheeks. She was perfect. In every way he could possibly hope for. Jackson's desire for her was a volatile, virulent thing, and Menes didn't blame him in the least. She was beautiful, intelligent, capable of deep emotions and equally capable of hiding them. That was important when one was in a position of authority. Like, say, a queen. Oh, he could see there were flaws, that she had control issues, and had very little ability to trust. However, he would never discover any of these things nor other more crucial answers if Jackson didn't stop locking down his needs and emotions where Marissa was concerned. All of the recent progress *he* had made up to date had been as a direct result of Menes's internal influence. Jackson was completely unaware of that fact, of course. Menes was a far more powerful soul than Jackson was, which allowed him to have his secrets in spite of the Blending. He wasn't subjugating Jackson in the least, merely . . . encouraging him to follow his natural instincts where she was concerned.

She was a beautiful creature, but she was in desperate need of a complex sort of wooing. An aggressive sort of wooing. She was too powerful a personality and had extremely strong walls for defense shored up against . . . well, that part was still a puzzle. Was it just Jackson or was it men in general? Or was it people that she mistrusted altogether?

"I imagine that, as a psychiatrist and as one that tends to the needs of police officers, you see and hear a great many terrible things," he said, watching her carefully to see how she reacted to his change in topic. It would throw her off, keep her off balance a little, which he suddenly realized was what he had been doing to her all along. He was keeping her from finding her footing, so she couldn't try to ward him off.

She frowned a little just before letting a professional mask slip over her features.

"It's part of the job, yes. The men and women on the force are very complex people, but for the most part, in spite of their strength and dominant personality traits, they became cops in order to do something good. For the most part they have very powerful moral compasses. Do some get lost along the way? Absolutely." Again a brief frown turned down the corners of her mouth. He would have missed it entirely if he hadn't been on high alert for it. "For people with such a powerful sense of right and wrong and a need for justice, it can be very psychologically damaging for them to see such terrible things. And to see those terrible things go unpunished makes it even worse."

"Yes. Believe me I know." Menes knew this not only from the parts of Jackson that were now a part of him, but he knew this from lifetimes of watching injustices occur right before his eyes. It was the essence of the war between the Politic and the Templars. He saw the horror of the crimes Odjit and her brethren committed and it made him righteously sick to his soul. He refused to leave the world open to her victimization. The only reason why it had been so easy for him to let go when Hatshepsut had been taken from him in their last incarnation was because Odjit was already dead herself. Had she not been killed he would have forced himself to remain. But he was a shell of himself without Hatshepsut. He was half the man he was capable of being when he was without her.

Of course Jackson knew nothing of this. He didn't understand at present the powerful depth of finding and craving a soul mate. But Menes believed he was beginning to. Jackson was far more attached to this pretty redhead than he realized . . . or was willing to admit to in any event. That was good. Important even. And he couldn't have chosen much better himself.

Menes reached out, unable to help himself as he envisioned Hatshepsut's soul within this beauty, and brushed back her hair from the side of her face. She startled, her skin flushing as she ducked to avoid the caress.

"Please don't do that."

"Why not?" he asked, genuinely curious. "Don't you like to be touched?"

"Of course I do, but . . . we're not . . . it's just not . . ."

"Not what? Ethical? I'm not your patient any longer, Marissa. Nor do I work with you anymore."

"The situation of the present doesn't erase what was. I am bound by ethics to not—"

"Not enjoy yourself? Not live? Just because we had the misfortune of crossing paths in an official capacity we should deny what I feel is a most incredible attraction? I see no logic in that. I see no logic to a lot of the laws and boundaries that are now in my mind because of Jackson."

"God, it's weird hearing you refer to yourself like that. And just because you don't like the rules doesn't mean we can break them."

"I disagree with you wholeheartedly, Marissa. Rules are a guide to seeing things done rightly. If I see that they interfere with what is right, then I change the rules."

"You can't just do that," she scoffed at him. "Jackson, being the boy scout he is . . . you are . . . I mean . . . well, he doesn't work that way."

"But he is not just the sum of himself anymore. And he is more inclined to the way I think than you realize. So," he reached to brush back her hair once more, taking no small pleasure in the fact that she didn't move away this time, "this idea that we must deny the attraction we feel is simply not an acceptable rule. I will summarily discard it and I will do everything in my power to see that you do as well."

She swallowed visibly and he saw the ghost of the fear she was feeling and trying so hard to hide behind a mask of coolness and control. *Oh Marissa,* he thought, *what has happened to you to make you thus?*

"It was you, wasn't it? You were the impetus behind what he said to me three weeks ago."

"I don't know what you—"

"Oh don't pretend like you don't know," she bit off. "I hate games. If you think I'm going to play you're sorely mistaken."

"Marissa, I am not playing a game. I honestly do not know what you are referring to. Three weeks ago I was extremely weak, having been harshly pulled from the Ether and expending energy I ought not to have done so immediately afterward. It numbed and paralyzed me from my connection with Jackson. It was part of the reason why this Blending has taken such a long time. If Jackson said something to you, I assure you it was not of my doing." Menes was genuinely curious now, especially since Jackson's memory conveniently shut down on the topic. More of the infamous Waverly recalcitrance. Honestly, if Menes didn't respect his strength of will so much it would be extremely irritating. "Tell me what he said to you."

"That doesn't matter," she said, beating a hasty retreat, sliding back off the barstool in such a way as to take herself out of his reach, rather than move forward and risk brushing up against him.

"But I think it does," he said, standing up and reaching for her wrist, preventing her from turning her back on him and their conversation. "Tell me what he said to you."

She was flushing that pretty fuchsia pink again. It was charming on her in spite of the fact that she was stubbornly shaking her head.

"Did he proposition you, Marissa?" he asked, taking a stab at it and watching it hit her like a ton of bricks, the entirety of her neck and shoulders blushing into that glorious color. "Ah, I see he did."

"Not . . . not a proposition as much as . . . a-an announcement of intentions."

Well, well. So Jackson had made bold with her all on his own. Menes wondered how Jackson had managed to keep that secret from him. Menes was supposed to be the stronger soul, considering the amount of time he had spent on this earth alone, never mind in the Ether. It took great strength of will to remain lucid while in the disembodied state of the Ether. It was so easy to get lost in the mists of forgetting, or rather the mists of *wanting* to forget. Wanting to forget the violence of emotion attached to their last death, and all the ones before it. Wanting to forget the loss of all those mortals left behind who would not be there when they returned once more.

Just the thought alone had the power to bring him to his knees. *So many. So many I have loved and lost over the centuries.*

"Are you all right?" she asked, reaching to wrap her hand over the rise of his shoulder, the strength of her touch anchoring him and telling him just how visibly he'd been reacting to his thoughts.

"I . . ." His professions of being just fine seemed to stick in his craw, held there tightly by the things left unfinished and unlamented. His comfort, his only comfort in all this turbulence of life and death, was his beloved queen. The longer she stayed trapped away from him in the Ether, the harder it became for him to push aside the darkness of his thoughts and centuries worth of memories. Of children lost, of friends gone to dust. "There is so much loss, when you live lifetimes the way we do," he said, surprising himself with his honesty. "Some moments leave their mark on my thoughts and heart more than others. In my previous lifetime humans were at war just as the Templars and the Politic were. I was in the new world . . . America . . . and a great many young people were going off to die or find glory in battle. I have long since evolved past the foolish idea that with war comes glory. With war comes death and nothing more. No matter who is in the wrong, no matter

whose cause is more just, to war means to reap death."
He felt the weight of his words like an oppression, as
though an elephant had taken up residence upon his
heart. "It is bad enough that as Bodywalkers we triple,
sometime quadruple, the life span of the host that car-
ries us, cultivating the opportunity for those we grow
fond of to turn to dust and leave us longing for them,
trying to fill the hole their passing has left inside of us.
Not just some . . . *all*." He looked into the concerned
warmth of her eyes. "All whom we touch in our new
lives will leave us. It is not unheard of for a Bodywalker
to take his own life when the grief of living without his
most beloved friends and family becomes far too difficult to manage."

She was listening to him very intently, as if what he
was saying was very important to her. He supposed that
was because it was her job to make others feel that way.
But the embittered thought didn't stand. He had come
to see the tenderness in her heart. She was genuinely
focused on him, and empathizing as best she could with
her limited mortal experiences. It was making his feelings all that much harder to keep control of. He wanted
to fully disclose everything to her, but he did not want
to have her thinking that being a Bodywalker was a
hateful experience.

"Grief. So much of it," she said softly. "You actually
have to watch those you love age and pass on, knowing
you will be left behind . . . forever. You can't even tell
yourself what so many human beings do—that you will
meet all your loved ones again someday in the afterlife.
You are denied that comfort because of the nature of
who and what you are. I can't even imagine how much
pain that causes you."

"It is . . . it is not an easy choice to come back from
the Ether. It takes great fortitude of spirit to encourage
ourselves to leave the relative safety of it. But that would

be like shutting yourself off from the beauty of loving relationships because there is the painful possibility it will fall apart. Right now my queen is struggling with this very problem. In spite of her devotion to our people, her commitment to seeing an end to this infinite war, she did not want us to be reborn because it would mean one of us would eventually have to watch the other die. When you love as deeply as we do, with every corner of the soul . . . the loss is incomprehensible. And even a hundred years in the Ether is not able to erase the agony of it."

"Y-your . . . queen?"

Menes looked at her in surprise, suddenly realizing how much he had confided in her. He had not wanted to mention Hatshepsut to her just yet, to lead her to believe that Jackson was unattainable because he was destined for another. It was bad enough that Jackson was struggling with his conscience on that one.

But perhaps it would be for the better, he mused thoughtfully.

"Yes. My queen. She is in the Ether, awaiting rebirth. She and I . . . there is nothing to compare it with, Marissa. Humans use the term 'soul mate' in order to try to make others understand the depth of feeling they harbor toward an individual that they love beyond all measure. But soul mate, in the case of my queen and myself, is woefully inadequate. And perhaps a little . . . inaccurate, since we are already mated with another soul when we exist in the flesh.

"In truth there is nothing capable of expressing what lies between me and my queen. She is beyond perfection in my eyes. She is that which holds all of the molecules of my physical self together. She is the only thing that can comfort my turbulent, enduring spirit when it begins to feel it has walked the world much too long." He drew breath, the delicious smell of Marissa provoking memories of her taste onto his tongue. His body tightened with excitement as he filled his physical senses with her and thought of his queen. His appreciation for Marissa was growing rapidly beyond just the physical. She was complex and delightful, always surprising him with how she wanted to project herself on one hand, and what ran deep and true inside of her on the other.

"You mean . . . you mean you're waiting for her?" He watched the light dawn in her eyes and had to work hard to suppress a smile at her sudden and glorious fury. "Of all the low-down dirty-dog things to do!" she erupted. "You have a woman waiting for you in those mists"—she waved a hand up toward the ceiling with an agitated flick of her wrist—"all alone up there and, by your account, in a state of grief and loneliness, and you're down here getting all handsy with *me?*"

"Yes, indeed, that does make me something of a scoundrel, wouldn't you say?" he said, not knowing why he was taking so much delight in her reaction. Perhaps it was because she was so indignant, so beautifully strong that the entire room practically resonated with her outrage. She was, he realized, a champion. She chose a side, most likely an underdog or someone who had somehow been wronged or victimized, and she became their protection . . . their armor . . . and with no regard for the damage she might suffer because of it. She was a glittering, impenetrable essence that repelled all enemies with all that she was, and would not abandon what she protected unless she was ripped away by force.

Oh yes. She was glorious.

And she was perfect.

A perfect queen and a perfect mate.

CHAPTER TEN

She was pissed. Really, really pissed. Probably because her whole body was burning with the embarrassment of having been made a fool of. It was bad enough that Jackson had been yanking her out of her comfort zone and rubbing her raw against her grating ethics, but to know that he knew there was no future between them and had manhandled her anyway?

Oh yes. She was furious. Her whole face and body burned with it, her heart sinking with shame for being so foolish even as her back rose into defensive hackles. Her fingers curled, as if they wanted to grab him around the neck and choke the life out of him. It was no wonder, because the impulse was not all that far off in that moment. And he was smiling at her still! That cocky, smug little smile that felt to her like he was thinking dirty, dirty thoughts about her.

The pig.

"It figures you would be proud of yourself for that! Quite the accomplishment, getting your hands on my ass. Wow. I see why you're the ruler of your people," she said, venom in every single word she spat at him. "With deception skills like that you are perfect for politics!"

"If you equate me with the politicians of your society you are mistaken," he said with serious intellectual contemplation in his tone. "They are renowned for their treachery and deceit. I, however, have never lied to you."

"Oh sure, you just decided to omit a few key details," she said bitterly.

He stepped closer to her then, invading her personal space and forcing her to look up. She tried to yank her wrist free of him and backpedal, but to her dismay the wall was at her back and his grip was not easy to break. After all, he was a titan. What chance did she have against such a powerful being?

Well, she might be outmatched physically, but in the matter of wits and, apparently, ethics, she had him in her dust.

"That's just as bad as lying," she railed at him, but awkwardly realizing it was very uncomfortable to argue and make a stand when being bathed by the overwhelming heat of a powerfully potent male. "It makes you even more of a pig because you can justify yourself in such a self-serving way. No wonder your people have been at war for eons!"

"I'm so surprised," he said in a soft, matter-of-fact manner, "to find you so harshly judgmental without even giving opportunity for explanations."

"I think the topic at hand is pretty self-evident!"

"How strange," he said with a soft, honest sense of musing as he reached out and caressed her temple lightly before running two fingers along the length of her hair, "that you profess such unequivocal knowledge about a person belonging to a species that, for you, had not existed before today. I had thought you much more thoughtful than that."

"Do not turn this around on me," she bit out, floored by his audacity.

"But it is about you. All of this is about you. You who are so fair-minded and so tolerant of so many people caught in so many difficult circumstances, and yet when you feel that a man might have potentially betrayed you, you do not even wish to slow down and think you might be misinterpreting. Tell me, hummingbird, why do you fly so swiftly? What makes you think you can't sit still for a moment lest a predator snatches you up and hurts you?"

"Stop touching me, Jackson!" She reached to shove him off of her but the moment she did so she felt the overwhelming strength of him through her palm and fingers. He would not move, she realized, until he wanted to be moved. She was weak and insignificant to him. Not just woman to man, but immortal to mortal.

"But I like to touch you. I like to look at you. And I very much like the way you smell, Marissa." The timbre of his voice dropped even lower on that last statement, making her breath catch as her lower legs went traitorously weak under her.

"Get off of me," she demanded through her clenched teeth.

"Ask me what my motives are, Marissa."

"Intimidation? Bullying? Selfishness? Why ask? I already know."

"Ask me," he said, his head lowering so he was breathing the request across her lips. Her entire body clenched, going weak as if she were a hormonal teenager about to be kissed for the first time. Damn him! Damn her. God, all she wanted to do was go back home, go to bed, and wake up knowing all of this had just been a ridiculous nightmare.

"Back. Off." She gritted both words out, using all of her strength of will to keep from lashing out and physically punching him in the eye. She wasn't by nature a violent person, and as mad as she was, the impulse still shocked her. When he didn't move, keeping himself that barest breath of distance away from her mouth, she was shocked to find her entire body reacting on a visceral, physical level, her chest rising and falling hard with each rapid breath, her mouth craving, as though wishing for him to close the distance between them. How could her body react one way when her mind and emotions were so powerfully motivated in the opposite direction? It was confusing and embarrassing because she felt as though he knew very, very well the effect he was having on her. "I won't ask because I don't want to know," she said, her eyes burning, the sting in her nose warning her that if she didn't regain control she was going to cry out of frustration.

"When I entered the Ether," Jackson said, "Menes was there waiting for me. A human can only enter the Ether when on the cusp of death . . . and only very specific kinds of impending deaths. Far enough to take life, but not so far it can't be reclaimed once the powerful strength and healing abilities of the Bodywalker has joined with its human host. When I came into the Ether, Menes, like all of the lawful Politic, asked permission to join with me. They make it as clear as possible, pull no punches, make you see the good and the bad of what you are about to become. Menes was especially careful, knowing that he is pharaoh over a warring race. It cannot be just anyone, you see, to Blend with a being of such heavy duty and responsibility . . . not to mention having a target painted on your back.

"But he asked, Marissa, and I said yes. And now I am asking. I'm telling you everything you need to know, I am seeking out in you everything I need to seek. Menes wasn't a part of me five minutes before he knew what I had been hiding from myself for so long now. He knew you were special. He knew I wanted you. And he knew that, had we not been restricted by ethics and protocol, I would have done anything to make you mine."

"You . . . b-but . . ." she stammered.

"Her name is Hatshepsut. In her original life she was one of the most powerful queens of Egypt. She is going to need a very precious host, a woman of strength and beauty. A woman of fire and passion. A woman of heart and wisdom. She is going to need you, Marissa, just like I need you."

He closed that last aching distance between their lips, catching her breath in his mouth before kissing her with a soft ferocity, the connection so gentle and yet the emotion behind it so fierce. She had never been kissed while inundated with so many thoughts and emotions warring through her. It made her feel like she was completely out of control. There was something thrilling and terrifying about that. Her first instinct should have been to flee, to run away far and fast and never, ever look back. But what she did in actuality was reach out for him, her palms flattening on his chest just before curling into it, pulling the soft cotton of the shirt he wore into the tightness of her fists. She was wedged between his muscled body and the wall, but she could swear he was the harder and more immovable of the two. The perception was due to the fact that she knew just how powerful he was, knew the strength he was capable of. And yet he touched her so gently, just the tips of his fingers drifting over the rise of her cheek before filtering into her hair. He still held her wrist in his opposite hand, holding her even though her hand was already against him. It was as though he were anticipating—

She gasped in shock as his words finally sank in, a stunning wash of cold dashing all the immediate heat he had inspired. She tried to jerk back and away, but there was simply nowhere for her to go. So instead she tore her mouth free of his and, panting hard for breath, turned her face down and used the press of her forehead against his chest to hide herself from him.

"No," she gasped on ragged breath. "No! You don't mean . . . but . . . you can't mean that! You barely know me! I don't . . . and don't I have to—?"

She was speaking incoherently because she wasn't thinking straight. How could she when he was pressed so close to her, overwhelming everything that she was, filling every breath with that so very *male* scent of him. His taste was on her lips, the burn of five o'clock shadow along the edges of them.

"How do you know what I mean and what I don't mean if we are such strangers?" he asked her, somehow confusing her with the logic. "Why do I feel like I am coming home when I kiss you if I barely know you?" He took a breath and she knew, she just knew he was drawing in her scent. His eyes were half-closed with the obvious pleasure of it. "We have just spent these past minutes talking of the enduring souls of my people and you, a nascent original who has only known one life, presumes to know everything there is to know about the soul and what it would be like if two souls of perfect complement came together? No. No, that's foolishness," he chided softly. "Even more foolish than a man who longs for a woman for over a year and yet stays seated at his desk, allowing her to walk by again and again, thinking he could be content with just the vision of her and the soft trailing eddies of her scent.

"I almost died three weeks ago and the moment I realized it, the moment it sank in, the first thing I thought was that I would have died without ever touching you the way you should be touched."

And that was when the ghosting touch of his hands came to an end. He pressed the weight of his body into her, and his hand slid down her chest until he had filled his palm with her breast, pressing her own flesh into herself, making her feel the intensity of his words and the desire riding hard behind them.

"I feel the soft shape of you like this and I can't decide whether to take you softly on my bed or take you hard, right here where we stand. And it doesn't matter because I know you'll be magnificent either way. It's going to come down to the impression I most want to leave on you, Marissa. It's going to come down to the understanding that I finally have you here. So," he said, his lips and breath hot against her hair as he continued to allow her to hide from him, "before you tell me we are strangers . . . before you tell me I haven't thought this through, I want you to think. Think about everything you've thought and felt since I announced my intentions to make you mine."

She looked up then, her whole body shaking from the impact of his words, his touch and his heat. She wanted to be outraged, but somewhere along the line it had abandoned her. Now all that was left was an overwhelming rush of curiosity, of possibilities . . . of things she never would have thought herself capable of thinking.

"You just . . . you never said anything . . . you were so . . ."

"So were you. And tell me now that you never thought the same thing. Tell me you never looked my way and wondered . . ."

"I wasn't allowed—"

"No," he said roughly, his grip on her breast tightening enough to get her attention and make her catch her breath. "We are done with bullshit and the shells of lies we armored ourselves with. Think, Marissa. Think . . . *I was dead*. If not for Menes, I was dead and gone from this world and from you. You were there at that moment. Do you remember? You think it was a dream, but you were there, holding me, screaming for me. I looked back from the Ether and could hear you." He leaned close to her ear and whispered fiercely against it, "I knew then that I had died without ever knowing what it meant to live. Knowing I'd had sex, but never made exquisite love, that I'd known lust, but never true passion. I knew longing, frustration, and craving much too well and satisfaction not at all. I came back for those reasons, but mostly, Marissa, I came back for you."

Tears burned at her eyes, clawed up her throat and suddenly, like a veil lifting away from her mind, she did remember. She remembered having a horrible nightmare about three weeks earlier, waking from the cold death of sleep with a gasp, feeling tears dried on her cheeks and rawness in her throat as if she had truly screamed, as if she had truly lost him. She had flown from bed, scrambled through her things, rummaging through clothes she couldn't remember taking off while in pajamas she couldn't remember putting on. She had found her cell and the work directory, searching frantically for his number and was about to hit SEND . . . until she realized what she was about to do and stopped, her breaths hard and ragged. She had realized how inappropriate it would be. Had realized she could never call him just to see if he was all right. Not then. Not ever. She had collapsed onto her knees then and wept. She told herself later that she had cried because she'd been rattled by fear, but in the face of his honesty with her, she didn't have it in her to lie to herself again. Now, knowing it had been real, that he'd almost slipped away from her forever . . .

"You see?" he breathed, when he saw the comprehension in her eyes, the dawning of the terrifying realization of what might have been if not for fate and the very unlikely choice of an Egyptian king thought long dead. "That was the exact feeling," he said, letting go of her and drifting fingers up over her breast, chest, and throat until he was touching the corner of her awakened eyes. "And to know that much grief without ever knowing that much passion of life is the stuff of too many human tragedies. Don't let this be another of those tragedies. We've been given a second chance, you and I. We can't waste it. If we do then we deserve every single moment of the pain we should suffer for it."

His kiss, as light as it was, was so incredibly poignant that she felt her throat closing up. When, she wondered, had anyone ever kissed her like this? As though she were a unique and precious thing, not to be toyed with lightly, but not to be shelved and untouched either. The answer was never. Even when she had fancied herself in love, even in what she had once considered her most loving relationship to date . . . as exciting or as hungry or as hormonal as anything might have been, none of it was in the same class of the way Jackson was making her feel. Every argument, every sound reason, every piece of shielding and armor she had ever erected to protect herself tried to crowd the understanding out. *You hardly know him. How can you even trust him? He's not even human!*

She gasped when that last thought sent leaps of forbidden excitement along her every major artery. Menes had saved Jackson's life. Had Blended with him and given him these incredible powers as well as making him nigh indestructible, but . . . what else had the Blending enhanced on him?

She flushed crimson, or so it felt, and she tried to turn her head. "Not this time," he scolded her softly. "Face it or embrace it, but whatever you're feeling in this moment, do not run away from it."

"I'm not running," she said softly, sounding no more convincing to herself than she must have sounded to him. "I'm just very overwhelmed, Jackson. The past forty-eight hours . . ."

With what sounded like a very reluctant sigh, Jackson eased back from her, giving her room to breathe and, coincidentally, room to catch a chill. The man was like a living furnace, giving off an almost volcanic heat. Or maybe that was just her perception because . . .

Marissa shook the thought away. There were more important things to worry about . . . and to say.

"How do I know you're not just saying all of this because . . ." She didn't know how to say it without sounding cold and accusatory, and some part of her acknowledged he'd never done anything to earn the blight on his character.

"Because you think I'm just looking for a vessel for my queen?" Even with him saying it for her it sounded awful, but it needed to be said. It needed to be addressed. "I came back here with many things on my agenda, Marissa, and I would be lying to you if I said that finding an original for my beloved wasn't the most crucial of all to me." He took yet another step away, and she had to tamp down the craziest urge to follow after him. *My god, if nothing else the man is utterly magnetic*, she thought fiercely. "And I do want you for Hatshepsut. But I want you for me as well," he said, the abiding craving in his tone running deep with truth. "You are thinking in a single and linear fashion when you consider my faithfulness to Hatshepsut. But, as you know, there is no singularity in any relationship I form. It is, if you will excuse the crude sketch of it, a ménage a quatre, Marissa," he said. "Multiple individuals coming together to enjoy the pleasure of one another. All have given permission and all understand there is no place for jealousies or peevishness. My queen would want me to find a woman not only for her to live with, but one I could live with as well. If I like her, that is good. If I admire her, all the better. If I lust for her, well, it will only add to the lust I already have for my queen, and I assure you that is quite significant."

With a flash of blinding realization she thought of all the possible combinations that existed when potentially four people were in bed together. The minute it raced through her mind she knew she was blushing straight to the roots of her hair.

"Ahh," he said on a soft exhalation of breath, his body reclaiming half the distance he had been putting between them. "Does the idea excite you, hummingbird? Does it make you curious? I can't see you being anything less than eaten up with curiosity. I'm beginning to see it is an essential part of who you are. After all, the job you do is all about seeing into other peoples' lives. You get to hear all their desires, all those secret things they would never tell anyone else. All the while, there you sit, living an experience like a voyeur where it is safe and secure. But safety is highly overrated, Marissa," he said, the richness of his tone flowing over her like a suggestive caress. "It is so much more exciting to live it firsthand. As long as you are with someone who will keep you safe."

That made her laugh, a nervous sound to stave off the tightening of her throat and the heat twisting inside her belly. "You are the furthest thing from safe that can possibly exist," she said, trying not to sound as breathless as she was. God, she could almost hear the excitement shivering in her own voice. "You're a target. You were always a dangerous man, Jackson. Anyone who has ever seen you in action knows that without a single doubt. But now, with Menes a part of you, that danger has literally doubled . . . and I don't know if I want to be anywhere near you when it all goes to hell. You said it yourself . . . you painted a bull's-eye on your back. You . . . I mean . . . by nature of the job being a police officer means going out there with a target painted on your back. The criminal element takes one look at that uniform and your life is instantly in danger. You are used to that. It's the job you signed on for. I didn't sign on for dangerous duty. I sit in my tidy little office, ordering my neat little thoughts in my crisp, clean files. The biggest danger I face is getting a paper cut!"

"Now that is a waist-high ditch full of horseshit. I was there, if you recall, when Leona Wright lost her shit in your office, leapt across the room and wrapped her talons around your pretty little neck." He touched a finger to her throat, right about where she'd sported deep, painful bruises for almost two weeks. "You could have been a school psychiatrist, sitting in an office in a cute little elementary school, the biggest risk getting a case of head lice. But no, you chose to dance with a melting pot of type-A personalities, being exposed to some of the worst shit mankind has ever seen. You got up in court in the Marscone racketeering case and told everyone flat-out that there was nothing crazy about him and that he was more than competent to go to trial. As I recall he was screaming death threats at you the whole time they were dragging him out of the courtroom."

"Actually," she muttered, "it was more of a 'you stupid fucking bitch whore' kind of a threat. Rewind. Repeat."

"Mmm. Not the point," he said with amusement in his peacock eyes. "You are just as much in the thick of things as I am. It's one of the things I admire about you. As well as your incredible grace under that sort of pressure. In fact, the first time I even saw you shaken was the night that I . . ."

Died. *Oh god, it had been real,* she thought again, feeling a little light-headed over all that had happened to her in these past whirlwind hours.

And maybe that was why it took her so long to . . .

Oh my god!

CHAPTER ELEVEN

Jackson was watching her face very closely at that point, waiting like a cat in front of a mouse hole, waiting for it to dawn on her what he was truly asking her to do.

And there it was. The widening of clear blue eyes and the sharp intake of breath.

"You mean you want me to *die?*" she asked him incredulously. "That is what you mean, right? In order for this queen or whatever to come and share space with me, I have to *die* first! You are out of your mind if you think any sane person is going to volunteer for something like that! And what in hell do you need *me* for? I'm sure there are dozens of gutsy, curvy little redheads running around dying all over the world! No!" She held up a hand and cut him off when he opened his mouth to speak. "Absolutely no! No talking. No touching." She pushed his hand away sharply. "No anything! I'm not letting you run roughshod over me and my life just because you need a vessel for some dead Egyptian queen. Sorry, mister, but you have got the wrong woman."

She shut him down completely by dodging out of his reach and marching off in fairly high temper. He ought to have been concerned for her, he supposed, but the truth was he was just too tickled to death by her. Everything she did gave him pleasure in one form or another. Be it intellectual, emotional, or physical, she lit him up on every single bumper.

But she did have a point. Jackson had become aware, at last, of Menes's plans for her almost at the same time she had. But it would be wrong to say they were all Menes's plans or all Jackson's plans. It was all boiling down together, a reduction of motives all pointing in the same direction. It was about wanting a woman and being willing to get her by any means necessary.

Of course he didn't like the dying part any more than she did. The thought of her going through that kind of trauma was not well received in his mind. Menes concurred on that, but he was more practical. One way or another she was going to die, be it now or many years from now. At least this way she would be saved and she would be his for as long as the fates allowed for them. And by the gods he prayed it would be longer than the last time. That was perhaps what had been the sharpest of the pain of losing Hatshepsut last time. She had only been reborn for a week before Odjit had taken her life. One week. It had been as heated and fervent as it always was, their spirits close in the Ether but lacking the physicality to touch. So when they were reborn they wanted nothing more than to feel each other in any way possible.

But one week had not been enough. Not by half. And he had not dealt with it well at all. He had failed her then, failed to protect her and keep her safe in life as well as in his heart. But this time he would not fail. This time Odjit had been dead for three weeks and this would be the safest incarnation they would enjoy in perhaps five or six hundred years.

But none of that would matter if he couldn't convince her to be a part of this future he found himself captain to. He was home now he thought, as he looked around the grand kitchen and the casual dining nook within it. Beyond was a large formal dining room and other rooms equally made for a big household. And the royal household was always quite large. Now that he was there, the house would fill with friends and staff, and the machinery of a government would begin to take place.

Not that Ramses did not do well in his stead. As far as he was concerned either of them could have been designated to rule over their people in perpetuity. But long ago the people of the Politic had chosen him. The Templars . . .

He despised this war, he thought with vehemence. He was sick to death of it. Why could they not see reason? Why did they fear the right to live their lives for themselves so much that they wished fervently for the god Amun to rise up and destroy them if they were not well behaved? It sickened him that half his people were wrapped up in this blind faith, this dark age of being oppressed by beliefs tempered into them by the fist of that zealot harpy who called herself a priestess. Why could they not see her for what she truly was?

He had asked himself these questions over and over, incarnation after incarnation and still there was no answer.

Except . . .

"Docia!" he called out as he moved from the kitchen into the main body of the house. The house was all new to him, so he wasn't exactly certain where he was going to find her. It was a great frustration for him, to feel like he wasn't completely in charge of matters close to him. But, he counseled himself, patience and time would see him where he needed to be, would help give him the strength and fortifications he would need if . . .

"Docia!"

"What?! Quit hollering at me! Jeez." Docia shot the

command at him with all the exasperation a baby sister could muster, though she was well into her twenties, and her Bodywalker Tameri was almost as ancient as he was.

"I had a question for Tameri. She has told you that there are others like her who want to defect from the Templars?" At her nod he hurried on. "Just exactly how many Templars are we speaking about?"

Since Docia was also only three weeks into her Blending, she had to go quiet for a moment and access her Bodywalker's memory. He watched as her face turned incredibly peaceful, so unlike the turbulent energy of his sister. He realized then that he had missed her terribly since she had done what he ought to have done from the start and had come out to New Mexico with Ramses. It tickled him, actually, that Ramses had, early on in their Blending, mistaken Tameri for Hatshepsut. True, these things were hard to discern at times, but the idea that his astounding and dynamic queen would choose someone like the adorable and slightly mousy persona of his sister . . . well, it wasn't a likely fit. Of course he and Hatshepsut had once altered sexes, he resurrecting in the body of a female and she in a male, just to see what it would be like. The novelty had made them ravenous for each other and the experience of seeing things from the other's perspective had been, in a word, wild. The sex alone had been outstanding. But he also remembered it as one of the most turbulent choices in their relationship.

God, he missed her. He craved her so terribly. Even now his body still ached with the arousal being close to Marissa had engendered. They must be together, he thought with no little amount of heat. Marissa and Hatshepsut must come together. It was the only solution he would be satisfied with. Yes, intelligent, curvy redheads were dying all the time, but he wanted this redhead and no other. This redhead had tormented Jackson with her very presence for so long . . . and there was a reason for that. She was very much a woman worth having. Now all he had to do was convince her of the same.

"There are at least thirty . . . but I sense there are quite a bit more, and that number will begin to grow once the news of my open defection to the Politic side filters through the ranks. That coupled with Odjit's rather untimely death at the hands of a mortal male . . . it will do a lot toward making those who are on the fence take a hard look at their priestess. If she were the all-powerful creature and destined ruler she was supposed to be, if she were truly the daughter of the gods and blessed and protected by them because of her devotion, then she would be here now, wouldn't she?"

"But she's dead. And honestly," she said, "I don't see Kamenwati taking the reins in her stead this time. There is talk, you know. He is . . . not quite right."

"What does that mean, 'not quite right'? Haven't we thought that Kamen and Odjit were off their nuts for some time now?"

"No, that isn't what I mean. I mean . . . we were in the Ether together and . . . touching his soul is like touching a great emptiness. I feel he is very lost, Jackson. I think he doesn't know what to believe anymore, but habit has him clinging desperately to what he wants Odjit to be for him."

"Perhaps it is time for him to come around and find faith in something new," Jackson said thoughtfully. "If Kamenwati were to defect to the Politic . . . Docia, do you know what that could mean?"

"Duh. It could mean the end of this stupid war." She rolled her eyes. "I'm not stupid you know. I wasn't Blended just yesterday . . . unlike some—"

"Shush," he said with a laugh as he grabbed hold of

her and covered her mouth with his hand. "Insolent. Disrespectful."

"Mmmk Mmu," she said against his hand.

"What was that? I didn't understand you." And he didn't lift his hand away either. She reached out and pinched him, making him laugh and letting her go.

"I said—"

"Uh-uh." He held a finger to her lips. "I know exactly what you said. No need to repeat." She grinned at him with satisfaction, folding her arms and looking like the victorious woman that she was. Damn her. She had always had him wrapped around her finger and that wasn't likely to change, Templar Bodywalker inside of her notwithstanding.

CHAPTER TWELVE

Awakening.

There it was, a small papyrus scroll, probably the most ancient piece of written history in the archive he was presently sitting in. Perhaps even the most ancient of all their written prayers, spells, and other such literature in any of their archives anywhere on Earth; *and to be sure, there were quite a few,* Kamenwati thought as he held open the reedy paper with the barest tips of his fingers, not wanting anything—such as bacteria or the natural oils of his skin—to come into contact with it. *Something this frail and old should not even be touched at all,* Kamen thought with a grimace. The Bodywalkers, both Politic and Templar, agreed on one thing, and that was that their history should be preserved at all costs and with all the respect it deserved. To that end there were a dozen of archives dotted across the world. The methods used to preserve what was in them outshone those of any antiquities museum. Light, temperature, limited contact. There had once been a single tremendous library, but after the great London fire had come within a hairsbreadth of claiming all they had collected, they had broken them down into twelve locations. And when the war had begun between the Templars and the Politic, there had been a huge series of battles over each and every one until all of the spoils were captured and relocated into secrecy, each keeping the other from accessing whatever parts of the archive they had wrested away.

It had hurt the Templars the most, however, when the Politic had ended up with just under seventy-five percent of the ancient written material, because much of their power came from the incantations and prayer spells such as the one he held so gingerly. Maybe if they had the larger majority of the works they would have gained the upper hand in this blasphemous war.

But there was no point in wasting so much time thinking about what might have been. He must now focus on what was.

It was perhaps preposterous to think a spell from ancient Egyptian times could have any kind of hand in reviving Odjit. It was more likely that Selena, Odjit's host, had suffered such severe brain damage from the dramatic loss of blood that had occurred when that lowborn mortal beast had nearly decapitated her. That was a physical result, not a magical one. And this spell seemed to be meant to awaken someone from a spell of sleeping or perhaps even paralysis. A useful spell to have regardless of what it did for Odjit, but it was still very much worth trying for her benefit.

He carefully returned the small scroll to its airtight container, then rose to make his way back to his mistress's side. Of course he made a small detour, stopping in to see what Chatha was up to. To his momentary pique, Kamen saw that the human male was no longer strapped down to the floor. All that was left of his having been there was a very wide lake of blood that was slowly making its way to the drain in the center of the floor. There was a reason Odjit called this her wetworks room.

After a moment he realized that the *pat pat pat* sound

of dripping blood was not that of the fluid draining away. He saw the droplets hitting the wet floor and looked up.

Apparently Chatha had grown bored of doing his bloodletting exercises on the floor. He had the human hung up by his ankles, ropes binding his arms down fast to his body in such a thick nonstop coil it was reminiscent of mummification bandaging. The mortal was unconscious, probably on the cusp of death yet again, while Chatha experimented on him for fascination's sake. To Kamen's sudden disgust, he realized Chatha had sewn the human's lips shut.

"Too loud," Chatha said by way of explanation as he gave the hanging man a push, sending him spinning and swinging, blood spattering everywhere. Kamen had to step back to avoid becoming part of the bath. "Is it time yet?" Chatha's eyes were feverish with the question. But Kamen knew Chatha was having far more fun toying with the man than he would if he were given permission to end the man's life.

Kamen's fury toward the insolent creature had eased somewhat, but he was still not satisfied. He could not be satisfied as long as his mistress lay still as death and trapped in an oblivion worse than the Ether.

And that was what was at the crux of this whole agonizing ordeal. At some point he was going to have to decide whether he should keep waiting, keep trying to bring her back to him . . . or take the life of her host and send Odjit back into the Ether for another hundred years so that she could then be reborn.

He must delay that choice as long as he could. He knew that if he were forced to push her back to the Ether, it would mean the end for him in this lifetime. Even with her there it had been an effort to keep a grasp on this existence. Had he not loathed having Odjit face the Politic alone, he wouldn't even have bothered with leaving the Ether in the first place.

"Do whatever you will," he said with a dismissive gesture. "Keep him or kill him, it no longer matters to me. He will suffer in the afterlife for what he has done— far worse than anything you have subjected him to."

Chatha's face widened into a beatific smile, all dimples and innocence, his eyes squinting shut. If those eyes had remained open, Kamen knew, there would be nothing innocent within them. The soul of the Down's male was completely subjugated, no doubt scarred into paralysis as the psychopathic monster dwelling inside of him showed him horrors his innocent mind and soul would never have dreamed of, never mind committing them with his own hand.

That left a sour taste in Kamenwati's mouth. On one hand he had to admire the wolf hiding in the innocent sheep's clothing. It was a stroke of brilliance that allowed him almost carte blanche entry into places and into peoples' trust that would normally not be so easy to access. On the other . . . Chatha was as evil an entity as anything he had ever seen. If there were a way to destroy Chatha's soul forever, Kamen would very much be inclined to see it done. And then he would see it done to Menes, an act that would end the war in a single stroke. Without Menes to flock to, the Politic would swiftly unravel . . . just as the Templars tended to unravel whenever Kamen and Odjit were killed and sent into the Ether. But to do so with permanence . . . to make a spirit rest once and for all in the afterlife . . .

Perhaps he would simply use the method where he craved using it most.

On himself.

"Listen, ya big hunk of ignoramus, if you don't put me down right this minute I'm going to kick you in the balls again and this time your kids are going to be born with black eyes! You feeling me, mister?"

The loud pronouncement rang throughout the house, alerting Marissa instantly of her sister's arrival. Marissa had been hiding from Jackson, keeping herself closed away in a sunroom just off the porch that wrapped around the entire house. She found that amusing, actually. What use would these people have for a sunroom? If the sun touched them . . .

She shuddered, thinking that he had actually had the gall to ask her if she wanted to be like him. To tell her that was his *plan*. Well, he could just take his plan and shove it where he didn't have to worry about the sunshine. She wanted no part of any of this. It infuriated her to think of how much he had screwed up her life and, by association, so many others. Leo Alvarez for one. Where was he? Was he even alive? If what Jackson had told her was true, then it wasn't very likely. She had met the darkly mysterious man only a few weeks ago . . . well, she had seen him many times before that, meeting up with Jackson, sitting in his chair with his feet up, looking for all the world like he owned the entire precinct. She had actually met him when Docia had gone missing and had found him to be quite intimidating when the fate of someone he loved was in jeopardy.

Now Marissa came hurrying through the rooms, the clicking of her heels sounding loud on the tiled foyer floor. She saw Lina up in the air, way *way* up over the shoulder of the gigantic man who was holding her. He had an arm bound tightly around her legs at the knees, presumably to keep her from kicking him, and she was hanging headfirst down his back.

"I swear to god, I would bite you on your ass if I was close enough!" Then she muttered. "Probably chip a tooth on the damn thing. What the hell have you got in these jeans, a coupla boulders for ass cheeks?"

"Lina!"

Hearing her sister's voice made Lina swing wildly

around, pulling herself upright in an impressive show of abdominal muscles and grabbing Asikri by the hair to hold herself up so she could see Marissa rushing toward her.

"Holy Hannah! They got you too? What the hell—" She broke off when Jackson came into the room. Her eyes widened and she zeroed in on Marissa. "Never gonna happen, huh?"

"Lina, will you be quiet?" Marissa hissed at her, working furiously to keep from blushing. So what? So she'd had a few illicit thoughts about a good-looking man. Big deal! An active imagination was perfectly normal. Sexual fantasies starring the good-looking man were also perfectly normal. The good-looking man himself? Not normal. Far from normal. Too damn not normal for her. "Will you put her down please?" she asked Asikri.

He growled, which she could only assume was a reluctant assent. Without giving her time to plan any lethal strikes on her way down, Asikri practically tossed Angelina onto her feet. Lina immediately ran up to hug her sister in a desperately tight embrace.

"He threw my phone away. A perfectly good iPhone!" she spat over her shoulder at him. "You owe me a new phone! And I want a pink case to go with it! Pink camouflage!"

"There is no such thing as pink camouflage," Asikri ground out. "Camouflage by nature of the word means an outfit worn to blend in to the surroundings. And unless you're in a cotton candy factory, sweetheart, pink doesn't blend in to your surroundings!"

"Great. Not only is he rude, inconsiderate, and a fine rendition of the Incredible Hulk, he has no imagination whatsoever!"

"Lina!"

Angelina started when Marissa's tone came out

sounding close to furious. Well, she was furious. This whole situation sucked and Lina being there only exacerbated her knowledge of it.

"Marissa, what are we doing here?" Lina asked with a very pronounced pout.

"There's . . . uh . . . been a development," she said carefully, not certain how much she could or should tell Lina.

"Your sister witnessed a crime," Jackson said, lying easily and using the cop voice that officers liked to adopt when they wanted to be seen as very official and very serious. "It involves some pretty bad people and when they find out what she knows and that she's willing to testify to it, it will put you both in a lot of danger. So . . . we're putting you both into witness protection."

"Witness pro—Oh, *hell* no! Mari, come on! I have a life! Shouldn't this be my choice?"

"No," Marissa said shortly.

The finality of the word made Lina go absolutely silent. And that was a very, very peculiar thing for her. Marissa felt everyone looking at her, most especially Jackson. The Egyptian pharaoh. God, this sounded like such a joke! But she had seen firsthand that it wasn't. And given that Jackson had just lied to her sister, it was very clear that he didn't want her to know who and what this house was filled with. It would be interesting to see how they were going to manage to keep her very bright and very nosy sister in the dark. She should just tell them to give it up from the start.

"Come on," she said, putting an arm around her sister's shoulders and leading her away from the group. "It's only temporary. It won't be that bad. I need to know you're safe, though."

"Tell me, what was it that you saw?"

Marissa lied by telling the truth. "I saw someone get

killed." Of course Jackson had been the one doing the killing, but understandably so.

"Oh honey, are you okay?" Lina asked with concern, wrapping her arm around Marissa and hugging her tight as they walked back to the sunroom. She'd love to see how they were going to explain the fact that no one was awake during daylight hours.

"I'm fine. It's just this whole situation is . . . I'm just a little rattled," she said truthfully.

"Does that have anything to do with Mr. Gorgeous in there?" Lina teased her, her trademark perceptiveness in full swing.

"I'm not even going to talk about that. Trust me, right now I'm so mad at him I could easily strap him down, pour honey on him, and stick him on an ant hill."

"At least the first part of that sounds like fun," she said with a giggle.

"You have a one-track mind!" Marissa groused.

"You have a no-track mind," Lina countered. "Come on, Mari. If I have to be stuck here let's make the most of it. At least, one of us should make the most of it."

"Knock it off, Lina. I'm honestly not in the mood for jokes."

She could tell her sister was biting her tongue to keep a sassy retort in check. It was reflective of her concern for her sister, as was her hug. "All right, I won't tease anymore. Well, not much anyway."

That made Marissa laugh. Honestly. Her sister absolutely couldn't help herself.

They were just sitting down when someone cleared their throat behind them. Marissa turned to see Jackson waiting there with a man she hadn't seen before.

"Angelina, this is Maxwell Turner. He'll be watching over you throughout the day, and I'll be taking care of you at night. I'm used to third shift and we tend to be nocturnal here. We're like a house full of vampires," he joked. He looked at Marissa as he said it. She had to admit, it was very clever. "You'll be in the guest house at the back of the property. We're not trying to keep you prisoner, but we don't want you to tell anyone who you are or make any contact with your friends until we think it's safe."

"And what if it's never safe?" Lina countered.

"I doubt it will come to that," Jackson lied. She knew it was a lie, just as she had known all along that he had no intention of letting her go back to her life in Saugerties.

Well, if he thought that meant she was going to be forced to stay with him, he had another think coming. She wasn't going to destroy everything she had worked for because he had some half-baked notion she was going to play party hostess to his queen. No way.

Never gonna happen.

CHAPTER THIRTEEN

"It'll be light soon. You think you've got this covered?" Jackson asked Max, who stood facing him, Ram, and Asikri. Max was one of the very few human mortals who knew exactly what his employers were. Throughout the years they had learned it was best to guard themselves while they slept. Not that Odjit and her kind could walk in daylight any more than they could, but she was not above using human assassins to come after them when they were most vulnerable. The house had sun-sensing glass in the windows that kept it dark during the day so they could defend themselves within the confines of their home. But of course, glass could easily break; it was best to have an alternate security force since the various Gargoyles sitting as sentries on the properties were as useless in daylight as the Bodywalkers, literally turned to stone at the touch of the sun.

But Maxwell was the son of a man whose family had been privy to the Bodywalker secret throughout the generations. His family had protected Menes and his loved ones through many centuries. It seemed strange sometimes that he knew more about Maxwell's lineage than Maxwell himself did. But Max didn't need to know where he had come from in order to do his job. And he was very good at his job.

"How hard can it be to keep a young lady entertained?" At Asikri's snort of derision he said, "I'm thinking as long as I don't throw her over my shoulder we should be fine." He smirked at Asikri. "I'll take her shopping on your credit card. It'll keep her very happy for at least a few days. She's damn pretty too. Maybe I'll take her to Bermuda."

"You'll show some respect," Asikri grumbled roughly.

"He's right, Max," Jackson said, although he was surprised Asikri had any opinion on the matter. Asikri tended to be the big grouchy type, never too pleased with what was going on around him and the tasks he was set to. Oh, he did everything efficiently, but Asikri and happiness were not words often used in the same sentence. Granted, there were reasons for that, but not necessarily reasons his friends agreed with. "Don't do anything that will complicate things. It's complicated enough on its own. Just keep her away from the main house during the day and keep her and her sister in your sights."

"You don't have to tell me how to do my job," Max said, sounding a little affronted.

"No. Of course not," Jackson conceded quickly. "I know you've been trained very well by your father and by Ram. He wouldn't have you here in the house if you weren't."

"You know, it's strange when I think of my great-granddad doing the job I'm now doing for you all those years ago," Max said. "I find that to be weirder, believe it or not, than knowing who and what you are. There's a sort of eeriness to it."

That made Jackson laugh. "You know, your grand-dad said something very similar to me when it was his turn to watch over us." That gave Jackson pause as he remembered Menes's memories and felt the things that Menes felt. It hadn't been until he was propositioning

Marissa that he had gotten an inkling of the grief that had led to Menes's last death. It disturbed him, the idea that he could be so swept away by the emotions of his counterpart. How had Menes's host felt about what was happening? How could he have possibly been in agreement with that course of action?

And yet, as the Blending took deeper root inside him, as Menes's memories and personality became a part of him, it was as though the lines between them were starting to blur. He felt it most in moments like this, when he fully felt a memory, such as speaking with Max's great-grandfather. And while Menes had instigated a lot of what had happened before with Marissa, he had been very present for all of it, and most definitely a part of the way he had taken command of her, touched her . . . wanted her until every cell was screaming for it.

But, of course, it was very likely that it would be a cold day in hell before that happened now. Being asked to die wasn't exactly whispering sweet nothings into a girl's ear.

No wait. Scratch that. A woman's ear. Marissa was all woman. There was no mistaking her for anything else. She had no sweet girlish behaviors, no naiveté. And perhaps that was a part of the problem. She was jaded on some level she refused to show him. Oh, she was still a believer in romance and true love, but not for herself. She would believe it for anyone else, she would counsel accordingly, but something was holding her back from allowing herself to feel what she wanted to feel. There was something . . . some intangible thing . . .

"Jackson?"

Jackson started when he realized Ram was talking to him. He had completely tuned him and Max out. Looking more than a little sheepish, he apologized. That seemed to amuse Ram to no end.

"It's like this every time. You never get tired of the chase, do you?" he asked.

That made Jackson grin like an idiot. Now here was something he agreed with Menes on fully. The chase. The seduction. The oh-so-sweet victory.

"This is only the second time I have come ahead of Hatshepsut with the intention of choosing a host for her. She was . . . very reluctant to return to the mortal world that time as well. It had hurt her deeply, leaving our child behind. She has not wanted another since then, and I doubt that will have changed now," he said with a dark sort of frown. Jackson had never really put much thought into it before, but he wanted children. When the time was appropriate of course, but if this queen of theirs did not want children, what could they possibly do to change her mind, knowing the grief and loss she had suffered? And that brought him to another question. Did Bodywalkers give birth to mortals or other Bodywalkers?

Our children spring from our host's mortal bodies. They are everything mortal and we leave them behind when we go, never to know them again unless, one day, we discover the actual death and find our way into the afterlife. We tend to outlive them before we pass, which is equally difficult. It takes ancient rituals and a complex mummification process, most of which are lost to us, to create more Bodywalkers. Odjit perhaps would be capable, since she was truly a priestess in her time and was well-versed in the Book of the Dead. And perhaps her niece, Tameri.

Tameri. Their unique defector with her extraordinary power. That defection had definitely fallen into the "good" column as far as things were concerned. He'd had no idea just how powerful she was. Nor had he realized how fearful Odjit had been of losing her. So afraid that she had come for Tameri herself, with all of her power brought to bear and every intention of destroying her if she did not come back to her willingly. And it was truly the power of fate at its finest that, in spite of all the massive Nightwalker power involved in that battle, Odjit had been felled by simple human hands.

Hands, he thought with a sudden choke of rage-filled emotion, that were presently unaccounted for. Jackson was loath to count Leo out without seeing an actual corpse, but it was hard to imagine that even Leo's strong and powerful body could recover from the bloodbath that had been left at his home. Next to protecting the women, this was Jackson's top priority. He was going to find Leo, dead or alive, and he was going to seek justice for whatever had been done to him.

"I need Ahnvil," he said abruptly. "I'm going to send him back to New York as soon as possible. And get me Diahmond. I don't know who has her in their care, but I want her well in place before her mistress is resurrected. She can help keep a closer eye on the women as well. No offense to Asikri or to you Max, but there are just some places you're not going to be able to follow them just by nature of your sex. When I say I want them watched, I mean every single minute. I'm not giving any opportunity for someone to get to them."

"I don't understand how you think you're going to keep all of this a secret from that girl," Asikri said. "And neither one of them looks like they'll have enough sense to obey whatever rules you set down for them. That spitfire alone will be hard to keep under wraps."

Jackson didn't bother to hide his amusement. "Did she really get you in the—?"

"She's lucky I didn't have bad intentions," Asikri groused. "Doing something like that could go a long way to pissing off an attacker and making what happens next a lot worse."

"Some would say it's better than just quietly letting someone do whatever they want to you. I know for a fact that every one of us would go down fighting. Why should it be any different for them just because they are women?" Jackson loosed a wry laugh. "I once arrested this guy who had gotten rough with his date and wasn't taking no for an answer. By the time we got there we were forced to pull her off of him and ended up having to rush him to the hospital with stab wounds to certain tender places."

Every man standing there winced.

"Never underestimate the power of a frightened woman," Ram said.

"I don't underestimate any of them," Jackson said, thinking about Marissa and how brave she had been in spite of being terrified. She didn't have to race him to safety the way she had. She could have just left him to rot. She might have had every right to it, too. That impulse to be of need, to help anyone in need of it was going to go a long way to convincing her to become a Bodywalker.

"I better get messages out to the Gargoyles. It's growing near dawn and we still have a lot to do," Ram said. "Max, take the women to the guest house and see they are comfortable. We'll touch base at dusk."

Jackson's first impulse was to tell Max to leave Marissa behind. It was strange, but he found himself craving her constant company now. It was as though, now that all secrets were out in the open and the walls of their respective jobs were no longer a hindrance, he was making up for lost time. And there was a lot of that time to account for. Jackson knew that Menes wasn't overly impressed by his performance so far with Marissa. To the ancient Egyptian it was simple. See something, want something, go after that something with all barrels blazing. Jackson realized that was in some ways a very good quality in a ruler. He was not very tolerant of the many human protocols that interfered with doing the best or the right thing. In this way they agreed that the right thing deserved to be done, but they were almost polar opposites when it came to how to execute it properly. Menes would have gone after Marissa without wasting time . . . or rather, without wasting life. How funny, Jackson thought, that this nearly immortal being was so much more appreciative of the shortness and preciousness of life than perhaps Jackson himself was. Perhaps because Jackson had always thought there would be time later to do certain things. Now, having tangoed so closely with death, he felt quite an understanding for Menes's straightforwardness.

"Dusk then," Jackson said, realizing after a long moment that they were waiting for his release. That was going to take a little getting used to. Not that he didn't know how to take command. Training Sargent and his predecessor had taught him a lot about that, much in the same way the Academy did. All things being equal, however, he had never shouldered a massive responsibility like the one he currently held as Politic ruler. Not many men would have. There were not very many monarchies anymore, and those that did exist rarely took place in a crucible of war and power of this magnitude.

"What about Kamenwati," Ram asked him once the others had moved out of earshot. "Docia said you were entertaining some idea that he might want to defect to our side? Do you know how insane that sounds?"

"When has any of this ever sounded sane? It's no more far-fetched than Tameri herself defecting. The niece of Odjit? I would never have believed it. I'm amazed that you did when she finally told you who she was."

"It was difficult," Ram said slowly. "But by then . . ."

"You'd already lost your heart to her?"

Ram smiled at that, very clearly enjoying a memory about the incident. "Something like that. It could easily have been a trap and I could just as easily be dead right now, a knife in my chest while I slept. But, as you know, your sister is very special and well worth the risk involved." Ram smiled wider then. "Well what do you know. I just realized that after all these lifetimes, I am finally going to be related to you."

"I see," Jackson said, equally delighted. "You're going to marry my sister then?"

"I had better. She won't stand for anything less. And . . . well . . . I don't want her to get pregnant out of wedlock and have her thinking I'm trying to be dutiful by doing the right thing by her only because of that. Your sister has odd notions about certain things."

"I don't think it's odd to demand respect," he said.

"Me neither. I mean it's odd for her to suddenly think being pregnant would make my love for her somehow less believable. Less true. She doesn't doubt me now, but her implication is that doubt would come into the picture at that point."

"I don't know. Just marry her quick and everyone will be happy. Especially because I left my shotgun in my house." Jackson frowned then. "But I guess none of that will be seen by me again."

"Nonsense. I'll have Max send some of the others out to pack up and move everything for you. Don't worry. No one has suspected you as yet of any wrongdoing. But it should be done today."

"I'd appreciate that. Especially the photo albums. Docia's whole life is documented in those things. She'll want them for her own kids one day." That brought his smile back. "You know, for a minute there I was getting worried. She kept dating these thoughtless bastards who treated her with about as much fascination as they did their furniture. Not disrespectfully, but with no appreciation for the treasure that she is. She was starting to believe she didn't deserve any better. Now she's got the best, and I couldn't be happier."

"Neither could I," Ram agreed. And although he said it quietly, there was no doubting the ferocity with which he meant it. He loved Jackson's sister. Like Hatshepsut and himself, Tameri and Ramses were souls meant to be cleaved together, for all they were in separate forms. And knowing of Ramses through the eyes of Menes, he had no question that Ram would be just as lost without Docia as he was whenever he lost Hatshepsut. And yet he knew he was extremely privileged to be one of the oh-so-rare individuals who knew, with evidence removing all doubt, that he would see his love one day again . . . and again . . . and again. It was sometimes the only thing that made this perpetual life of theirs worth living.

"I know I don't have to tell you this, but treat her well, my friend. Neither of us is worth a damn to anyone without our women by our side."

With that he took leave of Menes's lifelong friend and went off to plan how he was going to go about searching for his.

CHAPTER FOURTEEN

Marissa had to give these Bodywalkers credit, she thought with an exacerbated sigh. They sure knew how to pick them out. And by them she meant humans, mortals, of dependability and all-around good fiber. Max was everything that Asikri was not, and by showering her sister with his undivided attention, he had made great strides in making up for what the ruder man had done to get her there. Apparently Asikri hadn't bothered to do much in the way of explanation and hadn't really been able to understand why the old "your sister is in trouble and sent me to come get you" ploy was not the angle to take with a New York girl, native or not.

Now the two were sitting by the pool, catching the last rays of the unseasonably warm day. She could hear the low rumble of Max's voice, punctuated by her sister's uncontrollable laughter.

Marissa was making herself busy by inspecting the grounds of the house. Well, house was really putting it mildly. Even mansion wasn't exactly right. But it and its stone gardens of yucca plants and cacti were magnificent. Both, she realized, were dotted with very large statues of Gargoyles, all in varying degrees of crouches, spread wings, or even the impression of movement. Their faces ranged from ugly to absolutely grotesque, with varying wingspans, each one as distinctively different as one human was from another. It was funny but she'd imagined them all looking more uniform. If you knew one you knew them all kind of thing. There were other statues, too. Angels, Grecian goddesses, fauns, imps, and about a dozen other mythical creatures. The most unnerving was perhaps the behemoth-proportioned griffin Gargoyle in the front garden, the massive sentry looking very forbidding. She didn't think it was an actual Gargoyle, it being so big, but what the hell did she know? She was still very new to this whole creatures-of-the-night thing.

That's when it finally occurred to her to question the existence of other genuses and species. Hadn't he said they were one of the Nightwalkers? What exactly were the others, besides the Gargoyles? And since the Gargoyles had been created by the Templars, it was a good bet they weren't considered a Nightwalker species. But if they turned to stone in daylight and came to life at night, in her mind that made them uniquely qualified to be called Nightwalkers.

Just the thought of there being more creatures out there made her heart race. She sat down at the feet—or rather talons—of a Gargoyle, poking curiously at its leg to test its stoniness as she tried to calm herself with a little logical thinking.

Monsters were real. They had always been real. Whether human or otherwise. She shouldn't spend every moment fearing what might or might not happen to her or her sister. Today was no different than any other day they had walked out into the world. Expect the best, prepare for the worst, live life, and don't become paralyzed by fear. Which was easy to say, except now she was filled with the understanding that there very well might be a target painted on her back.

And Jackson wanted her to take on the spirit of this

dead queen? The same queen who'd been killed a week into her last existence? It was pure insanity. But what was odd was that she believed wholly that she would actually be in a fair partnership with Hatshepsut. She saw how Jackson and Menes shared a single body, mostly Blended but occasionally shifting from one dominance to the other. It was peculiar, and she would never have thought Jackson to be the type to sacrifice control of himself to anything. He was as type A as one could imagine. But then again, so was Menes. And considering absolute death had been Jackson's only other option . . .

She sighed and rubbed her neck, leaning back against the Gargoyle. She could appreciate how it must have felt, being given life only to know it wasn't your own life to live. With what Jackson was suggesting she would have no control of her life. Everything would have to be a consensus. But what if there wasn't agreement? Could the Bodywalker force her to comply?

She sat up, suddenly realizing where her thoughts had taken her. She wasn't really considering this, was she? No! Why even question or try to understand? It was absolutely out of the question!

Even if there was something compelling about the idea of a love that lived on and on with such utter devotion. To listen to Jackson talk about it . . . to listen to him talk about what he could see for them . . .

She stood up, shaking off the thought with a shudder. *Stop it, Marissa! You have too many reasons why this is a bad idea. Just think of Lina!* It wasn't only about putting herself in danger. She had already put Lina in danger because of her association with Jackson. Just imagine the danger if she were queen!

Oh god, why did she feel such thrilling excitement at the idea that she could be a queen? It was right within her grasp and that too had its appeals.

No! No! No! God, she'd gone insane. She couldn't stay here. The longer she stayed here the more she might be tempted to do something really, really stupid. And she was not a stupid person! The one thing she had all but beaten into herself was to not be a stupid person and not to allow herself the opportunity for any mistakes!

She turned her back on Max and her sister and began marching along the walkway to the main house. *No,* she thought. She would much rather take her chances out in the world than subject herself to this. She was going to find Jackson Waverly and tell him what he and his dead Egyptian pharaoh could go off and do with themselves.

She burst into the house and stopped dead in her tracks when she found herself in utter darkness. It was really eerie to walk from the late-day sun into pitch black, her eyes aching as they tried to adjust. She moved into the house, not yet familiar enough with its layout, fumbling for where the switches might be. She finally found one, lighting the kitchen and dining room in a flare of tandem light. Again her eyes were forced to adjust and she didn't have the patience for it. She was going to find Jackson and tell him to call off his watchdog. She knew without a doubt that Maxwell, for all his charms, would never let them leave without his boss's permission.

She found the living quarters—or one wing of them anyway—by throwing switches wherever she could find them. She wondered what kind of glass it was in the windows that allowed them to get so dark. Were they polarized? Where did one get windows like that exactly? What the hell did it matter to her anyway?

Getting herself angrier with every passing moment, she started opening doors. She realized quickly that the rooms were actually suites and she had just as much of a chance of walking in on one of the other people living in the house, like Docia and Ram. That slowed her down, making her more careful and encouraging her to move a little quieter. She turned the lights on in the outer suite of each room, then peeked into the actual bedroom with as much discretion as possible, using the light from the living area to reveal what was in the bedroom.

She was abashed with herself for being so disrespectful, but how had Jackson shown *her* any respect? All he had done was put her into increasing danger, literally asking her to give up her life for him.

She opened a bedroom door with new purpose and the light fell on Jackson's sleeping form. She wanted to storm into the room, slamming the door and waking him up. *But,* she began to wonder, *is he even able to wake up with it still being light out?* Leaving the door propped open so the light came in from the outer suite, she walked up beside the bed. The last time she had seen him during the day was when he'd been paralyzed by the daylight, and it was an image of him that, being reminded of it, chilled her to the core. He'd been so helpless, missing everything that made Jackson the vibrant and powerfully masculine man that he was. But with these darkened windows it should be better, shouldn't it? He had recovered when he'd been brought into the dark.

Unable to help herself, she reached out and touched his arm, almost as if she expected him to be as solid as stone like the Gargoyle in the gardens. And oh, was he ever, she realized. But not in the way she had been imagining, not in the rigid rigor mortis fashion of that previous time. She realized he was pure muscle under soft, warm skin, the feel of the combination so incredibly compelling. Before she realized what she was doing, she had her entire palm on his shoulder, running down the length of his arm. To wake him, she told herself. Not because she liked and wanted to feel him. Not because just touching him set memories of his kiss to flame inside her whole body. Memories of how he'd touched her, the confidence and aggression threaded all the way through him, which she could see even now as he slept.

That impact hit her that very instant as his hand was suddenly on her forearm, yanking her right off her feet and over his body. She hit the bed with a shout, feeling him roll her over as if she were a floppy little doll that didn't have any control of where her body was going to end up. She ended up on her back underneath him. He had rolled right on top of her, the covers trapped between their bodies, and the first thing she saw was the long, naked flank of him. She recognized it well enough, since it wasn't the first time she had seen him without his clothes on. Nor was it the first time she had felt him pressing his very very naked weight all against her.

Oh god. How had she ended up in this position again? What in hell had she been thinking?

"What in hell are you thinking, sneaking up on me like that?" he barked at her. "Jesus Christ, Marissa, I could have killed you!"

"Well that would solve all your problems then, wouldn't it?" she bit out. "Then whatshername could invade me and you'd be happy as a pig in shit! Get off of me, Jackson!"

"Like hell it would answer my problems. And it's not an invasion, Marissa! It's a partnership. For god's sake, if you don't want this then stop . . . just stop . . ." He was floundering for words, clearly furious and still waking up. She felt him shift his weight and even through the bedclothes she could feel him getting an erection. She gasped, wanting to be outraged, but then the doctor in her sheepishly realized she could hardly expect anything else after waking him up, what with this technically being his "morning."

He drove a hand into her hair, gripping her by the back of her skull and forcing her to look at him dead in his eyes. "I've told you," he said, his voice fierce and breathy. "I've told you how out of control I am when you're close to me! Haven't you been paying attention? Christ, every time I so much as smell you this is what happens to me." He moved his hips forward, pressing his solid erection into the softness of her stomach. "If you don't want me, then why are you here?"

She opened her mouth to tell him exactly why she had come there.

I'm leaving here. I don't want anything to do with any of this and I definitely don't want anything to do with you!

"Jackson," she said, shocked to hear how breathless she was. Shocked to feel how fast she was breathing, a way of supplying her thundering heart with the oxygen needed. Stunned to feel herself reacting to the feel and smell of *him*. "I can't . . ."

"Then don't," he hissed. "Get out of here and *stay* out." He rolled off of her, pulling her with him until she was lying across his body, her hands and knees scrambling for purchase. She was wearing a knee-length skirt she'd been given, care of Max, from a heavily filled wardrobe closet that, apparently, came equipped with a plentitude of sizes. Just in case, Max had said, but he hadn't said in case of what. But there was no slit in the skirt and no room for moving her knees up without the skirt riding up on her thighs. Her hands pressed against his bare chest as she struggled to sit upright. A moment later she found herself straddling him in what had to be the most universally provocative position known to any red-blooded man. He sucked in a breath and she felt his hands latch on to her hips, holding her where she was even as he said tightly, "You need to go, Marissa."

He was saying go, but the grip of his hands wasn't allowing for it. Not that she was pushing away like she should be.

"I know I do," she breathed. "I need to go. I need to leave, Jackson. I can't stay here. If I do . . . I can't let you talk me into something I'm just not . . . I'm just not the right person for this. You're so wrong about that. You think I'm this . . . that I'm more than I really am. I'm so flawed, so scared all of the time . . . and that was before you even entered my life. I know what you see is something different." She laughed, the sound low and bitter. "I'm the consummate actress, Jackson. I make everyone believe I'm a woman of confidence and control, but it's because I keep thinking if I pretend long enough then maybe it will come true. But it never does," she whispered. "It never does."

He was quiet for a moment, just looking at her. She couldn't bear it if she saw disappointment in his eyes, so she turned her head away and moved to leave him. But that same moment his hands came up to frame her head and face, his thumbs stroking up over the high bones of her cheeks, the touch so soft and gentle her eyes suddenly burned with the sting of tears. She wished then that she could be the person he thought she was. She wished she could be the brilliant, brave thing that her sister was. The real deal, not this pretense that she was so tired of.

"Marissa, you're lying to yourself," he said gently, making her look into his eyes again, making her realize just how often he did that. He always made sure to look directly at her, making her feel like he thought she deserved that respect at all times. It was so different from the way they had been when in the office environment, each of them pretending not to feel what they were feeling, each of them being harsher than necessary with one another because they were afraid to not be. "Do you think I don't feel fear every goddamn day of my life? Look at what I do, Marissa. Look at all the things I face day in and day out. I watched that bastard pull a gun on me, aiming dead between my eyes. I saw Chico leap for his throat, something I had spent hours teaching him *not* to do. Arms and legs only, Marissa. Minimal damage to keep liability down for the department. But he threw all of his training away for the instinct to protect me at all costs, and he willingly paid the ultimate price. Do you know how that made me *feel*?"

Tears suddenly blurred her vision as finally, *finally* he confessed to her what he'd needed to tell someone all along. She'd tried and tried to make him deal with it, but he'd been so shut down, pretending it was past him when it really wasn't.

"It wasn't your fault," she got to say to him at last. "Jackson, it wasn't your fault. You didn't pull the gun and you didn't fire it. It wasn't *your* fault."

"No. I know that. I do. Or I tell myself I do and hope that one day it will actually be the truth."

She smiled then, laughing softly as her tears shed off the tips of her lashes and rained down on him in two little droplets. One landed on his lips and she watched him lick the salt of it away. His hands were soft in her hair, his thumbs still touching her face as though she were the most precious thing he'd ever held in his life.

"I should go," she said, swallowing against the tightness in her throat and the fluttering excitement being birthed in her chest, the contrast shocking and inexplicable.

"But you're not going to, are you?" he asked her then, but it was more a statement than a question and it fanned the thrill growing inside of her.

"No," she whispered as though she were afraid to hear herself admit to it. "I'm not going to."

"Marissa . . ." He swallowed visibly. "Marissa, if I make love to you I'm never going to let you go. You have to understand that. I'm never going to let you go."

She waited for fear to come after those words, but it didn't. It just didn't. For the very first time in as long as she could remember, there wasn't a single ounce of the crippling emotion working through her.

"That's why I'm staying," she said softly.

Kamen stood in front of the large stone altar, looking down on the various containers holding the components the awakening spell called for. He was naked except for the pristine white loincloth of a true temple priest, the embroidered runic symbols on it done in turquoise and golden threads. He had laid Odjit on the flat surface of the altar, just a little bit beyond his ingredients, so that she was as close as possible to the magic that would be meant for her alone. He wanted there to be no doubt, no misdirection. He was no fool. He knew exactly how temperamental spells and prayer incantations could be. It was always a risk to enter into the use of one, especially one that was so unfamiliar and whose origin was completely lost in history. But he simply didn't see what choice he had.

He began the spell by casting sand across the altar, cleaning it of any residual magic that might be clinging to it from other incantations. There were almost a dozen mortars and pestles around him and he scattered each ingredient, from powdered charcoal to liquid Dragon's blood, and used each one's mortar to grind it into the stone. He also sprinkled each component onto Odjit's arm, and then very gently rubbed it into her skin. The Dragon's blood stained her an unusual ebony color, its iridescence very reminiscent of a snake's skin or a fish's scales. For the last component he used the sharp base of a large cat's whisker to draw blood at the crook of her elbow. Using the whisker as a quill he began to write the words of the spell in the sandy components and onto her skin. Then using his fingertip he wrote them once more in the gritty mixture that painted the altar.

There, he thought. There could be no mistaking who the spell was directed toward. Now all that was left was the spoken incantation. He read the words in the language it had been written in, the language he had been born to oh-so-many centuries ago. Strange how alien it felt after so many incarnations, so many languages and so many cultures he had been reborn into.

But his memory was long, just as it was far too keen for his liking. He remembered his first death, an ignominious one for a priest purported to be as powerful as the gods themselves. Dysentery. They had called it something else then, but the illness was the same.

There was a small sound, soft and barely there, but Kamen, like all other Bodywalkers, had extraordinary hearing. It was the sound of sand scrubbing against stone. The next sound was louder, but more important, he saw Odjit's finger twitch. He caught hold of his breath, afraid to make the slightest sound or move in any other way. *It's working!* he thought, the thrill of delight and pride in his abilities rushing through him for the first time in a very, very long time. When had he last cared about any kind of achievement? It was so long past that he couldn't even hazard a guess.

A twitch became a jolt, Odjit's arm where she had been painted flopping into the sandy, dark spell ingredients. Too late he thought of removing all the heavy stone mortars and pestles out of the way so she would have more room to move without potentially getting injured.

All of a sudden her entire body locked up, her spine arching up off the table so severely he feared it would snap her back in two. *But she is moving! Life is coming back into her!* His relief knew no bounds, so much so that an alien emotion stung his eyes, an oh-so-rare sensation of imminent tears. He curled his hands into tight, powerful fists until his large and muscular body was just as tight as hers.

Then a roar like that of a rough beast exploded out of Odjit's mouth and into the chamber.

And that was the first time he realized something was going seriously wrong. That sound chilled him straight to his spine. The way her hands were crooked like talons reaching for flesh, and right before his eyes her nails grew out about an inch in length, thickening and sharpening to a deadly point. About that same moment was when he realized she was becoming larger in her overall stature, her shoulders widening and thickening, her arm becoming more muscular, her height lengthening. Her hair began to change color from the midnight black the beautiful Selena, her host, had been born with. She did not grow grotesque in features, but they altered into something less delicate, more femininely rugged.

Then, in an instant, she snapped upright, eyes flying open to reveal them just as all the color bled out of them, leaving a negative of black so that the pupil was a milky white, the iris a pale gray, and the sclera around it black. They turned toward him with a scrutinizing look. Kamenwati felt himself grabbed as if by the hand of a giant, fingers tightening, crushing the air from his lungs. Before that could happen he incanted the words for the Curse of Ra, the searing red laserlike fire the Templars had learned to wield from another old scroll another time long ago. Without hands or gestures to direct the blast it burst out of him in all directions at once. It made the creature on the altar cry out as if in pain, but only for a moment. Then that massive hand threw him like a ball against the wall, the force of it like nothing he had ever felt before. He felt his shoulder wrench right out of its socket and the pain that followed was extraordinary. His head smacked into the wall so hard he saw stars, dizziness swimming quickly around him.

"Insolent mortal!" the thing screeched in that rough voice. "You think you can use the light of Ra on the god Amun?"

Amun. Amun risen? Amun . . . awakened? He got to his feet, staggering.

"Forgive me, great one," he said, taking a knee and bowing his head, shaking suddenly with excitement that finally, finally Amun had risen! And he had been the one to find the spell to do it! Moreover, he was, as was just and right, using the body of their most powerful and virtuous religious leader. "I did not recognize you in my mistress's form!"

"You call me forth yet say you do not recognize me?" The demand was followed by a deep-throated laugh . . . the dreadful kind of laugh a sadistic maniac like Chatha made before reaching to torment its latest victim. Then she turned soft, sliding off the altar and to her feet, walking toward him with a listing gait, showing Amun's weakness in this new mortal body. What of Odjit? Where was her ka in all of this? Had her soul been displaced or were there now three entities sharing space within that flesh? "So you called upon me. You are not merely mortal then. For only the powerful may beckon to a god. And I have chosen to listen to you. What is your plea?"

This time honest tears came to his eyes, his entire being shaking with relief. Both knees hit the floor now, the emotion in him as overwhelming as the pain in his mangled shoulder.

"We have been expecting you. We crave your judgment, to see which of your children are just and true to you, and which have lost their way. There is such a war among us that it has lasted millennia. I know, my lord god, that your prophecy says we will be punished if we have dissention amongst us, but there is no reasoning with the Politic. If my mistress still resides within you then you can see how devotedly she has tried to turn them to the true path. The faithful path."

She narrowed those cold, colorless eyes on him and he bowed his head again, hoping supplication would please Amun. Everything he had done had been in anticipation of this moment.

"She is, and I feel her ka within me, as well as another minuscule soul. No matter, I will destroy them for they weaken me."

"No! Please!" He threw a staying hand out, looking up in his panic. "She is a true priestess, she has sacrificed everything . . ."

"She has sacrificed nothing. She is insignificant. She is selfish and hungry for power. Think you know her better than the one sharing space with her soul?"

Kamen stared in silence, his jaw slack with shock. "But glorious one, she is faithful to you!"

"She is faithful to herself. Hmm. Perhaps I like her after all. Very well, she will keep me good company."

"Thank you, glorious one," he said, not knowing what address he should use otherwise. "I thank you."

"These other children of Amun, where are they?"

Kamen went still, hesitating as a niggling little alarm in the back of his brain suddenly grew louder. "They are everywhere. I thought . . . can you not sense them? We are all your children. The scrolls say—"

"I will tell you what to think!" the creature roared, coming up on him so fast he could never have hoped to move in defense of himself. The god grabbed him with that ephemeral hand once more and this time slammed him into the wall and held him there, crushing the air from his lungs and wrenching the dislocated arm on the right until he felt and heard the long bone snap. Kamen screamed from the pain of it, but the sound was garbled from lack of air.

"These other children of Amun, where are they?" The words echoed in his brain, trying to tell him what he did not want to realize. *Why*, it said, *would Amun refer to himself in the third person?* How was it possible that Amun didn't know where the everlasting souls of the children he had created were? Scripture said that he would know all of his children instantly, welcome them all in equanimity as long as there was no discord between them and no faithlessness.

"Tell me what I want to know," the beast demanded, its face eye level with Kamen, who was a good four feet off the floor. That meant the creature was at least seven feet in height, and though she was still shaped every bit like a woman, there was a statement of power and giant strength within her.

"They are everywhere," he repeated softly as shame and horror began to fill his damned soul. "But you are not Amun or you would know that."

The thing threw back its head, laughing roughly, gold and white hair curling all around her face and shoulders like some kind of demented Meg Ryan.

"I would, wouldn't I? No, no, little mortal speck, I am something you have never imagined in all of your days."

"My days have been many," Kamenwati hissed back at the thing, "and I have seen much in the way of evil. I know it when I see it . . . when it is touching me."

"Is this true?" It giggled at him almost girlishly, making the sound perverse. "But you don't believe me when

I say the witchlet inside me is evil? Then why am I enjoying her so? She is as wicked as that creature you have toying with the mortal man not two rooms from here. And you are not without sin to be sure." It turned its back on him, moving away as it inspected its body for a long minute. "It has been some time since we have enjoyed mortal form." It turned back to him. "Kamenwati. She says your name over and over, pleading like a lost girl, she who has made such a fool out of you. Kamenwati, the dark rebel. The misguided rebel is more like it. You have committed such sins that I should like you . . . however, you are ten times more pure than she inside me. You at least deluded yourself into thinking your cause was just. And do you know what is infinitely amusing?"—it turned back to him, the impish gleam in its eyes a licking, horrifying thing—"your precious god Amun cannot rise. You awakened me with this, yes?" It lifted a finger, the rewritten scroll he'd put on paper to protect the original fluttered up from the altar. The original was back in his quarters, its fragile spell in its protective tube. The spell went up in a sudden burst of flame. "You could have roused him from his sleep, had you a purer vessel. But didn't you know, like begets like?"

He did know now. Too late he realized what a fool he had been. He understood that his prophetess and presumed savior was nothing like what he had made her out to be in his mind. All of her flaws that she had excused as necessary things for her faith came rushing up at him.

Fool! Fool! Fool! It screamed at him, from every corner of his wakening mind. *What have I done? What have I done?*

"You have given birth to me," the imp replied. "That is why I am going to allow you to keep your life. Your guilt amuses me very much. As does your shame. I understand what you are now. As my power grows, I will understand even more. I know you will live endless lifetimes suffering with that guilt. Delightful. So delightful." It giggled again, continuing to inspect its naked body, fondling its breasts and pulling and poking at its nipples. "A woman. So different than the last time." It looked up at him as though suddenly remembering he was there. "You know, I like that one in there. You must bring him to me," she said, nodding toward the next room.

Kamen was released and he dropped to the ground hard, his legs buckling as his freedom caused a new scourge of pain to rocket through him. A breath inward told him he had likely cracked a couple of ribs as well. But that was so insignificant in the face of this unfolding horror.

"Who shall I say is calling him?" he asked weakly, hiding his true strength, however small it was at that point. It was obvious it could read his thoughts to some extent, so he kept his mind clear of all things except the act of going down the hall to fetch Chatha.

"Clever, clever." It shook a finger at him as though he were a naughty child. "Oh I shall tell you. It makes it more fun. Tell him Apep has come for him. That we will make great mischief together. Then put that toy he has out of its misery, won't you? It's far too gone to be of any enjoyment any longer."

"Yes, glorious one," Kamen rasped, staggering to the door. As he passed through the portal and left Apep behind, he understood that he had released the most foul of imp gods upon the earth. Apep, mortal enemy of the good and golden Amun. As opposite that god as ever there was.

And he had brought it down upon them all.

Once he was out of the sight of the thing he straightened up, the only sign of his pain the whitening of his lips and the stark truth in his eyes. He didn't risk going anywhere else but the room where Chatha was toying with the human.

The human. Yes . . . yes! The mortal was the key. It was the only way he could begin to right this thing.

He prayed to the gods that this time he was on the right path. And he knew now that leaving this existence was no longer an option for him. He had lost the privilege of peace.

He opened the door to Chatha's torture chamber.

"Chatha, heal it. I wish to play with it elsewhere," he commanded, looking down to see Chatha methodically tearing strips of skin off of his victim. Yes, he told himself fiercely, look upon the destruction you have caused and feel your guilt as you should! "Do we know its name?"

"Leo," Chatha breathed, looking put out that his game was coming to an end.

"Now now, Chatha. I have something better for you to do." *Yes go . . . go and entertain evil so much like yourself . . . the evil that was born out of my black, selfish heart.* "I have awakened the god Apep, maker of mischief and a great blackness . . . much like yourself. Go to her in the altar room. Make haste. I am certain she will not like to wait."

"Mischief . . ." Chatha smiled, beaming with that beautiful innocence, sickening him as he realized that permitting Chatha to live in the house of this Down syndrome innocent was but one of many sins he had allowed in the name of his mistress and his misguided cause. It was but one of the things he would make right.

Chatha hurriedly healed Leo, not even enough to bring him to consciousness. He closed all the wounds, knitting them just enough, but leaving him striped with angry ridges all down his chest, ribs, and stomach. Chatha then scampered to the door. "Come, come!" he beckoned Kamen.

"No, my friend," he said forcing a smile, "it's time for me to play."

Chatha barely waited for the denial to be finished before discarding Kamen's company. As soon as he was gone just long enough to have entered the altar room, Kamen bent to grab Leo by his arm and, kneeling, dragged that arm across his neck. The position lay all of Leo's weight against his dislocated shoulder and he ground his teeth together. He could have had Chatha heal him, but the pain was a good mask for his thoughts. He knew one or two telepathic Templars and they had both said the same thing to him. A target that was in agony was difficult to read because the pain took up so much space in their thoughts.

Besides, it was far less than what he deserved.

He hefted the man who was of equal weight and build, pulling him to his feet. Leo groaned and his eyes opened in a sticky pull of lashes. Cleansing the mortal of the bath of his own blood was not a luxury he had given the man. Leo's dark brown eyes swung to Kamen's face.

"I'm getting us out of here, my friend, before something far worse than Chatha comes down on us."

Leo's eyes were very swollen, his lips caked with blood. He cleared his throat, as if to speak.

He spit phlegm and blood in Kamen's face.

"I'm not your fucking friend," he rasped.

"No," Kamen agreed. "But I'm all that stands between us and almost certain death."

"So the fuck what? I'm happy to die," Leo ground out.

"No. I don't think you are. If you were, this torment would have ended your life long before this. It is your own resilience that kept this going as long as it has. I do not think you would give up now."

"Fine. But just so you know, motherfucker . . . I'm going to kill you as soon as I get the chance."

"I would be disappointed if you didn't," Kamen said, moving them to the door.

CHAPTER FIFTEEN

Jackson was out of his mind. Or that's what he thought. Crazy and probably hallucinating that he was holding Marissa in his hands, the soft coppery strands of her hair streaming between his fingers like magnificent red waterfalls, gleaming with a touch of gold. Her warmth was emanating into him—he'd never known such enticing warmth before. Pervasive. Steady. Patient. Waiting for him to recognize it. Waiting for him to take charge of his damn life and go about the business of living. Everything was in flux, everything was changing. His home. His job. Himself. Hell, even his sister had changed. Nothing was the same as it had been three weeks ago.

Nothing but Marissa. And even there Menes's proposal was to change her. To use her as a means to an end. A goal that meant far more to him than resolving this war, and he took that priority very seriously.

"I'm sorry I ever suggested . . ." he blurted out, trying to find some way of reassuring her that she wasn't anything insignificant in her own life or just exactly how she was.

"No. Don't be sorry. I . . . I'm actually flattered, I think. It sounds a lot like . . . oh Jackson, in a way it's incredibly romantic. Don't you think? Two people born dynasties apart . . . and then this thing, this magical thing happens and they get to meet and create, literally, a love for the ages. Imagine. It's as if you were Romeo asking me to become Juliet. Although perhaps that's a bad choice as a metaphor because they—" She broke off suddenly, her breath catching in her throat.

"They die." He finished it for her, not afraid of the stark truth of it. "Imagine," he said back to her, "if death were only the beginning for those lovers. Imagine if they knew that the other would always, *always* be there for them when next they were reborn." He touched a thumb to her lower lip, tracing the lushness of it. "What strength of purpose that can give them. What pain will come when one of them has to leave the other once more." He sighed softly, his breath stirring her hair. "The last time we were reborn, I came three months ahead of her. I chafed at the bit, fretted and stomped about. Nothing would satisfy . . . nothing could satisfy until my love was born again. But . . . it was only a single week after she finally came to me when Odjit found her and assassinated her before my very eyes. And I could not bear it, this world, without her. First I sent that faithless bitch back to the Ether, but then . . . I went back for my love, so she would have my soul next to hers in the Ether . . . and so I wouldn't have to bear a lifetime without her."

"Suicide." She breathed the word over him. "You committed suicide."

He nodded. "Had my host been a different sort of man it might not have been possible, but we were both swept away by our emotions. I will feel everything Menes feels just as sharply as he feels it. And he feels everything I feel, just as sharply as I feel it. He knew, better than I did myself, what I feel for you."

"Feel?" She whispered the word over him, like it was

a dirty little secret. "How can you trust what you feel? He could . . . he might be manipulating—"

"No!" The word was sharp, his hands tightening around her head. "Listen to me," he said as he brought her forehead into contact with his own. "For once . . . stop thinking with this loud head full of thoughts and just feel." He closed his eyes and breathed in deeply, dragging the smell of her into himself. A sweet shampoo made with vanilla, a musky floral perfume touched lightly to her skin as if she'd walked through a light cloud of fragrance. "Before anyone else . . . before Menes. Before all of this . . . before Chico . . ." He breathed her in again. "It was a Sunday. I remember because I was in a hurry to get to the flag football game at the park . . . we'd been beating the pants off of the Middletown PD the last two games."

She laughed. "That means it must have been a Sunday?" she asked.

"Yeah. Flag football gets you in the mood for Monday Night Football. Jesus, don't you have a brother? An uncle? Some guy somewhere in the family tree?"

She shook her head in between his hands. It made the silk of her hair slip back and forth between his fingers and he swallowed hard. Something about the sensation felt illicit. It felt like knowing her on an intimate level. Only someone close against her would know how her hair felt. And he knew she didn't let just anyone touch her hair.

"My father died when Lina was two. I was eight. I don't remember much about him. No brothers. I only have an aunt and she's been associated with . . . umm . . . about two dozen uncles . . . that I remember. Before she died my mother didn't let us spend too much time around them."

"Smart lady. When did she die?"

"I was nineteen."

"You . . ." He laughed then, turning up his chin and pressing his lips to her forehead as he squeezed his eyes tightly shut. "It was a Sunday," he whispered against her as his mind raced. She had raised her sister. Just like he had raised Docia. Only he had had Leo to help him. Leo had always been there, watching Docia when he had a test to study for or when he went to the Academy. Who had been there for *her*? How had she gone through medical school by herself with a kid sister to take care of? "And I came into the station with Chico. I had him off leash. Bad habit, really. I trusted him so much that I'd forget he was still an animal. I never forgot he was dangerous, don't get me wrong. I trained with him too much to let that happen. But he was still a dog, you know? And he smelled something. I was rushing through to get to the park, picking something up off my desk . . . I can't even remember what it was . . . and Chico got wind of something and did something he has never done before. He left my heel. Chico always stayed at my heel. *Always*.

"But something caught his nose and he left me. I saw it out of the corner of my eye . . . so I looked up and saw you. Do you remember now? He was at your feet and he growled. It's why you shied from Sargent the other day. You remember Chico growling. And it wasn't playing. You froze because you knew that was not a playful sound."

He heard her swallow and he pulled back so he could look into her eyes. "Yes," he said softly, "you remember. You were wearing something so loose. A skirt that swept your toes, full of fabric, light and whimsical, like a hippie girl straight out of Woodstock." It was a joke. Everyone in Saugerties knew that Woodstock wasn't held in Woodstock. It had been held in a little town called Saugerties, New York. "You looked so damn pretty. And I remember thinking, what's so wrong with us that you won't dress that way at work? A brief flash of thought before calling Chico to heel."

"But he didn't," she said, her voice as whisper soft as his was, as if they were in church telling secrets.

"No. He snarled and growled again. I dropped everything in my hands and flew . . . I mean flew across that room terrified he was going to bite you. And I remember thinking you stupid damn dog if you bite her she's *never* going to go out with me!"

She gasped, a small laughing sound. "You did not!"

"Did too," he said with a smile. "That was the minute I realized I was crushing on you big time. Of course I couldn't examine the feeling because—"

"Because your dog lunged for my throat?" she said dryly.

"Don't be a drama queen. You know full well it was the perp behind you he was gunning for. Deitz did a shit search on him *and* he cuffed him in front, the stupid lazy bastard. The guy had a knife and he was seconds away from sticking you. But he froze exactly the way you did when he saw Chico lunge. I called him out but he barreled right past you and went for the guy's arm. Took me a minute to realize why. Had my gun up the guy's nose two seconds later."

"I have to admit, as scared as I was . . . there was something kind of hot about you taking that guy down. It was my first time watching you actually face off with someone. I know it wasn't by the book," she whispered, "and I know Chico misbehaved. I confess he always scared me a little after that because it happened so close, but that was the day I first thought 'My god, that man is like a full dose of testosterone and adrenaline.' It was stunning because I never thought I'd be that kind of girl."

"The kind that finds me hot?" he teased.

"Oh, you . . ." She reached out and pinched him on his chest.

"Ow. Hey," he complained.

"Oh don't give me that. I doubt a—"

She was cut off with a wild gasp as he suddenly pushed off and rolled her beneath him, her hair spilling wildly across his bed and pillows. *Oh yes,* he thought, *I like that. Marissa in my bed.*

"So you thought I was hot, I thought you were gorgeous, and there was no one else between us save my dog. And that incident was the only reason why I chose to go to you instead of an off-site shrink. Because Chico saved you and I knew you'd get it. I knew you'd understand my loss."

"Of course I did. It was like losing an arm for you, Jackson. He was a sidearm no different from your gun or your taser. You felt naked without him. Vulnerable."

"I'm naked now. I'm vulnerable now," he said softly, unable to help himself from touching her hair again in a soft, reverent stroke.

"Yeah. The way a tank is vulnerable," she said dryly.

"I'm not talking physical, Marissa."

She fell quiet, her hands like gentle butterflies as they settled on his shoulders.

"I know," she said at last. "I know."

And he knew she did. What thrilled him was that she was facing it. Accepting it. Now if only she would accept him on a whole other level. He knew it was asking a lot of her. He knew she was trying to protect herself at all costs. He didn't know why exactly, and he hoped she would tell him one day. Perhaps it had to do with her having to raise her sister all alone, or just that she had a cruddy self esteem for god knew what reason. He just wanted to know so he could tell her she was wrong about herself. Tell her that she was incredibly beautiful and so much braver than she gave herself credit for.

He held her between his hands and bent to gently touch his mouth to hers. Just a touch, not a kiss, and there he waited for her, his breath quick and heated. It felt like a moment too long to him before she lifted that small increment into a kiss. He kissed her sweetly, a soft demure thing that was all she seemed to be asking for. But he wasn't going to let her get away with half measures. He pulled back and looked into her liquid blue eyes.

"Now kiss me the way you really feel," he said to her. "And know that it will decide whether you stay or I ask you once more to leave me, hummingbird."

He watched her catch her breath, felt her leg move up a fragment against his thigh, a subconscious gesture he knew. If her mind had any doubts, he knew her body did not. But she was expecting seduction and he wouldn't give it to her. He wouldn't take her as wildly and dominantly as he knew how so she could blame him for it later. No. No, this *she* had to demand from him.

"I want to," she said, a flush creeping over her cheeks. "You know that I want to s-stay."

"Prove it," he commanded of her. Her eyes widened as she licked her lips and let her gaze drop to his mouth. Then she lifted her head out of his hands and kissed him. Again, it was sweet. A pretty and shy kiss. But he didn't believe she couldn't find it in her to be more than that.

He broke off the kiss and moved to get off of her and send her packing. Disappointment lurched through him, a part of him crying out in frustration. He wouldn't aggress with her, sweeping her up in the passion he knew she craved. He'd tried that already and it had blown up in his face. But just as he was about to leave her hands tightened on his shoulders, trying to hold him to her.

"W-what's wrong? Why . . . ?" she stammered.

"What's wrong is I know exactly how passionate you are," he said fiercely. "I know how hot you can be when I make you that way. Why won't you admit to it? Why do you want to make me run roughshod over you with seduction just so you can hold yourself free of blame and heap it all on me? No, Marissa. I won't let that happen this time." He moved off of her but she tightened her grip even more, following him with a slide across and back beneath him.

"No! I don't know what you want!"

"You're already what I want," he said with a sigh. "That's the whole point. I want you, Marissa. You. Not just your body. Not just a vessel. But *you*. My Marissa. My sweet, delicious, passionate Marissa."

"I think you expect more than I'm capable of," she said softly, her cheeks so pink, like she was out in the freshest cold of winter.

"I think you underestimate yourself," he said back to her.

She seemed to think on that for a moment, but he could see the frustration in her. "Isn't it enough that I'm here? Doesn't that mean anything to you?" She was getting snappish, her annoyance with him for not seducing her very apparent. He would have smiled if he didn't think she'd deck him for it.

"I pulled you down. I put you under me. I'm here hard as a goddamn rock, Marissa. Doesn't *that* mean anything to *you*?" Damn. Now his frustration was showing. Well fine, he thought irritably. Better he fix the problem before it started. He swung himself away from her and got to his feet, pulling himself free of the grip of her hands, her nails trying to hold him until the very last second.

"Oh my god! Jackson, get back here!" she burst out. "Don't you dare make me beg! It's a shameful, dirty ploy to make me feel . . . to make me feel . . ."

"I'm not going to make you feel anything," he bit out. "You either feel it for yourself or you don't. And honestly, I'm not in the mood for any uncertainties. Not after—" He broke off, too sickened with disappointment to say it aloud. *Not after I've bared my soul to you completely. Why oh why won't you do as much for me?*

Marissa was completely flustered. Just minutes ago he was so warm and sweet. So obviously wanting her. What did he want from her? She had kissed him, hadn't she? She was there, in his bed, in spite of her original resolve when she'd entered the room. Did he want her to leave? Was . . . was she making a fool of herself?

"There," he said suddenly, pointing into her face. "That right there is what I'm talking about. I can read that expression clear as crystal. You don't trust me and you sure as hell don't trust yourself. I have more faith in you than you do, Marissa. I just don't get it. I know you're stronger than this!"

Marissa opened her mouth to retort, but he just moved away from the bed completely and was standing there naked and proud. He hadn't been lying to her when he'd said he was hard for her; his erection, just a couple of inches beneath that wicked tattoo, was an amazing, powerful thing to behold. And Marissa felt her mouth go dry and other places get completely wet. Places that were aching, begging her to do something. *Anything.*

She didn't know what happened next exactly. One minute she was on the bed, the next she was launching herself at him, her entire weight tackling into him so hard he almost fell over. And before he could say a word, she grabbed hold of him and crushed her mouth against his. She kissed him with everything she had. She begged him with her aching body and her craving heart. She reached down with one hand and yanked up that annoying skirt so she could wrap her leg around him and pull him in even closer. She felt him against her lower belly, his erection pressing against her uterus in all the wrong ways, she thought with frustration. He ought to be inside her, pressing against her that way. He ought to be holding her. He ought to be ravishing the hell out of her.

But he wasn't. So goddamn him she was going to make him do it. She opened her mouth beneath his, and slowly, provocatively ran her tongue over his lips.

"Let me in," she breathed against him.

Well hell. She didn't have to ask him twice, Jackson thought fiercely as he swept her mouth up against his, chasing after that silky, sexy tongue of hers. God, her natural seductiveness was treacherous and overpowering. This, he thought, was what he had seen every day walking past his desk in those CFM heels of hers. He'd probably had at least a hundred fantasies of bending her over her damn desk and fucking her to within an inch of her life, but this was so much better. He wanted her to make fierce love with him to within an inch of *his* life.

He lurched forward, tossing her back down on the bed, following roughly after her. He climbed right up between her thighs, helping her pull up that tight, ridiculous skirt of hers. God, the thing hugged her body the way he wanted to hug her body. But for now he settled for the feel of himself pressing against the warm, soft heat of her. He groaned as he rubbed himself against the fabric of her panties, listening to her gasp and feeling her grip him. She lifted her hips and moved against him in return, a seductive wriggle that just about made him lose his mind.

Take her. Take her!

He didn't need that voice in his head to motivate him. He was already on it. He reached down between their bodies and grabbed for her underwear, pulling it down her long thighs then pushing them away from her. She still had all her clothes on. She still had her shoes on, and it was exactly how he wanted to take her. No prelude. No more foreplay. They'd spent years toying with each other. Now it was over. He put himself back between her legs, his cock hard and eager, so eager for its mate.

"Fuck. Oh fuck," he hissed when he felt her heat and the purest wetness in the whole damn universe. His whole body tightened up and he wanted to . . . oh god, was this even right? Shouldn't he be—?

He disregarded all doubt and just gave in to Menes's forceful taunt to take her. He found her entrance and thrust into her all in the same movement. He gasped with the shock of how hot she felt around him. She was so freaking tight, so damn juicy wet.

He was honestly amazed he didn't make an idiot of himself by coming on the spot. No, he thought, that is not the way this is going to be. Not after waiting and wanting for so long.

She was gasping for every breath, her nails digging into his shoulders. Oh yes. Oh, god yes, he thought.

"Yes!" she cried out. "Oh god, yes!"

He laughed. "I couldn't have said it better myself." Then his hand left her thigh and reached to grab her blouse, ripping it open in two sharp movements. Her bra matched her discarded panties. A pristine white lace cami bra, the demure fabric meant to hide her from the world. But she reached beneath herself and had it unhooked and shucked off about three times faster than he could have done himself. Then he was touching her, his hands all over her bountiful breasts, her concave belly, her pretty neck and elegant shoulders. Christ, he didn't have enough adjectives to describe her or how it felt to be raw-fucking her. And that was what he was doing. Moving inside of her, thrusting hard and deep even as his teeth caught at one of her nipples.

Marissa cried out, gasping as though in shock, and then moaning and gripping him even closer. Yes. This had been what he wanted. Her aggression. Her passion being the impetus of what was happening between them. She drove her fingers through his hair making a tight fist, pulling just enough to get his attention. He let her drag him up to her mouth and then they sealed to each other's mouths with a heat and ferocity that couldn't be measured. He pulled out of her just so he could have the satisfaction of ramming home into her. Again. And yet again. And, oh god . . . oh god.

"Hard and fast this time," he gasped against her mouth. "This time."

"Yes. Yes! Please," she begged him savagely.

"As the lady demands," he said, his voice rough with his arousal. He could feel the virulent need to come clawing up through him as he rushed into her again and again, his speed as violent as his need. She began to cry out, successively louder, and he used everything he had to hold himself in check, to wait for it . . . to wait for her. He watched as his hard impacts shimmered through her body, listened greedily as it hoarsened her voice.

"On my god!" she cried out. "Oh my—"

She drew in a hard, sudden breath and then . . . magic. It had to be magic. Nothing real could ever feel as glorious as it felt when she tightened up around him and came hard, screaming like a banshee. You could just tell from listening to her how much she had needed this. How much she had craved him. And she would hear the same thing ejecting from him seconds later, fire burning a path out of him and ejaculating into her.

"Christ . . . Marissa!" He groaned, that act of spilling himself inside of her nearly painful, that was just how good it felt. He gasped for his breath, his forehead pressed to the bed near her ear as he listened to her do the same. He felt the wetness of their bodies oozing around him and oh it was so damn satisfying. So was the naughtily content look in her eyes when he finally lifted his head.

He bent to her mouth then and kissed her the way she should be kissed. The way he would kiss her from that moment onward. As though she were the most exquisite of cognacs, meant to be warmed and swept against the tongue again and again in order for its true beauty to be seen . . . to be felt. And oh, the burn that followed.

"That was then. This is now," he told her, "and always after. Whether I'm fucking you or making love to you, Marissa, you're going to damn well know how much I need you. You understand? You. I need *you*."

She nodded then, but before he could kiss her she reached to press her fingers to his lips.

"But Menes needs *her*," she said softly.

CHAPTER SIXTEEN

Jackson knew it was the truth, just as much as she did. But then again, he'd made no secret about his desires . . . on all fronts. He just was reluctant to talk about it right then, while he was still inside her and in desperate need to make love to her again, this time taking it slow and doing it right. Not that what they'd just done could be considered wrong on any level. More right, was possibly a better way of looking at it. He was afraid that if they started in on this topic once again everything would dissolve into defensive posturing and huge protective walls flying up in front of his face.

"You know, I'm going to have to stop referring to myself in the third person eventually," he said carefully. "Don't try to separate us, Marissa. We've very much become the same person. But there will always be the ability to do what I call a sidebar, where we can step apart from ourselves as a Blended being in order to debate an issue, voice a strong opinion, or when considering options. Sort of like having a very powerful conscience, I guess you could say."

"So you mean you want her, too," she said, an odd sort of flatness to her tone. Not petulant. Not curious. Just emotionless. Which led him to believe she was reacting to something with very strong emotion. It was a habit for her, he realized, this heavy curtain over her emotions. It might work very well for her in her profession, but he wasn't her patient any longer.

Very gently he eased away from her, moving to lie on his side right up against the length of her. She was rumpled and was wearing nothing but her skirt and heels and he schooled his features from smiling lest she mistake what was amusing him. The minute he was off of her though, she pulled down her skirt, smoothing it against her thighs. He saw her searching for her blouse with a turn of her head . . . either that or she was trying to hide some more.

"At the moment," he said, "everything I want is right here." He reached to run slow, gentle fingers along the path of her breastbone. His words and his touch must have gotten her attention because she looked back into his eyes.

"But he's not . . . I mean, if he wants me like this, doesn't that make him unfaithful to this woman he's supposed to love with every fiber of his being?"

"You're thinking in very black-and-white human ways. With the nature of who we are, Bodywalkers I mean, we have to flex to accommodate the fact that we're sharing the desires and needs of multiple souls."

"So it's carte blanche on cheating. How lovely for you," she said, sitting up suddenly. But Jackson took her by her arm and pulled her back down and even closer to his side.

"What I mean is, I know that Hatshepsut understands that by doing things this way, by trying to find a volunteer for her rather than letting her resurrect in the usual way of our people, things can't be left so black-and-white. She wants me to choose someone I would be very attracted to. It's . . . it's like a gift she's giving me, in some respects. However, once she is here, I would be taking my life in my hands if I even thought about another woman. I am a faithful man, Marissa. I always have been. I may not have had many long relationships, but when I was in one I didn't disrespect my significant other by sleeping around on her. And as you know, Menes has had what could potentially be the longest relationship on earth, and I assure you, he's never been unfaithful to Hatshepsut." He smiled a little. "That's not to say she hasn't occasionally over our lifetimes found a woman she's thought I would like and brought her into our bedroom as a gift to me."

Marissa gasped and flushed hot, indignation rising in her eyes. "I would never do that!"

"Never is not a word we use when we can potentially live hundreds of years in our mortal bodies . . . barring outside interference of course. And we come from a time when multiple wives were commonplace. We've been through every single sexual evolution and revolution known to mankind. What we've done here is blunt and rudimentary. And you're being very narrow-minded, Marissa. You're far too educated to start pretending you don't understand these things. And I assure you, if she does not have permission of her host, she wouldn't push or try to change the host's mind. Well"—he smiled a bit wolfishly—"not much anyway. She can be quite persuasive when arguing a point. Rather a lot like you. And she loves opportunities to put me in my place. Also a common trait between you."

That made her smile and laugh. "So she's convincing, kinky, and bossy."

He laughed as well. "In a nutshell, yes. But she's also incredibly kind, fierce when it comes to protecting her people and her family, and plays a mean game of chess."

"You make her sound so human," she said with a sigh. "But the truth is, she just isn't. And I don't know if I can be all the things that she is. A queen? A Body-walker? Your . . . your . . ."

"Wife," he said in a soft word. "We've been married over two dozen times, by everything from a priest to an island native that stomped and danced for the gods to take notice before playing a tune on a nose flute."

"Oh stop, now you're joking," she cried with a laugh, pushing at his chest in reprimand.

"I am not joking," he said almost seriously. "It's the truth. All of it."

She stopped smiling and turned pensive. "So, you're telling me that if I become Hatshepsut's host, then you'll want to marry me."

"As long as we all think it's agreeable, then yes."

"But you didn't seem like the marrying type," she hedged, her fingers smoothing her skirt down again even though it hadn't budged from the initial time. He was beginning to realize that her need to keep a perfect image at all times was like a protective armor for her. She was probably feeling very vulnerable right then, talking about difficult things without her armor on. It could very well be the reason why he'd never seen a single sign of a dating life from her in the two years she'd been on the force.

"I'm with Menes on this one," he told her quietly. "I'm waiting for the right woman. No one else will do."

"If I say no, then someone else will have to do," she said a bit sharply. "I don't see Menes giving up after the first try fails. You either for that matter. You're as tenacious as that dog of yours."

"Well, at least you're forewarned."

"About what?"

"My tenaciousness. I'm not the sort to give up easily, Marissa. I'll do whatever it takes to make you say yes to me."

Her expression was one of pure consternation. "Didn't anyone ever tell you that if you push too hard it makes people shove back?"

"I'm sure they did somewhere along the line. I think I disregarded it."

"Oh!" she exclaimed this time shoving at him harder.

Marissa wanted to be mad at him. She wanted to push back, push away and run. It was just too overwhelming. All of it. Everything he wanted from her was just asking so much. He probably wouldn't even be asking if he really knew who she was. She wasn't queen material. She just . . . wasn't.

"You're incorrigible," she said to him, unable to make it sound at all serious. She liked it when he teased her, although god only knew why. Just like she liked it when he acted like her hair was his favorite place for his fingers to be. And she damn well liked it when he threw her on the bed and took her like a man out of control with lust for her.

Oh yes, she liked that very much. Just like she was liking the way his fingers were drifting over her chest, tracing curling, lazy patterns over and between her breasts.

She had always thought that having sex that hastily was more about the man's pleasure and had very little to do with her own. Women needed more time, or so the textbooks said. But she had to admit she'd never felt anything so exciting in her life. There was something about knowing he was out of control and that it was because of her, and not because of his own selfish needs, that made it so incredibly hot. She'd had no doubt about it at that moment. And even now. And that was why, she supposed, he had refused to budge unless she was the aggressor. It had been very clever of him. No . . . no wait. Clever implied that she felt it had been manipulative. She didn't feel that way at all. She felt like he was beginning to understand her and the way she was. Of course, it was a far cry from them getting married . . . but still . . .

His fingertips skied up the slope of her breast and over her nipple just then and the sensation was electric. She could feel herself instantly going taut all over, including the nipple. She saw him smile and there was sudden hunger in those peacock eyes of his. He leaned his head forward, dipping down so he could touch his tongue to her and then quite boldly took her nipple into his mouth, the soft sucking sensation followed up with the scrape of his teeth as he let the turgid tip go once more.

"Jackson," she breathed softly, meeting his gaze and trying for all she was worth to say things without saying a word. She wanted him . . . no, needed him in her life. It had been quite some time since she'd let a man this close to her. Even then there was, to her, a proper sort of etiquette that she followed, which did not include making it to the bed only halfway clothed, not even taking the time to kick off her shoes. She did so now, toeing them off so they landed on the wood floor with two little clunking sounds.

"Getting ready for bed?" he asked her as he rose up and pulled her underneath himself; his big body covering her so completely that she actually felt small. What a peculiar thing, she thought. She was almost the same height as he was, and even without heels she was very tall for a woman. She found she liked the perception, although she would have thought it would have bothered her. She didn't like to feel overshadowed. She didn't like to feel out of control.

But she had already been out of control. She had let this happen in spite of her better judgment. She didn't know what to think about that and, thanks to his mouth returning to her breast she didn't think clarity would be coming anytime soon.

"I'm already in bed," she said, hearing the breathless quality of her voice, knowing it was because she was already eager for more, the stupid skirt she wore the only reason why she didn't raise her knees on either side of his hips and immediately cradle him between her thighs.

"Here, let me help you." He moved back, kneeling and levering himself up far enough to turn her over, exposing the zipper to her skirt. "God," he muttered, "you're poured into this thing." Then she felt his hand on her backside, slowly running down the length of her skirt, shaping her into his palm and clearly enjoying himself. He moved to the hem, then slipped his hand beneath it, instead of going for her zipper like she had thought he would. His hand crept up between her thighs, his fingers seeking and finding.

She gasped in a short breath, her face flushing with heat.

"Oh, I like this," he said breathily into her ear. "You're wet with me." He drew his fingers along the slickness of her flesh, his hand moving between her tightly compressed thighs and his fingers suddenly sliding into her. She tried so hard to catch her breath, to stop reacting like she'd never done this before. But she couldn't seem to help herself. There was something so illicit in their situation, with her being in serious breach of her ethics and him pushing her past her own tightly drawn lines at every single turn.

Then he was just as suddenly gone, moving away from her. She turned to see where he'd gone, but he went only as far as standing at her feet, putting his hands on her thighs and pulling her back up onto her knees, her hands scrambling to press into the bed for balance. Then he was pushing her skirt up over her thighs and backside, exposing her to the cool air of the room and making her realize just how hot her body was. He pulled her all the way back to the edge of the mattress, until her rear was pressed against his hips and the stellar erection he'd come up with. More than a little impressed with his recovery time, she turned her shoulders to look back at him, but a hand on the back of her head gently prevented her from doing so.

"I-I just think you should know . . . I don't, umm, respond well to this position." She was blushing again, wanting to hide her face against the mattress but unable to reconcile herself with the wanton position of having her ass in the air and pointed in his direction.

"I think you should know that I don't believe that for a second. It's not the position, hummingbird. It's the vulnerability you don't respond well to. But I'm going to teach you that being vulnerable can be a very good thing."

With that pronouncement, his hand slid between her legs once more, his fingers raking boldly through damp nether curls, on over a hypervigilant clit, pausing just long enough to acknowledge he knew exactly where it was and circling it as if with a promise to return later. He narrowed his stroke to two fingers, passing over the tender nerves at the entrance to her body and continuing to sweep back and up along the seam of her backside until he touched the tip of her tailbone.

Again, so deliciously naughty, so much hinting at the forbidden, and she realized she was eating up every sensation and every moment, eager to see what he was going to do next. What he did was trace right back the way he had come and those two fingers slid true and deep inside of her. She sucked in a breath and he chuckled softly.

"No, you don't respond well at all," he said, teasing her with his touch as well as his words.

"Shh!" she shot back at him. "I'm trying to concentrate here."

"Then I'm doing something wrong," he said with a

laugh, his free hand giving her exposed backside a little spank.

But when she would have protested once again that he was barking up the wrong tree with that, he curled those fingers inside her, massaging her deeply and stealing any ability to speak from her.

"Yeah, you know what, I think I need a more practical application of technique to test this out," he said, the words muttered, almost distracted. He withdrew from inside her, but before she could even miss him he was back up against her. She could feel the brace of his powerful thighs against the backs of hers, and looking over her shoulder just as he set himself to thrust into her she got the image of fierce virility and commanding male. His hands were suntanned to a light bronze and she saw them gripping the paleness of her hips. She cried out, unable to help the response, the sensation of him filling her like nothing she remembered from her previous and awkward attempts at the position they were in. But how? What was different? It shouldn't be . . .

"I can hear those wheels turning from here," he said with amusement. "Maybe this never worked for you before because you kept on thinking too much."

"Isn't it your job to keep me from doing that?" she asked, finding herself panting for breath as a wave of indescribable pleasure washed through her. Then, as if he weren't at all satisfied with her retort, clever though it might have been, he reached between them and found her clit, beginning to circle it slowly with every equally slow thrust inside of her.

"Oh my g—" She gasped, cutting herself off when he suddenly hilted hard into her, the smack of flesh on flesh filling the dark room, only the spill of light from the outer suite allowing her to see him. According to Max though, he would have perfect vision in the dark. Which made sense, considering they were a night breed or night something-or-other. She wasn't in her right mind enough to remember what it was called. She moaned long and loud when he picked up his pace, leaving off from touching her in order to grip both of her hips in his hands. For the first time she got the hint that he wasn't as in charge of everything as she had thought. He was starting to draw hard for breath, though not at all from exertion, she knew. She'd seen the man run laps with his dog keeping stride, seen him race around a training field in the hot sun with full body armor and hardly break a sweat. But the moisture between his palms and her skin spoke volumes, the thrill of knowing she excited him that much making her whole body sing.

She started to climax with alarming and unexpected speed. She curled her hands into fists, clutching at the bedding and squeezing her eyes shut tight.

And he smacked her backside once more, startling her.

"Stop thinking," he commanded her. "And quit resisting. There's nothing wrong with losing control, Marissa. Nothing at all. Christ . . . just let go. Because if you don't relax this tension in your body I'm going to come before I want to. Jesus, Mari, you feel so good it's killing me."

And somehow, for some reason, it was all she needed to hear. The empowerment that came with that statement was utterly unreal, and suddenly it no longer mattered whether or not she was in control . . . of the situation or of herself. She shouted out, realized it was his name on her lips, and he doubled his speed into her, a frenetic, frantic pace that told her he was losing control himself. He reached forward, his hand diving into her hair, twisting it up into his fist, though not enough to hurt. Just enough to make her lose all control, her body exploding in heat and spasms of the utmost in pleasure. She couldn't seem to keep quiet any longer, her whole existence tightening up and her body seizing him as if it knew he was close and didn't want things to end. But it was greed, pure and simple, because her pleasure was beyond anything she'd known before. And as he came with a shout that bordered on a roar, as he seemed to freeze in place in order to spill himself inside of her, she realized oh hell yeah, she really liked this position.

"Okay, that's three. Wanna go for four?" Jackson asked her breathlessly, making them both laugh. She'd finally made it out of her skirt. Not that it even mattered to her anymore. She was wantonly sprawled over his body and well into losing all sense of conservatism . . . and not regretting it in the least. Not just then anyway. She thought they both knew it was very possible that she would start second-guessing herself in the . . . well, it wouldn't be the light of day because she was pretty sure darkness had long since come calling. But then again, maybe she would surprise herself and decide that living in the moment without worrying about consequences or having total control over all of her actions was something she could really get used to.

"Maybe we might make it to good old-fashioned missionary this time," she speculated. They both waited a beat and looked at each other. "Nah," they said in unison. She giggled, in spite of her not ever having thought she was the giggling type. But she was discovering things about herself in leaps and bounds. It was amazing what could happen in such a short amount of time.

"Stop thinking. You're going to end up in a corner you don't want to be in and it'll shut you down like Fort Knox under a bomb threat."

"Okay," she said. She lay there for all of two seconds. "I have a question. Let's just say—"

"This is you not thinking?" he teased. "I hate to tell you but you're doing it wrong."

She made a face at him, coming just shy of sticking her tongue out. It made her take pause for another two seconds. There was something about him that relaxed her. *Well, beside orgasms,* she thought to herself. She'd had some nice relationships before meeting him, but . . . they hadn't exactly been fun. They were hardly what she'd call a relationship in the traditional sense, but just the same it wasn't "nice." It was more cordial. Intelligent. Mature. Sedate. All the things she usually looked for when trying a relationship on for size. She didn't like drama in her life . . . she had her ebullient sister providing more than enough of it, thank you very much. But all the push me, pull me emotions, the petty jealousies, the insecurities, they were not something she wanted to indulge in.

Since meeting him, she'd had nothing but drama where he was concerned. And the last couple of days had only exacerbated it. But she had thought she would have been very unhappy in a volatile relationship. Hell, she'd counseled enough people who were engaged in them. Some of them unhealthy to the point of danger and poisoning of the spirit. But . . . by trying to avoid all of the emotional pitfalls, she'd also managed to bleed out the joys, the passions, and the pleasure, she realized. The past hours in his bed had proven that to her. She'd spent so much time concerned about what type of life she didn't want to have that she'd not been living much at all. She'd schooled herself not to take chances, but chances were what life was all about. Taking them or passing up on them, those chances meant something.

"Let me ask you this," she said. "Let's make the wild assumption that I agree to do something like this, which, I'm still not inclined even the slightest to do. But let's say I was. How would she know? I mean, if you're down here and she's up there in the Ether or whatever, how would she know that I'm the one you want her to take. I could be dead and stay dead, no Bodywalker, if she gets it wrong. What if she's already found someone else and is on her way here?"

"She's not here," he said, reaching to smooth back the tumble of hair that seemed to be everywhere around them. "I would know. I always know. I can feel it almost instantly. It's a very powerful connection between us, with aspects that no other couple I know shares.

"Not even Ram and Docia. And they are very, very close to each other. And as to your first question, she will know. She knows everything I am feeling here, just as I know everything she is feeling there. She would feel me directing you toward her. She would feel how special you are to me. She will know instantly that you are my extraordinary gift to her . . . and she would be the most precious gift I could ever give to you. Oh I know it comes fraught with complexities and even danger, I won't pretend that it doesn't. But so does any other life, more or less. Look how this began . . . with Docia, a normal girl in a normal life, suddenly being pushed off a bridge. That should have been the end. It would have been the end."

"If not for a Bodywalker. And I understand that. I think it's . . . really something special to be given a gift like that. A second chance at life. But . . . it's not a natural death if I do this consciously. It's . . . just not."

It wasn't that he didn't understand what she meant. He did. She didn't want a second life because she wasn't done with the first one yet.

"I think you should know . . . it won't be safe for you to leave here for a while . . . if ever," he said, sitting up so he could put his back to her and not let her see the disappointment that was clutching at him. Disappointment, but not condemnation. He wanted her so badly his souls ached for it. But he understood why she felt it was a disrespectful thing to do, to simply throw away a life in order to try on a better one. These were not things that could be discarded and put on like clothes. He never thought it would be and he never once thought this would be easy. But now he was tangled up in her and it was getting really complicated really fast. He wished they could just shut it out for a few more—

The sensation that suddenly ran through him was like a scream, an alarming, screeching thing that propelled him to his feet.

"Jacks—?"

"Shh!" He was listening, listening to try to understand what he was hearing.

Gargoyles, his other half whispered to him. *The Gargoyles who are attached to us have arrived and there is something very wrong.*

Jackson grabbed for the nearest pair of jeans he could find and put them on as he was hurrying to the window. He couldn't remember how to work the smart glass, glass with particles inside of it that, when excited by an electric current, made it completely opaque, blocking out the daylight while he—

Electricity! He remembered the switch and turned it off. The glass became instantly clear and moonlight, bright and full, poured in. It lit the grounds very well, but even so it was amazing how much he could see, how much detail jumped out at him as though it were the light of day. Then he saw them, huge dark masses with wings, gliding to the ground in a deadly, beautiful grace of movement that should not have been present in creatures so big. And Menes knew these Gargoyles well.

Ahnvil, he thought as Jackson's eyes rested on the nearer Gargoyle. And as if he knew eyes were on him,

Ahnvil turned and looked straight up at the bedroom window. The Gargoyles' eyes were red, something that happened only when they were in battle mode or being threatened in some way. Suddenly Jackson found himself wishing he could open the window, except it was a solid sheet of glass in its casement.

"There's trouble," Jackson said, turning to look at her. "Promise me you'll stay right here," he demanded of her as he went for his gun in his dresser. He whistled sharply, more habit than anything, and he heard Sargent bark from farther inside the house. He ran out of the room before she answered him, instinctively knowing there was no time to waste. He didn't waste time with shirt or shoes. Sargent met him halfway down the hallway, whining excitedly, knowing something was happening as only an animal could know it. Jackson pointed to the bedroom door he'd just come through. "Stay, boy. You watch out for her."

Sargent actually looked put out by the order. He even whined, the doggy version of *"Oh, c'mon!! I wanna go too!"*

Marissa raced to the window, her heart in her throat as she watched for Jackson. This, she thought, is the other reason why I never wanted to date from within the police department. She knew she couldn't watch someone she loved run headfirst into danger every single day of her life, never knowing if that day was going to be the day his captain would be at her door in his stead because . . .

. . . loved? She hastily rewound her thoughts. Had she just said . . .

Love Jackson? No! Of course you don't love him! If for no other reason than he's a damn minefield full of trouble just waiting to erupt beneath you! Marissa Anderson, you are way too smart for that! Jesus, you'd think you were sixteen and crushing on the guy just because you'd just gone all the way with him!

Then the door to the house flew open, bright light flooding the frame for an instant and then it was gone again, Jackson having run through so fast he was hardly more than a blur. And that was when she saw who he was running toward. Or rather *what* he was running toward.

"Oh my god, they're really real," she breathed, her breath fogging against the glass as she pressed even closer to see. Despite the moonlight it was still dark out, but there was no mistaking the breadth of a wingspan on the back of a very large creature. Several creatures. What had Jackson said? That they belonged to him? Like possessions?

No. She remembered the story about the Gargoyles and their freedom. He meant . . . he meant that he was guardian over their touchstones for as long as he was on this earth. How many, she wondered, seeing three of them at present, did he have guardianship of? How many did he owe this great responsibility to? How many trusted Menes so implicitly that they pledged their loyalty to him generation after generation?

She heard the clicking of nails on the wood floor, then felt Sargent leaning his warm body and soft fur against her legs. He whined, clearly not happy his master took off without him. But Jackson would always look out for his dog first and he must know that whatever the trouble was, Sargent was too fragile a creature to get caught up in the middle of a situation that made powerful things like Bodywalkers and Gargoyles worry. He also thought she was too fragile a creature, she supposed, feeling a little put out by that realization. If she wasn't so terrified of what was beyond the window, she would have stomped down after him and told him to quit treating her like a precious commodity.

Oh, but it was kind of nice to feel like a precious commodity. There was something very compelling in the small, almost absentminded ways he took care of and with her. And she didn't just mean these past couple of days. As if suddenly becoming aware of it all, she remembered all those times he'd handed her the first cup of coffee from the pot, having figured out she liked it dangerously hot. Milk and three sugars. He had figured it out and had always remembered. He'd known when her sister's birthday was, she recalled. He'd walk her out to her car if she was working late, just to make sure she was safe. When she tried to decline he would ignore her. And he watched. She remembered all those times she'd felt him watching her. Especially since Chico had spotted the guy with a knife. He knew the precinct, even though it had a decent number of cops for a seemingly small town in upstate New York, was not as safe as one might think. Mainly because it doubled as central booking and holding cells until Ulster County Jail came and fetched them or they were transported out to them.

And now she knew why he had been watching her, what he had been feeling toward her. Or perhaps an impression of how he'd felt. It wasn't love of course. More like lust. And she didn't fault him for it because she had been lusting right back at him. But now she knew there was the potential for more, and as she watched him run out into the night bare-chested and barefooted and looking so damn in control and powerful she felt herself going weak in the knees and her breath becoming difficult to catch.

"God, let him be safe," she said fervently. Regardless, she just didn't have it in her to wait up in his room. He couldn't expect her to just watch as something or someone tried to hurt him. Oh, she knew she would be insignificant to these creatures of power, but she just couldn't stand there knowing he was going out into danger. Not from so far away that she couldn't get to him if he needed her. What someone like him would need some-one like her for wasn't even logically known. Then again, nothing she was feeling, thinking, or doing was rooted in logic anymore.

She hurried to the dresser, hoping that he had some clothes she could wear. Her blouse was tattered and torn, only her skirt remaining. She wriggled into it and her discarded panties as she checked every drawer and found them bare. Finally her eyes fell to his shirt where it lay draped over the back of a chair and she rushed into it, the garment big and as roomy as a night-shirt and, in spite of her height, it still dropped nearly to her knees. Rolling up the sleeves she raced out of the room and down the hall and stairs. She ran into one of the front rooms, shutting off the light so she could make out what was happening outside. She couldn't see any-thing now that she wasn't elevated and she found her-self drawn to go out. Sargent was whining in earnest now, looking to her to take some sort of action. But in the end it turned out that he was the reason why she proceeded with much more caution.

"Stay here," she tried to command the dog. He cocked his head and whined again. He sat down, but stood right back up again, his agitation enormous in the face of his craving to go to his master's side. She wholly un-derstood the feeling. But hers was the only life she was willing to be responsible for, so she made Sargent fol-low her to a nearby room, it too was at the front of the house with one of those large glass windows in it. But instead of looking to see if it was a better vantage point, she gently closed the door shut on Sargent, closing him safely inside. Then, after making sure the foyer light wasn't on so she wouldn't be seen leaving the house, she crept out of the front door.

* * *

Jackson ran up to Ahnvil who stood waiting for him, wings fully outspread, a mark of his tension. He looked as though he were spoiling for a fight. That was when a wave of fondness for the Gargoyle swept through him, as well as a few of the most prominent memories of him that Menes quickly gave him access to. They told him that Ahnvil was to be trusted implicitly, and that the Gargoyle was loyal to Menes, no matter who held his touchstone during those one hundred years he had to spend in the Ether between lives. Sometimes it had been Ram, other times Asikri. If not one of them then a powerful female who was less of a target than those in the governing seats.

"What is it?" he asked as soon as he was close enough.

"There is a powerful presence heading this way," Ahnvil told him, his voice like gravel crunching under feet. "We are all feeling it."

The Gargoyles were protectors for a reason. They could feel trouble coming, whatever it was. And though they were turned to stone by the touch of sunlight, the Templars could no sooner go out in daylight than any of them could, so their guardianship was only needed in the darkness. When they settled to their touchstones they could bear witness to everything crossing their path, to be reported at the full break of dusk.

"Powerful as in Templar?"

"Very close now. It won't be long." Ahnvil looked down at the gun in Jackson's hand and raised a stony brow. "That will not do much against Templars if they are this powerful. They will be very strongly shielded."

"I know. But until I got out here I didn't know the nature of the trouble. If it was human," Jackson retorted dryly, "I would think keeping a low profile and using a gun over my telekinesis would be the preferred course of action. You know, I wasn't just reborn yesterday," he said, the light of humor entering his eyes when he saw Ahnvil's sheepish discomfort. The big Gargoyle was known for his deep respect . . . as well as being hard on himself if he should fail in any way . . . even if it was just a simple misunderstanding. There was never a need to punish Ahnvil in any sense of the word, because the Gargoyle always proved to be much harder on himself than anyone else could be. The only exception, perhaps, being his former Templar master and creator. Ahnvil didn't talk much about it, but Jackson knew well enough it had not gone easy for him. For any of them.

"I know, Menes," he said. "Though you are still young I can see you are well Blended."

Another talent the Gargoyles had. Anyone who was a Bodywalker had a distinctive glow around them if seen through a Gargoyle's eyes. It was, Jackson supposed, the Templars' way of an early warning system. Until a human being did something to reveal his Nightwalker nature, it was virtually impossible for Templars to determine whether there was one or two souls in the body of a human approaching them. So, they had equipped their would-be slaves with the ability to see the difference so that they could warn their masters. And, apparently, the stronger the souls, the more enriched the Blend, the brighter they would glow.

"Jackson," Jackson corrected almost absently. "We think we prefer Jackson for this lifetime. Although I don't suppose it makes much difference to us either way." He shrugged and tucked the gun into the waistband at the back of his jeans. It wasn't an ideal holster if they were going to mix it up, but it would do.

"Odd," Ahnvil said, his head lifting and his large stone nostrils flaring wide. "The Templar is not on the air. Why would a Templar travel by foot onto the grounds when they all use their spell work to become airborne? And I . . ." Again, a wide flare of nostrils. "I smell blood. A great deal of blood."

That made the tension in Jackson's shoulders tighten even further. "An injured Templar?" Jackson looked back toward the house, wondering where Ram was and if, perhaps, this was one of the Templars Tameri had come to warn them about. A defector, of which she was one of many she had said. When Tameri and Docia's Blending had advanced enough for the former priestess to speak, those words had been like pure hope to Ram . . . and to Menes. Never in all these generations of war had they heard of such a thing. After all, no one dared to cross Odjit. But perhaps, if he let it be known that Templars would be welcomed back into the fold, they would begin to come in greater numbers. Before long they might all be on the Politic side of the line drawn between their two camps. It was a state wherein he could be very content should it come to pass.

"Is the Templar alone?" he asked his intuitive friend. There was no better tracker than a Gargoyle. Their specialized senses made it so.

"There are no other Templars in the area," Ahnvil assured him. "I do not even sense the energy of spells that might cloak them."

"Then I suggest we let our guest come to us and see what we see. Tameri's foot in our door is going to have to change our approach to things from now on," he warned Ahnvil, Ihron, and the female Gargoyle, Diahmond.

Ihron was a slightly leaner version of Ahnvil, which was unsurprising because they were not only from the same clan; they were rumored to have been born of the same maker. As for Diahmond . . . if a Gargoyle in its stone form could ever be considered beautiful, Jackson would have to say that Diahmond was exactly that. There were many stages of a Gargoyle's appearances.

There was the human appearance, meant to blend into the world, the human appearance with stone skin, worn like an armor that could be quickly donned and shed, and then the full Gargoyle form, which was that of a grotesque, winged beast. In any of his forms, Ahnvil was an enormous figure, and by the standards of a human woman, Diahmond was taller even than Marissa and quite muscular and fit. When human and wearing her stone skin she was as beautiful as a marble Aphrodite, smooth and graceful and powerful. Only when going into battle or when she flew did she turn into her grotesque form. Even so, she was compelling and a thing of fierce feminine strength, like a Valkyrie set for battle and convinced of her superiority.

"Should we not meet this Templar at the gate?" Ahnvil said, clearly chafing against the idea of letting a Templar simply walk onto the grounds of his king's home. Then again, Ahnvil was happiest when Templars were either not in his purview . . . or were being ground beneath his heel in battle. Getting the formerly enslaved Gargoyles on board with this new plan of acceptance was potentially going to be quite difficult. For good reason they did not trust any Templar.

That attitude had to change, if for no other reason than that his sister was Blended to a Templar and he would not have her treated like a pariah in her own home. Nor would Ram stand for it, and they could not afford to squabble among themselves. Their unity was the one thing they had always had over the Templars, who were actually greater in number than the Politic. It was unity that had kept their heads above water in the face of those greater numbers.

"Let them come," Jackson said. "I don't suggest letting them in the house or near the women, but let them come as far as they will as long as they behave. Speaking of women, Max, where is Angelina?"

"Sleeping I imagine. It's past midnight."

Jackson had not realized it was that late. He had spent far more time than he had realized making love to Marissa. It had seemed so incredibly short . . . so not long enough. "Let's not guess. Diahmond, Ahnvil, Ihron, please shift to human form. I don't need Angelina walking around the corner and seeing you in your present forms. Max, head back toward the guesthouse and see to it she's protected and that she stays away from the main house. I do seem to recall telling you not to leave her side."

"What am I supposed to do, get in her bed with her?" Max might have sounded more put out if the idea clearly didn't have merits in his estimation.

"Do refrain from that, too," Jackson warned him. "She is going to be a part of this family, so it would be wise not to play where you eat."

The statement made all eyes turn to him, each face staring at him in disbelief.

"But . . ."

"Let's talk about it later," Jackson said, glancing over to Diahmond. She was just as loyal to Hatshepsut as Ahnvil was to him. He knew that she would view him taking Marissa into his bed as an affront to her mistress's honor. And without the details of what was transpiring, he could see her becoming offended on her mistress's behalf. But since he didn't have time to spin long yarns of explanation, it was best to avoid the topic altogether for the moment. Diahmond was very thoughtful, exhibiting an even calmness of approach that was not present in very many Gargoyles. They had been built for battle and for rough work, and with that came aggression and fortitude and very little inner peace to temper it. A Gargoyle's temper was one of its greatest strengths and greatest weaknesses. In a rage they were nearly unstoppable, stone juggernauts that plowed through their enemies by the dozen . . . but that rage also blinded them to their moral compass, hazing the line between right and wrong.

They all waited until after Max hurriedly took his leave, all of their eyes trained on the dark reaches of the property in front of them. The landscaping was vast, from perfectly manicured to wild woods, and their potential enemy could come from anywhere before them.

"There," Ahnvil said, unsurprisingly being the first to spy the hulking figure on the drive. Not via the woods or over the walls, but the drive, with its white stones making it a bright beacon through the dark.

Jackson didn't wait any longer; he walked forward, the stones sharp beneath his bare feet and keeping him highly aware of his surroundings. That and almost ten years of being a cop. When he stopped, his phalanx of Gargoyles halted with him. Until Ahnvil suddenly changed form and leapt in front of Jackson, his huge bulk blocking Jackson's view of the approaching stranger.

"Ahnvil!" he barked.

"Kamenwati," Ahnvil snarled.

Kamenwati. Now he understood Ahnvil's reaction. To his right he saw Ihron bristle, his flesh turning to stone in a ripple of gray as he shook himself and snarled like a wolf in a pack, his blood running as high as his clansman. Of course any of them would bristle at Kamenwati's closeness. After all, he was Odjit's right arm. But for Ahnvil and for Ihron . . . Kamenwati was their creator. He had been the master of these hulking creatures and the gods only knew what humiliations and torments Kamen had forced upon his pet Gargoyles. Jackson placed a hand on Ahnvil's arm, feeling the rigid, immovable mass of stone that he was. But he knew Ahnvil could feel him.

"I know this is difficult for you, my friend," he said

softly, "but you must stand behind me and allow me to face him. There's nothing to fear. I have the three of you at my back and he is alone. He would be very foolish to provoke us." Although, he had often considered Kamen to be more than a little mentally unbalanced. Not necessarily in the avaricious, borderline psychopathic way that his mistress was . . . but not quite all there either.

Since there was no moving Ahnvil if he didn't want to be moved, Jackson was forced to step around him, his relatively slighter build slipping between the wall that was Ahnvil on one side and Ihron on the other. He turned his back on the approaching figure just long enough to give them a harsh look.

"You are independent beings and far be it from me to tell you how you should feel, but I am still ruler here and if you wish to remain with us you must listen to the commands I give you, no matter how distasteful it may be to you in that moment. You are free to leave, of course, but until you take your touchstones elsewhere and bid me farewell you will adhere to my rules and my wishes."

He turned to look back at Kamenwati, whom he had heard come to a halt several feet away. And that was when he saw the blood-soaked man Kamenwati held against himself. He was so drenched and caked in the stuff that he almost seemed like he had been thickly painted with it, making every part of him unrecognizable.

"I bring this man to you, for I believe he is yours and you call him friend," Kamen said, sounding as though he were in pain and out of strength himself. "But he is near death, so come and fetch him quickly."

The words made Jackson freeze in place for all of a heartbeat.

Leo.

Leo!

With a roar of fury Jackson ran forward, barreling into Kamenwati, ripping away his grasp on Leo even as he drove him into the stone drive, their bodies crunching over it as they slid to a stop. Jackson pulled his weapon out of pure habit, pushing up on his position across the other man's chest and shoving it into his eye socket.

"I don't give a fuck how powerful you are, you son of a bitch. This bullet will put an end to you in two seconds at this range. Now you tell me what the fuck is going on here or I swear to god . . ." Jackson wanted to scream a thousand things at the bastard, but there was nothing coming out of him. He found himself pressing his weapon hard against the Templar's eye socket while he looked over his shoulder at Leo's crumpled form. Diahmond had moved to him and was lifting him into her arms. She nodded to Jackson and he knew she would bring Leo somewhere safe and take care of him until Jackson was done where he was. Ahnvil had moved closer to Jackson once more, in full grotesque form, his vast wingspan overshadowing them, making him a black force interrupting the brightly moonlit night.

Jackson turned back to Kamenwati, focusing all of his attention on him, trying to put Leo's dance with death out of his mind until he could indulge in it.

"You will explain yourself," he hissed, leaning in close so he was staring straight into the other man's eyes.

"It is self-evident," he said softly, as if completely unconcerned. No. Not unconcerned. Resigned. "And I would beg you for that bullet myself," he went on. "But I do not have that right any longer. I've set loose an incredible evil on this earth, Menes. In seeking a cure for my mistress I—"

"Your mistress is dead," he spat.

"It might have been better if she were," he said. "Then none of this would have mattered. Take the bullet from the gun, etch my name upon it, and you may use it once my crime has been rectified. Make me that promise and I will stand beside you against the worst evil you could ever know."

It was Ahnvil's hand on his shoulder that made Jackson realize he was shaking with the urge to pull the trigger, a bloodthirsty instinct he would never have thought himself capable of. They, both Jackson and Menes, prided themselves on their sense of fair justice. To want to do this thing so coldly and so eagerly was a stunning experience for them both.

"You will forgive me if I demand a better explanation," Jackson hissed into the other man's face. It was streaked with Leo's blood, he realized, and he could smell the pungent tang of it rising off his clothes.

"Make me that promise, Politic, and I will tell you everything you need to know."

The cold and vast emptiness in Kamenwati's voice made Jackson hesitate for a beat and for the first time he really heard what Kamen was asking of him.

"Done." He said it sharply but with all the fierce sincerity he could manage so that Kamen knew he meant it. He pulled back, snapped the clip lock on the gun, letting the clip drop onto Kamen's chest. He racked back the slide of the .45, releasing the bullet in the chamber with a snap, the small metal projectile bouncing into the air. He caught it then slapped it down onto Kamen's breastbone, digging the metal down under his barely leashed strength. "It's yours now, Templar. Hand it to me when you are ready and I'll gladly take your life."

Kamen reached for the bullet, his arm and fingers obviously weak and shaking. He took the bullet in his hand, finding a fierce store of strength to clench it in his fist.

"Don't renege on this, Politic pharaoh," he said, the words more a plea than a command. Jackson had never seen him like this and didn't know what to make of it. His rage was faltering under his confusion. "If we don't die in the battle that is coming, then I will want this, make no mistake."

"You've heard his word," Ahnvil said sharply. "It may mean nothing to you Templars, but Menes does not fall away from his promises."

I promise you, my love, that I will be right behind you.

The last words Menes had spoken to Hatshepsut during her final moments of her most recent mortal life echoed into his mind. *No*, Jackson thought, *we do not make promises we do not keep.*

"Very well," Kamen said, an exhalation rushing out of him so much like relief. But then his eyes became troubled again. "I have awakened a monster. I thought . . . my mistress was lying in a coma and I thought to rouse her with an awakening spell . . . so ancient it was . . . I had no idea what it was supposed to awaken."

"Oh hell no," Ahnvil spat out. "What have you done, Templar scum?"

"I have roused Amun's enemy, Apep. I have set free pure evil on the world, Politic. He has been aroused in my mistress's body and his power will grow well beyond anything Odjit ever was. And he knows all of Odjit's thoughts. He will already be aware of you, and he will know that you are the biggest threat to his existence here on earth. Only you and others like you will have the power to stop Apep."

"The Politic is strong enough to repel any danger,"

Ahnvil said, his pride in his employers seething out of every word.

"Not just the Politic," Kamen hissed. "The Gargoyles. The Djynn. The Night Angels. Every Nightwalker both known and unknown to us will have to come together, only then will we be able to defeat Apep."

"Known and unknown?" Jackson echoed, that part of the statement somehow being what made the most impact on him. Battle he was used to. Joining other species in battle . . . while not a normal occurrence it had happened once or twice before. But how could there be unknown Nightwalkers?

"There is scripture, works in our vaults, that Odjit has been studying and trying to interpret. She was coming to believe there were twelve original Nightwalker nations. Or that at some point in the future there would be twelve. It was very unclear. But if they are out there we must find them because this is the god of chaos and destruction and his power is unlike anything we have ever thrown at one another. A rough beast has been born and he slouches toward us, Politic. Heed me . . . or discard me if you must. But whether or not you believe me, it *will* come."

Jackson sat back on his heels, sparing a glance up at Ahnvil and Ihron.

"I believe you," he said quietly. "What remains to be seen is whether or not you can be trusted. I will not turn my back on you in the name of a mutual enemy only for you to take the opportunity to slit my throat, as my friend did your mistress's. It is just the sort of justice you would seek, Templar."

Jackson pushed off of Kamen, grabbing up his clip as he made it to his feet. He shot the clip into place in the butt of the gun, then locked it in and chambered a round. He put on the safety and tucked it back into his waistband.

"Ahnvil," he said, turning his back on Kamen, "see to it our guest is given every comfort he doesn't deserve." Jackson put a hand on Ahnvil's arm to make sure the Gargoyle gave him his full attention. "He is not to be harmed, nor are we to treat him like he would have treated us. We're better than his kind for a reason. Have a care to remember that."

He saw the Gargoyle think about it for a moment, and it must have taken a great deal out of him to come to the right conclusion. It must be very difficult to fight the warring nature they had been born for, Jackson thought. But that thought was all he could spare for him. He took off across the lawn in the direction Diahmond had gone.

Marissa crept toward the men, feeling as though she were making far too much noise. She remained in the dark, though she realized that if their attention turned her way there would be no hiding from their extraordinary night vision. She envied it, especially after stubbing her toe on a rock. It would have been easier to follow the driveway, but it also would have been quite obvious as the sound of stones under her feet announced her arrival. She wasn't interested in becoming a part of what was happening. She wasn't foolish. She was mortal and they were quite a bit more hardy than she would be in an all-out battle with others of their ilk . . . namely Templars. And she had a feeling that was what this was about. Her heart was in her throat knowing Jackson was putting himself front and center for whatever was going to happen. Knowing him as she did, she knew he wouldn't let others take risks in his stead. She suspected Menes was made of similar stuff so that made them doubly foolhardy she supposed. Or brave. She would reserve opinion for after they got back to her in one piece.

She got close enough to see them clearly, keeping herself low to the ground against a nearby tree. She was probably just as ridiculous engaging in risky behavior as Jackson was, but she simply couldn't bring herself to wait behind safe walls without being able to know what was happening to him.

"Good god, Marissa Anderson, you are so damn stupid," she muttered to herself. Of course, she ignored her own logic, and her own warnings. None of that mattered to her as much as knowing Jackson was all right.

She saw them waiting, all attention forward, and wondered what it was they were waiting for. What did they know that she didn't? What could they see that she couldn't? For the first time she felt frustration and even anger over her human limitations. It was ridiculous if she thought about it. Two days ago she hadn't even known there was anything other than just human ability and sophistication out there. Now she was feeling just how insignificant the human species could be. Human hubris, their ideology that they were the be-all and end-all of intelligence in their part of the galaxy was now proved to be preposterous. What was more, it was proved to be so on their very own planet.

She saw a man break away from the group heading in her direction and she caught her breath. She was pretty sure it was Maxwell, and he probably was being sent to make sure she was safe and sound. But when he veered off away from the house she amended her thoughts. He was being sent to make certain Angelina was safe. The understanding that even in this highly volatile moment Jackson thought to protect her sister meant so very much more to Marissa than any declaration he had made to her thus far, and she had to admit those had been pretty damn compelling.

That was when she saw the figure coming up the drive, walking slowly and with some difficulty. She saw Jackson turn his back to him to say something in a hard tone to the Gargoyle next to him. She couldn't hear what it was, but it was clear Jackson was giving him a command. Then she saw him turn and—

He moved so fast he was like a streak of shadow. She saw him tackle the interloper with such force that she heard the echo of their connecting bodies. She gasped, rising almost to her full height before remembering herself and keeping low. She saw Jackson pressing his gun to the other man's face and his body language screamed with his desire to destroy the man beneath him.

"No," she breathed. "Oh god, Jackson, please don't."

The Jackson she knew would never harm an unarmed person . . . but he wasn't entirely the Jackson she had known any longer. But did Menes enhance or detract from the moral fiber she knew was so much a part of Jackson? She had already seen him kill, but that had been extraordinary circumstances and that individual had most definitely been intending to do them great bodily harm.

Marissa then saw the smaller of the three Gargoyles kneel to retrieve something from the ground, and then it turned and walked in her direction. Caught in the open, knowing she would be spotted, she froze and didn't know what else she could do but wait and face whatever condemnation was about to come her way. She stood up and the Gargoyle hesitated for a moment. That was when she realized it was female. She almost laughed with her incredulity. Why had she assumed that all Gargoyles were male? Why had it never occurred to her that there could be female counterparts?

And that was when she realized the Gargoyle held a human male in her arms. She cradled him like a child, as though he weren't a full-grown and very bulky

weight to carry. However, the limpness of his arm as it
hung free and the lolling of his head told her that he was
badly injured.

"Let's bring him into the light where I can see him,"
she said authoritatively. After all, she was very likely to
be the only doctor on the premises. She could be wrong,
but she wasn't about to wait and see when it was clear
someone was in imminent need of her. The Gargoyle
hesitated and Marissa got the feeling she was trying not
to look over her shoulder for some kind of permission
from Jackson. But it was clear they both knew it wasn't
going to be forthcoming anytime soon as Jackson dealt
with whoever it was that had brought the injured man.
The Gargoyle nodded to her at last and they hurried
back to the house.

As soon as she could she threw some light onto them.
"Put him down right here," she said, pointing to the
floor. The couch would only get in her way, and she was
fairly certain he was beyond complaining about creature comforts. The Gargoyle female knelt down and
laid her burden out on the floor. Marissa leaned over
the man and drew in a breath of shock. He was caked
in dried blood. So much so that it couldn't possibly be
all his own. There couldn't be any way he would be
alive if it were his own blood loss. Unless of course
he was like these other supernatural beings. God only
knew what it was they were capable of. A part of her
was fretting about leaving Jackson out there on his
own, as if her watching him from afar in the trees could
provide him with some sort of strength or a moral compass.

So she did her best to discard her concerns about
Jackson and focused on her patient.

"God, it's been a few years since medical school," she
muttered. "I need to wash away some of this blood. I
can't see a damn thing." She looked up at the imposing

figure of the female Gargoyle. She was in human form, but her skin was a dark gray sheet of stone and she had no doubt it felt like it as well. She didn't look like rough stone as she might have expected. In actuality it was more the smooth glassiness of highly polished marble. "Can you . . . I'm sorry your name is . . . ?"

"Diahmond, please," she said. And for some reason it surprised her to hear such a normal woman's voice coming from what was clearly such an extraordinary woman.

"Diahmond, can you bring me a lot of water and find some towels?"

"Yes, of course."

"This man needs a trauma room. You need to call 911 for me as well," she said as she gingerly tried to inspect the man for the source of the bleeding.

"I'm sorry. I can't do that. We must keep a very low profile here," she said by way of an apology when Marissa narrowed her eyes on her.

"I don't give a damn about your profile! This man needs help and I intend to see that he gets it."

"He needs a healer," Diahmond said just as stubbornly. "You will have to suffice until one can be brought here."

Marissa realized they were just wasting time arguing, so she nodded stiffly to the Gargoyle. Diahmond went quickly into the rear reaches of the house.

"Don't worry, my friend," she said in a whisper as she gingerly brushed at the blood scabbed thick over his eyes. "I will see to it you get the help you need."

She didn't expect a reply because he was completely limp with unconsciousness. He had black hair, she believed, but that was the only discernable trait. He was in a pair of boxer shorts and nothing else so he was cold to the touch. It was still too early in the spring for the nights to be anything close to warm. Diahmond returned quickly with a tub of water and some towels of varying sizes.

"We have to find his injuries so we can stop the bleeding." She didn't state the obvious, which was that they were looking at a catastrophic loss of blood. Much in the same way Jackson had assumed Leo Alvarez was dead by sheer volume of—

Marissa felt a cold finger of ice running down her spine. She took her towel to the man's face, wiping frantically to be able to distinguish—

"Leo!" Jackson slammed into the house and, seeing them on the floor, he hurried over to them and dropped to his knees. "Diahmond, we need a healer here ASAP."

"Already taken care of. I called Nané, but it will be several hours before she can get here."

"He won't last that long," Marissa said harshly. "Why won't you just take him to a hospital? Jackson, come on! I know how much he means to you!" It was evident in the way Jackson had reached to grip Leo's hand, the fear that was in his eyes that he, too, thought he might lose his friend.

"I want to . . . but we could never explain this and it would bring undue attention on us," Jackson hissed at her. "Don't think I'm not doing all I can! Nané can save him; modern medicine cannot. Look at him and tell me honestly if you think the medicine of the normal world will save his life! It's been two days since he went missing, Marissa. For two days he has been at the mercy of the Templars and god only knows what they've done to him in that time."

It was self-evident what they had done to him, but Marissa became subdued, biting anxiously at her lip as she tried to clean away some more of the blood. She began to find his injuries and—

"Oh my god," she exclaimed, horror lacing her words. Under all of that blood were furrows . . . gouges in his flesh, as though someone had taken a melon-baller to him and stripped him of chunks of his skin. Somehow they were in varying stages of healing . . . and none of it seemed to be a source of free-flowing blood.

"Kamenwati must have done a hasty healing job on him just to get him out of there. It didn't sound like there was much room for finesse," Jackson said tightly. But Marissa could see the burn in his eyes. She knew what he wanted most was to make the Templar who had done this to a man he loved as a brother and visit him in kind.

"Did he . . . did he do this? This Kamenwati?"

"Probably. Maybe . . ." Jackson prevaricated. "I don't know. Instinct tells me Kamen had a hand in it . . . although I have to admit, firsthand torture doesn't seem like his style. But he isn't above hiring the job out to another." There was hard contempt in his words and listening to him talk about the other man had her looking anxiously about.

"Where is he?"

"Ahnvil and Ihron have him. Let's just say they will keep him safe until we need him again."

"More torture?" she snapped at him, her blue eyes full of fire. "One person isn't enough?"

He blinked, looking incredibly surprised at her sudden release of ichor in his direction. Then he looked hurt. Really hurt. She knew it because he didn't jump down her throat with equal force, defending himself to the core. Instead he sighed and looked away from her.

"I thought you knew me better than that," he said, sounding so very lost. "But that's been your point all along, hasn't it? That we're strangers to one another. That perhaps it would be best to maintain the status quo." Then he was looking at her, the peacock blue and green of his eyes full of the fire of his temper, though he did not raise his voice. "But if I were to do that," he said tightly, "it will be you who next lies on this floor in a bath of blood and at that point there would be nothing I could do about it! Now you see? You see what can become of you if you go off on your own? Hate this place if you will, hate me if you will, but do yourself a favor, Dr. Anderson, and stay where I can help."

Because he couldn't bear being helpless, she thought, her throat tight with self-recrimination. She did know him better than this. She knew damn well he deserved much more respect from her than she was giving him.

"I'm sorry," she said softly to him, reaching out to cover the hand that held Leo's. "I'm sorry. You're right. I know that. And I do know you as well. Menes notwithstanding, you are a strong man with a great focus on doing what's right. And I should know after these past couple of days that there are things in this world of which you have a far better understanding than I do. Jackson, I'll take care of him until your help arrives. You know that I will and I know you know me and just how stubborn I can be."

By the time she said that last part his anger was visibly gone and he even spared her a small smile as he reached for a cloth and began to help her clean the blood away from his friend's wounds.

Kamenwati let Ahnvil shove him into the small bedroom. Judging by the size of the house and the grand appointments within it, it was probably intended as servant's quarters. Ahnvil shut the door, the rough stone beast shifting form from grotesque to human with a wide shrug of his shoulders, his wings collapsing to his back and then disappearing altogether. He did not, however, rid himself of his stone skin. Kamen might have told him there was no need for it, as he wasn't planning on battling him or escaping his present situation. No. Kamen was not always a fool. He knew he was, at present, in the safest place on earth.

But neither did he hold out much hope that they would be any match up against a god. Spell work had conjured him from the depths of obscurity, perhaps magic could reverse that. But even if there were an enchantment that could be applied to the situation, Kamen didn't know what it was. In the end that was what this would boil down to. Finding the spell to reverse his foul stupidity, and then finding magic users powerful enough to wield the spell and yet manage to keep themselves alive throughout the process.

But outside of himself and Odjit, he didn't know of anyone else strong enough. Perhaps Tameri, Odjit's powerful niece, but by his count she was only three weeks Blended. It would take much longer than that before Tameri's power had grown to full strength. And that was the problem with the Blending. While it was different for everyone, whether it went easy or hard, it left them very vulnerable . . . and often didn't reach full strength before they were hunted down and assassinated.

"Leave it to you," Ahnvil growled at him, "to loose hell on earth with no regard for the long term. That's the problem with you Templars. You're impulsive, shortsighted, and selfish. You care nothing for anything besides your personal agendas."

"Show me a single creature on this earth that does not crave. Show me one that will not go to great lengths to appease that craving, even if only to ignore it."

Kamen spoke quietly. He was stating fact, not defending his position. It didn't matter anymore what he felt, what he needed, or what he wanted. All that mattered was righting the wrong he had done. Oh, it could never make up for all the thousands of other wrongs he had committed throughout his many lives as he had allowed

Odjit to put blinders on him so that all he could see was her. Although it had not been her inasmuch as it was what she represented. He had been devoted to Odjit and the ideal he believed she stood for. To confess the ill in her would be to recognize the poison he himself had become by association.

He had only wanted unity. The scrolls decreed there must be unity among the Bodywalkers when Amun rose, or else he would be enraged and would punish them. Many scholars had found this on the most ancient papers in their vaults. Many believed that if there were unity then Amun would eagerly rise and bestow the afterlife on them. An end to this cursed living at last. All its violence, all its emotion, all its petty, scraping misery, all of it would be withdrawn from them and this time when they let go there would no longer be the agony of knowing they would have to do it all over again.

"Always with your justifications," Ahnvil growled at him, his large body making the room seem even smaller as he restlessly paced the length of it. Kamen knew very well what the Gargoyle thought of him, and he supposed he knew what Ahnvil would do to him if ever given permission to do so by Menes.

"Just the same, Gargoyle. It's just the same."

"What are you talking about?" Ahnvil barked irritably.

Kamen gave him a look and all Ahnvil could think right then was that there was utter emptiness in the eyes he was looking in. Not soullessness as he often enjoyed accusing his maker of, but literally a chasm . . . a void where there was nothing that mattered any longer. Nothing worth mattering.

"The bullet. Or, if you like, your hands around my throat. Or, if it pleases you to gut me stem to stern." Kamen drew a line down the front of his body, his finger brushing over bloodstained fabric. "Then as you like it. Death is death, whatever the method. Perhaps this time I will just stay in the Ether. I will wait there until Amun comes to us . . . and I will pray he will look at me and know all I ever wanted was for him to come for me and set me free. Don't you see?" He leaned forward in his chair, "You can devise no torture for me Gargoyle, that I am not already suffering. Fate has done the job far better than you ever could."

"Well, you don't mind if I try, do you?" Ahnvil sneered at him. "We all need our entertainments."

"I think you are going to have your fill of blood and war before this is over, Gargoyle. It will drain you of your friends, your loved ones and maybe even your life. Direct your rage and lust for the fight toward Odjit and the demon-god born inside of her. Think you she was bad? Think you she was powerful?"

Kamenwati laughed, the lowest of punctuations. Ahnvil had to consciously stop the shiver that walked up his spine. He had never heard anything so dead . . . so empty. That was when he realized that the physical form before him was merely a manifestation. There was no longer any substance to the man Kamenwati was. The chill, however, was because he found himself actually looking for the man of fire, the zealot he had always attributed to Kamenwati's makeup. It had been several generations now . . . about three hundred years since he had been Kamenwati's pet dog. Back then the man had been deadly in an almost beautiful sort of way. Kamen did one thing very well. He preached . . . and he lived what he preached. He toiled to understand what the gods wanted of him, and fought for what he thought was right when he came to a conclusion.

Ahnvil shook himself. No! He would not feel sorry for this man! He would engage in no empathy! The bastard had *enslaved* him!

He also gave birth to you . . .

With a savage growl, Ahnvil stormed out of the room, slamming the door behind him so hard that the wood cracked.

Kamen didn't move. Didn't react. He sat there, unraveling the centuries before himself, looking for all the things that had slipped past him . . . looking for how he had come so far from his own ideals. He didn't blame Odjit. That would be too easy. He made no mistake about where blame belonged.

Now, all he could do was rectify at least one small corner of the hell he had wrought.

Until then, he simply sat, and breathed, and waited . . .

CHAPTER SEVENTEEN

Some time later Jackson found himself sitting in a chair at Leo's bedside, watching him while he slept and, Nané reassured him, healed. After she had healed him she had said he was doing very well, considering the trauma he had gone through. Nané did what she did very well, her innate healing ability allowing her to bring Leo much further along. But her skills were only so strong and she had tired quickly. He had given her his leave once he knew Leo was out of danger and no longer in any pain.

He needed to go to Kamen and rip some answers out of the son of a bitch. He needed to know if this was his fault. Had they gone gunning for Leo to try to get to Jackson? Did they pursue his friend after the altercation in the woods and then put him through this horror because of him?

And he was thinking of putting Marissa in this kind of danger?

"Oh god, Leo, she's right. It's insane to tell her I care for her one minute and then the next throw her in the middle of this train wreck our lives have become. But when I think of moving into the future without her by my side, it devastates me in a way I never thought I could feel for anyone other than you and Docia. It would cut my heart out if I lost either of you. You're the closest thing Docia and I have to a brother . . . hell, Docia even tells people you're our brother when in casual conversation. It just doesn't occur to her that you aren't."

And it wasn't until that moment that he realized how much he had been missing Leo these past few weeks. Leo remembered nothing of the night Jackson had met death and reawakened as Menes's host, so he hadn't been able to discuss it with him. With his best friend and, yes, for all intents and purposes, his brother. And that had been hard. Keeping this secret, Jackson realized, had put Leo in jeopardy by not forewarning him he might have some dangers to face because of it.

"Jackson, please, stop."

Jackson startled, standing up and swinging around to see Marissa standing in the doorway. He hadn't even heard her, he who had this supernaturally acute hearing. He had been too wrapped up in his grief.

She moved over to him quickly, surprising him yet again when she wrapped her arms around him and hugged herself to him. His hands fell hesitantly on her shoulders. He wasn't quite used to this affectionate, warm side of her. She had always been so professional and crisp. It was funny, but he'd once fantasized about her . . . doing just this. Coming over to him and hugging him and telling him it was going to be all right.

"You aren't responsible for this," she said, her voice whisper-soft in his ear. "The evil that did this to him is responsible. Leo will know that, I suspect. He always struck me . . . well, I don't know him personally, but he's ex-military . . . a war veteran . . . so he knows."

"Yes, but will he understand why I now have to make friends with that evil?"

She pulled back. "You think that man did this?"

"I . . . don't know yet. I have to talk to him. And I have to talk to Leo."

"So talk." The gravelly command came from the bed and Jackson whipped around so fast he nearly pulled her off her feet. But he was reflexively holding her against him as he moved closer to the bed and leaned toward Leo.

"Dude, you look like shit," Jackson said frankly.

"At least *I* have an excuse," he said, chuckling gingerly. "What's yours?" It was clear he was sore and uncomfortable, and when he moved to sit upright, Jackson instinctively wanted to tell him to relax and just lie down . . . but he knew the reaction he'd get from Leo and how he himself would behave if the tables were turned. Leo was going to come out fighting, rushing to get back to himself . . . to be something other than a victim.

Luckily there was a trained psychiatrist in the room.

"Mr. Alvarez," she said sharply as she pulled away from Jackson. "You are far from well enough to bounce onto your feet and hit the ground running. Lay back down and heal," she said, pointing to the bed authoritatively.

"You know, that would be more compelling if I hadn't seen you snuggling with Officer Huggy Bear over here." Leo nodded toward Jackson.

"Would it be more compelling if I sat on your chest?" Jackson bit out. The last thing he needed was Leo making her feel self-conscious, even if it was just a defense mechanism on his part.

"No, but it would be compelling if *she* did." Leo chuckled again, finding himself genuinely funny. And Jackson had to admit, no one did a one liner or a potshot better than Leo did.

"Behave yourself. Do what the doctor says," Jackson said, reading the pain Leo was putting himself in by the white, tight lines around his lips and the clench of his jaw. "Besides, I need you to tell me what happened."

"Fine. I'll talk." But Leo would be damned if he would do it lying down in a bed. He'd been strapped down long enough, now he needed to move. Then he needed to get his desert eagle and stick the muzzle right down the throat of the prick bastard who had done this to him. "It was that kid. From when Docia disappeared. The Down syndrome kid."

"Andy?" Jackson was aghast with shock and horror as he remembered what Leo had looked like an hour ago.

That was when dizziness and his pal weakness paid Leo a visit, lecturing him about how much blood he'd lost. He gritted his teeth with anger, but stayed seated on the bed. He knew it wouldn't do him any good to stand up only to end up back on the floor again.

"Yeah, him. I turned my back on him because I thought he was harmless." He laughed, full of wry self-recrimination. "He jumped me and . . . he's a psychopath. A sadistic psychopath. I didn't even think it was possible. But I should have known better than to turn my back on anyone. Won't make that mistake twice, I'll guarantee you."

"Come on, Leo," Marissa scolded. "Down syndrome children and adults are some of the sweetest and more beautiful souls walking this earth. And because of their distinctive features it's like an instant trigger for us to not see them as a threat." She shivered visibly, rubbing at her arms. "My god. That poor baby has that kind of evil subjugating him? Isn't there any way you can get the Templar soul out?"

"Templar soul?" Leo echoed. "What the hell does that mean?"

"No," Jackson answered her. "At least, not that we've discovered." Then Jackson took a breath and said to Leo, "This is going to take a little bit of explanation."

* * *

"Holy shit" was Leo's response after a long minute of sitting in stunned silence. "You know, normally I would have called you insane for a story like that and rung up the crazy police to come get you," he said, his resignation evident in his tone. "But the truth is, after what I've just seen and experienced, I'm a believer." The last part came out of him in a bitter tone.

"I'm sorry, Leo," Marissa heard Jackson say softly. "Leo, I'm so goddamn sorry I put you in the middle of this. I think they were trying to get information on me; kidnapping you with the hope I'd beat the bushes frantically in a search for you and give myself away. I should have warned you. I should have confided in you."

"Listen, hotshot, before you start beating yourself up, I don't think that's why they came after me. I can tell you with a huge amount of certainty that this was revenge motivated. The South African prick who dragged me out of there told me as much." His mouth went tight around the edges. "And as much as I would love his head on a plate . . . it sounds like a better tactical advantage to keep him alive . . . for now anyway. No, I'm far more interested in dealing with that little fuck who holds the real Andy a prisoner in his own body."

"There's no way of changing it . . . the only way to get rid of Chatha is to kill the innocent kid," Jackson said gravely. And he raised a quick hand to silence Marissa with a finger on her lips. "I don't like it any more than you do, but there's no way of destroying one without destroying the other. The most we could do is . . ." He hesitated, and she could see how distasteful this was for him. "We could catch him and force-feed him a modern psychotropic drug. It's one of the only ways a Blending can be prevented and the only way it can be reversed. Modern mental health meds act like a trap, numbing the Bodywalker inside from being able to access the host's mind and body. It's like a paralysis. We can see and hear everything, but can't so much as move a muscle."

"That sounds horrible," she said, disgust over the whole situation climbing up from her belly and into her throat. She swallowed when the urge to throw up swam over her. "But it also sounds like the perfect prison for Chatha. If we can retrieve Andy, keep him here under our control, he could return himself to normal."

"Only, he's been trapped all this time . . . seeing and hearing, a witness to heinous acts and crimes. It could be there's nothing left of the original's psyche after all of that," Jackson said.

"Well, it's at least something to try," she snapped at him, reaching a level of frustration that couldn't be contained. "God! Why can't you people just stay in that Ether of yours and just leave us alone!"

She watched Jackson's entire demeanor change, his jaw clenching as he obviously bit back a sharp retort. Instead he took a breath in slowly to calm himself a little. "Some of us would," he said tightly. "But that existence, that never-ending numbness, can drive a soul mad. We may be incorporeal, but still have all our human urges. To live, to laugh, to love. What right do you have to say we don't deserve that? We should stay in purgatory indefinitely? Do you know what that's like? Do you know what it's like to love someone with everything that you are and be this close to them and unable to fucking touch them? No. Clearly you don't. You don't know a damn thing about it because you're so afraid of losing your precious damn self-control that it's completely starved you of any goddamn empathy." He turned to Leo while she stood there with her mouth open in shock. "Sorry, Leo. I'll come back later."

He brushed past her and left the room, slamming the door in his wake and making her wince.

"Oh man, has he got it bad," Leo drawled, moving to

lean back against the headboard. She could tell he was wearing out. She knew she should let him rest, but that remark compelled her to stay.

"What do you mean?" she asked warily, not sure she wanted to hear the answer.

"Seriously? How can you not see it? He's more than a little crazy about you, Doc. He has been for a while."

"For . . . a-a while?" This was Jackson's best friend. His confidant. If anyone would know anything personal about Jackson and his feelings on a subject it would most likely be this man. "You're mistaken. He only just . . . it's because he wants me to die or whatever and let his queen come and take me over," she said with no small amount of bitterness entering her tone.

"Yeah? And what about the past year when he's been mooning over you from afar? Doesn't that count? I mean sure, he never crossed the line . . . You know," he added thoughtfully, "maybe it was more like a year and a half. Yeah. That's it. You've been here two years, right?"

"Well I—yes but I . . ." She nervously licked her lips. "Did he tell you that?"

"Did he ever say it to me straight out? Not on your life. He'd have died first before admitting he wanted something he couldn't have. Oh. Hey. There ya go," he said, smirking at her. "He did die first before admitting to it."

Marissa blanched, the understanding making her heart race like she was on some kind of thrill ride. "Because," she said a bit breathlessly, "we worked together."

"Yeah. And this is a small town with a small precinct. People talk. So Jacks kept his mouth shut and respected you enough to keep his hands to himself. But I guess all that doesn't matter anymore." Leo paused as he eyed the shirt she was wearing. Jackson's shirt. "So I'm assuming he's making up for lost time. Dead queen or no dead queen, you're very special to him Marissa. If you weren't he would have gone after you with all his barrels blazing. He would have taken you to bed, scratched his itch as it were, and be on his way shortly after. It's what he's done all of his life. Has been ever since his parents died anyway. He doesn't like to get too close to people. He doesn't want to cope with any more loss if it can at all be avoided."

Of course. *Of course*, her mind cried out, forcing her to resist the urge to smack her palm to her forehead. *What the hell kind of a shrink are you, Marissa Anderson?* It was one of the reasons why he had taken losing Chico so hard. And the reason why he'd gone ballistic when Docia had died. It must have just about killed him to walk into Leo's place and see all that blood, thinking his best friend was most certainly dead. Christ, and all she'd been doing was worrying about protecting herself.

"You're going to want to go after him now," Leo prompted her.

"Yes. Yes I am," she said absently. "You rest and I'll . . ." She didn't finish because she was already hurrying after Jackson.

In the bed, Leo chuckled. *At least something good might come out of this,* he thought. Leo wasn't feeling so hot, but preferred not to get comfortable. The pain would keep him awake for a while. Maybe that would protect him from the nightmares he knew were going to come for him. It had happened in the war. It had happened three years back in Nicaragua. It most certainly would happen again.

Damn.

He would have killed for some cold hard Jack Daniel's right about then.

*   *   *

Why is this house so damn big? she thought with frustration as she searched for Jackson. She didn't find him in his room or the kitchen or the main living areas, and she wasn't about to poke into rooms she didn't belong in. It had been wrong of her to do so the first time. She had known that but she had let her temper get the best of her . . . just like she had done now.

He was right. She did try to keep her emotions in check. She had thought it made her a better psychiatrist, more professional, able to see a bigger picture rather than getting mired down in the emotions of her patients. What it had done was completely desensitize her to anyone and everything save her sister. Maybe she would have noticed . . .

"Jackson?" she called, venturing out onto the deck and the moonlit night. She didn't know where the switch was, so she was hoping the moon would provide enough light to find him if he was there.

"Nope. Too busty to be Jackson."

"Oh! I'm sorry," she said to the woman sitting in the shadows.

"Don't be. You don't have the same ability to see in the dark as we do," Diahmond said. "There's not much in the way of privacy in a house with this many people in it."

"I don't know how everyone does it. I think I'd go mad if I didn't have some sense of privacy."

The Gargoyle regarded her for a moment, her eyes—a cool gray that could be seen in the moonlight almost as if they were aglow—moving over her briefly. "It's the life of a royal," she told her, almost pointedly. "It's a price you pay for the good of your people. You bear with all the fuss and limitations it puts on your freedom because the people and their well-being means more to you than yours does. It takes a very special sort of person to be able to make that kind of sacrifice."

Call her crazy, but Marissa got the feeling Diahmond didn't think she fit that bill. She shrugged internally. What did she care what the Gargoyle thought of her?

"You don't like me very much, do you?" she asked her, moving farther out into the night, turning her face up to the moon. She had to admit, the night wasn't necessarily a bad thing to wake up to. It was cool and crisp and full of curious sounds.

"I am merely at a loss to understand you. That is all."

"What is so perplexing? That I won't readily alter my life away so I can share it with someone else whom I hardly know anything about?"

"What would you like to know about her that could possibly change your mind?"

Ouch. Two points to the Gargoyle. The way she had said it implied there were circumstances she might approve of. Had she really meant it to sound that way?

"What is she like, your queen? I'm assuming you know her . . . you sound like you do."

"I don't know her half as well as her husband does. If he cannot convince you of her worth, then what can I say to convince you? I will not argue with you or wheedle with you, mortal girl. You do not understand this world, and I see that you fear what you don't understand."

Zing. Four points total. Wow. She hadn't lost a battle of wits like this in ages. And never so resoundingly.

"What's to understand," Marissa said petulantly. "I die. She lives. Period."

Diahmond smiled. "So simple. Yet so complex. Each Bodywalker comes equipped with a special ability. My lord pharaoh is telekinetic. Ramses can control the weather. Do you know what hers is?"

"I don't . . ." Marissa said a bit lamely.

"Empathy. Emotions, mortal girl. She feels what others feel so keenly, that sometimes all that keeps her balanced is the man you are looking for now. Menes. Jackson. Call him what you will. Now, do you know what I fail to understand?"

"Do tell," Marissa invited dryly.

"Here you have this proposition laid before you . . . a man who loves you and wants you to do something that will increase his passion for you a thousandfold. He has chosen you—I can only assume he sees something of worth in you—over every other woman in the world. And if you think he makes this choice lightly you would be terribly mistaken, so know that now. The last time he was sent to choose for her it took him eleven years before he found someone he deemed worthy enough. Do you know what that must have done to him? To wait so long? This man has offered you something that will make you stronger, make your senses keener, and will add untold amount of time to your life. I'm not saying it doesn't have its pitfalls. It does. And to say otherwise would insult your intelligence. I don't know you but I'm assuming you have some."

All right, now that one was just low, Marissa thought with a sigh.

"Here he offers you this, and then on top of all of that . . ." she said, leaning forward and resting her elbows on her knees, "a love for all time. A love of the ages. Something no mortal woman on earth can lay claim to. A relationship with no doubt. No questioning. No insecurity. I know this because I have seen it. I have seen it through two incarnations. It mattered not how long it was . . . they live lifetimes with every single day. They live more in a week than you or I can know how to do in years. I would give my right arm to know even an hour of what they have, and yet you cast it off as though something better will come along. That is the trouble with you humans. You never thrill in the now, always you grasp for the future."

"But I . . ." Marissa trailed off, not knowing what she could really say to argue with her except the one clear truth. "I'm afraid of dying," she said softly.

"Ah." Diahmond seemed to think on that for a moment. "I die every single day," she said. "The sun touches me and claws the breath from my body, turning my lungs to stone before the rest of me follows suit. Oh, I logically know I will awaken with the night . . . but I also know that I am helpless until then . . . that a bulldozer or sledgehammer can be applied to me and there is nothing I will be able to do to defend myself. I die every single day. I suffocate, and I fear. So yes, I do understand. But at least you are guaranteed to come back this time. How many others on the earth can say the same . . . including me? And of those few . . . those chosen few . . . how many of them know about it in advance?"

Marissa stood quietly, not knowing what to say. She had never considered any of these things. All she had been focused on was whether Jackson cared for her because of what she was . . . or because of what she could become. And if she'd been unsure of that, she certainly wasn't anymore. After all, how many hoops did he have to jump through to convince her? When would it be enough? Maybe the problem wasn't with her doubting him . . . but just with her not being able to believe someone could really feel that way about her.

"Excuse me," she said. But before entering the house she hesitated. "Thank you," she said to the Gargoyle. "Your mistress is very lucky to have you in her corner. Very rarely have I seen anyone talk about their faith in another person with so much conviction. I suppose . . . people come to me with their troubles, talk about all the dark things in their lives. It's so easy to listen to that day in and day out and begin to think . . . begin to think that there really is no such thing as a good relationship.

And that's unfair," she amended quickly, to herself as much as to Diahmond, "because there is a very beautiful person in my life and my relationship with her, while trying at times, is one of the healthiest and most wonderful I know. I am very stupid for not realizing that as much as I should. Maybe . . . maybe I'm so stupid I haven't realized you can't have the good if you aren't willing to go through the bad."

Diahmond smiled at her softly. "Maybe there's hope for you after all," she said, clearly teasing her.

"Maybe," she agreed with an answering smile.

She went into the house, and suddenly realized her heart was pounding and an exhilarating mix of fear and excitement was bleeding through her. She wasn't looking for Jackson anymore, although she would find him next. No. There was someone else she needed to see first before she could even allow her mind to think the frightening exciting things it wanted to think. She ran out of the house and into the darkness, following the drive around toward the guesthouse. She stumbled on the steps, her anxious feet putting themselves all wrong as she neared her goal. She knew that once she crossed this threshold there was a chance she would be leaving a completely different person. Someone braver than she ever had been before. Someone who wasn't acting at being strong, but really was strong on the inside and the out.

"Lina!" She slammed the door behind her and hit the lights. After all, she wasn't a supernatural creature yet.

Yet . . .

The word was so terrifying.

"Crazy," she muttered to herself. "You're crazy. Even your crazy sister is going to tell you this is crazy," she said as she burst into Angelina's bedroom, waking her with a start.

CHAPTER EIGHTEEN

"This is so cool!" Angelina cried after her sister dumped the entire story of what had been happening, what was happening, and what she was actually considering doing into her sister's lap. After all, she couldn't do any of this without her. She couldn't give up her sister as well as daylight and her job and everything else.

"It's not cool, it's insane!" Marissa argued breathlessly. "You need to tell me it's insane!"

"Look," Lina said dryly, "if you came here wanting *me* to be the voice of reason, then clearly you don't really want to be talked out of this."

Well, she had a point there.

"I guess I don't," she confessed aloud, as if it were a dirty little secret that shouldn't be spoken of, because saying it made it real. "But what about the whole dying part? I mean, surely . . ."

"You're looking at it all wrong," Lina said, her eagerness almost infectious. "It's not dying, it's . . . it's . . . metamorphosis. You're a pretty, fuzzy warm little caterpillar . . . and when you take this step you'll be this magnificent, powerful, beautiful butterfly that will be so deeply loved and . . . oh, I'm so jealous I could spit! The only thing that kind of sucks is the sunlight part. I don't know what I'd do if I couldn't see the world in daylight every day." Then she shrugged. "But from the sound of it you'll be able to see in the dark almost as if it were daylight, so maybe it won't really matter. Anyway . . ." She looked down at the bedspread and tugged at the fabric a little. "Anyway, it'll be nice knowing that you're safe, you'll be happy, and that I won't lose you anytime soon. From the sound of it you'll potentially outlive me."

"Believe me, some of those things are the ones I question. But . . . I'm realizing something. These people here are in pieces right now. With Jackson only just now becoming fully Blended, coming here to take on the reins of his government, they've been without the leaders they depend on for a very long time. Especially her. She only lived a week, as I understand it, before the Templars got to her last time. That means it's been almost two hundred years since they were truly together." She sighed in tandem with her sister. It really was terribly romantic, the idea of two souls striving for centuries for the opportunity to simply be with each other. To be able to touch one another. It made it easy to understand why Menes's grief had outweighed his sense of duty to his people when he had lost his bride after only a few days. "And provided I can keep out of reach of the Templars, I could maybe help."

"Think about it," Lina said eagerly. "You're a psychiatrist! Who better to have an empathic ability? How are you going to do it? Bullet to the brain? Or poison, like Cleopatra, dying in beautiful repose." She laid back in the bed, one arm thrown dramatically over her head.

"Okay, it really creeps me out that you are excitedly talking about my suicide." Marissa frowned. "I don't know. I hadn't thought that far ahead. I mean the bullet thing . . ." She shuddered. "No. It might be fast but . . . no. I think I'll stick with the poison idea. Write myself a script for some heavy-duty sleep meds. I guess I have to talk to Jackson about it. I don't know what the rules are here. Oh my god, I'm really doing this." Marissa felt her throat clench tight even as the rest of her squirmed with excitement. "Provided he still wants me." She sighed. "I haven't been very nice to him."

"He'll forgive ya. They always do."

"What if . . ." she began.

"Oh stop thinking and for once in your life just do," her sister said with sudden vehemence. "Do what you really want to do and stop analyzing it. Stop trying to control it. Just . . . stop."

Marissa took a breath and nodded. Angelina smiled and, wrapping her arms around her sister's neck, hugged her tight. "Now . . . drop dead."

She sniggered and Marissa pushed her away with a laugh, getting up and smoothing her skirt. "All right," she said. "Here goes nothing . . . and everything. This is me, just doing. Going with those instincts and emotions and . . ."

"Leave!"

"Oh fine," Marissa said, sticking her tongue out at Lina, dissolving their maturity completely back to when they'd been kids, making fun and teasing each other. Then she took another breath and hurried out of Lina's bedroom and out of the guesthouse.

She found him rather unexpectedly as she was approaching the house around the southwest corner of the building. Actually she heard his voice first and the sentence that hit her ears made her freeze in her tracks.

"I know you need to get to bed, Max, but I need you to do me a favor and bring Sargent back to the SPD. Tell them . . . just tell them he's going to need a new trainer," he said, his tone low and his words tight with the emotion he was refusing to show. "Tell them that I had to move away due to an unexpected family crisis that won't resolve itself anytime soon. I'll write a resignation letter to make it official and have one of the Gargoyles send it from another state. Just in case they are looking for me. In a few weeks Leo can go home and make them understand that he's not dead and I had nothing to do with it."

"Jackson, no!" she burst out, unable to control herself due to her outright shock.

Jackson turned slowly, his eyes sweeping to hers, the anger in them hard and very evident. He didn't say a word, just pointedly turned his back to her to speak to Max once more. "He's to travel in the cabin of the jet, Max. Don't crate him and put him in the hold."

"I wouldn't do that," Max said, clearly protesting the idea that Jackson thought he might.

"I know. It just . . . needed to be said. I had to make sure."

"Jackson!" She barked his name out as she marched up to his side. When he didn't acknowledge her she shoved herself between the two men and grabbed him by his shirt, wishing she could shake him. "You cannot give up that dog! What are you thinking? You know how much he means to—"

"What I know," he bit off into her face, "is that someone just reminded me that anyone and anything near me risks themselves just by knowing me. Someone reminded me that what I am turns an innocent soul into a target, brings stress and heartache and horrible things into the life of that innocent. So excuse me, but I'll be damned if Sargent is going to get himself killed while trying to protect me from a supernatural creature he has no defense for! And he's been trained for a job that he loves. That he's eager for. This is me being unselfish, Marissa. But I can see why you wouldn't recognize it."

All right, Marissa thought with irritation, just when had she become the designated asshole in the house?

Everyone was taking these mean little potshots at her and she'd had just about enough of it.

"Don't you dare fault me for taking the time to understand and evaluate something before jumping in with both feet! And you!" She whirled to face Max who was trying to discreetly leave the argument. She pointed to the ground and let out an imperious, "Stay!" Max went still, lifting a brow in curiosity and Sargent's butt hit the ground in a very obedient staying position. "If I'm going to be queen around here, I'm going to expect to be fully . . . and I mean *fully* . . . informed of any important decisions! I'm not going to be a figurehead or something pretty sitting on a throne while all the big strong men take care of all the business." She whipped back around to face Jackson. "I don't know what Hatshepsut's feelings are on the subject, but I suspect all this high-handed bullying bullshit doesn't fly with her, and it doesn't fly with me either. So with the both of us together you're in for a major attitude adjustment. We aren't going to put up with it!"

She stopped talking, breathing hard and glaring at Jackson as her temper started to cool. She hadn't noticed his eyes going wide, hadn't noticed the slight slack in his jaw.

"Did . . ." He cleared his throat of an unidentifiable emotion. "Did you just say *we?*"

She could have knocked him on his ass with a feather, that was how numb with shock Jackson was. Surely she didn't mean . . . ? Yes, he thought quickly before he got his hopes up, she was just speaking hypothetically.

"Yes, I said we, provided you can quit being an ass long enough to kill me. And what's the deal with that anyway? The rules, I mean. Can I just overdose or lick mustard off a spoon or . . . what are the rules to this dying thing, because I know there has to be rules and you can damn well bet I'm going to get it right."

"Oh my god." It was all he could think of to say. He knew he was staring at her, knew he was looking like an ass because he couldn't form a single coherent thought in his head about what to do next. He couldn't because his heart was racing with fear and excitement. Fear that he was dreaming, excitement that he wasn't.

"Jackson," she said dryly, "when a woman offers to kill herself for you she kind of expects a little more than 'Oh my god.'"

"Oh my fucking god," he shouted at her right before letting every single impulse flowing through him loose. He grabbed for her with both hands, dragged her up against his chest, wrapping her in a suffocating hug while crushing her mouth under his. He kissed her as hard and as deep as he dared, overjoyed to feel her whole body softening and relaxing, her lips parting to allow him to do ravishing things to her mouth. He kissed her so long and so intensely that he thought he was getting light-headed from lack of oxygen. When he finally pulled back from her it was to her smiling eyes, watching her lick her lips clean of their mutual flavors.

"Max, you can go now," she said, dismissing the man with a wave but never once looking away from Jackson. "Back at the house, *not* on a plane. Understood?"

"Yup." Max chuckled and headed off with Sargent in tow.

"I can't believe," Jackson stammered, still not knowing what to say. "Are you one hundred percent . . . ?"

"Are you ever going to finish your sentences?" she teased him.

"My god, I'm going to kill you," he said fiercely, wanting to shake her for taking delight in his flabbergasted state.

"Well, that's kind of the idea, right?"

In lieu of shaking the hell out of her he yanked her back up against himself. This time it was she who leapt for the kiss, meshing her mouth to his as if they were a single being, then breaking again and again as each successive contact grew hotter and hotter and faster. Before he knew it she was climbing up his body, arms wrapping around his head and neck and legs wrapping around his waist. It took four blind, heated steps before he found the side of the house and slammed her up against it, following hard with the press of his body. God. Oh god, what was it about her that made him want to forget every nicety he'd ever learned as a lover and just . . . fuck her crazy. And then take her slower, sweeter, afterward. But it was always this first. This hunger. This rapacious need to just be inside her however he could manage it and as soon as was humanly possible.

Together they pulled up her skirt, his hands running hot beneath it and letting her fill them with soft, sleek flesh. Her backside was curvy enough to earn the title "booty," but it was always played down with the sharp lines of professional clothing. Sexy yet conservative. The kind of conservative sexy that made you want to un-conservative her. Unwrap her. Undo her. Just as he was coming undone, he realized. Not just the way she was feverishly working to open his jeans and push them down off his hips, but just undone. If she knew how devastated he had been when she'd said those things to him earlier . . . even now it choked him to think of her wishing he'd actually died. Because that was what it had been. If not for Menes, he would have died. Of course, if not for Tameri saving his sister he wouldn't have even been in that place and time, but that was splitting hairs.

And that didn't matter now. With one hand on her backside he reached to take himself in hand and aimed himself in the direction he desired to go. He notched himself against her and, gripping her hard to keep her still, he lunged up into her in a single, stunning thrust. She broke from his mouth to cry out, her hands reaching for his hair, grabbing it up into her fists and doing everything but pulling. He didn't pause, didn't wait. He had no time for that. He was completely blindsided by the knowledge that he could come in just a couple more strokes. He didn't understand it really. He had no experience with which to judge this desperation. He'd always been in total control of his relationships, headlong feelings and undue attachments not anything he'd ever indulged in or craved.

He was just as bad as she was, he realized. He was the pot and she the kettle. At least she had an excuse. A bid to be more professional. What was his reasoning? *It was just safer that way*, he thought. And there was nothing safe about this. For all they would be immortal and nearly unbreakable, this was akin to taking his life in his hands. Or giving it into hers. And god, but it terrified him.

But it didn't keep him from taking her hard right then and there, both of them moaning with pleasure loud enough to be heard . . . well, just about anywhere. He wished he could make himself be self-conscious about that. Make himself show her more respect than he felt he was doing just then, but he couldn't. Didn't. Wouldn't.

All he could do was thrust himself into her again and again, as fast as he could humanly manage, sucking air in through his teeth when the urge to climax grabbed him by the balls and ripped through him. It happened so fast. So blindingly fast. And it pulled out of him until it hurt. He was barely aware of the fingernails dug deep into his shoulders, or the way she gasped to catch her breath, or the way she was like liquid in his arms and against the wall.

The wall.

Holy hell! He'd just taken her against the side of the damn house! In *public*! Well, nearly anyway. He knew no one would have dared come in the direction of the ruckus they'd just made. In that way, he realized, it was damn good to be the king.

"Death by sex," she breathed into his ear. "Oh yes. I hadn't considered that one."

That made him snort a laugh out his nose. Sometimes she just tickled the heck out of him. Like the time she'd taken umbrage with Howard Redman's lewd assessment of her ass every single time she walked past his desk. Any other woman might have found another path. But not his Marissa. She had leaned over the desk, he could swear she was purposely giving him a peep down her blouse, and had whispered very loudly that what he was doing was called sexual harassment and that the department had a zero-tolerance policy and that he better be careful before some gutsy pissed-off chick decided to sue him right down to his saggy, baggy little boxer shorts.

"Now, Mr. Redman," she'd said, "if you want to talk about the inadequacies you are feeling that are compelling you to behave this way, you know my door is always open."

And Jackson had just about died laughing, along with the rest of the bullpen. Redman hadn't said a single word to her since then.

That's right. You don't mess with my woman.

"There are easier ways," he said breathlessly. "Although, none more fun. And there are rules," he agreed with her assumption. "You can't blow yourself up or cut off your head. It has to be something that, had it been a little less serious, modern medicine might have saved you."

"No beheading. Check."

"Although, it's a classic."

He looked around, double-checking that they were alone. But he knew that wouldn't last with such a big household moving around the place. The Gargoyles patrolling the grounds would catch them soon enough and he absolutely did not want to embarrass her. When Hatshepsut was on board it might be different, but right now he had potentially more fragile sensibilities to worry about. He moved himself out of her, the feel of leaving her bittersweet, the night air cold on his hot, wet flesh. He realized she was probably cold, half naked in little more than his shirt. He reached for the hem of her skirt, pulling it down over her backside.

"I suppose you have a particular method chosen?" he said, trying to ease her back onto her feet but finding himself thwarted by the persistent vise of her thighs. He looked into her eyes, raising a brow.

"I told you I prefer death by sex. But if you aren't willing to help a poor girl out, well, then you're not the man I thought you were," she said, amusement written across her kiss-swollen lips.

He caught up her mouth with his, kissing her slow and dark, deep and beautiful. It was, he thought, the most delicious kiss of his whole life.

"Being a doctor," she breathed softly against his mouth when he lifted away from her for a moment, "I think an overdose is best. Just . . . a cocktail of the right pills and I fall asleep. Before you know it I'm in the . . . what'd you call it?"

"Ether."

"What's it like? Is it like it sounds? All misty and foggy?"

"In a way, yes. Mostly, it's . . . very quiet. It's void of anything except our souls brushing against each other, only half of the time able to connect in some way. It's very intimate, being up there all together, existing only as consciousness and emotion. It's very exposed and yet very lonely."

"It sounds lonely," she agreed. "I'm glad I'm not staying very long. And by the way, how long does this whole thing take?"

"For however long it takes you to die, Marissa. Once you are pulled into the Ether, Hatshepsut will meet you instantly. She will know you are for her. I wish I could explain the why and the how of it, but I can't. It's just the way it is."

"As long as you're sure she'll like me enough to . . . well, what if she doesn't? I mean, we can't just say 'oops' here." She reached with her soft fingers to brush his mussed hair into whatever order it was that made sense to her.

"She'll like you. She trusts me implicitly to know her and her needs. She trusts me to send her perfection."

"Perfection?" She dropped her gaze. "I think after all of this we both should know my 'perfection' is an illusion. I'm not perfect. Not even close."

"You're perfect for us," he said. "And that's all that matters. There is no other choice, Marissa. Not for us. We don't want anyone else but you."

That made her soft smile return and she looked at him again.

"Then let's get this show on the road!" she said.

"Yeah, about that. You think I could pull my pants up first?"

She laughed, the sound of it echoing into the cold New Mexico night.

CHAPTER NINETEEN

"That's the last of them," she said, her hand trembling as she put the glass of water down by the empty pill bottles. She nervously licked her lips and then straightened the collar of yet another one of his shirts against her throat.

"Come and sit back," he invited her, patting the bed beside him. He was sitting back against the headboard, where an empty pillow was waiting for her.

She slid over to him, the cotton sheet and its remarkably smooth thread count feeling incredibly soft. She curled up against him.

"I'm so scared I'm nauseous," she said as she wrapped her arms tightly around him and hugged herself to his warmth and strength. "Or maybe that's the medication. I've never swallowed that many pills all at once before."

"I don't blame you for being scared. And I'm not going to tell you not to be. This is your process and you are going to go through it any way you want to. It's not every day you get to commit suicide."

"I know. And I'm warning you now, if this gets messed up I'm coming back to haunt you. And I'm going to be a jealous ghost. I'm going to be there especially when you try to touch someone else."

He smiled. She could feel the way his lips moved

against her scalp and hair. How strange that every feeling, every sensation seemed so incredibly acute. She was noticing the way he smelled. Clean and freshly showered. They'd gone in together, bathed together, made love together. Then he had donned a clean pair of jeans and she had put on a clean shirt. But it was still his. It felt, she thought, like being covered by him. The touch of cotton against the hairs of her body was like a petting touch all over all at once. Her legs and feet were bare. She hadn't even put on any underwear. Just his shirt.

"What will we do first? When I come back?" she asked.

He chuckled. "I'm thinking sex might be involved. That seems to be the way of it lately."

"You're probably right." She smiled up at him, tipping her head back so she could see the peacock green of his eyes. "After all, we kind of had over a year of long-distance flirting, however subconscious it might have been."

"True." He drew soft fingers along the side of her face, drawing on her as though tracing her image. "Can you try to remember something for me?" She nodded. "Just be yourself. When you meet her? She's not a pharaoh. She's not a figure of a larger than life romance. And she's not even a Bodywalker when she's there. She's at the purest form of her soul, and she will want to know you on the same level. She won't expect more than you can give. She won't try to bully you or subjugate you. That doesn't interest her. Next to her relationship with me, her relationship with you is going to mean everything to her."

"That's . . . it's comforting to hear you say that," she confessed. "I'm still nervous as hell." She glanced down at her hand, rubbing her fingers together. They were starting to feel a little numb and she felt the first hint that she was being affected. She'd never tried recreational drugs, but the sensation lapping like a soft tide throughout her face and body was probably what getting stoned felt like. Suddenly she wished she knew.

"I've never been drunk. I should have done that," she observed. "I don't suppose a Bodywalker gets drunk?"

"No. We process the alcohol too quickly. It's fun to try. Sometimes if you work hard at it you can catch a good buzz."

"That's what I have at the moment. A good buzz." She was silent for a moment, focusing inward to the sensations walking sluggishly through her. "Promise me something? If something goes wrong—"

"It won't," he said sharply. "I'm not promising you a damn thing until you come back and make me."

"Okay." She paused for a beat. "But you'll take care of Lina, right? So that she's safe? She needs a keeper, you know."

"I got that feeling," he agreed dryly. "And we'll take care of her together. We'll keep her here with us and try to keep her from getting into too much trouble."

"Ihron. Or no, better yet, Ahnvil. He's big and strong and damn serious. She needs some seriousness to countermand her special kind of crazy." She smiled, thinking of all the things Lina had done over the years. In a way she had been jealous of her sister. She just threw herself into her every passion, chased after anything if it seemed interesting enough, and dug her feet in for whatever cause she deemed justified her loyalty. Marissa had spent her entire life trying to be what was expected of her. Trying to be the steady. The rock. And now, suddenly, here she was doing the craziest thing of all, outstripping her sister.

"I'll make sure she gets an appropriate bodyguard."

"Not Max," they said in unison. She laughed, the sound resonating muzzily and warmly inside of her, clearly an effect of the drugs wending their way through her system.

"No," he agreed. "I think Max likes her a little too much. We'll find someone else for her daytime endeavors. Although she might find herself becoming more nocturnal if she hangs around us constantly." He paused for a moment. "You're feeling it, aren't you?"

"Yes I . . . can you tell?"

"Your pupils are dilating. Come now, rest your head, and close your eyes. You'll just go to sleep."

She hoped so. She had seen some drug overdoses in the past. They didn't always go quietly and peacefully. She didn't want him to suffer while she went away from him. She just wanted to go to sleep and then wake up in his arms exactly the way she was.

"I feel like Juliet," she whispered. "But I hope we won't end up as tragic as that."

"No. I'm going to wait for you."

"You did this, didn't you?" she asked him suddenly. "You said something before . . . you killed yourself when you lost her last time, didn't you?"

He was silent for a long moment, his breath warm in her hair and against her scalp. "I couldn't bear living without her after waiting so long to touch her again. And then she was with me . . . and we had a week. Just one week in two hundred years. A hundred before and a hundred after. I don't know why it takes us so long to come back, but it does. And then suddenly it's like our eyes are opened, and we can sense souls that are leaving the living world as they brush against the Ether. Then we reach out and grab hold of them and we come back if they agree to live with us."

"It's almost unfair, to ask someone if they want to die or live with you. Does anyone ever choose against you?"

"All the time. Or we realize we aren't going to be

compatible souls. There are no absolutes. I think you've learned that lately."

She yawned and nodded. She felt herself drifting. Almost floating and spinning.

"Jackson?" she said softly.

"Mmm?"

"I'm going now."

"Yes, love, I know. I'll be here waiting for you."

"Okay," she said.

And then she fell asleep.

Blue. The misty fog of the Ether was the most beautiful cerulean blue. Like a vast fluffy ocean, mist scudding to and fro. She felt as though she were in her own body, living, breathing, touching, and feeling, but she knew she had no substance. It was just her. No frills. No clothes. No words to define herself as a woman or a professional. All of that didn't matter anymore. All that mattered was finding Hatshepsut and going back to Jackson.

"I am here," a soft, dulcet voice said, the accent so beautiful and rich with a culture completely alien to her. "I am here. Has Menes sent you to me then?" An apparition appeared in the form of a tall, dark-skinned and dark-haired woman. Her hair was dressed up in braids, coarse beads woven within. "Have you come to give yourself over to me? Will you let me show you a new life and a new world?"

It was odd how off-puttingly dramatic it sounded. Was this the woman, the soul Menes loved? Now that she was incorporeal, all she had was the senses of her soul, and something told her the woman before her was not complementary to her. It felt wrong. So when the woman reached out for her she pulled back and moved away.

"What's wrong with you, mortal female? If you do

not accept me and bring me to my king you will die. You will not come back to the man your heart broadcasts love for."

"I . . ." It was weird speaking without a mouth, lips, and tongue to do so. It was more an emanation of thought, like telepathy. "I don't believe you!" she burst out. "You cannot be the woman that man professes to love!"

She smiled then, softening her approach. "I am sorry. I have been here so long and my last lifetime was not a good one. I didn't wish to be born again. But Menes has talked me into it. Now come. Touch your soul to mine and we will fulfill this love story you so aspire to. I will let you know how a queen should be revered and how a king should beg for her love."

She reached for her again and Marissa wavered with indecision. If she refused this woman she would lose her life. She would lose Angelina and Jackson and everything that meant anything to her. She will have let go of all of it for nothing. She didn't see what choice she had. Perhaps, with time, Hatshepsut wouldn't seem so harsh. So . . . cold and autocratic. But Jackson had told her that the Ether made things feel strange. Perhaps she was making harsh judgments because she was still scared of what was about to happen to her.

Enough, she told herself. You committed to this course, now finish it.

Slowly she reached out to touch the other woman's soul.

"No!" The scream raced in on the mists, screeching from the left all the way to the right. "Do not touch her!"

Marissa jerked back, barely in time, all acceptance leaving her and blocking her soul from this other one. Permission, she remembered. They couldn't join without the host soul's permission.

"Do not touch this false beast," a powerful feminine voice said, belonging to a second woman, stunningly beautiful and bald. Gold and tourmaline earrings flashed in her ears, a golden collar sat at her throat. She was strong without being autocratic in her bearing. She was confident as she swept between Marissa and the other soul. "She lies. She is not Hatshepsut. She is one of Odjit's breed. A Templar." She spat the word like a curse. "Be gone from here, Kemisi! Be glad I was here to stop you, because my love would know you false the moment you awoke within this innocent woman."

"A fine act," the first soul said. "Do not believe her. She is not Hatshepsut. I am. You must beware. So many Templars are here and crowding me out in order to get to you!"

"She lies," said the bald beauty. "Listen to your heart, Marissa. It loves the same man that I do. Feel of both our souls and know which of us is true."

Marissa knew if she had a heart it would be pounding in terror. What had she almost done? Oh god, how was she to know who was true and who was false? Could she trust herself to know something like that while in a state she had so little control of? And Jackson had said this would happen quickly, that the cusp between life and permanent death was fleeting. She had only a matter of moments to decide.

"Let me help you," the second soul said softly. "When last I was alive, Menes and I loved in a week what others spend lifetimes missing. When he took his own life in order to be by my side, he made a promise to me. He said that next time he would find a woman of great strength and sure spirit. And," she said with a smile, "that he wanted me to choose someone with most delicious curves. Of course, he knew we had no control over that. Here we are just spirits and we only have impressions of what we once looked like."

"This is preposterous," the first Hatshepsut . . . or Kemisi . . . said. "I could wax eloquent just as she does, but I will not. I am the queen and pharaoh of the Bodywalkers and true mate to your lover. Choose me and be done with it, or choose her and awaken the host of a Templar witch who has deceived you."

"Listen," the second spirit said softly. "Not to me. Not to her. Listen to yourself. Do not be afraid to trust yourself. You have struggled all your life trying to find your own strength and trying to make others believe in it even when you couldn't. Yes," she breathed, closing her eyes for a moment, her brow furrowing slightly. "I feel it all now. But you are strong. And with me guiding you, you will learn to trust that strength. Trust it now. Choose."

"She pretends to be an empath," the other spirit scoffed. "It's like watching a play. You are a bad actress, Templar witch."

Choose. Trust herself and choose. She was afraid. Deathly afraid. But she *was* strong, she realized. At some point the acting had become the truth and she had become stronger than she realized. She was confident. She made choices and affected people's lives for the better. She was looked to for her strength and it was not just an illusion.

And that was why she reached for the second spirit.

"You have lost, Kemisi," the second spirit said simply as she reached and touched herself to Marissa. And in a blinding flash of impression and sensation, she knew she had chosen right. This was Hatshepsut. The love she felt for Menes shone into every corner of her soul. It was so bright and brilliant it almost hurt to know it. "You should thank me for keeping you from my lover's wrath."

"That's was rather the point, now wasn't it," the other soul sneered. "It would be worth my immediate death to see Menes kill this creature his other soul loves so dearly. It would rend them apart and he would be back by your side in an instant. Just like last time. And we always grow stronger when you are here with him, wallowing in your incorporeal love." The spirit hissed in their direction, then scudded away on the next breeze, clouds of blue curling in her wake.

"Come now," Hatshepsut soothed her. "You are safe now. It's over. Let us concentrate on what we are to become together."

Marissa nodded, painful relief echoing through her.

"I'm sorry I was not here for you immediately. Other souls were crowding me out. Templars, no doubt, trying to see Menes fall. But I think you and I know that the Templars are now the least of our problems. Our lover will need us now more than ever." She smiled then, a warm sensation Marissa felt spinning through her. "Let us return to him. And let us endeavor to stay alive more than a week this time, shall we?"

Marissa laughed, reaching again for the stunning spirit and her warm humor. *Yes*, she thought. *This is who I want to be.*

And so they reached into each other and began the process of letting their souls Blend.

CHAPTER TWENTY

Nothing had devastated Jackson as much as watching her last breath escape from her body. Even knowing what was happening, even with Menes's complete faith in what was taking place, he found himself painfully bereft and a weight of grief settled on his heart.

God. Please God. Bring her back safe.

And now, Menes thought within him, *you know exactly how I felt when Hatshepsut last left me.*

And he did. He felt it so keenly it just about killed him. And now he understood why Menes's previous host had willingly allowed Menes to follow her into death. When first he'd come to understand what Menes had done for the sake of a woman, he had been appalled and had warned him there was no way in hell he was agreeing to suicide if something like that should happen again.

He had been so wrong. He knew . . . he knew he would be very easy to convince if something were to happen to Marissa. He hadn't fully realized it before, but he knew now.

"Goddamn it, I didn't tell her I love her," he whispered to the empty room as he remained bent over her, touching her face, waiting for her to draw breath again.

She knew. Do you think she would have done this for

*you if she had thought otherwise? You know. In your
heart you know that she loves us and she never spoke
the words. Words are not necessary when it comes to
love of this depth.*

And Jackson knew Menes was right. He knew it in
his soul that his other half was far more of an expert in
these matters than he was, and that Menes was right. At
this point love was implied. Words meant nothing, and
actions meant everything.

She sucked in a breath, startling him. The emotion
that raced through him had no name. It was too powerful, too encompassing to be given a mere word to describe it. Painful tears burned into his eyes as his hands
framed her face . . . her beautiful, brave face. And it
floored him that she thought her strength was an act.
Well, she wouldn't think that any longer. Not after
what she had just done on faith. It left him speechless
that she had trusted him so much, when he knew she
was so cautious with her trust along with everything
else. He wasn't sure he deserved it, but he was infinitely
delighted to have it.

"Am I alive?" she asked tentatively. Then she opened
her eyes, looked into his and saw his emotion-filled
eyes.

"My god, can I tell you how much that sucked?" he
said, laughing unsteadily and scrubbing a hand across
his wet lashes.

"Yeah, for me too!" she shot back. "I'm the one who
died here. Oh, and thanks for not telling me what she
looked like or anything so I didn't almost come back
with the right damn Bodywalker."

That made him go still. It hadn't even occurred to
him that someone would try to deceive her. It was a
tactic he had never heard of before. He hadn't thought
any of the Templars would be so profane as to interrupt

the joining of two destined souls. God, how low they had sunk.

"Well, Menes says you can rest assured you have the right damn Bodywalker. Jesus, it's like he's singing in here." He tapped his forehead. And then his heart. "And in here. All this talk of love, but I never thought he would be emotional. He's utterly beside himself with joy. As am I."

"Well . . ." She hesitated. "I don't feel her."

"The Blend takes time. You will feel her soon. Menes feels her, and that is enough for now. That and the fact that you said we would have sex after you came back." He grinned at her, lecherously wriggling his brows. It made her laugh out loud.

"Can we do it in the shower again?" she asked, her hands eager on his shoulders. He swung himself out of bed, scooping her up and striding into the bathroom with her.

"I like the shower. It's messy and clean at the same time."

She laughed. "That makes no sense."

"Hummingbird, if you're waiting around here for things to make sense, then you definitely are with the wrong guy."

She smiled at that, pulling herself up closer to him so she could kiss his cheek gently.

"Oh," she said, "I am very much with the right guy."

He stopped his progress toward the shower and looked into her pretty blue eyes.

"I love you, too," he said. "And don't you ever stop making me say it to you."

"You have a deal," she breathed.

EPILOGUE

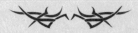

"Where is it? I wonder where it has gone!" sang the deviant god. "Where has the priest hidden? I think I know. I think I do!"

"He ran away with my toy," Chatha said with a pout. He plopped down on the floor ready for a good sulk.

"Oh, do not despair," the god soothed gently. "I can find him and your toy very easily. Shall I do it?"

Chatha nodded furiously, clasping his hands together and rocking back and forth with excitement.

"Where? Where?" he asked.

"Let me see . . ." the god drew out slowly, obviously thinking as he seemed to search the ceiling. "Aha! There it is!" He pointed to the ceiling. "The flat lands, warm like the desert, and so close by. Like our homeland. Hiding away!" The god sighed. "We shall get him later. Him and your toy. I must wait until I have a better hold over this corporeal state. If I should go and they should kill this mortal body I will be banished back to where I came from. The place with no name. The darkest Ether where only the damned survive." He shuddered. "Those who dwell there are my disciples. Much like you, my friend. But I do not like it there. No. It will be much more entertaining here, I think." The god moved forward and patted Chatha on the head. "And I think I would like some followers. I am in the mood to be adulated. Yes. Very much so. Adulation brings a god power. Adulation manifests my strength. I will mold these Templars into my acolytes."

Chatha nodded. "That's a great idea!" he said eagerly, beaming up at the god with his innocent smile.

The praise pleased the god greatly. But suddenly something scraped at his subconscious. It was not a pleasant feeling. "There is something out there," he whispered to Chatha. "There is a great power. I feel it. I fear it." He wondered what it was and was frustrated that he could not see it. But perhaps in time, as he grew ever stronger, he would.

But in the meantime, he would find Chatha's toy and the priest that had escaped and correct them for their disloyalty to his magnificence.

Yes.

That would do just fine.

Read on for an exciting sneak peek of

FORSAKEN
BY
JACQUELYN FRANK

The next book
in The World of Nightwalkers series

. . . why hast thou forsaken me? . . .

Leo Alvarez was not a religious man. He had been anything but for as long as he could remember. He had come such a long way from communion and the catechism lessons his mother had demanded of him.

Such a long way.

He was not what one could call a good man. He wasn't evil, surprisingly far from it considering the harsh realities of his life. But he most certainly was not an angel. He was not free of sin, and many of those sins were very heavy indeed. But Leo figured that if there really were a point where he would be judged for them, he would not be apologetic for the things he had done. He had a code, followed it with powerful efficiency, and felt it would speak for him.

But however serious his sins, he knew he didn't deserve the punishment that was presently being dealt out to him. No one deserved the cruel and excruciating torment he was swimming in.

Leo rolled in and out of consciousness, but the bliss of unconsciousness would be robbed from him violently when the blade sinking into his flesh found the nerves and receptors so readily available. The message was received in a burning explosion of pain, forcing him to clench his jaw until his teeth creaked under the stress of it.

But he would not scream again. He was hoarse from all that had come previous to this new onslaught. He didn't worry about whether or not it made him seem weak. No. None of that mattered at the moment. Nothing mattered to Leo outside of one single word. One single objective.

Live.

Live, Alvarez, he demanded of himself for the thousandth time. Although, by now it was obvious that the twisted demon who orchestrated his agony had no intention of killing him.

No.

That would be far too merciful, and this evil thing—the creature that had lashed him down to the coarse cemented floor, his wrists torn to shreds inside the cuffs of heavy metal manacles—was everything opposite of mercy. But these wounds would be healed shortly. As would the newest carving that the beast was drawing into his body. But healing would come only after the thing called Chatha was through lifting Leo's organs out of his body to present them to him, just before he would begin to dissect them before his prisoner's very eyes.

This time he reached deep and Leo could feel him fumbling around inside his gut, moving lower, slick fingers having difficulty gaining purchase at first. But eventually Chatha found his kidney and ripped it out of him, giggling as he held it up, prodding at it with a finger, not caring that Leo was quickly dying of blood loss.

Maybe . . . maybe this time I will die before he can heal me, Leo thought. But he struggled to tamp the hope down, knowing that it was a part of the creature's tormenting ritual. To make him think he was going to find release. Make him think that, after days of this torture it would finally be over. And he was fading. He was reaching for something . . . something beyond life. Something waiting for him. Something of infinite, blissful peace.

Then Chatha dropped the kidney, and scrambled up over his body on hands and knees. His face pressed close to Leo's, filing his darkening vision with that innocent and maniacal visage.

"No, no." he tsked, wagging a blood-wet finger before Leo's nose. "No fair!"

And that was when tears would burn into Leo's eyes, hope dashed all to hell as the beast laid hands on him like an Evangelical preacher touched by God, and healed him.

Leo awoke with a savage shout, his body lurching out of bed, forcing him to stumble and fall as his sleeping muscles refused to awaken and do their duty. He fell to the floor, his hands barely reaching out in time to keep him from landing face-first into the luxurious carpeting. The jarring of his body shook sweat from the tips of his hair, a shower of salt and water spraying everywhere. He was soaked in it, his bare chest slick with wet and his boxers plastered to him in their drenched state.

He tried to slow his breathing, tried to make himself understand that he was awake and, for the moment, safe. This house was the home of his best friend. The friend who had seen him healed and who was patiently waiting for him to open up and talk about the horror that he had been through.

But he would be waiting a very long time because Leo would never, *never* speak a word about it to anyone. He would not resurrect those moments in the bright light of day. He would never burden another soul with the horror he had survived . . . somehow.

No. He would go to his grave with it. He would drag it into the afterlife with him, and this time it would be the one kicking and screaming.

She tilted her head, listening on the wind, feeling the eddy of how it flowed freely or, better yet, washed around things. Like sonar it told her where everything was just by the way it shifted. When there was no wind she was as good as blind to what was happening in the world, and those were the moments that she found as terrifying as humans would feel if only they knew what was out there. What was out there living and breathing beside them without their knowledge.

Knowledge. Knowledge was key and it was her job to deliver information. Her people could feel and sense things all around . . . just like she could with the actual wind right at that moment. But unlike the surety of knowing there was a cow twenty paces to her left and a church with a steeple twenty miles due south, the future had murky eddies. The wind of the future was blowing in bad directions, and if the wind blew one way tragedy and horror would reign. If it blew another, there would be tragedy and survival. And yet another would bring victory and joy. It was the first that must be avoided at all cost. The others . . . the others would fall as they would and that was as it should be.

"Whistle and blow, whistle and blow," she murmured, the phrase like second nature, her people's way of saying "What will be will be."

She pushed off, letting the wind wash over her, letting it lift her up. The feel of it flowing over her skin was the most comforting sensation she knew. Sometimes, when she was bound to the wingless earth, she felt like crying in frustration, missing this feeling. Longing for this feeling. There was nothing like it in all the world, nothing more freeing. She had no idea how anyone could take it for granted or how mortals bore being bound to the earth. Then again, they tried to fight it, didn't they, in their great lumbering metal machines? Poor things. She supposed it was their comfortable and safe way of doing things. But the wind was not safe and as much as it buoyed up it was the sudden plummeting sweeps down toward soil that made life course through the veins. Those humans who flew on silk wings . . . yes, they were the braver sort. They she felt affinity with. To know that a single tear in that silk could end their fragile mortal lives . . . it was delightful. Those were humans she longed to know better.

But that was impossible. Contact with humans was strictly prohibited. Well . . . in truform anyway. You could hardly swing a cat without bumping into a mortal these days. It was why they lived so distant from the nearest human dwelling. But other things had the same inclination and the world was growing small.

But that would cease to be a worry for very much longer if the wind kept blowing so ill. She moved low and fast, marveling at the cacti and other strange vegetation. She had never been in this part of the United States before. Which was strange really. She loved to travel and see the world, to see how very different one place was from another. And when she was glutted on the topography of a region she would move deeper into the area, mixing with humans, learning all about the differing cultures involved and the almost rhythmic beauty of their languages. And food. God, how she loved food.

She shook the thought off. She was letting herself get distracted. There was business to be done. Sightseeing would have to wait for a different day and a very different set of circumstances.